THE
HALF-LIFE
EMPIRE

BOOK 3

THE HALF-LIFE EMPIRE

BOOK ☢ 3

SHAMI STOVALL

Podium

Podium

RECAP OF EVENTS

Long ago, three clans of aliens arrived on Earth—the Teth, the Vay, and the Frest. They were different species within the same biological family, like cats in the scientific family of Felidae, each with their own society.

When the aliens first arrived on Earth, they were met with the full spectrum of emotion from the humans who greeted them. Truths were called into question, beliefs thrown out the window.

Immediately some nations on Earth welcomed the aliens. One of the largest nations before the firestorm bombs—the People's Republic of China—took in the Vay and made them citizens.

It was then that a new technology race began.

The aliens had many advancements, and the technology they gifted to humanity was called "A-tech" to stand for "alien technology," as uncreative as that was. Any nation that didn't embrace A-tech fell behind, quickly becoming a third-world country.

But the Vay didn't value what humanity valued. They didn't believe in freedoms; they hated the human way of life. They quickly controlled the nations into which they were introduced, and then fought for dominance over the planet, hoping to subjugate humans and have the Vay rule supreme. The Frest—a gentler clan of aliens—was completely killed off through the Vay's systematic genocide. The Teth allied with nations across North America, offering A-tech to their new allies so they could grow strong enough to oppose the Vay.

To no one's surprise, the war between the Vay and Teth involved nuclear weapons. The resulting fallout created the "Forever Winter," a period in history when the skies were blotted out with clouds, and the temperatures sank all over the globe.

Contrary to its name, the Forever Winter eventually ended, and the remaining humans and aliens struggled to create something from the ashes of the previous civilization.

Kita Yamasaki, a granddaughter to the great doctor Benjamin Yamasaki, has lived in a post-apocalyptic North America for her entire life. After run-ins with the Iron-Blooded, a group of alien-worshipping cultists, and a Teth nest, Kita decided to make her home in a human settlement known as Richfield.

She relied on Bishop, the man she loved; Gascoigne, the woman who had once hunted her; and Crouton, her adopted daughter, in order to start a new life. As they were gathering supplies, Kita and the others ran afoul of the Iron-Blooded once again, but this time, they had advanced Mark VI power armor.

Kita desperately wanted a suit of power armor for her own purposes. However, after stealing from the Iron-Blooded's weapon factory, Bishop was taken captive. In a desperate attempt to get him back, Kita headed off to one of their bases of operation. On the way, she met a man and one of the Teth, both of whom had lived in an underground facility their entire lives.

Brecht, the human, and Vega, the Teth.

Brecht was under the impression the CCP (Chinese Communist Party) was behind the devastation, but nothing could be further from the truth. He was unaware of what was happening on the "surface world," but was familiar with the Teth due to his training. Because of that, Kita decided to take Brecht and Vega with her.

After regrouping in Richfield, Kita, Gascoigne, Brecht, and Vega infiltrated one Iron-Blooded facility after another in an attempt to find Bishop. However, after acquiring a suit of Mark VI armor for themselves, and shutting down several of the Iron-Blooded's operations, they failed to locate Bishop. Kita, convinced he was dead, had almost given up hope.

Fortunately, the last location they searched—a mining facility—had several imprisoned individuals, including Bishop. It turned out the Iron-Blooded were gathering materials for their own massive improvement project, which involved gathering as much A-tech and skilled individuals as they could find.

When Kita rescued Bishop, she also found information for more underground sanctuaries—places the Iron-Blooded would love to raid. So, once

Bishop was safe, they went north in search of one such facility—only to find Vay aliens in the woodlands around an old United States underground bunker.

After fighting off the aliens and securing the location, Kita took the fission battery powering Richfield and used it to give life to *US Sanctuary Housing #4*, known simply as "Sanctuary," an underground bunker constructed before the Forever Winter. Inside, Kita not only found supplies for rebuilding a small civilization, but actual nuclear weapons.

Firestorm bombs. A-tech-infused warheads capable of leveling an entire coast of a continent.

Kita also discovered a lone Winter Survivor in the facility—a scientist driven mad by decades of isolation. It appeared that US Sanctuary Housing #4 had been a site of experimentation, though it was unclear what exactly they had been trying to learn.

Determined to take advantage of the underground greenhouse, Kita and the others moved the one hundred and fifty residents of Richfield up to Sanctuary. During this process, the Iron-Blooded discovered their location. Equipped with her Mark VI suit, Kita and the others had to fend off an ambush intended to annihilate everyone in Richfield.

During the fight, it became apparent that the Vay were still in the area, and several aliens joined in on the fighting. The Iron-Blooded went for Kita's power armor, but were unsuccessful at retrieving it.

Thankfully, Kita and her companions managed to defeat most of the attacking forces. The majority of the Richfield citizens reached Sanctuary, and now they face the daunting task of rebuilding.

Lastly, it seems the weather has been nicer, and as long-time readers will know, perhaps Architect Riven used the Meteorological Plexus to correct the world's satellites because the Iron-Blooded were left with no other option but to live on Earth.

This is where the story left off . . .

THE
HALF-LIFE
EMPIRE

BOOK 3

CHAPTER ONE

I had been hit with shrapnel from a grenade, buried alive, and even irradiated, but nothing compared to the horror of my current conversation.

"We need more babies," Gascoigne said, deadpan.

I sat at the computer desk at our underground facility, staring at the glowing monitor. *Babies* was never a problem I thought I would have to face. For most of my life, I had actively tried to avoid people—now I was supposed to try and make more of them? How did this fall to me?

"What do you want me to do?" I asked as I poked away at the old keyboard.

The whole machine was ancient, but it was made with alien technology—A-tech, for short—and constructed using some of the most advanced techniques and materials possible. Supposedly, this computer would last hundreds of years, powered by a fission battery.

Supposedly.

Gascoigne clenched her teeth. "Kita, you're the one in charge, remember? The others aren't listening to me. I'm just the bitch from Ex Cathedra. *You* have to be the one to tell them that we'll die off unless these people start breeding."

I swiveled around in my chair, my gaze distant. She was right—this was the role I had chosen. I couldn't give up on it now that it was bothersome. I'd rather just sit here on the computer, though, and learn everything I could about our new home.

US Sanctuary Housing #4.

That was its official name. Everyone—including myself—just called it *Sanctuary*. And Sanctuary wasn't going to make it unless we had higher population growth numbers, apparently.

We had less than one hundred and fifty people here, and half of them were older. Sanctuary could easily hold thousands without much effort, but unless we gathered individuals from the surrounding wasteland, we'd have to make our own.

And no one wanted that. The wasteland around here was filled with rail gangs, junk hunters, and the Iron-Blooded. Any of those lunatics would steal our A-tech and flee in the dead of night. They certainly wouldn't help us *build*.

Gascoigne snapped her fingers, obviously attempting to get my full attention. "Stop playing with your machines and deal with the situation."

Her appearance was as rough as her words. Despite the fact that she carried scars from both battlefield and butcher, Gascoigne wore them openly. She also wore a pair of tight black shorts and a white tank top over a black bra. I never would've had the courage to wear that outfit, but I also didn't look like her.

Months of nonstop training had left her rather muscled. The nanites in her blood—the tiny machines that repaired the body whenever it took the slightest injury, even microtears to the muscles—made it easier than normal to bulk up. And Gascoigne had taken advantage of that, as her abs attested.

"Isn't everyone still getting situated?" I asked with a nervous laugh. "Now might not be the time to bring up their failures to procreate."

Gascoigne ran a hand through her short brown hair, her hazel eyes glaring at me.

I spun in my chair and returned my attention to the monitor. "As a matter of fact, we should stick to the original plan. First, we clear out the first two warehouses, and then we get everyone their own designated *home area*."

"It takes nine months for those babes to bake," Gascoigne drawled. "We should be incentivizing it now."

I tapped away on the keyboard and then stopped. It occurred to me that Gascoigne *was* from Ex Cathedra. It was a country to the east of us, beyond the mountains, and made from the last remnants of the United States of America. Because of their military equipment and fortified bases, they were the best positioned to take advantage after the Forever Winter ended.

They had conquered all the nearby "independent" cities and rounded up stray gangs of people roaming the plains or hiding out in the woodlands. Ex Cathedra made slaves of anyone who didn't swear allegiance to their cause.

I slowly resumed my typing. "I take it forcing people to have children is a regular tactic where you're from?"

Gascoigne had once been a *judge*—the military soldiers who wore power-armor exoskeletons and acted as battlefield commanders. They were the worst of the worst, only because they were nearly impossible to stop. Well, if someone *else* had power armor, they could be stopped, but that was exceedingly rare.

I touched the back of my neck. Connectors had been grafted into my body, allowing me to interface with those marvelous power suits. Gascoigne had them, too, obviously.

Judge Gascoigne . . .

"Ex Cathedra makes it a big deal to have children, yeah," Gascoigne casually replied. "And for good reason. They're going to beat U-Cali in the coming war, and it's all going to be because they have the numbers."

To the south, below the mountains, a war raged between the two largest nations formed on North America. *United California* and *Ex Cathedra* were at each other's throats. I wondered, briefly, if we could convince deserters to come to Sanctuary, but that was probably too risky.

"I'll handle the situation," I whispered. Even though I was staring at my computer screen, I saw nothing. My mind filled with images of a potential future, but I would need to start taking the first steps.

"Tch. Good."

Gascoigne stomped out of the room, her footfalls echoing around the mostly metal and empty space. Sanctuary was hollow, really. It was a gigantic facility with five empty warehouses, some filled with useful tech, some filled with terrible things no one should have.

I stood from my chair.

This office . . . The walls were as white as untouched snow, their pristine surfaces reflecting the soft, ambient light that seemed to emanate from nowhere and everywhere at once. There was A-tech lighting built into most corners and between metal paneling, to be both convenient and creepy.

Everyone currently in Sanctuary had complained it didn't feel like home. Some said it didn't feel livable—the air was so sterile it was as if the very molecules had been scrubbed of all earthly taint.

At least no one had gone into the fourth or fifth warehouse, where it was a horror show of blood and weaponry.

I doubted anyone was ready for that . . .

Everyone here had come from Richfield, a small town to the south. They had lived a comfortable life of seclusion in the wasteland, with small farms, tiny homes, and a wall that only partially kept out the gangs. Sanctuary was almost the polar opposite. A huge place to live, safe from the elements, with vast underground farms . . .

I had thought they would be overjoyed for the improvement.

Obviously, I just didn't understand people.

"Kita, it's time," I said to myself in a low voice. "You can't make everyone happy. You have to just do what's best for the future."

The solution was obvious, even if I didn't like it.

I walked to the far corner of my office, where a sleek refrigerator was built straight into the wall. The door had a mirror-like sheen that allowed it to blend with the perfectly white room. I grabbed the cold handle and pulled the door open. A waft of icy air rushed over me and I shivered.

While the refrigerator *could* hold hundreds of items, it currently only had three things inside.

Three metal canisters with thick, glass windows on one side. Inside the canisters were leathery eggs the size of my arm. Each glass window had a bumpy plaque that labeled them in Teth language, Tethlite. It was a form of braille, since the aliens didn't have eyes.

An architect egg.

A warrior egg.

An innovator egg.

These were Teth children of three different castes, suspended in blue cryostasis gel. Once the canisters were broken open, the gel would mix with oxygen and act as a resuscitator for the eggs.

I wrapped my hand with the long sleeve of my sweatshirt and removed the canister with the architect egg. Unlike humans, who, in theory, mated for life with one partner, had children one at a time, and required nine months of gestation, the Teth operated on an entirely different system.

The architect caste could command other castes to mate and have children, sometimes at a shockingly high rate.

They would reproduce quickly. Our population would grow. And with the Teth's intelligence, and human creativity, we could become an unstoppable nation.

Also, in theory.

"Hello, little one," I whispered to the canister as I walked it over to my computer desk. "Are you ready for the world?"

I probably looked and sounded insane. The thing hadn't even hatched yet.

I removed the other two canisters as well. Warrior Teth were strong and imposing, and the innovators were hyperintelligent. Normally, if Teth reproduced without an architect nearby, they didn't create more of their caste—they created mindless drones that acted like animals. The architect was essential to the production process.

After a deep breath, I turned the handle on the top of the architect canister and broke the seal. It hissed as it opened, and oxygen rushed inside. The blue gel shifted to a light orange color as it brought the egg back from the brink of death. It was no longer held in stasis.

Now it would hatch.

I did the same with the other canisters. They hissed, and the gel transformed in coloration, indicating that everything had gone correctly.

This meant we would have three Teth babies on our hands. Again, unlike humans, Teth weren't in their "child phase" for long. Only two years, on average, before they were fully grown. And the drones had a shorter timeframe than that . . .

If the humans wouldn't reproduce, the Teth would. It would solve our population problem in no time.

"Okay, time to get active." I leaned down to examine the architect egg a little closer. It resembled a snake egg, with its odd, wrinkly exterior. When nothing happened, I frowned. "I hope you're not dead. I, uh, would dislike that."

Everything looked like it had gone correctly, but strange things could happen with older A-tech. And if the eggs died, I wasn't entirely sure how I would know that.

I had stolen the eggs from Architect Riven. What if I had accidentally harmed them in some way? It could've happened, and I never would've known. I had never seen Teth eggs hatch before. I had only ever seen what happens on videos or read about the process in articles written by my grandfather.

"Perhaps I should think of a name," I said as I leaned my face ever closer to the canister glass. "What would be the name of an epic architect? One that will lead us into a new future of human and alien relations?"

No pressure.

I chuckled to myself. It probably wasn't best to raise a Teth architect with such stresses. Probably better to raise it with solid values—and empathy—before telling it that it's the most important creature in the whole facility.

Probably.

Then I thought of a great name. It was human in origin, and from a general who lived long before the Forever Winter, but that was fine. I wanted the Teth to have human names. It would help attach them to Earth, and to Sanctuary.

"What do you think about the name *Agrippa*?" I held my breath after the question.

The egg didn't move.

And after saying the name aloud, I realized it didn't sound very modernly human. It sounded ancient. No one was named Agrippa anymore.

I ran a finger up and down the glass of the canister. "Maybe *Marcus* . . . Or if we want to get really weird . . . *Vipsanius*."

"Is this what you do when you say you're *very busy* and need the office to yourself?" someone asked, startling me to the point my heart leapt into my throat.

I whirled around, about to keel over from a heart attack, when I realized Bishop was standing next to me. When had he gotten here? Why didn't I hear him enter? Had I been too busy thinking about the Teth eggs?

"I, uh, well, um . . ." My words abandoned me.

"Don't worry, Kit-Kat—I won't tell anyone you were slacking off." He playfully patted my shoulder and then glanced over at the canisters. "Finally letting the eggs get some fresh air, I see." Bishop then flashed me a smile.

I stared up at him, unsure of what to say.

Bishop was a good foot taller than me. I was short, though, so perhaps it didn't mean much, but he always seemed like a mountain from my perspective. He wore a pair of cargo pants, all the pockets stuffed to the brim with odd things. Tools, plants, a whole handbook's worth of paper—each pocket was different, but each pocket was equally full.

I was surprised he didn't have a backpack or a coat. Instead, he walked around in a tank top that showed off his many tally mark scars. Each one he carved into his own body, but only after he killed someone.

Most of those tally marks were gang members or Iron-Blooded lunatics, but not all. I had been there when his junk hunter friends had turned on us, and when he had sliced up his arm to remember the occasion.

I shook my head, dispelling those thoughts.

Now that Bishop was here, I could speak with him about important things.

"Gascoigne thinks we should have more babies," I muttered, my gaze falling to the floor.

"Oh, *finally*." Bishop laughed as he unfastened his belt. "I've been preparing for this mission. I haven't touched myself in three days."

"N-Not *us*," I said, my face growing hot. "I meant the whole of Sanctuary." I placed my hand on his chest. "I don't have time for that right now. You understand. I have this whole facility to look after."

Bishop begrudgingly fastened his belt back in place, his expression aggressively neutral. "Right. We wouldn't want to disappoint the facility now, would we?"

I sarcastically motioned to the three canisters filled with orange gel. "We should also set a good example for the children."

Bishop quirked half a smile. Then he shrugged at the nearest canister. "Do the eggs hatch in those things? Or what?"

"I . . . I don't know."

"Seems to me like you'd take them out, so they had room to stretch their six legs or whatever the hell Teth have."

I nodded once, but I hesitated as I reached for the architect's canister. What if I did this wrong? What if I removed the architect and that wasn't correct? What if it died? It was the only architect I had—and the only one we'd probably ever find. They were the rarest caste, and extremely important.

Instead, I scooped up the canister with the warrior egg. I'd use this one as a test. If I removed the egg and it hatched outside of the gel, then I'd remove the others.

Hopefully, I wasn't about to kill it.

CHAPTER TWO

With my breath held, I moved my hand over the orange gel. Before I could reach in, Bishop grabbed my wrist. I jerked my attention upward, until our gazes met.

"Why don't we invite Vega to your exclusive office?" he asked with a shrug. "Ya know—the one Teth we have living with us."

"He was raised by humans in an underground facility." And he wasn't one of the architect caste. He was just a warrior. I figured he wouldn't know anything, but that was probably me jumping to conclusions. Perhaps Vega *did* know something. "All right," I finally muttered. "That's probably for the best."

Bishop smirked as he released my arm. "Good. Wait right here. I'll be back in a jiff with our resident Teth." He turned and left me in the white office with only my shadow as company.

The eggs didn't move while he was gone. I knew—I watched them closely, never looking away and rarely blinking. The Teth eggs were crucial to my plan. I had been telling the people of Sanctuary that we would be a human-alien civilization, and while there had been some resistance, everyone had agreed to the transition.

If the people here grew accustomed to the Teth, then I might have a chance of rescuing "wild" Teth from the wasteland. Additionally, the Teth of the wasteland were more likely to listen if I had an architect.

Everything was a cascade of contingencies.

I glanced at the innovator egg.

"You're the smart one," I whispered to it.

Then I squinted at the warrior egg.

"You're the big sibling that needs to watch the others."

My mind drifted back to the aspect of naming. Perhaps I could use all three of the names I had joked about earlier. *Marcus Vipsanius Agrippa* had been an old-world general. Ancient, really—leading armies for a nation that was buried long before the nuclear fire.

But then it struck me. My grandfather was the man who had really forged ahead to bring the Teth and humans together.

I grabbed the architect canister. "Your name will be *Benjamin*." After my grandfather. Then I grabbed the warrior canister. "And you'll be *Joel*." After the man who left me his underground bunkers. Finally, I scooped up the innovator canister. "And you'll be *Tamura*."

My sister.

I rarely ever said her name.

I swallowed down my pain as the memories of her death washed over me. I had shot my own sister. It had been an accident—but still. She had died because of me.

Now, I supposed I could honor her memory by giving her name to one of my new baby Teth.

Tamura.

The door to the office opened and closed. This time I had been paying attention. I didn't want to think of my sister's death, and I was thankful for any distraction. I whirled around on my heel to find Bishop strolling in with one of the Teth.

This was Vega.

Since Teth were hermaphrodites, capable of switching their gender depending on the needs of the architect, most didn't use pronouns. However, since he had lived with the humans all his life, Vega had insisted we start using "he" when referring to him. Which was weird, but it made the residents of Richfield feel better, so we all agreed.

Vega was one of the warrior caste, all right. They were the tallest and most muscular of all the Teth. Vega in particular was defined by the muscles that rippled across his body. He stood on two thick tree-stump legs and was nearly ten feet tall.

His skin was shiny black and glistened under the lights as though wet. Although, today he was wearing clothing. A tailor-made pair of pants and a shirt that covered most of his broad shoulders and chest.

Like all Teth, Vega had four arms—two that were thick with muscle and ended in claws, and two that were small, thin, and capable of fine motor skills. The hands on the smaller arms had long fingers for manipulating things.

Those were his *crafter arms*. Innovator Teth used them to great effect, either as artists or scientists. The warrior caste had little need for them, since they didn't have fearsome claws, but Vega used his while interacting with the humans of Sanctuary.

Vega held out a hand to shake. I awkwardly reached out and grabbed his slender fingers.

"Greetings," he said, his English garbled since Teth mostly spoke with their tongues and not any lips.

"*We should speak easier,*" I said in Tethlite.

Vega nodded once.

None of the Teth had eyes—including Vega.

Since most humans made eye contact when speaking, or used their eyes for nonverbal communication, it was often difficult for people to make friends with the Teth.

I didn't mind, though. Looking people in the eyes wasn't my favorite pastime, either.

"Are you sure you two don't want to speak something normal?" Bishop glanced between us. He still hadn't learned Tethlite. "I mean, I think the little ones should primarily speak English—to get along with the humans."

Vega growled deep in his throat. When he spoke, it was in cleaner and more precise English, as though he was focusing all his energy on getting each syllable correct. "I learned both languages when I was young. As did Brecht and the others. If we are raising Teth young, we should make sure they are exposed to both at all times."

That wasn't what Bishop wanted to hear. His response was nothing more than a groan.

"Vega . . ." I switched back to English so Bishop wouldn't be left out. "Do you recognize these types of canisters?" I handed one to him, so he could feel the metal, glass, and name plaque.

After a brief examination, Vega placed the canister on the table and then snorted. "Yes. I've felt these before. The gel is a nutrient paste after its exposure to oxygen."

"Do we take the eggs out? Or leave them within?"

"Leave them." Vega lowered his fang-filled maw closer to me. I figured it was to be *polite*, since humans tended to conduct themselves in closer quarters, but I didn't appreciate it. "Once most of the gel has been absorbed through the egg's membrane, the young will emerge."

"I see . . ." I touched the canister with the innovator inside. "How long do you think it'll take?"

"Less than a week." Vega stood straight and then rotated his large shoulders. "Will they be kin, then? Our family?"

I wanted to just nod, but Vega wouldn't see that. The Teth always had to verbalize responses—or they touched one another. That was actually more common. They were touchy-feely with those they considered friends and family.

But I hated that, so I simply replied, "Yes."

"Who made you that outfit, Vega?" Bishop asked with a smile. "You're lookin' fine."

The hulking monster flexed his larger hands, his claws extending slightly. "Himiko made this for me. She has been designated as a tailor, it seems. She insisted I wear clothing."

Vega wore a plain white shirt made of thick material that wouldn't easily rip. Heavy cotton? I wasn't certain. His pants were clearly a burlap sack, and it made me wonder if Himiko intentionally gave Vega bizarre makeshift clothing or if these were really all she had to work with.

Bishop whistled. "You like it, right? I mean, I've seen you aliens wear clothes before. Just not . . . many clothes."

"It limits my ability to feel the air around me," Vega said with a growl. "But, yes, Teth have clothing, both for space travel and for planet-side living. I learned about them, but I've never worn any myself."

I wrung my hands, my thoughts buzzing. My grandfather knew everything about the Teth. He'd taught me Tethlite, and how the caste system worked, and how the aliens read and communicate. But now I would need to raise them? Teach them things?

My nerves were getting the better of me.

"Vega," I whispered. Then I switched to Tethlite. "*Would you and Brecht be willing to help me raise the babes? I want them to be emotionally stable, and well-educated. A-And they must love, or at least appreciate, humans.*"

Vega tilted his head; his nostrils—which resembled a snake's—flared slightly. "*I am a warrior,*" he stated. "*I am not designed for such work. An innovator or a caretaker would be best.*"

I wanted to sarcastically glance around, to emphasize that we didn't have either of those here, but Vega wouldn't be able to see that. Instead, I sighed. "I'll speak with Brecht," I said in English.

"Certainly."

Then the Teth nodded his head to me—an acknowledgment of my authority over him. It was also a sign I had given a command. The aliens were very hierarchical. Like ants. They needed a chain of command, and they preferred to "stay in their lane" when it came to their caste.

Which was the exact opposite of humans. We tended to flit from one career to the next, ever growing and ever changing our horizons.

Raising Teth was going to be a harder challenge than I originally suspected.

"I'll help you raise kids, Kit-Kat," Bishop said, always smiling. "I'll be a great dad." Then his face lit up. "Wait. Let's ask the doctor. She's old. Very old. I bet she mingled with the Teth before the Forever Winter."

"They say it takes a village to raise a child."

Bishop snorted back a laugh. "My grandmother used to say that."

I had been repeating a phrase Joel had written in his survival guides. Although I had lived many places, I had never known the sense of community found in a village. Richfield was the closest I had ever found.

And while we clearly had enough people here to raise the Teth babes, Vega shifted his weight awkwardly from one massive foot to the other. He tilted his head and then said, "There are Vay in the area."

I nodded. "We fought some of the Vay when we came to Sanctuary, but I don't know how many are in the surrounding area."

"They have made it clear they intend to genocide the Teth, just as they did with the Frest."

Vega's words were haunting and quiet.

Our new home was nestled in unfamiliar territory. While the surrounding area had been cleared, and many of the Vay dead, I knew it wasn't the last of them. There were more. And if they knew we were hatching Teth eggs, I suspected they would get more violent with their attacks.

"For now, we'll raise our little Teth indoors," I whispered. "All right, Vega? I won't allow the Vay to harm them."

He bowed his head again. *"Please, speak with Brecht on the matter."*

CHAPTER THREE

While Sanctuary was our new home, it wasn't really a *home*.

Not yet, anyway.

I walked around the first underground warehouse—everyone had dubbed it *Section One*—and I kept to myself as I observed the people of Richfield in their new environment. Brecht was here somewhere, and he had grown up with aliens, so he was the obvious choice to help me with the new babies.

Section One was gigantic, and had enough space to house at least a hundred families all by its lonesome. It also had greenhouse areas for plants, though people seemed less interested in those at the moment.

It was just . . . one big, long warehouse, that seemed to stretch on for some time. The walls were white, the ceiling gray, and the floor a series of artistically designed tiles. It appeared to be marble, but it was a sturdier, and more lightweight, material than that.

There were "living quarters" and an industrial kitchen, but the quarters weren't for entire families, they were for individuals, so the warehouse section needed to be partitioned into homes for everyone. That would work in the long run, but until all the construction was done, it was a bit cramped and a difficult place to live.

When I walked by, I kept my coat up to hide most of my face.

Everyone knew me, but it was still easy to hide. I was small. Short in stature, and barely a hundred pounds.

While I searched for Brecht, I wanted to gauge how everyone was doing, and be the "Sanctuary Leader" everyone had dubbed me. It didn't feel right, though. It was like trying to use a glove as a sock. Maybe it could work, but it'd always be uncomfortable.

"Move that over there," someone shouted.

Another person hauled a large aluminum shelf to the side, creating a makeshift wall. "Like this?"

"To the left!"

Everyone was engaged in making a living space for themselves and their families.

Then the screech of metal on metal filled all of Section One. It was worse than nails on a chalkboard—worse than the sounds of screams during a midnight raid.

The denizens of Sanctuary clamped their hands over their ears. They shot their glares and glowers to the very back of Section One.

There were two giant machine vehicles in the very back of the warehouse. They were here when we had arrived—construction vehicles that had clearly been used to build portions of Sanctuary. The vehicles resembled gigantic cranes, though they had the capacity to fold into themselves for convenient storage.

One was vibrating, obviously in use.

I headed in that direction, curious to see what was going on.

Two residents of Richfield, Westley and Grizzled Garret, had been assigned to deal with these vehicles, and sure enough—there they were. Ideally, Westley and Garret would've moved them out of the way . . .

"What's going on?" I asked a man as I squeezed by him to get to the back end of Section One.

"*They're trying to build the fish farms,*" the man shouted over the sounds of metal shrieking. "*But the crane's not workin'!*"

I glanced around, surveying the area. The tanks for the fish were the size of small houses. Currently, they were stacked together, away from the new potential housing areas. The tanks needed to be positioned near the water pipes and drainage systems if they were to function properly.

Hence, the crane.

The goal was clearly to lift the fish tank up, move it to the pipes, and set it down.

The screech and groan of the crane filled all of Section One with unease, though. Obviously, these vehicles needed some maintenance. The vehicles probably hadn't been touched in over fifty years, but due to the A-tech in their design, they were still capable of functioning.

I hurried over, curious as to the progress.

"Got-damn it, Westley, be careful with that!"

Grizzled Garret stood outside the crane, his calloused hands on his hips. He was the type of man who looked like he could wrestle a bear—or two. Thick. Muscled. But also stocky. He could hibernate, if he wanted.

That was how he earned the nickname "Grizzled," after all. It was better than "old man," since some of his hair was graying already.

Westley, inside the crane, yanked on a lever. The long arm of the crane moved to the left, the screech of metal on metal growing louder. Something was wrong, but it would be more sarcastic than helpful to point that out.

After yanking a second lever, the crane stopped moving. Westley sighed. His seat in the vehicle was at least ten feet up, and the crane arm was another ten above that. Section One's ceiling was only a foot or two higher—and I feared for Sanctuary's integrity. What if they smashed the crane arm into the wall? Or lifted it so high as to punch a hole in the ceiling?

My overactive imagination wasn't helping in this instance.

"I don't know what's wrong with this thing," Westley called down.

Garret huffed and waved one of his burly arms. "What did I tell ya? First the shifter, then the movement. The hunk o' junk is strugglin' but it should be able to move a couple things all right."

"The tanks are mostly made of glass. Unless we can fix this shaking, I don't feel comfortable moving them."

"Don't be such a ninny! Just get it done!"

Westley was the quintessential wasteland bookworm. He was wiry—lean with muscle, but also lean on the amount of food he had gotten over his life. He wore glasses, but they were the kind made from the back-alley lens crafters in the larger settlements. They helped, just not as much as you'd want.

He was intelligent, though. He could rebuild old computers or take them apart on a whim. Despite that, Westley sometimes struggled to navigate the complex circuitry of a casual conversation.

It didn't surprise me that Garret's shouting was flustering the man.

Westley never responded to the last shout. He just focused his attention on the levers in front of him.

"Got-damn it," Garret muttered under his breath, glaring up at the wiry engineer. "He never listens."

Westley pulled another lever, and the crane sputtered. The whole machine jerked as the arm of the vehicle swung closer to the fish tanks.

"Be careful!" I held up a hand as I ran over. "Wait, wait, wait." I flailed both my arms to make sure Westley saw. "Turn off the machine."

Westley flipped the engine switch, and the crane powered down after a long whirl that was akin to a soft sigh. He slid out of the crane cockpit and then climbed down the side ladder to the floor.

At least the screeching stopped echoing throughout Section One.

"K-Kita. Hello." Westley had oily brown hair that remained slicked back no matter what he did with it. He combed his hair with his fingers as he approached me. "I think we can get the tanks in order. It'll just take—"

Garret stomped over, every bit a grizzled old bear. "Why'd you quit, huh? *Why?* This junk will struggle to turn on again, mark my words." He wore a gun holster on his belt I hadn't noticed until that moment. While it was common to carry weapons, the sight of it once again reminded me of my sister.

I needed to stop thinking of her.

"Listen," I said, stepping between them. "Something is wrong with the cranes. I'll look at them. Maybe it's something I can fix."

"How?" Garret barked.

He was more angry dog than man in his current state.

"I've fixed a lot of A-tech machines in the past." I rolled my hand around. "I've lived in a lot of bizarre places, and I studied a lot of the tech designs."

I'd even had to study a few of their mining cranes for when I broke into an Ex Cathedra silver mine. There was a piece of me that already knew the problem. The cranes used large gears and pistons, and occasionally something would get caught between them. The screeching usually indicated that.

"Do you have any tools?" I asked.

Garret huffed, grumbled some curse words, and then grabbed me a belt full of tools. He had basic things—like screwdrivers—but also more advanced things, like A-tech drills and an atomic battery. They were can-sized objects filled with radioactive isotopes. The decay of the isotopes generated electricity, and the atomic batteries could last for generations.

I attached the belt to my waist.

Then I pulled myself onto the ladder that led up to the driver's seat. The rungs were well-worn. The crane was older. "And if this doesn't work, I'll still be able to move the fish tanks for you," I called down.

"And how will you do that?" Garret shouted up at me, still grumpy.

"I have an exoskeleton."

And while those suits of exoskeleton power armor were mostly used for combat, they were originally built with construction in mind. I could power my suit, pick up one of the fish tanks, and set it into place without much trouble.

Garret and Westley exchanged glances.

Then Garret huffed. "We can't just wait for you to decide everything, girl. You wanted us to move? We did. But we have to have control over our environment. We can't sit on our thumbs while you, *personally*, handle every damn thing."

I pulled myself up into the crane's cab. Then I glanced down at the man. "I apologize. It's not my intention to be the sole person fixing things—I'll, uh, learn to delegate. But until then, we need this fixed now."

There was a hatch that led into the engine of the machine from the cab. I leaned down near the floor, popped open the hatch, and slipped into the crane itself. Fortunately, a light flickered to life near the engine. Unfortunately, it was dim.

And I instantly knew the real problem—the battery for the engine was dying.

Thankfully, Garret had given me one.

Atomic batteries were a great boon back when they were first introduced to the world, right after the Teth arrived. They were shaped like tuna cans, basically, and just like the USB port, were designed to plug and play with most electronic objects.

I sifted around through the engine, found the old atomic battery, and carefully removed it using the screwdriver Garret had given me. Once I popped it out, the light in the engine died. The instant I popped in the new one, the light flickered back to life, twice as bright as before.

Atomic batteries could last a long time—upward of fifty years. Had this one just been in constant use?

"*Is it working yet?*" Garret shouted.

"Give me a moment," I yelled, my voice echoing throughout the crane. "I need to check the pistons."

"If one of the pistons is broken, we're fucked!"

"Don't worry, we'll get through this," I shouted as I scooted through the crane. What would a real leader say to motivate this man? I tried to recall some great speeches throughout human history. "The, uh, human spirit has been tested throughout history and we've found its indominable, and—"

"*What?*" Garret yelled. "What kind of gibberish are you spoutin'?"

I reached the pistons and the main turning gears and frowned. Leaders were inspiring. I needed to be more inspiring. "I'm just trying to say we have a lot going for us! We should remain optimistic."

"Oh, yeah," Garret said, his voice thick with sarcasm. "I have a *lot* going for me. My eyes are going. My knees are going. My back is going. If I wait for you to handle everything, I'm sure my memory will be going!"

I decided not to engage any further. Garret was in a mood. That was fine. I couldn't let it fluster me. Instead, I poked around the crane. There were four pistons, and after I inspected all of them, I found exactly what I was looking for. One of the crane's screws had come loose, and was stuck on one of the piston tracks, no doubt screeching every time one pumped back and forth.

The gears looked okay, and once I had cleaned everything up, I made sure the remaining nuts and bolts were all perfectly in place.

Then I scooted out of the crane's small engine compartment, shut the hatch, and sat up in the driver's seat.

"Okay," I called down. "It should work now."

"*What?*" Garret seemed flabbergasted. "It's fixed? Already?"

I nodded and then headed down the ladder. Once at the bottom, I unhooked his toolbelt from my waist and handed it back over. "I really appreciate the effort you two are giving Sanctuary. I'm sorry things aren't perfect yet, but I'll try to make sure this place is ten times better than Richfield."

Garret slowly took the toolbelt from me. "Oh."

"Thank you for finding this place," Westley chimed in. "I know you're trying really hard. And Dr. Claire said you're always doing something. This was probably minor—we probably should've been able to handle it ourselves." He sheepishly rubbed the back of his neck.

"If you ever have problems, you should come to me." With a chuckle, I added, "Just mechanical problems, though. I don't know anything about dating. Or personal drama. Or anything like that. Just . . . the machines. I like the machines."

Westley smiled. "Right."

Then he climbed up the ladder, slid onto the driver's seat, and started up the engine.

The crane flared to life. And it purred—a glorious sound that made it seem like the vehicle itself was happy this ordeal was over. The pistons were no longer scraping against a screw. The screeching had stopped.

"Well, I'll be got-damned," Garret muttered. He rubbed his chin as he turned his gaze down to me. "Scrapyard Pete said he didn't want to touch this baby because he didn't know anything about it. I'm glad we got a resident A-tech expert."

I forced a chuckle. "It's nothing."

But then understanding dawned on Garret. He glanced around to our surroundings. Our A-tech surroundings. When he returned his attention to me, his anger was gone. "Oh. I see. You have big plans."

"I think this place could be much better than Richfield," I said.

Garret hefted the belt and pointed to the pocket where the atomic battery had once been. "Not if we keep running out of supplies, though. That was our last one."

"It was?"

Damn.

Sanctuary was old. Perhaps the others had been replacing batteries left and right. Thankfully, we had a fission battery at the heart—and that would last us hundreds of years. The smaller batteries, however . . .

"I'll get more," I stated.

That was what a leader did, after all.

Garret, the bear of a man, actually smiled at me. "Good." He straightened his pants and then pointed to the crane Westley was operating. "And I'll do my part here."

I nodded, and was about to leave, but that was when Garret held out a hand. "Yes?" I asked.

"Sorry about . . . all that." Garret half shrugged. "It's been stressful."

"Don't worry about it. I'll get those batteries, and soon this place will feel just like home."

Hopefully no one would mind that home also having a lot of Teth.

Instead of walking around and interacting with people—because I was clearly terrible at that—I sat in one of Sanctuary's computer rooms. This was a place made with some of the greatest A-tech before the Forever Winter, which meant some of the best cameras I had ever seen.

Perhaps I could call Brecht on Sanctuary's intercoms . . . I'd have to figure out how to work them, however . . .

Sanctuary had three total computer rooms, one situated right next to Section One, and one acting like a control hub for the entire facility. The room next to Section One was the worst, however. It smelled of sweat and urine, and I suspected it was because it was used as a house for the previous resident—the sole scientist who had live here before.

Dr. Jack Matthews.

He was a Winter Survivor, and had lived alone in Sanctuary for decades. He'd used this computer room liberally, it seemed.

Jack was currently being held as one of our "prisoners," which reminded me that I would need to deal with him at some point. I added his name to my mental list of ever-growing problems I needed to handle.

First, I had to get supplies for the cranes in case they broke down again. I told Garret I would get that done.

Second, I had to check the perimeter for the Vay. I'd promised Vega that our newest Teth babies wouldn't be in danger.

Third, I wanted to speak with Brecht about the best way to raise humans and Teth in the same environment. Plus, I wanted to give him the title of *caretaker*. He was the only one I trusted with this task, now that Vega had turned it down.

Fourth, I needed to speak with that lunatic, Jack Matthews, about what his plans for the future were. Because that was the humane thing to do.

Lastly, I would definitely need to figure out what I was doing with the fourth and fifth warehouses in Sanctuary. They were filled with . . . dangerous things. Bombs. Weapons. Experiments.

If the others knew about the dangers here, they might honestly want to leave. The real key would be using them to our advantage. How could I do that?

The computer room was spacious, even if it was dull. There were several screens, five in total, with three being dedicated to the cameras around Sanctuary. Two of them were used for work, and both were honestly the size of a large window.

The keyboards were the type favored by the Teth. They were basically braille. You had to feel your way around them in order to get them to work. When the screens changed, the keyboards rippled to display the information in a way that could be felt, so that both humans with eyes, and Teth with advanced tactile sense, could use the computers.

I tapped away on the keyboard, and shuffled through the computer cameras. Instead of interacting with the denizens of Sanctuary, I'd just find Brecht here.

It didn't take me long to find his room. He had set up in a storage space off Section One. It was large enough for him and for Vega, since the two often shared quarters.

Unfortunately for him, I switched the security camera on right as he was rolling around in his bed. With Gascoigne. And none of their clothes.

CHAPTER FOUR

O-Oh, sorry about that," I said aloud, as though Brecht and Gascoigne could hear me.

Obviously, they couldn't.

I fumbled with the keyboard, my hands shaky as I tried to shuffle to another camera. Instead, the image of Brecht and Gascoigne was just switched to another one of the monitors. The anxiety of the situation caused me to nervously chuckle.

They were rather aggressive with each other in a way Bishop and I weren't. Pornography was commonly traded in all the major cities, but I had never purchased anything like that. I preferred books. The words allowed me to fall into imagination, and the secondhand embarrassment of watching other people—real people—wasn't present in books.

So why was I watching Gascoigne and Brecht now?

"What're you doing, Kita?" I asked myself. "Just don't look at the screen and turn this off."

But curiosity did get the better of me. Gascoigne wasn't really the loving or caring type. And apparently, that held true in the bedroom. If they had been wearing clothes, I would've said they were wrestling—attempting to strangle each other—but given the circumstances, perhaps they just liked it rough?

Thankfully, there was no sound.

My face burned as I dragged my gaze down to the keyboard.

What was wrong with me?

Then the door to the computer room flew open and my heart lunged into my throat. When I glanced over my shoulder, and saw who had entered, I almost died of sheer embarrassment.

Chelsy sprang into my computer room. If it had been anyone else, I probably could've talked my way out of the situation, but Chelsy was only eight years old. There was no explaining this without also explaining a myriad of concepts that no eight-year-old should be mulling over.

In a desperate attempt to hide my shame, I leapt up onto the desk with the computer monitors. Yes, I physically threw myself up, sat on the desk, and practically hugged the offending screen to block the contents from view. It was . . . weird.

But I was weird, so this all evened out.

Chelsy stopped in the middle of the room, her eyes big, her smile fading into half a grin, as though she wasn't certain if she should be happy or not.

She wore a white dress, large black boots, a backpack, and a pair of pink leggings. In one hand she held a pen, and in the other, she held her standard notebook. Chelsy had been born mute, and often used the notebook to communicate with people around her.

"Hello," I said as I hugged the screen tighter.

Chelsy was my adopted daughter. I couldn't—under any circumstance—allow her to see what I was doing. I was a role model. The leader of Sanctuary. The person Chelsy looked up to.

I didn't want to ruin those images.

She had dark, lustrous hair that fell in gentle waves around her shoulders, framing her expressive, curious eyes that spoke louder than words ever could. When she glanced between me and the computer, she clearly knew something was up.

Instead of prying, Chelsy smiled and then held up her notebook. The paper already had a message. It read: *Kita, look! They're teaching me to speak with my hands.*

Chelsy made some movements, curling her fingers into vague letter-shaped positions. I suspected she spelled out her name, but I wasn't entirely sure. I knew English and Tethlite, but nothing else.

"*Who* is teaching you?" I asked.

Instead of using her hands, Chelsy grabbed her notebook, wrote a name, and then showed me. *Himiko.*

That was twice I'd heard that name. I knew her—she had lived in Rich-field with the rest of us—but I didn't really *know* her. For most of my life, I preferred to be alone, and it was only just recently that I was expected to be a leader of sorts.

"I'm glad she knows how to do that," I muttered.

Chelsy, once again, glanced from me to the corner of the computer screen I was hiding. When I didn't move, she grabbed her notebook and wrote something else. Her message was: *Miss Himiko teaches the kids. She thinks they're getting sick. Do you have more meds?*

The town of Richfield had been stocked on antibiotics, but those wouldn't cure the common cold. I shook my head. "What kind of sickness?"

Miss Himiko doesn't know. We had to go home early.

I didn't need this right now. For many reasons. I couldn't allow the few human children we had to die, especially not right before we had new Tethlite babies. And in general, I just couldn't sit by and let this happen. As the one in charge, I was supposed to have solutions.

"What did DC say?" I asked. My grip on the computer monitor loos-ened. I caught Chelsy attempting to sneak a peek, so I decided to end this.

I unplugged the monitor from the back. The screen flickered and then powered down. With a thankful sigh, I slid off the desk.

Chelsy narrowed her eyes into a suspicious glare. Then she wrote her next message with speed and intensity that betrayed some of her annoy-ance. She clearly wanted to know what I was hiding from her.

Too bad.

DC is with the kids now, Chelsy wrote.

DC stood for *Dr. Claire.* She was old, but she had lived during human-ity's golden age, back when the aliens provided us with copious amounts of A-tech straight from their hyper-advanced civilization. She was the only one in Sanctuary with vast amounts of medical knowledge.

Still, no amount of book smarts could eliminate a virus. Sometimes intervention was necessary.

"I need to leave Sanctuary to do a few things," I muttered, more to myself than to Chelsy. "I'll speak to DC before I leave to see if there's any-thing she would need from outside."

In theory, there were other human civilizations around. Dodge City wasn't too far from here, and if we used a railroad, we could get even far-ther west.

But first I would search the surrounding territory. Vega was right—our enemies were too close. I had to make sure we were safe first. Then I could head out—get some atomic batteries for everyone around Sanctuary, and medicine for the children—and hopefully be back to Sanctuary before the end of the week, when the eggs would hatch.

I had a habit of disappearing into my own thoughts. I hadn't even realized I was exiting the room, and leaving Chelsy behind, until she clapped her hands to get my attention. I stopped halfway through the door, frozen in place as I came to the realization of where I was.

"O-Oh, sorry, Chelsy. Did you have something else to tell me?"

The little girl frantically wrote another message. This time it read: *Take me with you!*

I caught my breath. Taking a small girl out on a dangerous mission seemed like a terrible idea. Why would I ever do that?

Then again, she had been stuck in Richfield without me for months. Now she would be stuck in Sanctuary—without me—because I'd be too busy dealing with everything else. But what if there were Vay aliens out in the woods? What if I ran into rail gangers? Or what if the Iron-Blooded were planning another attack?

I didn't want to put Chelsy, my little crouton, in danger.

"How about this," I said, still in the doorway. "I'll, uh, take you somewhere special when I get back from my errands, okay? And I'll show you some Teth babies. You'd like that, right?"

If Chelsy had a voice, it would be bouncing off all the walls. Her face lit up, and she did a little twirl.

She liked the Teth, ever since she had seen one of the drones. They were incapable of speaking—just like her—and I suspected she thought of them as family because of it. Chelsy also really liked babies, and I suspected it was for the same reason.

They couldn't speak.

Over and over again, Chelsey seemed drawn to those things and individuals. Now I would have Teth babies? I knew it was pulling on all her heartstrings.

"But you have to wait here for me." I held up a finger. "And stay healthy. And do what DC tells you, okay? If you're good, I'll take you somewhere when I get back. It'll just be us."

Normally, I'd never do anything with *just me*. I was too awkward. But I suspected Chelsy was missing me.

She nodded vigorously to my proposal. Even without her notebook or sign language, I knew this was something she absolutely adored.

It wasn't just the children who were sick.

I entered Sanctuary's impromptu infirmary to a symphony of sneezes and coughs. At least a dozen individuals were waiting around on cots, each draped in a thin blanket, some with hot water bottles, and others clutching handkerchiefs like they were prized possessions.

The scent in the air was a bizarre cocktail of eucalyptus and menthol.

DC walked from patient to patient, taking their names and smiling like a saint. She even looked like one. Her golden hair cascaded over her shoulders like waterfalls of molten honey. Her heart-shaped face was free of blemishes and wrinkles. Even her clothes were white, as though somehow holy.

She was over seventy, but somehow looked younger and healthier than me.

That was because the aliens had brought with them all sorts of tissue-altering science when they arrived on Earth nearly a century ago. They had simple ways to stave off the disease of aging, and most of their leaders had altered themselves long ago with implants straight to the brain that forced the body to maintain a certain status quo, rather than falling apart.

Dr. Claire had one such implant. But they were rare for humans to have before the Forever Winter—only the elite and wealthy, those lucky enough to get the first and second generation of implants numbered less than a few thousand. Those who had them, and lived through the Forever Winter, were always called Winter Survivors.

"Dr. Claire," someone shouted. "My nose is getting stuffed."

She nodded in the person's direction. "I'll get to you shortly, Alan."

No hint of irritation in her voice, just a chipper and upbeat tone.

I made my way into the infirmary, taking special care not to touch anyone. I couldn't afford to get sick at the moment. I had too much to do.

"Do you think this is a plague?" someone asked.

"It's just a cold," DC replied in a singsong voice.

Everywhere I looked, someone needed reassurance. Yes, they had colds. No, it wasn't anything serious. DC took down people's names and how long they had been experiencing these symptoms, all while people wrapped themselves in their blankets and self-pity.

The five children in the room were less dramatic. They were huddled together on the back cots, playing a game with their hands. I couldn't hear them, but they occasionally laughed between wheezes.

I waited my turn to speak with her, standing near the door.

The infirmary had once been an office facility in Sanctuary, but cots had been moved in so we would have a place for injured or sick individuals to recover. We only had a total of fourteen cots, and they just barely fit in the room. Some were pressed up against the others, and a couple were practically shoved into the far corner.

I was content to wait until DC was done, but she stopped halfway through her notes and walked straight toward me. I straightened my posture as she approached, sad I wasn't as tall and athletic looking as she was.

"Kita," she said, smiling. "Are you feeling under the weather as well?"

"N-No. I came to see if you needed anything. I'll be heading out to gather some materials, and I just want to, uh, see if I could find something for you."

DC held up a notepad. She had written everyone's various symptoms, as well as circled the time they had been sick.

"This is likely a virus." DC chuckled as she said, " Since you're from Ex Cathedra, you probably call it *trench cough*."

"Yeah," I muttered.

"The best treatment is rest, hydration, and perhaps some steam. Most people fully recover from the common cold within ten to fourteen days. Unless they develop complications from the illness, nothing permanently bad should happen. You don't have to go out of your way for any sort of medications, but . . ."

"But what?" I asked.

"I believe the amount of illness is a sign that this underground greenhouse is home to airborne viruses." DC folded her arms over her chest. "It's not medications we need—but ways to filter the air. No underground bunker would be complete without an air purification system. I suggest you find Sanctuary's and activate it until the particle levels are reduced."

Damn.

I hadn't thought of that.

She was right, of course. One of the biggest dangers of these abandoned facilities was the air quality. I thought, since Dr. Matthews had been living here, he would've kept the place clean, but he was clearly insane.

I would need to handle this as well.

"Do you need anything else?" I asked.

DC glanced around. The infirmary did have surgical tools, as well as antibiotics, syringes, and a spectrum infusion pump. If DC needed, she could operate on people and have everything required on hand.

"This is a beautiful place," DC whispered. But then her smile faded. "I think it's important to make sure it's secure. As soon as word gets out of the supplies that were hidden here, we'll no doubt be inundated with trouble."

I shook my head. "I intend to handle that while I'm out." No one would bother us if they knew I piloted such an advanced suit of power armor.

"Excellent. Then, please let me know if you need anything from *me*." DC placed a gentle hand on my shoulder. "I'm here to help."

"Thank you."

But she couldn't pilot the power armor—only individuals with the implants in their neck could do that. I rubbed the holes on my spine, just below the hairline on my neck, and I shivered.

I just had to handle all our enemies . . .

CHAPTER FIVE

Night within Sanctuary was tense.

Since no one had really settled into comfortable homes, there was a lot of noise at all hours of the evening. A couple of babies shrieked, some of the men continued setting up faux walls, and the scrape of metal on metal created a disturbing melody that echoed throughout Section One. The noises there could be heard from every corner of our underground facility.

Bishop and I shared an office in Section Three and treated it like a home. It was the last office before the horror show that was Section Four, and allowed me to keep an eye on the place. Bishop and I were cleaning the labs before allowing the rest of the Richfield citizens into the area.

In my mind, Section One—which was mostly a warehouse with lots of equipment—was perfect for living. It had the kitchen, and the barracks, and lots of machinery to make life easier. Section Two had all the plants and underground farms. Another perfect place for people to live and spend their days.

Section Three was just filled with supplies and random things Sanctuary needed. I kept everyone out of it in order to put lots of space between them and Section Four, which was a lab.

Here in the Section Three office, we had a desk, a computer terminal with several monitors, and a makeshift bed made of blankets and sleeping bags. Very fancy. And the place was tidy—because of me. I sat at the computer searching through the information while all of Sanctuary tried to settle themselves into a night of sleep.

Bishop sat on our bed. He had a mirror, a knife, and a bowl of water. He shaved the stubble on his chin, carefully brushing the blade over his skin.

"Kit-Kat," he said while he worked, "are you tired yet?"

"Not quite," I whispered.

The Sanctuary computer had a lot of information. I wanted to sift through it all, but during the day, I had other responsibilities. I could sleep when I was dead—right now, I needed to work.

Bishop finished his shaving, cleaned his blade in the water, and then stood. He tucked his knife into its sheath on his belt, and then, after a loud yawn, he sauntered over to the desk. Then he stood behind me.

That . . .

Unnerved me.

I didn't like people looming in areas where I couldn't see them. Years of living across the wasteland had taught me to keep people within my sights at all times. Obviously, Bishop was trustworthy, but that didn't stop my skin from crawling when he placed his hands on the back of my chair.

"You shuddered," Bishop said. "You okay?"

I continued poking at the keyboard, my eyes glued to the screen. "Yes. I'm just . . . tense."

"I can help with that."

Bishop placed his powerful hands on my shoulders and dug his fingers into my muscles. With slow and controlled movements, he massaged the base of my neck, and then down my spine, between my shoulder blades.

It felt good, but I jerked out of his grip. Leaning forward on the desk, I muttered, "Bishop, please. I don't want to relax."

I had work to do.

"You don't want to relax?" Bishop playfully asked. "I can *also* help with that."

He unsheathed his knife and then brought it around to my throat. I caught my breath, my heart hammering. Before I could find my words— and demand to know what was going on—he lowered the blade, gently grazing it across my skin until he came to the collar of my shirt. Then he sliced the fabric with a clean and easy motion.

It was just a T-shirt, and he had only cut it so that it was now a V-neck, but it was so unexpected, I didn't know how to act.

It was exciting. How did Bishop always do this? He had a gift for completely flipping the script—making me feel sexy, even if I never did on my own. I hadn't been in the mood for anything other than work, but now . . .

Bishop ran his hand down my side, feeling me up as he went all the way down to my hips. My heart beat so hard, and my work was completely forgotten.

Then he brought the blade back to my throat. It was tilted in such a way that it would be difficult to cut me, but I still felt the cold steel against my skin.

Bishop leaned down until his mouth was close to my ear. "It's been a while since we've done stuff," he whispered, somehow threateningly, somehow playful. "A man can only wait so long . . . And you're so very beautiful."

My face was hot, and my heart just kept hammering.

I . . . didn't know what to say.

How was he so good at this?

He was always so sexy. I wished I was more like him. Should I say something back to him? When Bishop brought the knife down a second time, he slowly cut more of my T-shirt. I tilted my head back, and then he moved his hand between my legs.

Bishop was confident.

That kind of self-assured and positive attitude was what attracted me to him in the first place.

When he cut through the front of my bra, I half gasped. It probably sounded like a yipe or a yelp—because I wasn't the sexiest individual—but that didn't matter to Bishop.

He chuckled into my ear, and in a sweet tone, said, "Tense enough, Kit-Kat? Because I'd love to help you relax now."

I swallowed hard as he sliced through the rest of my shirt and tugged it from my arms. I shivered, because it was cold, but my body felt hotter than ever.

"B-Bishop," I stammered. "I . . ."

He let go of me, stood straight, and then spun my chair around. I crossed my arms over my chest and stared up at him. The look in his eyes was a mix of hungry and adoring. After he put away his knife, he ran a hand through my black hair.

"You wanna do it on the bed?" Bishop whispered. Then he placed his hands on the armrests of my chair, posting himself above me. "Or right here? But you gotta pick fast, because I'm not gonna wait long."

My face burned so much, I could barely look him in the eye. But I knew this was a kindness. Bishop understood I was particular about things. Fastidious. Cleanly. A few times we had done "stuff" in places that made me feel sullied afterward, and Bishop always went out of his way to never do that again.

We bathed together frequently—and it was probably the location we did most of our intimate activities.

"The bed," I forced myself to say, though my words were barely a whisper.

Bishop chuckled. He was always easy to make laugh. Then he scooped me up in his arms—like I weighed nothing—and I leaned onto his chest. It was easy to be with Bishop. Effortless.

I loved him.

Bishop fell asleep promptly after everything was over.

But I wasn't tired. I had too much to do, and my restless mind punished me if ever I attempted to take time for myself.

I had led people to Sanctuary. If I sat around, wasting my time with sleep, I was failing them.

My grandfather never slept, either. That was why his name was in all the history books. Why he was the one who first welcomed the aliens to Earth. The reason he was the first to learn their language, Tethlite, and teach it to others.

So, while most of Sanctuary's denizens struggled to get a good night's rest despite the symphony of irritations, I headed to our makeshift prison. I wore a new T-shirt and a pair of jeans, though Bishop had threatened to cut them up as well. I had told him no. I needed them. We didn't have a lot of spare clothing my size.

Bishop didn't wake when I left the bed. It was fine, though. I could handle people locked behind bars without an escort.

Thankfully for me, the prison was in Section Three, away from the others, and down into a deeper level of Sanctuary. It was colder there, and I suspected it had once been a basement storage unit for some of the bio-material used in all the experiments.

I didn't want to think about research that was once conducted here, though. That was a mystery I could solve *after* I had solved all the current fires.

With slow and careful steps, I walked down the metal stairway to the subbasement. The air here was heavy with the weight of silence, and each time I disturbed that with a breath or scuff of my boot, I tensed. When I reached the bottom, I stopped.

There had once been two alcoves with shelves that faced one another. Scrapyard Pete had welded some bars to the ceiling and floor, and created a couple doors from sheets of silver tin. Everyone said Pete was our resident handyman, but I was starting to suspect he was our resident engineer. The cells of our prison were expertly crafted.

Each one mirrored to the next and was a world unto itself—a small, stark space where light dared only to trickle in, as if afraid of what it might reveal. The corners housed the darkest of shadows.

"Hello?" someone asked as I walked the small hallway between the two makeshift cells.

I turned toward the speaker.

Jack Matthews.

He wore a pair of gray sweatpants and a white shirt—our prison "uniform" cobbled together from the leftover clothing inside Sanctuary. Jack had a brown and gray beard that was the longest I had ever seen on a person. It went from his chin all the way down to his waistband. The faint lines near his eyes said he was in his early fifties, but they were liars.

This scientist was a Winter Survivor. He was close to a hundred years old. At least.

Jack kept his oily brown hair in a ponytail. He tugged on the end as he stood and stepped out of the darkness of his cell.

"Hello?" he repeated.

I took a deep breath. Then I mentally prepared myself. "Jack? My name is Kita. I'm here to ask you a few questions."

"Are my plants okay?" he asked the moment I stopped talking. "Are they all in the same place? You haven't touched them, have you?"

Jack rushed to the bars. He grabbed them with both hands and leaned his weight onto them. With wild eyes, he searched my expression.

"They're still where you left them," I said. "And we've been watering them."

That was a lie. Most of them had, unfortunately, died or been moved during the process of getting the people from Richfield into the bunker. Thankfully, I was rather good at lying—it was the only real social skill I had—and the doctor relaxed a bit in his cell.

My third rule to lying: avoid contradictions and easily verified facts.

Since he couldn't verify anything, all I had to do was avoid contradicting myself and it would be easy to maintain this charade.

I straightened my posture. "Dr. Matthews, I came here to speak with you. I've, uh, explored the facility and I've found some disturbing—and interesting—items."

The man stared at me, unblinking.

I wrung my hands and paused. While I was confident with my lying, and even had rules to maintain an elaborate fabrication, I hated moments like this.

Jack Matthews wasn't normal.

I wasn't normal.

That made for a terrible combination.

And when I said "normal," I meant in the interaction department. Most people could deal with this level of strange, but I felt myself butting up against a rock. With my breath held for a moment, I decided to push through.

"What were you planning to do with those items?" I asked.

"You're not welcome here," Jack said. "You should get out."

After a sigh, I said, "Why aren't we welcome here?"

"This is a safe place. My place. Away from the nuclear fire. *Purifying flames.*" Jack rubbed the bars, his eyes as wild as ever. "Miri made sure the world would burn, and he—or she, the aliens are a strange lot—gave me this place as a reward for helping. This is *my* place. *Mine.*"

"Miri?" I asked.

Hearing that name seemed to calm Jack down. He released the bars and nodded once. "Miri'Cova."

That name was Teth in origin. I had heard it before several times. First, the name was used in a message to my grandfather that was from before the Forever Winter. Now, it was being used in conjunction with biological warfare that was being developed in this very facility. Both times, the name was tied to treachery.

This was a fifty-year-old mystery, though. I kept trying to ignore it, but the evidence continued to jump up and slap me across the face.

"Can you tell me anything else about this Miri'Cova?" I asked.

Jack chuckled, like this was actually an amusing topic of conversation. "The Teth developed the firestorm bombs. They made the technology. They're not just *nuclear bombs*—they have staying power. Fire. Destructive forces made specifically to terminate life. The Teth were going to use them against the Vay, wipe them from the planet."

While this was all disturbing, and Jack said every word as if it were a delight, I mostly knew that already. "That had nothing to do with Miri'Cova."

"Miri leaked all that information to the Vay. He—or she, again, it's confusing, they're hermaphrodites—Miri gave them the research and the materials to make their own firestorm bombs. Then Miri tried to leave the planet on one of the few remaining Teth starships."

I nodded once.

A while back—more than a year ago now, perhaps more—I had found recordings meant for my grandfather. In those recordings, there were details about Miri'Cova's escape, and about how his starship was actually sabotaged before it left Earth. Apparently, the engines wouldn't work correctly, and it would float aimlessly.

Miri'Cova would be forced to consume his own children to survive. And probably eventually perish, once the food supply ran low.

A dark fate, but probably one appropriate for the traitor.

But again, I already knew this. "Anything else about Miri?" I asked.

Jack laughed once. "Miri was friends with the Vay. He, she, it, brought some of them to North America to start a secret nest up in the north, away from any of the major cities, or any detection, really."

"Really? Where?" This was *new* information, and would explain why there were Vay in this area. We were much farther north than I had ever lived.

Jack shrugged. "I dunno. I never met them. And who would want to?" He smiled, flashing his yellow teeth. "I haven't spoken to anyone in years, and I would've preferred that. My plants are all that matters now. Once the humans and aliens are all dead . . . It'll be the plants that rule. And they'll remember me."

Why was he on the verge of being coherent? Perhaps this was all a game to him.

"What about the *items* here?" I slowly asked. "What were you going to do with them?"

"Items?"

I had been vague on purpose.

"The bombs," I whispered.

But the moment the words escaped my lips, the person in the second cell stirred. Our other permanent prisoner was none other than Quern, a power armor pilot for the Iron-Blooded. Like me, he had connectors on the back of his neck that would allow him to control one of the exoskeletons.

I glanced over my shoulder. Quern was by the bars of his cell, his expression unreadable.

He was a muscular man, and the uniform we gave him didn't quite fit because of it. His T-shirt was on the verge of giving up the ghost and tearing at the seams. His dark tan skin and light-colored eyes were striking, nearly beautiful. It was the intelligence behind his gaze that worried me the most, though.

He was also missing his left thumb—thanks to me. I had ordered it be removed so we could use his fingerprint to access Iron-Blooded tech. Now, Quern kept his mutilated hand mostly balled into a fist, and it was difficult to notice, but I always kept it in mind.

I didn't want to discuss the specifics of the firestorm bombs with Quern nearby. Not unless we were going to kill him. He probably hated me with all his being.

And the Iron-Blooded could never be allowed to know we had bombs at this facility.

"The bombs," Jack said, so loud his voice echoed throughout the room. "They're ready to strike. Fully armed and operational—each with a fuel source that is hundreds of years from expiring. Miri said to keep them in case the purifying fire failed."

"You have firestorm bombs?" Quern asked. Then in Tethlite, he added, *"They're the reason everything went to hell. You can blame the Teth, but after hearing that madman talk for hours on end, I'm convinced the humans pressured the Teth to make those weapons."*

Quern was . . . a bit fanatical.

All the Iron-Blooded were.

"Humanity has done nothing wrong," Jack shouted. He spoke in English, but it was obvious he understood Quern's statement.

I wondered if the two of them had been conversing with each other. They had nothing but time, after all.

"Quiet, old man," Quern hissed in Tethlite. *"You don't know what you're talking about."*

"It's the aliens who are to blame. The Teth and the Vay—even the Frest—brought all their problems with them. Our planet, our plants . . . they were caught up in a war that wasn't meant for them."

Until the last few statements, I'd almost thought Jack had regained some of his sanity.

"*Don't talk about the Teth that way,*" Quern whispered. "*They're our superiors. Better than us in every way.*"

Jack stretched his arms through the bars and then pointed at Quern. "I've got heartaches by the number," he said in a singsong voice. "Heartache number one was when you left me, and heartache two was when you came back!"

I . . . wasn't sure why he was singing. Was this his delusional way of ending the conversation? It was working.

I pinched the bridge of my nose, wondering why I even bothered. Jack and Quern were both unstable in their own ways, and I probably should've left well enough alone.

However, interacting with both of them got me worried. I walked over to the makeshift door of Jack's cell and eyed the hinges. Then I turned around, walked across the narrow hall, and inspected Quern's door, though I tried to hide what I was doing by panning my gaze over the entirety of his living area.

His door was thinner than Jack's but it still seemed in place. I couldn't get too good a look at it while hiding my actions, though.

Quern glowered down at me, never moving.

"*When are you going to kill me?*" he whispered in Tethlite.

"I'm not," I casually replied.

My plan had been to release him back to the Iron-Blooded once we were secure here in Sanctuary. It was probably stupid of me—Gascoigne had advocated for Quern's death many times—but I was trying to lead by example. If I wanted humanity to recover, I needed humanity to stick around. And Quern was a little more agreeable than most Iron-Blooded.

Just a little.

"*You're not going to get my hopes up by lying to me,*" he said.

I shook my head. "Believe whatever you want to believe."

"*If you were smart, you'd end me now. And I know you're the brains of this outfit. Do us both a favor and drop the charade.*"

I didn't know how to answer that, so I didn't. Was he *trying* to convince me to kill him? I wondered why—but not for long. My mind was better dedicated to more pressing problems.

Like how this facility had had a purpose before the bombs went off.

It seemed major players from before the Forever Winter knew about that mysterious purpose. That worried me. Winter Survivors could know about Sanctuary as well. I made a mental note to discuss that with the others.

I stared at Quern. He stood half in the shadows, half in the artificial lighting. He always had this intense look about him. I met his gaze, wondering what he thought about this whole situation—but I knew better than to ask him about it.

Quern loved to preach about the evils of humanity, and how we should hand over all control to the Teth. He would hate my plan to integrate Teth babies into our society. He would want them to rule over us—like they ruled over the Iron-Blooded.

"*If you don't kill me, you'll regret it,*" he whispered, almost threateningly.

That was a little surprising, but I wasn't worried. I sarcastically glanced around and then shrugged. "I hate to break this to you, but it looks like I have the upper hand."

Quern said nothing in response.

I didn't usually like provoking people, because sometimes it gave them the motivation to do audacious things, but Quern was our prisoner. He had been locked away for weeks now. And he wasn't saying *he* would get me, he was implying the Iron-Blooded would eventually get us.

At least, that was what I hoped he was implying.

I turned and headed out of the prison. "Thank you both," I called out over my shoulder.

But neither Jack nor Quern replied.

That was fine. I had gathered all the information I possibly could from the interaction. Now I needed to get some sleep so I could patrol the perimeter tomorrow.

I decided to sleep in the computer room with the Teth eggs. Was it some sort of mothering instinct? I didn't know. All I knew was that my imagination continually tortured me with visions of their destruction. What if an earthquake happened and the canisters fell to the ground? What if one of the eggs couldn't absorb all the nutrient goo? What if they were too cold?

While most of Sanctuary slept, I gathered the eggs off the table and placed them on the floor under the desk. I was probably being insane. I knew that. But that was the only place that allowed my imagination to rest. If they were on the floor, they couldn't fall. If they were under the desk, nothing could fall on them. And if they were in a nice sheltered location, perhaps they wouldn't get too cold.

"Goodnight, Benjamin, Joel, Tamura," I whispered.

The orange gel containers didn't move.

I liked to imagine they could hear me in their eggs, though. And since I disliked Tethlite so much, I was hoping they would learn English first.

Again, I knew I was crazy, but as long as there was no one around to see it, I could deny it until my dying breath.

With a sigh, I stood from the desk and paced around the quiet room. Pacing helped me think. And I needed that.

What could I use firestorm bombs for? Obviously, devastation on a grand scale, but what else? Ex Cathedra and United California were locked in a stalemate war. Could I be an arms dealer? Sell one side the tool needed for instant victory? What could they possibly offer me? People? Teth? Supplies?

Maybe all three.

But if I did that, they *would* use the bomb. And the previous bombs had been so horrific, humanity still hadn't recovered . . .

The cost would take a toll on us all.

After a couple hours of mulling over the problem, fatigue took me. I pressed my back up against the metal wall and then slid down into a sitting position. It wasn't comfortable, but I didn't care. As long as I was close to the eggs, everything would be fine.

So I closed my eyes and tilted my head back until it rested against the cold wall. I wished Bishop was here with me, though.

As I took some deep breaths, I found myself on the edge of sleep. Years of living in an underground bunker had prepared me for even the most rock-like of sleeping environments.

But then someone pressed icy steel against my throat.

I snapped my eyes open. To my horror, Quern was here in the office. He was kneeling next to me, a knife held against my flesh, his gaze drilling down onto mine.

CHAPTER SIX

I didn't move, but my mind raced.

Bishop was in our office room. Gascoigne and Brecht had been together. DC was swamped with people in the infirmary.

No one who I truly trusted was nearby.

And the eggs . . . they were here, under my desk. I almost glanced over to them—I would give away their position if I did that!—but I stopped myself before I turned my head. Instead, I met Quern's intense gaze, my heart hammering against my ribs.

Did he know about the eggs? What if he took them?

"I told you that you'd regret not killing me," he said.

Quern was so close, I felt his hot breath on my chin, and smelled the boiled stew he had for dinner. The blade he had was one of the tools brought over from Richfield. It was some sort of woodworking knife, but the blade had been sharpened to a fine point. He kept it pressed against my neck, and I felt a line of my skin burning as the weapon slowly cut my flesh.

A small part of me thought it was statistically improbable that two different men, using two different knives, would be holding them to my throat in the same night.

I almost laughed.

Almost.

But besides wanting to voice the improbability of the situation, I didn't know what to say, so I remained quiet. In my experience, it was always unnerving when the other person kept their motives hidden.

Quern grabbed my left arm near the shoulder and then stood, hauling me up in the process. Even though we had cut off his left thumb, he still had a nub that dug into my flesh. In one fluid motion that betrayed his years of combat training, he yanked me close and twisted me around so my back was pressed against him.

"*Stay quiet,*" he whispered in Tethlite. "*Do what I say, and I won't kill you.*"

Quern kept his knife against my throat, while also maintaining a blood-choking grip on my bicep. I muttered an acceptance of his terms, but my heart was beating so loudly in my ears, I didn't hear my own statement.

"*Good. Now show me to the area with the bombs. Don't disturb the others. The moment you alert anyone, I'll end us both.*"

I took a deep breath.

Quern wouldn't hesitate to kill us both. This wasn't an empty threat.

And even if he saw the bombs, it wasn't like he would walk away with them. They were huge. They required a delivery system—a massive truck or plane or turret—in order to be functional. One man couldn't carry them away.

So, with a shaky hand, I pointed to the door. Quern practically lifted my weight off the floor as he headed in the direction I indicated. We exited my office, and into the dark hallway. He shut the door with careful movement, mindful of the noise.

Thank whatever gods were left he didn't see the canisters.

I was pressed so tightly against him, I felt every ripple of his muscles. Even his heartbeat wasn't a mystery. He seemed calm, but tense. Quern had likely been thinking about this moment for a long time.

"*Straight to the bombs,*" he commanded.

I moved my head to the left, and we took off down the hall. My feet barely touched the floor, but Quern's echoed through the hollow corridors, a lonely sound as we made our way away from Sections One and Two.

Section Three didn't really have people in it—but maybe Bishop was awake and outside our office room. Unfortunately, while it was night, most of Sanctuary's lights were dimmed. It was darker here, and my anxieties got the better of me. The sharp blade at my throat probably wasn't helping things, either.

I trembled the whole way.

Bishop wasn't in the hallway.

Once we reached a door, Quern loosened his hold on my arm—just slightly.

Quern opened the door and pointed in the direction we needed to head. Sanctuary was practically a subterranean labyrinth, and the deeper we got the more it was obvious the place hadn't been cared for. Jack had lived here for decades, but the paint was peeling in some areas, revealing the cold, unfeeling steel beneath.

The air grew heavier as we neared Section Four.

It was also filled with the scent of metal and something else—something indefinable but ever-present.

"This is it," I whispered as I pointed to the door that led to the warehouse used for lab research.

It was locked with a computer terminal. Instead of trying his hand at it, Quern shoved me close. "*Unlock it.*"

I placed my hand on the old keyboard. Without needing to look, I unlocked the door. Quern pushed it open and the hinges groaned the entire way. Cursing under his breath, Quern dragged me inside and then shut the door behind us.

The labs . . .

Abandoned equipment lay scattered around us, all left to the mercy of time. Desks were laden with sheets of yellowed paper, and overturned chairs and glass shards decorated the area.

Every wall was lined with cages, though.

On either side of the vast warehouse were dozens of glass enclosures. They were impressive, since each one had their own little environment inside, ranging from the deserts to the rainforests.

"*What the fuck?*" Quern asked as he eyed the zoo-like environment with a disgusted sneer.

The glass enclosures once housed animals. Now they just had corpses.

Animal carcasses filled the lab, all of them in various stages of decay. It definitely explained the smell. Sanctuary had a life-support system, but DC was right. We needed to fix the air filtration system, because I was certain this massive graveyard of animals wasn't helping anything.

Maybe . . .

This was why so many people were getting sick.

Bishop and I had cleared away some of the corpses, but since we were the only ones coming back here, it had been a slow process. Perhaps the stink was getting into the air vents, and the decayed material was floating on the air into the other sections.

Quern pressed his knife against my throat, bringing me back to the present. "*What is this?*" he growled.

"I was trying to ask Jack about it," I replied. "But he was getting crazier with each question."

"*You don't know?*"

"He was a researcher . . ."

I was trying to formulate my words—to better describe what I had found here—when Quern tightened his grip once again, the nub on his left hand a constant reminder that he likely despised my very existence. He leaned his head down, his hot and angry breath on my ear.

"*If you don't want me to cut you up,*" he said, his Tethlite rather thick and menacing, "*tell me what they were researching here.*"

"Illnesses," I murmured, solidifying my earlier theory. "Specifically, for the Teth."

"*You're planning on killing the Teth?*" The anger in his words was enough to tell me that he was giving serious thoughts to killing me and then burning Sanctuary to the ground.

"No."

Quern pressed the knife closer, and a hot trickle of blood slid down my neck and then onto my collarbone.

I touched his wrist, silently urging him to restrain himself.

When Quern pulled back, just slightly, I managed to say, "It's fifty-year-old research. Done by other people. I haven't touched it."

The corpses around the room vouched for my statement with their silence.

Quern didn't move for a long time. Then, he slowly glanced around, as if taking everything in for the first time. I wondered what he thought of all this, but I wasn't about to ask. The blood soaking into the collar of my shirt, though minor, was still at the forefront of my thoughts.

Thankfully, the tiny machines in my blood, the nanites that had been developed before the Forever Winter, stitched my skin back up.

"The humans here were trying to kill the Teth?" Quern asked in English, his voice gravelly.

He rarely spoke English.

"I think Teth were involved, too," I whispered. "The computers have most of their notes about it. I . . . I don't know what they were going to do, because it seems everything was interrupted."

Quern gritted his teeth. Then his presence of mind seemed to return all at once. "*Where are the bombs?*" he asked, switching back to Tethlite.

I pointed to a far door. "In the next section over."

Quern didn't speak. He hurried me through the labs, around the glass enclosures with the many bodies. I tried not to gag as we went by the worst of it. Quern didn't seem to have trouble. His gut was as iron as his heart, his gaze locked on the far door, and his gait taking us there as fast as possible without straight running.

The computers here, the ones with the research data, were on. Quern did glance at one as we went by, and I felt the hesitation throughout his body. He was considering stopping, but he turned away and led me to another locked door.

Well, not *any* locked door.

It was something special. It was a *vault* door, one with multiple locks and a timed release. This type of door would have been very useful at stopping someone like Quern.

If I had locked it . . .

Instead, I had left the door open. I had wanted to do something with the bombs inside, and dealing with the hassle of the vault door seemed superfluous. We were the only ones here, after all, and in my head, I could've shut the door before our enemies got to it.

I hadn't thought about the enemies within Sanctuary. I should've been more mindful. I should've dealt with them in a better manner than locking them away—pushing them out of sight and mind.

Quern slipped in through the crack of the open vault door and dragged me with him the whole way. Once inside, the lights flickered to life, humming until the illumination was enough for us to see everything in the fifth and final warehouse.

There were rows upon rows of large, industrial racks, each made of solid steel. They were anchored to the floor and covered in boxes, crates, and canisters of all sizes. I had opened most of them when I wanted to make an inventory, but since it was just me allowed in this back area, half the containers were still closed.

At least Section Five didn't smell of death. I took a deep breath and relaxed a little, though Quern's grip never allowed me to forget the peril I was in.

On the far shelf, in plain sight, were several firestorm bombs. They were old-world warheads, the type meant for smaller operations. Even if they were tactically tiny, each was the size of a motorcycle.

All of them were sealed and covered in warning signs and hazmat symbols.

Despite the clear indictor of their deadly purpose, Quern glanced around, his eyes not really focusing on any one thing. When he spotted the warheads, he squinted, as though unsure of what he was looking at.

"That's them," I said.

Quern straightened his posture. "*Those? I thought . . .*" But he never finished his statement.

Unless someone had studied history—like I had—most people in the wasteland had no idea what a warhead looked like. Quern was probably used to the tiny square-shaped bombs that an individual could carry and plant.

But the firestorm bombs were nothing like that.

Had he been hoping to carry a bomb out of Sanctuary? Probably. That was likely why he had me bring him here.

Quern dragged me over to the warhead. He stopped in front of it and glared. With the knife still held to my neck, he leaned in close.

"*Are the insides dangerous?*"

I nodded once, careful not to cut myself. "They're radioactive. See the casing? That shields us from the worst of it. If we unsealed these, we'd put everyone nearby in danger of radiation poisoning. Also, if the bombs are damaged themselves, they could prematurely explode."

Quern leaned away and growled a curse under his breath. Then he exhaled. "*You know how to use them?*"

"I do. That's why we can't unseal them."

The first rule to lying—tell them what they already believe first, then everything that came after seemed more plausible.

I *did* know all about the firestorm bombs, but I wasn't sure if unsealing them would do all that damage. I just didn't want Quern to even think it was a possibility. In my heart, I knew we should leave these bombs alone unless we had a good use for them—or we were going to sell them. If I attempted to open one, I had no idea the kinds of fallout that we would have to deal with.

"*Very well,*" Quern muttered. "*We're leaving. Show me the fastest way out of this hellhole. And quickly—before the whole place starts to wake up.*"

CHAPTER SEVEN

Quern dragged me out of Section Five, and then back into the room with the glass cages filled with animal bodies. He stopped at a computer, sneering.

Most people struggled to use computers with Teth keyboards. The tactile typing wasn't suited for most humans. Quern had grown up with the Teth, though. He was one of their Iron-Blooded cultists—he probably preferred A-tech over human-made tools and technology.

He quickly typed away, pulling up files until he reached the results of the research.

Then he moved away from the computer and yanked me over to the Section Three door. I said nothing and didn't resist. I was worried about my life, but I was more worried about the others. Quern was a trained military combatant. Most of the people of Richfield weren't.

I couldn't risk putting them in danger.

So Quern led me through the dimly lit corridors, careful not to make much noise. When we reached Section Two, he tightened his grip on my arm, silently warning me. Again, I said nothing.

I had been in worse situations.

While my heart thumped in my ribs, I reminded myself I had lived through everything else—if I kept my eyes open for an opportunity to end this, I'd likely find something.

Quern took me to the walls. They were steel, cold, and mostly gray—a perfect reflection of my mood. While most people slept, we hurried into Section One.

It was here that Quern hesitated. We'd brought him through here at one point, but it was obvious he didn't recognize the place.

We had been busy building, after all.

"Do you need me to lead you out?" I whispered.

He gritted his teeth so powerfully I could hear it.

Instead of answering me, he made his way through the "paths" between proto-buildings. Everyone was setting up a home or an area to call home, but the walkways were always kept clear.

People were sleeping, but a few lights glowed in the "dwellings."

Quern avoided them. And before long, he made it to the entranceway. There was a large door, which led to a massive stairway up to the surface, that was both locked by Sanctuary's computer system and also held secure with a padlock on the handles. This was to prevent someone from hacking their way inside, like I had.

Quern shoved me over and grabbed the thick, steel padlock. It rattled against the handle.

Someone would hear if he kept that up.

He stopped, growled some sort of curse under his breath, and then fished through his gray sweatpants. He withdrew pieces of scrap metal from his pocket. One was sharp, one was thin and pointed, and another reminded me of a level.

A lockpick set. He probably had cobbled it together from the scrap that had been used to make the jail. Scrapyard Pete had probably been careless with cleaning up, and Quern capitalized on that.

However, it was nearly impossible to pick a lock with one hand. Quern exhaled, and then shoved me up against the door itself, the front of my body squished against the unforgiving metal. Then he leaned his weight on me while he attempted to unlock the first lock on the door.

Normally, I would've have been hypercritical of my captor attempting to do something, but since I had difficulty breathing, every second felt like a minor agony.

Quern fiddled with the lock for at least a few solid minutes.

"Do you need help?" I whispered.

"*Don't patronize me,*" he hissed in Tethlite. "*I've been trained in escape operations. This is how it's done.*"

I waggled a hand back and forth. "I don't know. I've seen this done better—but definitely not slower."

"Shut up. This is just some fancy old-world lock. Anyone would have difficulty with it. Obviously, that's why you've used it."

His Tethlite came out flustered, and his work on the lock definitely suffered. I almost laughed. Was Quern easily unnerved, or had I injured his pride?

The lights would come on soon. It would honestly make me laugh if he took so long that he was just caught. On his own. Without me doing anything.

But I wasn't that lucky. Quern, true to his word, managed to unlock that damn padlock with just his tools. That was impressive, given how complicated that lock had been.

"Now use the computer and get us out of here," Quern commanded in Tethlite.

He gently set the steel lock on the ground, careful not to make any noise. He never took a hand from me, not even while he half knelt.

I scooted over to the computer terminal and easily opened the entrance. Wind from the outside swept into Sanctuary, and the tarps over some people's dwellings rustled. Quern shoved me out before I could see if anyone awoke.

Then the door shut behind us with a groan and creak. A gigantic stairway led up to the surface. Since we were so far from anyone else, and with a wall between us, Quern dropped the stealth. He practically hauled me forward by my shoulder, his knife in the other hand and vaguely pointed in my direction as he ran up the stairs, taking them two at a time.

Once we reached the welcome entrance, I was sucking down air. Running up stairs wasn't a skill I would've boasted about. Quern, on the other hand, was rather athletic. He jogged to the entrance door and pulled me along without much trouble at all.

Then we exited the building and stood at the edge of an asphalt parking lot covered in a spiderweb of cracks.

Pine trees stood like tall sentinels all around us. Small beams of moonlight pierced through the cloud cover, offering small pillars of illumination in the otherwise dense and dark forest.

Metal posts outlined the edge of the parking lot. A small road, still visible, was just beyond that. And standing between a few nearby trees was a sign that read: *US Sanctuary Housing #4.*

I thought Quern might stab me and then make a run for it, but he didn't do that. Instead, he kept me close and ran forward. I held his arm tightly, trying to keep his pace. It was difficult, though. It was dark, and the ground was uneven.

"Where are you taking me?" I asked in English.

"*Keep quiet,*" he hissed in Tethlite.

That wasn't helpful.

Instead of trying to engage with him, I tried to memorize our route. If I knew where we were going, perhaps I could deduce his plan. If he went south, I would know he was trying to get back to his Iron-Blooded friends. And if he went west, I would know he wanted to get into United California.

To my surprise, Quern headed *east*.

There wasn't much to the east besides rail gangs. And if he went east enough, we'd run into Ex Cathedra.

What was his plan?

Pine needles rustled in the evening wind and our footsteps crunched the detritus underfoot. The air was cool and crisp. Perhaps too cold. My breath came out as a fog, though I kept warm from the sheer amount of movement we were doing.

This whole forest smelled of fresh pine mixed with an earthy musk. It was as though it hadn't been disturbed in a long time.

In the distance, the howl of a lone wolf created a haunting melody that reverberated through the trees. Several owls hooted from their hidden perches.

The sound of wildlife eased my tension. If the Vay were close—or any of their mindless drones—the animals would've fled.

Perhaps Quern thought the same thing, because he started to run, his breathing heavier than before. He didn't seem to care if we were making any noise or not.

"Where are we going?" I dared to ask again. "There's nothing out this way. Not for miles."

"*I said to stay quiet,*" he growled.

And he offered nothing else. So again, I kept track of our direction, and every slight shift Quern did as he took us deeper and deeper into the darkness of the woods. Occasionally, he had to slow down to get over obstacles. There were a surprising number of rusted cars we had to climb over. There had once been a road through this forest, but it was destroyed by overachieving trees, and now it functioned as a vehicle graveyard.

And Quern had no problem hoisting himself—and me—over each and every truck that stood planted in our way. He hefted me up, practically slung me over his shoulder, and then leapt down on the other side.

The road that was once here had been multiple lanes, and by the time we reached the other side, it felt as though we had made it over a minor mountain.

"We shouldn't go too far," I said, the cold air stinging the tip of my nose. "There are gangs, and wild animals if you go too far into the wilderness. The radio DJ talked about bears pretty frequently."

Quern shot me a glare. "I can handle a bear," he said in English. "I told you to stay quiet. If you don't fuck with me, I'll let you live."

"Why?" I asked, not because I wanted him to kill me, but because I didn't understand his motivation. Was he taking me as a hostage? Was he going to bring me to the Iron-Blooded? Would he torture me for what we had done to him?

But Quern didn't elaborate.

I had been held hostage by the Iron-Blooded before, and it had been a terrible experience. However, this time I was stronger. Better. My blood was filled with nanites. I could handle them.

I hoped.

With his knife still in hand, and his other hand firmly on my arm, Quern took me farther and farther east.

The sun started to rise, but the overcast skies made it difficult to see. Plus, the pine tree canopy above us was like nature's roof. It remained dark, even as the morning approached.

But then we reached a dirt road. It was clean, and the tire divots told me it was used often. Quern stopped us before we took a step onto the dirt itself. Our footprints would be more noticeable if we walked along the road—even if that meant an easier time walking.

He eyed the length of the road, his gaze shifting from left to right.

"We shouldn't mess with anyone using this," I whispered. "We don't have any weapons."

If I had my power armor, I could handle anything that came our way. But that wasn't a possibility at the moment.

Quern narrowed his eyes and turned so we were heading north along the side of the road.

Which was seriously the worst option he could pick. Because apparently the Vay were up north—and those war-hungry aliens would gladly rip up the both of us.

CHAPTER EIGHT

For several hours, Quern took me north, weaving a way through the pine trees.

By the time it was late into the afternoon, the wind was harsher, and my clothes sweaty. Quern finally slowed his pace, his own breathing heavier. Then he stopped, jerked to me a halt, and listened. A *clanking* sound echoed off in the distance, along with the *crack* of gunfire.

Dammit.

One of the things I loved about having lived in Richfield, and now in Sanctuary, was that I hadn't needed to deal with the darkness of the wasteland. It was nerve-racking to meet new people out in the open, considering there was no law here.

Quern and I had a single rusty knife between us.

It would go poorly if we ran across anyone with a gun.

"I'd love to know what we're doing," I whispered. "So that I'm not constantly confused by all of your decisions."

Quern glowered down at me. Then he returned his sights to the road. "We need to find a working vehicle."

In a playful tone, so that I wouldn't anger him too much, I said, "I hope you're not planning on taking us farther north."

"I hope you're not hoping too hard," he darkly quipped.

"The Vay are up there. We can't—we shouldn't—go anywhere near them."

Quern yanked me down the road, never meeting my eyes. "The Davis Space Force Base is farther north. That's where we need to go."

A space force base? From what I had seen, there were only half a dozen of those across all of North America. They were places to construct starship parts, or build weather satellites. Technically, I had been to the Thompson Space Force Base—that was where the Teth architect, Riven, had been hiding.

Now a lot of things made sense.

If we managed to get to the Davis Space Force Base, Quern could likely communicate with the heart of the Iron-Blooded. He would probably tell them all about our firestorm bombs. And everything inside Sanctuary.

Another *crack* of a gunshot caused me to flinch.

"Stick close," Quern muttered. "There are people ahead, but from what I've been told about the area, they're likely not friendly."

I appreciated he was speaking in English now, though I didn't question why. Perhaps it was just to make me feel better.

He pulled me along as he picked up his pace. It wasn't long before the road led to a clearing. Instead of walking out into the wide open, Quern took me into the trees. We crept through the shadows and the wooded area, but close enough to the clearing to get a view of where it led.

To my surprise, there was a large building in the middle of the clearing, and actual roads with asphalt that led away from it.

The building . . .

It was an old-world prison.

A group of people were living and working around it, their pace slow. The prison, with its rusted bars and weathered stone, was the perfect fortress. Sure, the iron gates had once meant to keep people in, but now that made for a perfect fortified entranceway.

Even from our spot in the woods, I could see that some of the cells had been repurposed into living quarters, workshops, and storage spaces. There were at least a few dozen individuals going about their lives.

Although, it seemed some of the cells were still used as prisons. The windows were reinforced, and the courtyard beyond the gate was littered with chains and posts. If I had to guess, the people here probably took captives. Maybe even sold them off to others. It was a common practice in the backwaters of the wasteland, especially in overgrown woods or forests.

And each of the people here were blatantly carrying firearms, which only added to my theory. Most of them had handguns, but a few had rifles with leather straps. They kept the rifles close, slung on one shoulder, as they meandered throughout the prison.

These people were a gang.

Just beyond the prison, the skeletal remains of a highway system stretched like the veins of a forgotten megacity. A few vehicles were parked along the cracked asphalt near the prison, including some motorcycles and a large truck.

A couple of these gun-toting lunatics were actually in the process of fixing up a few smaller cars. As they worked, they made a *clack-clack, clank* sound, their tools cutting through the steel frames of the ancient vehicles.

The *crack* of gunshots came from a few individuals practicing their aim. They were taking turns shooting a few upside-down tin cans that were positioned on top of a chain-link fence.

Quern and I observed them for a moment. One thug shot a can off the fence. Then another one ran forward to grab it, even though the first man was still taking shots.

If their collective IQ was channeled together into electricity, it *might* be able to toast a piece of bread.

Quern pulled me close. "You don't want their attention," he whispered.

"I know," I whispered back.

He eyed me as he asked, "Is that why you didn't immediately call for help?"

"In my experience, most people aren't going to help you out of the goodness of their hearts. And this place . . . This looks like a hellhole."

Quern darkly chuckled. "That's my assessment as well."

I didn't see any women here. That was always a warning sign.

If they had been a coed group, I would've assumed they were a town, or a settlement attempting to carve a place for themselves in the wasteland. But whenever it was just men, all carrying guns, it was always because they were a gang—and they wouldn't be keen on just helping me.

I also didn't see any farms or animals.

These people got their food from someone, and I suspected it was all stolen.

The open yard, just beyond the front gates, seemed to serve as the communal area. There were barrels with fires, long tables, and a few idiots who appeared to be boiling chemicals. I wasn't entirely sure if it was to make a caustic substance they could use as a gas, or if they were just bored, but it seemed completely counterproductive to anything I would call "constructive."

"We're going to steal one of their vehicles," Quern stated.

"With your little baby knife? Or do you have a real weapon hidden somewhere?"

Quern gritted his teeth. When he turned to me, his eyes were narrowed in irritation. Then he smirked. "Heh. And here I was thinking I had the perfect weapon—a distraction." He unsheathed his knife and pointed it at me.

I opened my mouth, ready to make another quip, but then I swallowed my words before I spoke them. Quern wanted to use *me* as bait? How so? I didn't even want to ask. I had no desire to get anywhere near the prison gangsters.

"I'm not going to be your distraction," I stated.

Quern waved the tip of the knife around in a circle. "You're not going to have much choice. Either you help me get a vehicle—and we both leave this place. Or you trade one captor for a whole group of captors. And they don't look as forgiving or intelligent, to be frank."

Before I could protest, Quern grabbed the collar of my shirt and yanked me forward. He took me all the way to the edge of the trees. In a harsh whisper, he said, "Keep them occupied."

Then Quern shoved me with all his might. I flew out of the tree line and hit the dirt. I kept myself from shouting in pain—it was a habit I had developed when I lived alone, as making too much noise often led to unwanted attention.

But that didn't prevent me from getting spotted.

"We got a visitor!" one of the rifle-carrying men shouted.

He ran over, with two others flanking him. They held up their rifles, but quickly pointed them to the ground once they got a good look at me.

I wasn't particularly intimidating. I was five and a half feet, rather small, and had no visible weapons. As I stood, I kept my hands in the air, hoping none of them would get trigger-happy. "I'm sorry," I forced myself to say. "I got lost. Turned around. I didn't mean to, uh, disturb you."

The others around the old prison turned their attention to me. A man near the gate walked over, and the idiots with the tin cans stopped their target practice. It was a slow day, apparently, and everyone needed a good look at the fresh meat.

"Where'd you come from?" the thug asked.

He spoke rather eloquently for someone who was missing half his teeth on his right side.

"I found a road, and I followed it. I didn't know where I was going."

My rules of lying always helped me out.

The men glanced between each other. Their attire was a patchwork of post-apocalyptic practicality. Many of them wore bandanas or makeshift hats fashioned from scraps of fabric. There was a lot of dust and debris in ruined cities, and having something to cover your face was essential.

The core of their outfits consisted of sturdy, long-sleeved shirts made of denim, now faded and frayed from constant use. Their pants are typically heavy-duty cargo or work trousers secured with thick belts they had likely made themselves.

I suspected they gathered most of this from the same place, since they were all matchy-matchy. Perhaps an old-world factory was nearby, or the prison itself had been packed with outfits meant for the people of a world long since dead.

"You're traveling alone?" the man with the missing teeth asked. He stepped closer to me and then grabbed my arm and yanked me close. "No bag? No supplies?"

Two others surrounded me, preventing any sort of escape.

"I . . ."

Although I was mildly afraid, I tried to ham it all up. I choked back a sob.

The thug growled and then shoved the end of the rifle into my face. "Who's with you, girl?"

"I got separated," I said, my voice strained. "My sisters went after our horse, and he had our packs. I'm so sorry—I'll just leave. Please let me go."

Obviously, none of that was true. But since it was all plausible, and something they wanted to hear, I had their full attention.

The men shot each other side glances. Then they smirked.

After removing his rifle from my face, the man pulled me toward the prison. "We can't let a cute little girl like you wander out in the woods all by yourself. You'll stay here. With me—Jecket."

"My sisters should be around here somewhere," I said, trying to sound flustered.

Unfortunately, the doofuses who had been practicing their aim started to head back to the fence. And the thugs near the gate of the prison were a little more disinterested as well. I wasn't a very good distraction if they weren't focusing on me.

"Th-They could be in trouble," I stammered out, loud enough for every-one to hear. "Because there was a bear. That's what spooked our horse." I threw out one of my arms, trying to demonstrate the size. "It was a man-killer. Huge. I . . . I think it's nearby. My sisters are probably in danger."

That got everyone's attention.

The bears in these woods were monstrous. I assumed it was due to some sort of mutation caused by ambient radiation, but I wasn't entirely certain. Radiation stayed low to the ground, and often fell into pits, caves, or crags and stayed there longer than other locations. Bears that hibernated in radioactive caves often gave birth to freaks of nature—if their offspring lived at all.

Jecket gritted what little he had left of his teeth. Then he glared at me, his eyes slightly bloodshot.

The smell of burnt chemicals lingered on the air.

And then it hit me. These thugs were making addictive substances—chems they would sell to others, or just take for themselves.

"There's a bear, huh?" Jecket asked. "All right. You're gonna help us find it."

"What?" I asked. "But—"

"We can't have no damn bear on the roads around here. We're gonna have to put that fucker down for good. And you're gonna help us."

CHAPTER NINE

I regretted every decision that had brought me to this point.

Lying typically got me out of situations, not created them.

Jecket whistled. A few men in the prison whistled back, their screeching bird calls so shrill they hurt my ears. They were clearly communicating with each other, because a few more men from the prison came hurrying out, some slinging backpacks onto their shoulders.

"We're goin' on a hunt," Jecket shouted. "Round 'em up, boys. We got a bear to skin, a couple girls to find, and a horse to corral."

Hm. Perhaps I had lied *too* well. Or perhaps my impromptu story was too enticing to leave uninvestigated. Either way, these idiots were convinced there was treasure in the forest, and we needed to find it.

Was that distraction enough?

I hoped Quern would be able to capitalize on this.

When Jecket started hauling me toward the tree line, my heart pounded.

What would they do when they discovered I had been lying? There would be no horse tracks. No signs of a bear. Nothing. Would they become angry? Yell at me? Or worse? And if I was out in the woods, I wouldn't be here when Quern finally managed to steal a vehicle.

I grabbed Jecket by his denim shirt. With as much anxiety as I could muster, I made my words warble. "W-Wait. I don't want to face a bear! Please. I'm too frightened."

Jecket grumbled something, his irritation on full display. Then he whistled again, this time harsher, and the call shorter. Another man exited the prison, this one older, his hair graying, his clothing stained with splatters of blood. He walked with a slight limp, and since I had lived with one for years, I could tell it was due to an old injury.

"Martin, take this girl. We're goin' on a hunt."

Martin grunted as he picked up his pace. Once he was close, I took note of the beard that dominated most of his face. He turned his icy gaze down on me, one eye brown, the other milky.

"I'll take her," Martin said.

I didn't protest. Even as he grabbed me by my elbow, and dragged me toward the prison, I remained on "good behavior." In my experience, if I acted meek and dumb, everyone would assume I was meek and dumb. Then, when I found an opening, I could exploit it without much trouble.

Martin smelled of tobacco and chems. He walked me through the prison gate, and then across the ramshackle courtyard without saying a word. When he brought me to a large metal door, he glared.

"Don't cause me any trouble," he growled.

I shook my head. "Will they find my sisters?" I tried to act innocent, but it was more difficult than acting frightened.

Martin narrowed his eyes, and I wondered if he was suspicious of me. Instead, he said, "Your sisters will be fine."

He led me inside, and I had to hold back a cough. Thick dust hung on the air. It smelled of broken stone and sawdust, and I wondered if they were constructing something. Martin walked me down a long hall, where there were barred doors on either side of us. The lights overhead were A-tech, and glowed with a soft white that was gentle on the eyes, but definitely highlighted the junk in the air.

As we walked, I saw a few workbenches with tools on them.

And a few atomic batteries. They were distinct and can-like—difficult to miss. I was surprised they weren't locked away.

My gaze lingered on one for a long while as we passed.

Martin noticed.

He yanked my arm, shaking me out of my thoughts. "Don't touch anything," he said as he squeezed my arm. His grip hurt, and I grimaced as I felt my skin bruising.

"I won't," I said in a tiny voice. Then I stared up at him through my eyelashes. "I just haven't seen a building like this before."

"It was built before the Forever Winter. That's all you need to know."

But I barely heard the man. The instant he turned his eyes forward, I glanced around to take stock. Everything about this prison screamed *minimalist design, maximalist survival.* The gang obviously slept in a patch-work of salvaged mattresses, hammocks strung up between cell bars, and a couple of bunk beds with only a few springs missing. The color scheme? *Early 21st-century rust.*

I didn't need any of that—but I was impressed by the fact every room had electricity. They probably had dozens of batteries.

Martin walked me by a large dining room. A cafeteria? The tables were an eclectic mix of whatever furniture survived the Forever Winter, and the walls were decorated with a charming collage of graffiti.

As we walked, I counted twenty-two people here, and that wasn't including Jecket and the ten or so that went off into the woods looking for a bear.

Which was an impressive size for a gang out in the wilderness.

"What's your name?" Martin asked. He turned me down a hallway and walked me through a security point, complete with a barred door.

"My name is Kita," I said.

There was no point in lying. This man wouldn't know who I was—and if he did know, he would probably let me go immediately.

I could only imagine what Bishop, Gascoigne, and the others were planning. They knew I was missing by now. They would come for me.

But Martin clearly didn't recognize my name. "Kita is a pretty name for a pretty girl."

And I didn't like where *this* was going. Although I hadn't dealt with much sexual aggression—since I had been a hermit for so long—I rec-ognized the hallmarks whenever they showed up. I didn't answer him. Instead, I glanced away and continued to count everything. The number of people. The lights. The steps we had taken since coming inside.

Which was beginning to really add up. How deep into prison was he going to take me? Would Quern even search for me in this part of the prison?

There was a chance Quern would just take a vehicle and go. Honestly, it was my preferred outcome. This prison was close enough to Sanctuary that Bishop was sure to find it before long. Or I could just escape and make it back to them. Either or.

Then Martin stopped.

He jerked me to his side and motioned to an empty cell. He dragged me in, and I tensed. There was just a cot and a tin bucket with a thin handle.

That was it.

"You'll stay here," he said.

Again, I didn't answer.

Martin took two steps backward out of the cell, and then shut the barred door. It *clicked* into place, the lock shutting fully.

"And you're not going to hurt me, are you?" I asked.

"I'll come by to check on you," Martin said with a smile—though it wasn't a friendly one.

"Do you have anything to eat?" What I wanted was more information. Where did they get their food?

"When I come back, I'll bring some dinner. And we'll talk about what you're willing to do to pay for it."

Again, I didn't like that—so I didn't respond.

These thugs clearly took people against their will on the regular. If I had known they were so close, I would've taken my power armor out and paid a visit.

As it stood . . .

Martin chortled as he left me. He headed down the hallway, limping as he went, his gait rather awkward. I remained silent until I couldn't hear him anymore. Instead of waiting for Quern—who I honestly thought might've left already—I turned around and faced the little metal bucket.

It was obviously meant to be the toilet. All I saw was a tool waiting to be transformed.

Most people weren't aware of the metaphysical changes metal was capable of going through. Rust caused metal to expand, which was what caused it to be weak and brittle. Rust corrodes, and since this whole prison was one gigantic rusty mess, I knew the bars were nothing more than stale candy canes at this point.

I had removed the handle of the bucket and sharpened the end into a semi-fine point. Then I took the whole bucket and headed over to the rusted bars of my cell.

After a few hours, one side of the bucket had sufficiently chipped away at the rusted bars, cracking through the layers of brittle metal. The noises I made were nothing to the construction and shouting from the thugs around me. If it ever became quiet, I took a break, and only resumed once all the ruckus resumed again.

When night fell, the prison became a fish tank—the glow of lights here kept the darkness at bay, but everything could see in, and we couldn't see out.

Quern had left me. That was the only explanation for why I was here for so long.

And while I hated every minute I was here, I knew I would escape soon. I just had to chip my way through one more bar.

But then I heard the strange gait of someone limping. I stopped my work and placed the bucket in the corner of the cell.

Fortunately, I'd figured someone would come by, so I had broken two bars down at the base, near the floor, where it would be difficult to tell that they were no longer connected to anything. If someone leaned on the bars, they'd instantly be able to tell, but I was banking on that never happening.

Martin came walking back with a plate half covered in hardtack—which was a kind of biscuit made out of the most tasteless substances possible. The only upside to hardtack was how long it lasted without rotting.

That was all he had, and made me wonder if the prison gang here actually ate well.

"Here's your dinner," Martin said.

"Did Jecket find my sisters?" I asked.

"No. But everyone is still searching."

Wow. Dumb *and* persistent. I almost laughed.

Martin shook the tray. The hardtack rattled around. They had the consistency of rocks.

"You're hungry, yes?" he asked.

I was. My stomach had been grumbling, but the pain wasn't too bad. I'd feel it tomorrow, but now I could ignore the ache.

"You want this?" Martin stepped closer to the door. "Maybe you should come over here and get it."

As casually as I could, I slipped my hand into the back pocket of my pants. The sharpened bucket handle was still there, waiting to be used as an impromptu weapon. I would only get one surprise attack, though. If I fucked this up, Martin would fuck *me* up—and I couldn't afford that.

Sanctuary couldn't afford that.

Martin banged the plate against one of the rusted bars of the door. "Well? You want it? Come over here, lamb. I won't charge you much."

"I don't really have much to barter with," I said as I sarcastically glanced over at the bucket.

"You can work off your debt." He smirked, like he was so clever. "With your mouth."

I exhaled. "Yeah, well, now I'm not even in the mood to quip around with you. Girls like a little buildup before they commit. I was hoping for some more repartee—but I don't think you can handle that."

A part of me thought it was funny that I had no troubles being frank, mean, or lying. But when it came to being honest, building real relationships, and assuming the role of the leader, it felt awkward.

I blamed the wasteland. Living alone made it easy to develop antisocial skills.

"I don't care what you're in the mood for," Martin said. "We haven't had a girl stop by in a while, and you're *my* responsibility. Either you get on your knees and ask nicely for the food, or you're not eating."

CHAPTER TEN

I didn't want trouble—but I *definitely* wasn't going to get on my knees for the man. And if *trouble* or *pleasing Martin* were my only two options, I was going to pick trouble every time.

I clicked my tongue in disapproval and shook my head. "Do you have fat in your ears? Or maybe you're so old that your hearing is going. I'm not in the mood. I'd rather be slowly consumed by the fleas that infest this place rather than touch your disgusting body."

That was just the truth. I was hoping he would taunt me some more and then leave, but the man's face was twisting into hatred.

Martin griped the sides of the tray until his knuckles were white. Then he tossed the whole thing, hardtack and all, onto the floor. When he came for the cell door, I backed into the corner and tensed.

I probably shouldn't have been so harsh.

"I was bein' nice," Martin said, practically a whisper if it weren't for his seething rage.

He pulled out keys and unlocked the cell door. Then he placed the keys back in his coat pocket.

Unfortunately for me, the man then dug into his jacket and withdrew a handgun. It was a 9mm thing, not the most powerful, but it would still do the trick. I pressed my back against the wall, almost regretting my decision to antagonize him.

Everyone knew it was idiotic to bring a homemade shiv to a gun fight.

He sauntered in, tall and confident.

"I think you owe me an apology," Martin said. He stopped in the middle of my cell, his considerable bear-like body in between me and the exit.

I nodded as I hesitatingly stepped forward. "Y-You're right," I said, putting the quaver in my words. "I shouldn't have been that rude."

"Get over here and apologize properly."

I stepped close. Martin lowered his firearm, though he kept it tight in his hands. Once I was next to him, I placed my free hand on his chest. He relaxed a bit and even chuckled, like this was going to be a glorious night.

And then I pulled the sharpened bucket handle out of my pocket and stabbed the man straight in the throat.

Not the side of the throat. Not with only half my strength. I went as hard as I could, directly for his windpipe. And I felt no guilt—the thug had imprisoned me and was going to force himself on me. Or worse.

Blood squirted from the puncture wound as he stumbled backward. He gurgled out a croak, obviously trying to shout. In his panic, he must've forgot he had a gun, because he just flailed his firearm around while grasping at the injury with his other hand.

In the confusion, I shoved my hand in his coat pocket and stole his keys. His eyes were practically bugging out of his skull, his face turning a dark red, and then slightly purple. I darted around him, leapt out of the cell, and then locked it behind me.

During that time, Martin regained some of his senses. He leveled the gun and fired.

The sound of the shot echoed throughout the prison, and I knew everyone was now aware of our scuffle. The bullet ricocheted off the walls. I flinched, and then tried to run.

Another shot.

Something burned my arm, and I yelled out in pain. Blood wept from my shoulder. The bullet had cut through me—cut through muscle, but not bone.

I ran as fast as I could, my body dulling the pain through copious amounts of adrenaline. Martin fired off six more shots, but the farther away I got, the more useless all of his efforts became.

"What's going on?" someone shouted down the halls of the prison.

Someone else called back. "We've got problems! That was gunfire!"

"Fuckin' search this place!"

I remembered my way through the prison thanks to Martin. I turned down the hall, went through a security gate, and then slowed when I neared one of the workbenches. There were tools scattered across the top, including a screwdriver, and two atomic batteries. I grabbed the batteries, shoved them into my pockets.

"Hold it!"

I tensed and whirled on my heel. Some thug stood down the hallway from me. He held a shotgun in both hands, the butt of his firearm pressed against his shoulder as he aimed down the barrel.

I tried to lift both my hands, but my injured shoulder refused to cooperate. I lifted one hand and then half lifted the other, gritting back a sudden sting of pain. "Don't shoot," I breathed.

He stepped forward and glared. Something about the man screamed *inbred.* Maybe it was because his eyes were so far apart it was like they were trying to escape his face, or maybe it was his oversized forehead—I wasn't certain. All I hoped for was that he wasn't a trigger-happy inbred lunatic.

"I found the problem," the inbred man shouted. His voice carried throughout the prison. "Someone get over here!"

Although no one directly answered, I knew others would be here soon. My heart pounded so hard in my chest, I wasn't sure if I could breathe properly. My own blood soaked my shirt.

But then someone slipped quietly into the hall behind my inbred "buddy."

The shotgun-wielding thug never turned around. He kept his firearm pointed straight at me, taking small steps forward, like he was cautious, but still excited to apprehend me.

The person behind him . . .

It was Quern.

With all the silent agility of a trained assassin, Quern snuck over to the man, yanked his shoulder so the man turned around halfway, and then ripped the shotgun from his grasp. In the next half second, Quern planted the barrel of the gun into the man's jaw and pulled the trigger. The buckshot exploded through the man's face, destroying a good portion of his skull.

He collapsed to the floor in a welter of blood.

With the shotgun still in his hands, Quern turned to me. Some of the inbred man's blood was splattered on his white shirt, but Quern either didn't notice or didn't mind.

"*You were supposed to cause a distraction and then run back into the woods,*" he growled in Tethlite.

I honestly chuckled. "W-Well, it wasn't like you articulated that to me. You fucking shoved me out in front of a bunch of gun-toting, drug-addled *thugs* and—"

Someone else rounded the corner into our hallway. All I had time to do was point. Quern spun around and fired his shotgun. He struck the man in the chest with the full force of buckshot. The man crumpled backward, a handgun hitting the floor next to him.

I hurried forward, patted the man's pockets with my one good hand, searching for anything useful, and then picked up the 9mm. This thug didn't have any extra bullets—it was just what he had in the firearm.

But when I turned around, Quern slammed me against the wall.

More pain flared through my injured shoulder and I shouted. Quern ripped the 9mm from me, his expression icy. "I'll hold the weapons," he whispered in English.

"R-Right."

I held my injured shoulder, trying to stop the flow of blood. The nanites in my system were already stitching me back up, but it would take a little while. Until then, I had to be careful.

Quern released me, and I took a moment to catch my breath.

There was more shouting, but it honestly was distant and rather confused. No one knew what the hell was going on. These were low-level criminals, after all, not a hypercompetent organization like the Iron-Blooded or the judges in Ex Cathedra. They didn't even have a radio system in place to speak to other members of the prison in a quick and efficient manner.

Quern motioned with a tilt of his head. "This way."

He took off down the hall and I followed him. The lights of the prison stayed illuminated; it made navigating the inside of the prison rather easy. When we came to the courtyard, however, it was a different story.

It was pitch black outside.

The lights for the courtyard were obviously damaged and inoperable. That didn't deter Quern. He shoved the handgun into his pocket, and then grabbed my arm. Together, we ran out into the darkness. I spotted the silhouettes of individuals running around the inside of the prison, but they were still frantically trying to piece together what had happened.

In this chaos, there was no one to stop us.

Quern was clearly familiar with the layout of the prison, because he guided me through the gloom without problem. When we made it to the front gate, he slipped out and then dragged me to a nearby vehicle. It was still on, but the headlights were off. Only tiny lights near the driver's seat were blinking, but it was enough for me to make my way inside. I sat in the passenger's seat.

Quern had stolen a jeep, and the chair was surprisingly comfy. I belted up. Then I glanced around.

This vehicle didn't have proper doors or a roof. It was open and exposed to the elements. The chill night wind whipped over us, stealing my warmth.

The back of the jeep was packed with a few bags, and even a box.

"Did you get all this?" I whispered.

"We needed supplies," he said. Quern then hauled himself into the driver's seat.

He had taken the whole day to swipe things from the prison gang? I was almost impressed—but since that gang was clearly deficient, I assumed these supplies were going to be subpar.

"Did you pick up any batteries?" I ran my hand over the bags, hoping I could feel some. It was difficult, though. All the bags were stuffed to the brim.

"Why?" he hissed.

I didn't answer him. In my heart, I was planning for the moment I would escape, and then make my way back to Sanctuary. Any and all batteries I found I would take with me and hand over to the denizens of my new civilization. They needed them, and if I was going on a hostage adventure, I might as well make good use of my stolen time.

"We might need them," I forced myself to say—just to give him an answer.

Quern put the vehicle in reverse. "I got some."

I exhaled and kept my hand over the injury.

Quern backed the jeep away from the prison, and then turned the vehicle onto the dirt road. Once facing away from the prison, he flipped on the headlights and slammed his foot on the gas. The vehicle lurched forward, the tires kicking up dirt. We sped away from the gang and their fortified base of operations.

The forest road was bumpy with branches and cracks. I gritted my teeth as the jeep jostled me around. The seatbelt dug into my injured shoulder. I sucked in air and then tucked the belt into my armpit. The cold air stung worse as it blasted through the unprotected jeep.

Quern didn't seem to care. He kept going at the fastest pace he could muster, obviously trying to put distance between us and the thugs. He focused on the shattered road, staying on the cracked asphalt as much as possible, and only swerving to avoid some of the largest branches.

I thought we were going to make it without a problem.

But then the headlights shone over a group of people crossing the road. It was Jecket, and a few other thugs—the ones searching for my "sisters."

"Careful," I shouted.

But Quern didn't lift his feet from the pedal. Instead, he turned the steering wheel slightly so that he was pointed directly at Jecket himself. The man stared with wide eyes, the perfect imitation of a startled deer.

I threw my good hand over my face and closed my eyes to avoid watching what was about to happen.

The jeep plowed into Jecket and the whole vehicle shook. The resulting *crash* was enough to send a shudder down my spine. The *crack, crack, crack* of gunfire sounded afterward, and a *ka-thunk* echoed from the undercarriage of our vehicle as Jecket was tangled in the right-side wheel for a few rotations before coming loose.

I opened my eyes to see our hood was dented and coated in a fine misting of blood. When I glanced back, I just barely caught the silhouettes of the lunatics all crowding around their fallen leader.

With a shaky hand, I gripped my injured shoulder tighter. "You really didn't like him, I take it."

"Human waste," Quern drawled. "The world is better now that he's dead."

I envied his conviction, but it reminded me I was dealing with someone so fanatical, anything in his way was just a dead body.

I needed to get away from him as soon as possible.

CHAPTER ELEVEN

Quern drove the jeep for several hours.

The evening winds washed over us, never allowing me to get warm. I shivered the whole time, my teeth clattering. My stomach churned and knotted, and I hated the way the vehicle treated every crack like it was a canyon. This jeep's suspension was shot.

For some reason, the gunshot wound on my arm wasn't healing as quickly. The pain lingered, and whenever the jeep flew around too much, my shoulder throbbed in agony.

Quern glanced over from time to time, and eventually slowed the vehicle. Without so many bumps, I managed to breathe a little easier. I kept myself balled in the passenger seat, my eyes closed, but my mind working overtime. My thoughts lingered on Sanctuary. I had told Chelsy we would explore. I had guaranteed Vega I would protect them from the Vay.

Then the jeep came to a stop.

I opened my eyes, but it was still dark. Everything outside of the vehicle was just . . . darkness.

The headlights shone on a building, though. Quern stared at this new location, his eyes narrowing.

It was an eerie relic of the world before the Forever Winter.

A gas station.

They were used to fuel up vehicles that required liquid fuel and combustion engines. Those vehicles didn't work anymore. The only cars and vans we had access to were the ones that used A-tech engines that ran off batteries.

Abandoned pumps dotted the outside of the building, their hoses sprawled on the cracked concrete. A faded sign, creaking in the evening wind, read: *WELCOME TO MONTANA.* There were some other words, and a number, but those were all too faded to read properly.

"What're we doing here?" I whispered. "This is a long way from the military base."

Quern shot me a glower. "We're going to take a rest."

I supposed even the Iron-Blooded needed a break from time to time. With a sigh, I glanced over my shoulder. Where were Bishop and Gascoigne? Brecht and Vega? Anyone?

This gas station was still on the road, so my hopes remained high. Perhaps, if we slept here long enough, the others would catch up.

"Resting is a good idea." I turned so he could see my blood-soaked shirt and injury. "I think I might need to do something about this."

Quern, armed with his stolen shotgun and 9mm, slid out of the driver's seat. He walked around the vehicle and motioned for me to come with him. After a deep breath, I complied. Then Quern led me toward the gas station, one hand on my uninjured arm and one hand carrying his shotgun.

The top of the barrel had a little flashlight. Quern flipped it on and used the weapon as our guide.

The windows of the gas station, frosted with dust, offered a glimpse into a bizarre museum of Montana souvenirs. There were shelves and shelves of snow globes containing scenes of the rugged Montana landscape, postcards depicting majestic mountains and sprawling plains, and adorable figurines of bears and moose, both staring blankly into the void.

The gas station had no front door. It had either been destroyed, or this building never had one.

Quern led me in, flashing his shotgun light at every corner, as though to make sure we were alone. His eyes scanned the shelves, though his gaze lingered on nothing. Then he let me go and headed for the rusted cash register.

While my creepy companion searched for . . . something . . . I turned my attention to the bears and moose. I loved figurines. I had once made dozens in my free time. And Chelsy still appreciated them.

I slowly crept over to the shelf, and with my good hand, I picked up both a baby bear, and the little moose. Chelsy would enjoy them, so I stuffed them into my pockets. They rattled against the atomic batteries.

Quern banged around behind the register for a moment. Then he leapt over the counter and made it back to my side. He used the shotgun light to illuminate my injury. With a sneer of disgust, he led me out of the decrepit gas station.

"Nanites don't work as efficiently when you're cold," he said, anger in his tone.

"Why is that?" I asked.

But before Quern could answer, I had already concocted a theory. The tiny machines traveled through the bloodstream, and when a human body was cold, the smallest blood vessels—the capillaries—constricted and closed. That would make it difficult for the nanites to stitch up injuries and heal muscles.

"Just . . . trust me," was all Quern managed to say. "We should treat the injury, and then you should remain warm for a bit."

"We're going to treat my injury?" I stared up at him. The outside of the gas station was creepy, and I hated not being able to see beyond the shadows. "Why? I thought you were just dragging me back to the other Iron-Blooded. To Commander Dannik or Architect Riven."

I really didn't understand Quern's plans. Probably because he wasn't talking about them.

Quern shook his head and frowned. He yanked me toward the jeep. "Don't you remember when I was injured? When you had me captive on the train?"

That had been a while ago—back when we first took Quern hostage. And when we had cut off his thumb.

"I remember," I whispered.

"You took the time to use your first aid on me." Quern met my gaze. "Even when your companions were calling for my death. So, think of this as just returning the favor."

"What're you going to do after that? Are you going to . . . torture me?"

Quern darkly chuckled. "Do you *want* me to torture you?"

I didn't dignify that with a response. Of course I didn't.

He smirked as he said, "You should be really thankful I don't need any of your fingers to accomplish my goals." He jerked me close. "Because I *would* return that favor if it were necessary." After another chuckle, he said, "But for right now, I'm just going to make sure you don't die. I need you."

Needed me?

I already knew he wouldn't elaborate, so I stopped my line of question-ing. Still, it made me feel a little better about the situation knowing he wasn't going to torture me or mutilate my hands. This just gave me more time and opportunities to think a way out of this.

Quern flashed his light around the area.

The air was heavy with an unnerving silence.

I shivered. Quern held me against his body. Then he shone his light over another building—a small restroom that was attached to the gas station. The restroom was made mostly out of cinderblocks, but the tiny signs for MEN and WOMEN were still nailed in place, letting me know what this was.

Quern walked over to the jeep, grabbed one of the backpacks, and then hauled me over to the restroom. He entered through the MEN door, and I almost made a joke, but I held back. My shoulder was hurting too much for me to laugh.

We stepped into one of the most cramped spaces I had ever been in my life.

The tiles were cracked, and stained with God only knew what—especially near the only toilet. A small, makeshift bed lay next to it, cobbled together from old blankets and rags. A plastic ten-liter bottle was upside down and wedged into a hole in the roof, complete with a stopper. The large bottle was cut in half so that rainwater could collect in it, and a grate had been strapped over it, to keep solid objects or creatures from getting in.

Once the stopper was removed, the water would pour down onto the tiles in the corner of the bathroom closest to the drain.

Someone had once made their home here.

"Cozy," I quipped.

Quern glanced over. Did he find that funny? I didn't know—he had an unreadable expression.

The place wasn't livable, though, obviously. This whole bathroom was cold, barren, and lifeless. No one had been here in ages. The dust and mud were here to attest to that fact.

Quern shoved me toward the "shower" in the corner of the restroom. "Undress. We'll use the rainwater to wash you off."

He didn't leave. He just waited.

When I didn't immediately comply with his demand, Quern stepped forward, like he was ready to just do it himself. I backed away.

"I never treated you like an animal," I said in low tone.

That stopped Quern in his tracks. He narrowed his eyes at me, practically glaring. They were light-colored and icy, like our surroundings. For a long moment, he said nothing. Then Quern stepped toward the door.

He yanked the flashlight off the end of his shotgun, and placed it on the floor so that it shone into the corner of the restroom.

"There's nowhere to run," Quern said. "Wash up. I'll be right here when you're done."

He stepped through the door, leaving it open a slight crack, and then waited.

I let out a long exhale. While this wasn't "nice," it was better than nothing. I appreciated that Quern wasn't a heartless lunatic, but I knew if I gave him too much grief, he'd probably just shoot me and get this over with.

Instead of complaining, I walked into the corner of the grimy restroom. I stood over the drain, shivering. After I collected my thoughts, I pulled off my clothing and set it down in the cracked sink that was still clinging to the cinderblock wall.

It was so cold.

My teeth clattered loud enough to fill the whole restroom.

Then I reached up and uncorked the plastic bottle. I shouted when the frigid water splashed over me.

"*Are you alright?*" Quern hissed in Tethlite.

"Y-Y-Yes," I managed to say, my body practically quaking with shivers.

I stood under the flow of ice water, making sure to clean my injury, until all the water was gone. With blue lips, colorless fingers, and skin completely covered in goosebumps, I turned for my clothes.

"Q-Quern," I whispered, my voice practically frozen. "I need a t-t-towel. Something to d-dry off with."

I held myself tight, my injury no longer hurting. All I felt was the sting of a chilly night.

The door opened slightly, and Quern held up a large towel. He didn't step into the restroom, not even when I made my way over and took the cloth.

"Th-Thank you."

He said nothing.

Then I dried myself, my hands numb. Once I was certain the water was gone, I pulled my pants back on, checked the batteries and figurines, and then reached for my shirt.

It was so bloody, it felt silly to wear it again.

"I need a new shirt," I said, louder than before.

"We should tend to your injury first."

I crossed both my arms over my chest and then turned so my back was to the door. "All right. Do you have anything?"

The door opened, and Quern stepped inside. He picked up the flashlight and shone it onto my bare shoulder. I shivered, both from the chill and his gaze. I tried not to think about how vulnerable I was, or how much I wanted to put a shirt on at that moment.

Quern set his backpack on the ground and removed things from inside. I glanced over and saw he had some rubbing alcohol and bandages.

He was really going to dress the wound.

I turned away before he could spot me watching him. When he touched my shoulder, I loosened enough for him to gently pat the bullet wound. It had closed somewhat, from the nanites who were overachievers, but it was still bad.

And it stung when he dabbed the wound with alcohol. I sucked in air through my teeth and just gritted through it all, though. The pain didn't last long. Quern quickly wrapped my shoulder with a bandage, careful to go under my arm, but only at my pace. His hands were rough, yet somehow gentle.

They were also warm. So delightfully warm.

I was almost sad when he finished.

"Thank you," I whispered, my breath visible.

Again, he said nothing.

"I need a shirt." I eyed the bloody rag in the sink and knew I wasn't putting that back on.

Quern reached into his pack and withdrew a denim shirt, just like all the members of the prison gang had worn, and I took it with a frown. No bra, either, but I didn't blame Quern for that. It was surprisingly difficult to find women's clothing that fit while out and about on the wasteland.

Instead, I went back to my bloody clothing, and attempted to clean my bra as much as possible before donning it once again.

Quern left me alone in the restroom, and while he wasn't looking, I intentionally placed my blood-soaked shirt on the faucet of the sink. Then I placed a moose figurine on top. If Bishop and Gascoigne came here looking for me, they would understand what this meant.

I didn't know how to leave a clearer, message, though. I didn't have anything to write with, and if I took too long, Quern would surely come in and see what I had done.

So I hoped this was enough.

Then I slid on my denim shirt, no warmer now than I was before. Ice practically coursed through my veins.

"I'm all done," I said, my voice shaky from the chill.

"Good." Quern opened the door and flashed his light to guide me over. "Now let's leave this place. We'll make camp up the road, and you can stay warm to recover."

CHAPTER TWELVE

We drove for a short distance on the road, and then Quern turned off.

I hated that, but maybe the jeep would leave tracks in the mud, and the others would be able to follow us. Again, I hoped.

When we came to a step in a grove between the trees, Quern killed the engine, hopped out, and immediately set up a tarp on the ground and then overhead, creating a simple tent secured between tree trunks. He was fast, and efficient, like he had trained for this moment his whole life and was looking to get a gold medal.

Then he grabbed a pack, pulled out some hardtack, and passed me a few bits of the crumbling bread.

"Eat this," he commanded.

Then Quern took a bite and grimaced. After a long exhale, he forced himself to swallow a whole mouthful more. After, he returned to setting up a simple sleeping location.

I nibbled on the hardtack, not particularly hungry, but I knew I needed the sustenance. The nanites in my system would only heal me so much, and they used reserves found in adipose tissue—fat tissue—to create the cells required for body restoration. I didn't have much fat reserve, so calories would have to do.

As Quern worked, I would've recommended we stay in the jeep, but it was stuffed with things he had clearly pilfered from the prison gang. It would take Quern longer to unpack everything, then repack everything once we woke up, than to set up a camp spot.

Part of me wondered if someone would come along and kill us for our vehicle, though. It was always risky business sleeping out in the wilderness.

Too risky for comfort.

"Shouldn't we find a safer place?" I whispered.

"We won't stay here long." Quern finished and then stood back to admire his work. "Four hours. Max."

A perfect sleep cycle. The Iron-Blooded really did train their men to handle the wasteland like it would forever be their home.

"I only have six shotgun rounds left," Quern said aloud. "But plenty of ammo with the smaller gun. Should we be approached by anyone, I'll handle it."

That wasn't the best arsenal I'd ever seen, but it was something.

Quern grabbed a blanket from the back of the jeep and then took me by my uninjured arm. I flinched, but he didn't let go. Instead, he dragged me over to the tent and practically shoved me inside.

"Stop wasting time," he growled.

I crawled into the tent. There was nothing here other than the tarp across the lumpy ground. Quern got into the tent, secured the tarp flap shut, and switched off the flashlight. With all the haste and gruffness of a child wrapping themselves up with their favorite teddy bear, Quern grabbed me and then burrito-ed us together in the one blanket. My back was pressed up against his chest as he lowered down on the floor of the tent.

I felt his heart beating, we were pressed up so tightly. He was warm. This could work—if it weren't so nerve-racking.

The batteries in my pants pocket dug into my legs. I tried to move, which caused Quern to curse under his breath.

"*What the fuck is your problem?*" he hissed in Tethlite.

"I have things," I said, irritated.

He reached into my pants pockets and withdrew the two batteries and bear figurine. It was pitch black in the tent, but I heard him fumble with the objects, clearly trying to visualize them through touch alone. Teth did it all the time, and I suspected the Iron-Blooded were rather adept at the skill, since they learned most everything from the Teth themselves.

Sure enough, without turning on the light, Quern said, "You took one of those toy bears from the abandoned storefront?"

"Yes."

                    SHAMI STOVALL

"And these batteries?"

"From the prison. Because I wanted them."

Quern ground his teeth loud enough to fill the tent. He shoved the items off to the side, then patted me down, checking for anything else. I tensed, but said nothing, even as he slid a hand over my inner thigh.

"Relax," he said through gritted teeth. "If I was going to do anything to you, I would've done it already."

"Yeah, really putting me at ease," I sarcastically muttered.

"I've seen you fight—I know what you're capable of. I don't need to baby you." Once he was done with his inspection, Quern tightly wrapped the blanket a second time and lay down. "Now stop moving and sleep. I'm not going to slow our trek down if you get tired."

He pulled me close, and his heat enveloped me.

Quern's breathing evened out like this were just part of any other mission. The blanket was so thoroughly wrapped around us that it would be impossible for me to just pull it off and flee. Wiggling slightly would wake Quern in an instant. He was the type of soldier who slept and woke at the drop of a hat.

At least I was warm now. I closed my eyes, and took even breaths, the tarp smelling of plastic.

I had been exhausted.

The moment I had closed my eyes, I had fallen asleep. Now, I only awoke because I heard something outside of the tent. I opened my eyes, but the sleep crust made that difficult. I rubbed my face, wiping away the sweat and fatigue. All that greeted me was a wall of solid blackness. I saw nothing.

The noises from outside sounded like something scraping across the pine needles that lined the floor of the forest.

I tried to turn, but Quern wrapped his arm around my midsection and held me in place.

He was awake, and just as tense as I was.

"Stay quiet," he whispered, his teeth close to my ear.

I swallowed hard and tried to remember where we were. In the middle of the woods? Away from the road? Maybe this was Bishop. Maybe he and the others had finally found me. I hoped. I hoped with everything I had.

But then I heard a loud *huff* and I knew that wasn't the case.

It was an animal. Something with four legs. Something large. Something sniffing through the fallen pine needles.

It was shifting its way closer to us, its footfalls heavier than I would've liked—its breathing loud and its breaths harsh. This wasn't a fox or boar. Its breathing was far too loud for that.

"It's a bear," I said under my breath, my mind filling in all the blanks.

Quern cursed in Tethlite. "*Why do I run into literally every problem imaginable?*" he said, clearly speaking to himself rather than me.

He slowly released me, and then untucked the blanket from around our bodies. The creature outside—most definitely a bear—bumped into our jeep. The vehicle rocked on its rusty axles, and the monster huffed again.

Quern quietly searched around the tent. He grabbed the flashlight, and the 9mm, but I was certain he hadn't brought the shotgun into the tent with us. Where was it? The jeep? Or had Quern put it somewhere close, just out of my reach?

I sat up, and I marveled at how much better my shoulder felt.

The nanites had done their job. I was mostly healed—now I just needed to stay alive.

But the blood . . .

My blood. Still on bandages and my undergarments, and no doubt still carried an odor. My heart slammed against my ribcage as I realized the real problem here.

And as soon as I had that revelation, the snout of the creature poked into the tent near the bottom of the flap, sniffling and snorting so loud I didn't need to see it to know exactly where and what it was.

"Oh, fuck me," I whispered.

Quern grabbed my arm, pulled me back, and then opened fire with his 9mm. *Crack, crack, crack*—the rapid fire of the handgun was infinitely louder when it shattered the silence of the woods. The creature outside roared and reared up on hind legs, taking the roof of our tarp tent with it.

Quern switched on the flashlight, pointing it directly at our monster attacker.

It was a bear.

I knew it. *I goddamn knew it.*

And not just *any* bear—it was some sort of freak mutant grizzly bear, a grotesque perversion of nature's design. Its brown fur was a patchwork of matted clumps and bald, scarred patches, where the skin beneath was sickly and weeping pus.

Its face was a distorted canvas of aggression and pain, one eye blown out by Quern's shots, and the other alight with rage. The monster's jaws were oversized and lined with rows of jagged, mismatched fangs.

The thing stood at least nine feet tall while on two legs. It towered over us. The thing was larger than our jeep.

I found it difficult to breathe . . .

"Run!" Quern shouted.

The mutant grizzly slammed its claws forward, like it wanted to bury us in one powerful attack. Quern pushed me out of the way, and we tumbled backward, just out of the bear's reach. We almost tripped and slammed into a pine tree, but Quern was fast. Despite having just woken up, the man was more alert than I was. He yanked me away from the tent and practically carried me around one of the nearest trees.

The bear roared, blood splattering from its head as it whipped around to get a better look at us.

The bear's limbs, all four of them, were elongated and twisted. Its claws resembled rusty, serrated daggers, and it had a neck covered in thicker fur, as though it had some sort of mane.

And it moved like every gesture was torment. One moment it seemed sluggish, then it would whip its head around, its body limber, and also stiff, as though the creature itself was at odds with its mutated form.

Quern headed for the jeep, but that was a mistake.

The mutant bear lunged with frightening speed. It swiped at Quern, barely hitting him, but it was powerful enough to send the man into the trunk of a tree. The bear's claws had dug furrows into Quern's torso, and Quern stumbled to the ground, onto one knee.

I shouted, picked up a pine cone and then threw it. The small object struck the bear in the side of the head. The monster turned its one monster eye on me.

I turned and leapt between a cluster of trees. The bear huffed and lunged. I thought the trees would stop its advance—but nope! *I was wrong.*

The fucking monster hit the trees so hard it practically shattered their trunks. The bear roared again as it tore its way through the woods, its claws slashing up branches and cutting away obstacles. I ran a little farther into the darkness, between trees that were growing closer and closer together, hoping to slow the bear's pursuit.

Eventually, it became too dark for me to see. I held my arms out, trying to feel my way forward, but the bear wasn't having as much difficulty.

It knew exactly where I was, and the moment I slowed my pace, its hot breath was waving over my whole body.

It swiped, and one of its claws slashed the back of my left leg. I shouted again, but kept upright and pushed forward. The trees did slow its pursuit, but not as much as I would've hoped.

Then I hit a tree, practically winding myself. I didn't know where I was, and the darkness was so thick, a part of me wondered if this was just some sort of horrific nightmare.

The grizzly's growl was guttural and close, the echo of its rage reverberating through the forsaken forest all around me.

CHAPTER THIRTEEN

I turned around and frantically searched at my feet for *anything* to use as a weapon or a distraction. Perhaps I could wrap my bloodied bandages on a stick or—

The *bang* of a shotgun filled the forest. The bear screeched and then attempted to whirl around. The trees were its enemy, and the monster savaged everything it touched as it thrashed its claws, ripping and tearing nature itself.

How many bullets—and how much buckshot—could this fucking monster take?

Quern's flashlight shone through the trees, enough for me to scrabble around and pick up a tough branch. Quern shot again, and again, unloading as much as he could into the massive mutant bear. The monster lunged away from me—toward Quern—and I leapt into the trees in an attempt to put some distance between me and the beast.

Quern shot a fourth time and blew most of the bear's face clean from its skull, including one whole ear.

The bear swiped with its claw, but it was clearly distressed. It reared back, and then roared so loud the trees shook.

The bear patted at its missing face, its blood splattering across the forest floor, soaking into the icy dirt. I ran over to Quern, barely able to see our environment, but the tiny light he had was enough. I grabbed his arm, and motioned to the shattered trees—the path that would lead back to the jeep.

"We need to go," I said.

Quern, bleeding from multiple claw marks across the chest, half smirked. "Get running. I'll catch up."

I didn't argue with him because that would be insane. We had to go right now. I took off as fast as I could, sucking down icy air as I sprinted through the half-ruined forest. Occasionally the splintered tree trunks caught me, cutting my legs, even through my pants. I didn't care. With single-minded focus I made it to our campsite, and then rushed over to the tarp.

I grabbed it, my batteries, and the bear figurine. I threw them in the back of the jeep, and secured them down with a rope that had been left undone. Then I jumped into the passenger seat and secured my belt.

Quern still wasn't back.

The angry grunts of the bear filled the woods around me. It snorted and huffed, its breaths wet, its shouts ferocious.

My heart beat so hard I almost couldn't hear anything else. I glanced over at the driver's seat. The jeep used an old-world key to turn on. I cursed my luck as I gripped the seat. If Quern wasn't back soon, I'd grab a pack and—

But then Quern flew out of the darkness, leapt over the hood of our vehicle, and threw himself into the driver's seat. He was soaked in blood and sap, as though he had massacred a whole crew of lumberjacks.

He threw his shotgun on the center console and didn't bother buckling his seatbelt.

"Hold on," Quern said, breathless.

Which I was already doing—wildly.

Quern got the jeep going just as the mutant bear emerged from the shadows.

With its one eye, the beast lunged for us. It had all the hatred of a monster with a grudge, and even though Quern managed to drive past it, the bear took a swipe at the back tire, practically knocking the jeep around with just a single tap of its massive claws.

The sky rumbled overhead.

The headlights only showed us ten feet ahead, maybe twenty if there weren't many trees, and by sheer luck of the post-apocalyptic lottery, we managed not to slam into anything. Or maybe Quern was just that good a driver—I didn't know.

The bear—that fucking bear—kept chasing us. We couldn't get to full speed because of the terrain, but that mutant didn't have the same problem. It roared as it chased us, running on all four elongated limbs, its exhales a ravenous sound made of pure hatred.

Quern, gripping the wheel with the determination of a man who refused to die in the woods, kept his full attention on the woods, weaving when he could, threatening to roll our jeep if ever he went too hard to the left or right.

"*Shoot it,*" he commanded in Tethlite.

I grabbed the shotgun.

For half a second, I considered shooting Quern. It wouldn't take much to kill him now. But once I glanced down at the shells still ready to go, I realized we only had two shots left. And if I killed the driver, this jeep would surely career into a tree, and I would die either from the crash or the jaws of a bear, perhaps a combination of both.

So I unbuckled my belt, turned around in my seat, used the headrest as a mount to steady my shots, and took aim. I only had the red taillights to help me, and they illuminated the mangled face of the grizzly like it was possessed by a demon.

I pulled the trigger.

The *bang* was loud, but my heart still sounded in my ear.

The buckshot splattered the bear on the side of the face that was already damaged. The skull was visible now, and that still didn't stop the animal.

Quern hit a branch, or maybe a fallen tree, and most of the jeep lurched into the air. We landed with a bone-jarring thud, and I almost lost my grip on the shotgun. With my whole body shaking, and my soul ready to ditch my body, I took aim again.

I had been through worse.

A damn bear wasn't going to end me now.

I fired again, this time striking the bear's only good eye. It howled and fell back, clearly blinded. The jeep sped away at such a pace that soon the monstrous animal was lost in the darkness of the woods.

Quern gulped down air as though he hadn't been breathing for most of this mad dash out of the forest.

With a nervous chuckle, I slid into the passenger side and re-buckled my belt.

Neither of us spoke. That was fine. I was busy running my hands over my body to make sure I wasn't missing anything.

For several minutes, we drove in silence, until Quern found another road, this one made of packed dirt. He slowed his speed and took even breaths. Then he reached an unsteady hand for his chest, his nanites stitching together his wounds, but not fast enough to stop all the bleeding.

"We should probably stop somewhere," I said. "Maybe there's another ratty gas station with some rainwater."

He laughed once at that, and shot me a serious glance. "I'm not sure where we are anymore."

I leaned over to get a better look at the dirt road. It was clean, and free of rocks and branches. Someone maintained this pathway—which meant it was probably in active use.

"If we follow this, I think we might find some people."

Quern cursed under his breath. He kept one hand on his chest, holding his body together, and his other hand tightly gripping the steering wheel. "Fuck people."

"They might have supplies." I motioned to the back of the jeep. "We could trade some of this for better food. Or bandages and medicine. Probably some antibiotics."

"Or they'll see we're both injured and try to kill us." Quern shook his head, his eyes narrowed in an icy glare. "Humans are always like that—trust me. We're better not stopping. We should head to some place far from the fucking wilderness, and tend to any injuries on our own."

I exhaled. For a moment, I almost didn't argue, because Quern was more injured than I was. If anyone was going to suffer, it was going to be him. But after a few moments of quiet contemplation, I decided to make my case.

"That bear was probably irradiated," I muttered. "And if we were exposed to even slight amounts of radiation—from the environment or that monster—the first thing to get compromised is your immune system. Then your hematopoietic system. Then your gastrointestinal tract."

Quern didn't reply to me. He didn't nod—he didn't even glance over. But he was quiet, and perhaps mulling over the information, so I continued.

"Even if you have nanites in your blood, you still run the risk of your most vital systems taking a hit. You should clean your injuries. That's a must."

He slowed the jeep as we turned with the road. The lights shone across dozens of pine trees. Not a soul was around, not even any nocturnal animals.

"Most people aren't bad," I said.

Quern snorted back a laugh. "*They're disgusting animals no better than that bear,*" he said in Tethlite. "*Once we reach the Davis Space Force Base, I'll be able to get plenty of medical attention.*"

"How much longer until we get there?"

He didn't reply—because he didn't know where we were.

"Are you really *that* afraid of humans?" I sarcastically asked.

Quern gritted his teeth. "You want to risk it that badly?" He had switched back to English, and I silently wondered why he kept flipping.

"I happen to like humans a lot more than I like the Teth."

"Yeah, I bet you had fun with the prison gang. They were extremely trustworthy. Probably treated you with kindness and respect."

His sardonic tone almost made me laugh. Quern had a mild point. Those weren't the best people to interact with.

"Random raiders and thugs don't keep roads maintained," I said as I gestured to the well-packed dirt we were driving on. Even with terrible suspension, it was a smooth ride.

"You'd be surprised," he whispered.

I didn't say anything further. If he didn't want to listen to reason, I couldn't force him.

We traveled the dark trail through the woods until we finally reached the tree line. More rumbles overhead told me it would rain soon. Quern cursed under his breath, and I suspected this was the last straw. We needed to find shelter.

So he kept on the road.

We drove past a grassy field, and then a few fences. I didn't see any people, but the signs of civilization were at least around us.

Then I spotted something in the distance. It looked like a wooden wall made of pine tree trunks. It was at least six feet tall, with the trunks sharpened at the top. The wall was obviously a fortification for a small town, just as Richfield once had a trash wall to keep out the "riffraff."

"We should stop there," I said.

"We don't know who they are," Quern growled.

"It's fine. They'll see we need help—and we can pay them for it."

"They'll turn on us."

I gave him a sidelong glance. "The people of Sanctuary wouldn't have attacked two individuals who needed help."

I didn't say this, but I also knew they wouldn't have helped, either. Richfield had had been an isolationist city that turned people away all the time. And as an underground civilization, I suspected Sanctuary wasn't about to let random people on the road in through the front doors, either.

But . . .

I did intend on bringing people in, and since I was the leader, I could make those decisions. Which meant not *all* of humanity was terrible.

Quern slowed the jeep as he approached the wooden wall. The highlights shone over the carved tree trunks. Holes were cut between some of the logs—so people could point guns and rifles through them.

No one came to greet us, though.

The rumble in the clouds overhead, and the wicked howl of the wind, told me a storm was likely on its way.

"Don't alert these bumpkins to my allegiance—or to the fact you're my prisoner," Quern said, his tone low and threatening. "Because if you do, I'm just going to shoot my way out of the situation. Do I make myself clear?"

"I understand." I glanced up at the sky. "But I think it'll do us both good to wait out the storm."

I didn't think the people of this podunk town would save me. Once Bishop and Gascoigne arrived, I would be out of here. I just needed to make sure Quern was slowed down until then.

CHAPTER FOURTEEN

Quern drove around the wooden barricade until we came to the front gate. The sky continued its low rumble, warning us that we didn't have much time.

When we reached the gate, the headlights flashed over a single guard positioned by a door in the wall. The young man—maybe seventeen or eighteen?—practically gasped when he spotted our jeep. He held a long rifle, his hands shaking. With a few quick movements, he aimed his weapon at us, but kept the barrel low, pointing at the tires rather than our heads.

"H-Halt," he shouted.

The boy wore jeans with holes on the knees, likely from wear and not as any fashion statement. His jacket was thick, and his chin marked with spots of stubble.

Quern brought the jeep to a stop. He glanced over at me, and then motioned to the young man. Did Quern expect me to speak for us? He really *did* hate humans, it seemed.

I stood from my seat and leaned half my body out the window. My legs were sore, not only from the running, but also the many small injuries. I held on to the door as I said, "Hello. My name is Kita Yamasaki. This is my friend, Quern, and we're in need of a place to stay for the night."

The young man slowly lowered his weapon until it practically slipped from his hands. "My name is Roger. Uh, Roger Black. This here is Eagle Nest. Our town. We don't normally let people inside. Not unless we know them a bit first."

The sky thundered, as if agitated by the conversation.

Then rain burst from the dark clouds. At first, it was a small trickle, but that only lasted seconds. A complete downpour erupted from the sky, drenching us all in a matter of moments.

Our jeep had no proper roof.

And Roger didn't have a guard station.

As we stood there, everyone getting wet, I wasn't sure what to follow up his statement with. Finally, in a moment of sarcastic frustration, I said, "My blood type is O negative, I'm afraid of the Vay, my favorite food is wheat noodles, and I hate getting wet. Do you know enough about me yet? Or should I keep going?"

Roger blinked back all the water on his face. With a shake of his head, he motioned us forward. "I'll let you in."

Then he disappeared through the door. A few moments later, a portion of the wall creaked open wide enough for the jeep to drive through. Quern, also soaking wet, drove our vehicle into Eagle Nest, his posture stiff and his grip on the steering wheel tighter than ever.

I didn't blame him.

This place was . . . quiet. Even in the midst of a storm. No one came to greet us.

The whole city was a gigantic circle, with a single road down the middle. Houses and workshops were built on either side of the main street, with places to load and unload large objects, perhaps even livestock. At the end of the road, on the far opposite side of the town, were a few empty buildings.

Roger led us to one and pointed to a large garage door. He pulled it up, opening it like a large shutter. Quern drove inside.

I suspected these buildings were once meant for horses. As Quern drove in, my suspicions were confirmed—the floor was lined with hay, and there were horse-height windows all along one side of the stable. A few stalls for horses to sleep were built into two of the corners.

"You can stay here," Roger said, his voice echoing throughout the mostly empty stable.

He flipped a light switch that was attached to a grand total of three bulbs. They flickered to life and brought a bit of illumination to the inside of our stable.

The metal walls and concrete floors were the opposite of welcoming, but they beat sleeping out in the rain. The only real downside was the odor. The horses who lived here must've died here as well.

"Once the rain dies down, my father will come to see you."

Roger rubbed his arm as he backed away toward the garage door. I slid out of the passenger's seat and held up a hand. "Wait. We're injured. Do you have any bandages or medicine? We can trade. I have bullets. Or, uh, whatever is in this box."

Not my most convincing pitch.

Roger shifted his weight from one foot to the other. Then he sighed. "Uh. I'll see what I can do."

"Thank you. Even just some water and alcohol would be great."

He backed out of the empty stable and then pulled down the garage door.

Quern didn't move. He sat in the driver's seat, even after killing the engine. I glanced around, hoping to find something useful. There wasn't anything here. It was just us and the jeep. The cacophony of rain battered the roof, and we were out of the weather now, but there were no blankets, no chairs—nothing.

"I think we should just sleep sitting in the jeep," I muttered.

It was warmer here than the forest. It could work this time around.

Quern didn't answer.

Then the garage door opened again, but only a small amount. Roger ducked under, one arm full of minor medical supplies, including some small jars of what looked like moonshine.

"I got some things." He shoved them toward me, never really getting too close.

I took them. "Thank you so much."

"You said you had bullets?"

"Yeah."

I set his supplies on the jeep and then rummaged through one of the packs that Quern had packed. Sure enough, 9mm clips were stuffed to the brim of one. I passed two over to Roger, hoping he would accept that. The man happily snatched them from my grasp.

With a nervous smile, he once again backed out under the garage door. No goodbye or commentary—he just slipped away into the rain and shut the door behind him.

"That was weird," I muttered.

"They're planning on killing us," Quern said, deadpan.

I shook my head. "I doubt it. That's a little bleak. He knows we have weapons—and the ammo to use them. Places like this don't like to get bloody in the heart of their home."

He turned to face me, his eyes narrowed in irritation. "You're naïve—and I'm surprised you've lived this long."

Although I wanted to counter his statement, I couldn't in good conscience do that. For the longest time, I lived life as a recluse hermit. I *did* consider everyone and everything a threat. But loneliness ate at me. I think I suffered from all my time away from others.

Plus, I had things to live for now. I had nothing when I was alone. A whole city was waiting on me.

"I'm confident I know the vague direction this town is in relation to Sanctuary," I said as I spread out the supplies Roger had given us. "Once I get back, I can have some people come here and deliver a message. We can help each other—maybe even absorb the citizens of Eagle Nest into our burgeoning civilization."

Quern didn't answer me.

He had simply lifted an eyebrow when I had said, *once I get back.*

But now that I could properly examine the supplies in the back of the jeep, I was making more mental notes. I unfolded our tarps, removed my batteries and bear figurine, and grabbed a pack. I dumped out the contents and made it "my pack." Then I shoved in the batteries, some moonshine, the figurine, and some 9mm clips.

Quern had packed enough hardtack for thirty people. It seemed a shame to eat it, but it was better than nothing. I took some of that, too. Then I grabbed a few bottles of water, rounding out everything.

I'd want all this.

"What're you doing?" Quern asked from the driver's seat.

I sifted through Roger's gifts once again. "I'm getting you bandages. One second."

With as much haste as I could muster, I grabbed some bandages and alcohol and walked over to Quern. He was still holding his injuries. His face had paled, and I wondered if he had lost too much blood.

"Let me help," I said, holding up the bandages.

Quern practically knocked them from my hand. He turned with an icy glare. In Tethlite, he hissed, "*I don't want their medicine. It's probably poison. Fuck them.*"

I flinched away from him, baffled he was this irrational. I tossed the supplies into the back of the jeep. The bottle of moonshine—which had been the size of my fist—shattered. I cringed and let out a long exhale. Probably shouldn't have done that.

"Did humans harm you in some way?" I asked. "Or are you just really indoctrinated?"

"*I was a slave in Ex Cathedra,*" Quern said, lowering his voice into something threatening. He had given up on English completely. "*For years I worked under the boot of a judge. They hate the Teth—they killed so many in their wars, it was practically a genocide.*"

I knew.

I had lived in Ex Cathedra.

They were powerful and single-minded. They wanted to unite humanity, rebuild a nation lost, but also purify it. The judges and their power armor were making that a reality.

"*I . . .*" Quern took in a deep breath and visibly calmed. In a quieter voice, he continued, "*I ran away. The Iron-Blooded took me in, but it wasn't until I was housed with the Teth warriors that I understood. The Teth are better than us. They work as a unit. As a hive. They protected me. I protected them.*"

He was right. The Teth did live in a hierarchy. And they all knew their place from birth, which was convenient.

"How old were you when you joined them?" I asked.

Quern didn't respond. He didn't even look at me.

I cleared my throat and switched to Tethlite. "*How old were you?*"

"*Ten.*"

"*So they raised you?*" That was a little surprising. "*You lived and worked with humans and Teth for most your life?*"

When he glanced over, his expression was an aggressive neutral. "*Why does it matter?*"

"Because I want a civilization where we both live in harmony," I stated, switching back to English. "Brecht and Vega did it. You did it. I know the Iron-Blooded teach that humanity is evil and murderous—"

"*They are.*"

"—but there's a reason the Teth allied with us when they arrived. They liked humanity, and worked to combine our technologies. My grandfather thought it was an amazing idea, and I'm going to continue his legacy."

Quern . . .

Stifled a laugh.

"*Why are you telling me this?*" he asked, sardonic in tone.

Why?

Well, I had been hoping to intrigue and convince him. Maybe—just *maybe*—he would change his mind and *want* to return to Sanctuary with me. If that were the case, we'd gain a new ally. And since Quern knew so much about the inner workings of the Iron-Blooded, and had grown up with Teth, he would be a great boon to our community.

Quern turned his gaze down to his left hand. The nub of a thumb was chilling. "*Humans are the only ones I've regretted coming into contact with. No matter what story you spin, you're not going to convince me.*" With gritted teeth, he motioned to the back of the jeep with a jerk of his head. "*There are bandages from the prison in the box. Use those.*"

Perhaps out of guilt for what I had done to him, I sighed and went to the box. Sure enough, he had collected a lot of bandages. I pulled out half and brought them over. Quern carefully removed his shirt, sucking in air between his teeth, and then showed me the claw marks.

They were . . . the opposite of okay.

Had the bear been badly irradiated? I hoped not—but the back of my leg still stung, so it was a real possibility.

With shaky hands, I wrapped the bandages around Quern's chest. He never flinched or made any noise. He just allowed me to do my work. I attempted to be gentle—again, out of a sense of guilt—and perhaps he felt it, because he stopped me halfway by grabbing my wrist.

"What's with you?" he asked in English. "If you really want to build your perfect civilization, you're going to kill everyone who threatens it." Quern eyed the bandages, and then me again, now glaring. "You never should've let me live."

"My grandfather once said that truly good ideas convince people." I half chuckled. "He said that was why people left their homeland to move to the United States during its infancy. Because the US was such a good idea—so much better than everything that had come before it."

And sometimes, in my wildest imaginings . . .

I thought I could make something even better. And once people heard about it, they would want to be a part of it as well.

I pulled my wrist from his grip. "But words are cheap. I need to work hard. I need to make this work. If I want Teth and humans to get along, I have to make it a reality."

Each word was spoken more for my benefit, not for Quern's.

I wanted to convince myself to keep going.

"I'm not the only enemy," Quern muttered. "There are already new nations collecting power. Ex Cathedra and U-Cali aren't going to let your new little civilization grow."

His words reflected one of my greatest fears.

How would I deal with them? Diplomacy? No. Not with Ex Cathedra. They would never listen. They already were powerful, and their military formidable.

"The Iron-Blooded ran into this problem before, and they basically were forced into hiding because of it." Quern turned away from me, dismissive. "You'll be the same way. No one will listen. You'll have your tiny community, but once you die, your ideals and dreams will go with you."

Damn.

He was so negative.

But I refused to give up. I had options.

Once finished with Quern's bandages, I stepped away from the jeep. The man appeared more relaxed than before. Or maybe he was just tired. After a long sigh, he slid out of the jeep and went to the back. He gathered a tarp and then our only blanket.

With casual confidence, he laid the tarp on the ground. Then Quern gathered up some of the spare hay. He was obviously in pain, because he grimaced more than once, but that didn't stop him from hauling it into two piles, each person-shaped.

Quern put the piles on the tarp, patted them until they were definitely human-shaped—and snuggled together—and then wrapped them tightly in the blanket, making sure to tuck around every edge.

"What the hell are you doing?" I asked.

Now we would never be able to use that blanket ever again.

"It's time to sleep." Quern motioned to the jeep. "Clean off the broken bottle, and let's sleep between the packs. Out of sight."

"Oh." I crossed my arms. "You think the people of Eagle Nest are going to kill us while we're sleeping?"

He eyed me like I had asked him a ridiculous question. "How many times do I have to tell you I don't trust them? Should I say it slower? I can explain my reasons, but I can't understand them for you."

That caused me to snort back a laugh. He was snarky now?

"They're not going to hurt us."

"Let's make a bet," Quern said.

"Fine. I bet they won't even come into this garage. They'll wait for us to exit, and they'll be perfectly nice."

Quern shook his head and chortled. Then he pointed to the back of the jeep. "Let's get some sleep. Maybe you'll wake up with more sense."

CHAPTER FIFTEEN

We sat in the middle of the jeep. I slipped in and out of wakefulness, struggling with dreams. Once again, Quern practically slept on top of me, making sure I wouldn't just bolt in the middle of the night. His head was on my shoulder, and most of his weight on my side. He was clearly more fatigued than I was.

I had cleaned the moonshine, but now the jeep reeked of alcohol. It was better than eau-de-horse-poop, though.

As I sat there, I had a pretend argument with myself, going back and forth for both me and then Quern. I wanted to convince him humans were good. Why did I believe that so thoroughly?

Because of my grandfather . . .

In my head, I explained it all to Quern.

My grandfather *believed* in mankind. He believed the majority of individuals were good, even if most were susceptible to laziness or ignorance. When people asked him if technology would outpace our morals, he told them that personal responsibility was the key. If we kept our morals, our ideals, our values, then we wouldn't have to discuss hypothetical futures or shadowy problems no one could fully pin down.

Meritocracy. Equality of opportunity. Freedom.

He spoke of those the most.

They were just words until I understood. The beauty of humanity was that talent could come from anywhere—any person—so long as they had the drive to see it through. My grandfather was a proud American, born to a second-generation Japanese man and an immigrant woman from

Finland. Through hard work, they lived well, but that didn't stop them from striving further.

My grandfather had nothing but reverence when he spoke of how his parents encouraged him to go beyond merely acceptable levels of success and to never blame anyone else for his shortcomings.

Real ideals, he said, required the strength of the individual to carry them, not the strength of someone else.

So when my grandfather became a human ambassador—one of the first humans ever to deal with the Teth—he went beyond mere acceptable levels of investigation and understanding. My grandfather befriended Architect Riven and came to an understanding—the Teth would fit into our society as equals. They would accept nothing more, and nothing less.

But my grandfather didn't stop with that. He planned and built and advocated for cooperation at every level. He said we, as a society, couldn't become complacent or second best. Humanity had to rise to the occasion, meet the visitors as equals, and leap forward without doubt. If we remained ignorant or weak, we would be ruled by the Vay and our way of life destroyed.

He championed advancement because he kept mankind first and foremost in his heart—he wanted what was best—and he made decisions accordingly.

My grandfather was a diplomat and a scholar and an engineer who worked tirelessly to see his vision of the future made into a reality. In a way, it advanced both humanity and the Teth. Aliens found life on Earth challenging, but with mankind's hospitality and knowledge, a new coalition was born.

In my head, I totally won the argument.

But . . . then imaginary Quern would bring up that humans and aliens still fought. The Forever Winter happened, and now we lived in a world of ruin . . .

"Touché," I said to myself—and the imaginary argument I had semi-lost.

Despite that, I knew I had to be more like my grandfather.

I had to be better.

Quern would never convince me otherwise.

My dreams soured into nightmares as I tossed and turned. Visions of the townspeople entering the stable left me in a cold sweat. In my dream, there was a squeak at the garage door. I held my breath, straining my ears to listen for more, but the rain made it difficult.

Quern stiffened, obviously roused from his slumber by even the slightest of change in the environment. Then he grabbed my shoulder, his fingers digging into my bicep. "They're here," he whispered.

That was when I heard it. Soft footfalls.

With tense movements, I glanced around the bags and peered over the edge of the jeep. It was risky, because someone might spot me, but I wanted to know what was going on. The three overworked lights in the stable offered enough illumination for me to see the blanket and tarp stuffed with hay not too far from our vehicle.

Quern reached for the waistband of his pants and pulled out his 9mm.

Then I spotted two individuals creeping over to the hay-stuffed blanket. I watched, with terrified realization, as both individuals lifted personal rifles and pointed them at the mounds behind the cloth.

They really were planning to kill us.

The two resulting shots echoed throughout the stable and sent a shiver down my spine.

I jerked awake, my heart pounding.

The rain had ended, and the garage was still. With ice in my veins, I peered over the edge of the jeep and glanced at the piles of hay. They were undisturbed. It really had been just a nightmare.

Quern was already sitting up, his expression neutral.

"Did something happen while I was asleep?" I whispered.

He glanced over and nodded. "Some people came into the stable."

"They didn't shoot us?"

He lifted an eyebrow in blatant bewilderment. "Obviously they didn't."

"What happened?"

"They checked the area, and then left us."

Ah. I understood. The people of Eagle Nest were worried. We were strangers, and we could've been doing anything in their stable, including preparing to kill them all while they slept. Perhaps we had even been using the storm as cover for all our activities.

But once they came in, and saw we had done none of that, the denizens of this small town left us alone.

"I told you they wouldn't kill us," I said.

Quern exhaled. "They could've."

"They could've *tried*." I motioned to our vehicle. "If they really had come in here, we could've run them over. Or something. Point is, we had options. And I think most of these small cities don't actually want conflict. They just want to rebuild."

Quern listened, but I didn't know if he was actually listening to my words. He seemed distant—lost in thought. Part of me wondered if he actually had *wanted* someone to try and kill us.

"We're leaving," he muttered.

"You don't want to stay and trade for more supplies?"

Quern climbed up into the driver's seat. "No. We've already wasted too much time. I want out of this place as soon as possible."

After stretching, and blinking away all the sleep in my eyes, I leapt out of the jeep and headed for the garage door. The door squeaked as I opened it.

Quern backed up, turned the jeep in a tight circle, and then faced the garage. He motioned with a jut of his chin, and I went straight to the passenger's seat.

Without so much as another word, Quern accelerated down the main street. The citizens of Eagle Nest glanced over, their eyebrows high. I suspected they wanted to speak with us now—the storm was over and we hadn't been a threat—but no one went out of their way to stop us. They just watched as Quern sped past, barely looking at anyone or anything.

With the wind whipping through my short, black hair, I took a seat and buckled my belt.

There was a wall around Eagle Nest . . . When I glanced over at Quern, he didn't meet my gaze. What were we going to do? It was a quick and easy ride all the way to the edge of town, where the gate was closed, but he hadn't stopped to ask anyone for help.

Was he just going to drive through it?

What a very Iron-Blooded thing to do.

"Please don't hurt the town," I said.

He glowered at me. "These aren't your people."

"Anyone interested in rebuilding the world for the better is *my people*."

Despite the irritation in my voice, Quern didn't let it affect him. He slowed as he approached the gate, parked, got out, and then used the lever himself, even though there were plenty of Eagle Nest citizens nearby. No one said anything to us—Quern didn't look like a man to mess with, frankly—and once the gate *click-clicked* open, he pulled himself back in the driver's seat.

As he headed out the gate, he glanced over. "Why didn't you try to take the vehicle?"

"You still have a gun, and the vehicle was parked," I replied matter-of-factly. "It would've given you plenty of time to aim and fire—and you're a pretty good shot. Not really worth taking the risk of escape, given that situation."

Quern seemed to mull this over as we exited Eagle Nest. Then he nodded, almost approvingly, as though he thought my assessment of the situation were correct.

"Why are we taking this road?" I asked. It was the road that led from Eagle Nest, and seemed well-worn.

"This is Plan B," he snapped. He said that like he'd once had a Plan A, but that seemed unlikely.

"We don't need more supplies?"

He shook his head, his gaze straight forward. "I have everything we need—and the Iron-Blooded's base of operations is nearby."

"Howdy, folks. I'm your radio host, Weatherbean, here to give you all the local news for the Wastewoods."

As Quern drove, I listened to the radio. It was different here, since most broadcasts could only reach about a hundred miles. That made it "fun" to discover people in different parts of the wasteland. Or, in this case, the Wastewoods, as the radio host liked to call it.

"First up, we have more word from the east. It seems Ex Cathedra is moving along at a nice clip, making headway through the woods. Hopefully their tanks will run over the grave of my dead whore wife as they make their way here."

I frowned, already missing the cringe-antics of DJ Slam back in the region around Sanctuary. This radio host was more . . . dour. And perhaps unhinged.

"The trains haven't been runnin' right for months now, and some folks believe it's because of gang fightin'," Weatherbean said, his voice tinged in static. Wherever he was, it was far from us, or perhaps his equipment was beat-up. "Let them fight, I say! My *new* wife, Rita, hates those rail gangs. They took all her chems and left her locked in a shed for two days. That's actually how we met."

To my amusement, Quern dragged a hand down his face and groaned. Then he reached for the radio's volume.

I blocked his hand. "No. I want to hear if there's anything important."

He shot me a sidelong glance, but he didn't argue. I suspected he was still on the mend, and didn't want to argue about the damn radio, but I didn't know that for certain.

"If you're having problems with raiders or gangs, remember that here in the Wastewoods we offer protection at militia stations. You'll see their flags around, each a bright yellow and depicting a bobcat. They'll provide you with food and shelter."

I glanced over to Quern with a lifted eyebrow. "See? We weren't killed by Eagle Nest, *and* there are militia around to help people. Humanity has a lot of camaraderie."

"It's a trick," Quern said, practically exhaling every word. "Those places are the *prime* location to take advantage of someone."

"It was the ideal situation to kill us back in Eagle Nest, too."

Quern didn't follow up with any commentary after that. He just gripped the steering wheel and kept his attention on the road.

"Wastewood Militia gets it done!" Weatherbean shouted with a whoop. Afterward, he coughed and simmered down. "Now on to the weather, right? Has anyone else noticed it's not as gloomy as it used to be? And there's less acid rain to go around? It might just be my old-man brain imagining things, but the clouds seem thinner than usual . . ."

He wasn't wrong. When I turned my attention to the landscape, I took note of the brighter skies. It seemed the world was finally healing.

The majestic mountains in the distance sported a coat of white, but I turned my attention in the other direction, wondering when Ex Cathedra would be here.

The jeep hiccupped. I focused my attention on the hood as the engine coughed worse than a chain-smoking toad. Quern grumbled something and then shook his head. Given the way the jeep was reacting, I imagined it wouldn't turn on again once we turned it off. This was the vehicle's last trek.

"We're almost to a point of safety," Quern said, as if he were reassuring me.

"We're getting farther and farther from everything I consider safe," I muttered.

He didn't respond to that.

That probably meant we were drawing closer to the Iron-Blooded, or at least their base of operations.

"In other news, I heard about a man who controls alien drones *with his mind*," Weatherbean said. He slammed his hand on something and a *thump* issued through the radio. "Now that's a superpower. I wish I had that with my goats. Damn things keep runnin' off, even though I treat them all like princesses, and got them all dresses. Ungrateful meat bags, I say."

I sat forward in my seat, my heart pounding.

I knew who that was. I had fought him in the city of Boulder—him *and* his drones. He was a "human architect" and an experiment created by Architect Riven to help control humans. And I had almost killed them all when I escaped the Hoover Dam.

The human architect was still alive? And he was here? In the Wastewoods?

Quern turned to me, his brow furrowed in concern. "What's wrong?"

"Oh, fuck me," I whispered. "Theon Sellers is here."

CHAPTER SIXTEEN

The weather seemed to brighten, which was nice, and I wondered if the clouds overhead might possibly split apart for just a moment, to allow for the sun to greet us in full force. Years ago, that would've been an impossibility, but now . . .

It got me hopeful.

When Quern turned the jeep toward a ruined old-world city, I knew this was our real destination. And sure enough, as he drove down a road riddled with cracks and potholes, I spotted dozens of Teth drones sifting through the rubble. They walked on all their limbs, like alien dogs, sniffing around for anything useful.

They were intelligent, but not like how humans classified animals. Teth drones did whatever they were told by other castes of the Teth. They were controlled by pheromones and typically had no ability to govern themselves.

If they were ever left with no orders, they tended to repeat whatever was last given to them—which was why some drones continued to guard places years after all the other Teth in the area had died.

"You've met Theon Sellers before?" Quern eventually asked me as we drove between the deserted husks of skyscrapers. I assumed he hated the silence between us.

The radio broadcast had stopped thirty minutes back, after all. We were now in places more humans had thoroughly abandoned.

"Theon used to run the city of Boulder," I muttered.

"Up until you destroyed his operations." Quern tensed. "Which is why I need to bring you back. The Iron-Blooded want you to pay for what you've done. And after everything I've seen, I need to give them all the information I know they can't get through torture."

"Really nice of you to explain all your plans," I darkly quipped. "I assume you're going to get in on the torture? Take a couple of fingers? For old time's sake?"

Quern glanced over at me with a glare. "You're pushing your luck with an attitude like that."

"This is the attitude I take whenever the world is fucked up."

If Bishop were here, he would understand. He made jokes like I made sarcastic comments. It helped to brighten the gloom.

The silence between us turned bitter.

Which was fine. I kept my attention on our surroundings, and suddenly, my hopes rose. This city was decrepit, and larger than I had imagined for someplace this far north. The Forever Winter had been rough everywhere, but especially north of the 39th parallel.

And that was where we were, but this city was more intact than expected. Sure, it was bad. The weeds were reclaiming everything with the attitude of, "Hey, why not a hostile takeover?" and the penthouses at the top level of the skyscrapers were going full open concept. Walls were so pre-apocalypse.

But everything else, even the smaller houses, and even some of the rickety churches, were still standing. There were plenty of places here that still had the feel of a world before the aliens. If I managed to get away from Quern, I could probably find useful items and a way to stay hidden.

How would I get away from him, though?

With a subtle glance, I eyed the 9mm he kept tucked into his waistband. Shooting him was an option, but he was larger and stronger than me. If I got the drop on him, however, I could probably shoot him, race into the city, and find my way through the ruined buildings.

It was a solid plan, and I hammered out the details in my imagination as he drove.

As we moved deeper into the city—I still didn't know its name—the remnants of the old world's last moments were more evident. Burnt-out vehicles, barricades that had long since failed, graffiti screaming defiance and despair in equal measure. The air was thick with the ghosts of the past.

"I suppose humanity is impressive," Quern said, jarring me from my thoughts.

I glanced over, surprised he had even a little bit to say. "What?"

"These buildings. They're impressive. For humans."

I nodded once. "Yeah. Humans are natural architects, really. And our strength comes from versatility, which the Teth lack. But don't tell the Iron-Blooded I said that or else they'll torture me double."

The Teth's genetic code dictated their caste, and their caste dictated everything about their personality. The Iron-Blooded hated when anyone spoke poorly of that, though.

"You said you're going to build a city with humans and Teth?" Quern asked.

"Yes," I confidently replied.

"What about the illness? The one I found inside the depths of Sanctuary? You said it targeted the Teth."

"I didn't make that." I held up a finger. "I found that research, and it could be more than one illness, so it isn't really safe. And I don't intend to do anything with it—as a matter of fact, I think the corpses are causing the people of Sanctuary to become ill, and I need to get rid of it all."

"Why not keep it?" Quern narrowed his eyes, his gaze on the cracked roads in front of us. "Why not use it on the Iron-Blooded? Or the Vay?"

"First off, I don't know if it'll work on the Vay." I glanced over, half intrigued by scientific matters, half in the mood to instruct him. "Are you aware of genetic illnesses? How certain humans are more prone to certain diseases? Like sickle-cell anemia? Well, the Teth and Vay are similar—and can cross breed—but they're not identical. Since I don't know much about this illness other than it was made to kill the Teth, there's a good chance it won't actually do that to the Vay. Additionally, wanton destruction in the form of biological warfare will result in a world far more crippled than it already is."

Quern shook his head. "And you care about that? There's a good chance you'll die long before you see the world change."

"All the great leaders of history didn't set their sights on the immediate. They set their sights on the tomorrows only their children would see."

I said every word slowly and passionately, my mind and heart in agreement.

A disease that killed the Teth wasn't the best route. Not for my planned future.

Quern didn't respond, but I could tell my moment for escape was drawing close.

The trick was timing. Quern, ever vigilant, rarely let his guard down—but I had seen it a few times now. I needed to be patient, wait for the right moment when his focus shifted just enough. Maybe when he was navigating a particularly nasty pothole or distracted by one of those Teth drones or maybe even—

Quern stopped the jeep.

I gripped the edge of my seat, my heart racing. When I glanced around, I didn't see Theon, or any other Teth besides the distant drones. We weren't even *anywhere*—we were just in the middle of a cracked road with rusted vehicles on either side of us.

"Get out," Quern said. He tightened his grip on the steering wheel, his eyes straight ahead on the road and not on me at all. "Take a pack. Go the way we came. Leave."

I waited with bated breath.

A part of me figured he would follow that statement up with something. Or maybe he was joking? What was he even talking about?

"Are you deaf now?" Quern glanced over with a sardonic glare. "I said, *get out.*"

"What're you doing?" I asked.

"I'm letting you go before any of the Iron-Blooded see you in my custody."

"I . . ."

He was releasing me? But why?

I must've been too stunned, because Quern half turned in his seat and pulled his handgun from his waistband. "Do I have to give you more incentive? Do I have to threaten you?" In Tethlite, he said, *"I'm not a patient man."*

While I had been planning my escape, this scenario never entered my imagination.

In my head, something would've happened. A drone would've jumped in front of the jeep, and Quern would've swerved, and I would've taken his gun, and perhaps shot him in the foot, and then said a Bishop line, like, "Now you have extra iron in your blood, Quern!" before disappearing off into the city.

That was insane. I knew it was, because I never made quips like Bishop, but in my imagination it was wonderful.

Quern letting me go? I never would've imagined that.

"Thank you," I whispered.

He grunted something but didn't actually answer me.

I didn't argue with him. I slid out of the passenger seat and then slowly walked around to the back of the jeep. I reached for my pack, my hands shaky, my veins filled with adrenaline. Was this a trick? No. It couldn't be. Quern didn't actually need me . . .

He already had information on Sanctuary.

And he was going to provide it to all my enemies.

Was that the price I was going to pay for allowing him to live? His escape, my kidnapping, and even this situation was all my fault. If I had killed him like Gascoigne had said, this wouldn't have happened.

I scrunched my eyes as I grabbed a few more hardtack from another pack.

But then the hard breaths of something large caught my attention. I stiffened as hot breath washed over me, starting with the top of my head. The air stank of blood, and I already knew what was behind me.

One of the Teth.

With my breath caught in my throat, I slowly turned around.

Sure enough, standing before me was one of the aliens—one of the Teth. It had no eyes, just a long "face" that ended in an elongated mouth filled with fangs. Its skin was a matte black, darker than the sky, and with a wet shine. Everything about the Teth reminded me of a monster, and years ago, I had been deeply afraid of them.

But now . . .

I gulped down air.

"*Hello,*" I said in Tethlite.

Four more of these aliens slipped from the darkness between the large buildings, each quieter than the last. Most of the Teth stayed to the shadows, since bright lights often caused them irritation. They had four arms—two large, two thin and fine—but these Teth weren't bulky, like Vega, which meant they weren't warriors.

Their bodies were skeletal thin.

When their smaller arms reached for the ground so they could feel their environment, I noticed their long, spindly fingers, nearly twice the length of my own.

"*What's going on?*" Quern slid out of the jeep and then stopped.

We had been caught by a Teth scouting group. These were all members of the *outrider* caste. They were pawns to the warrior caste, just above drones in terms of usefulness and importance to the overall hierarchy.

They were some of the least intelligent Teth, in my humble opinion, but they were often fast, nimble, and made for great scouts.

These five outriders had been so quiet and sneaky, I hadn't even heard them approach. The one behind me was only two feet away, its hot breath on my skin, and if it wanted, it could've gutted me.

"*Quern, kin of different blood,*" the first outrider said in Tethlite. "*We were told of your death, and mourned it. Yet here you are, with a female, at the edge of our new domain. Explain yourself, so that we may take it to the architect.*"

Quern slowly glanced between the five outriders, his shoulders tense and his stance wide. He looked uncomfortable. Considering he had been about to let me go—for some reason—I supposed he was caught off guard and didn't like that.

He remained silent.

When the lead outrider stood to its full height, the alien was nearly seven feet tall and wiry with corded muscles.

"*Who is this?*" the outrider asked.

I glanced over at Quern, and our gazes locked for half a second. Then he turned away, his expression unreadable.

If he told these Teth who I was, then they wouldn't hesitate bringing me straight to the Iron-Blooded ruling command. Theon, Architect Riven—all of them. And they really would torture me to death. If Quern was having second thoughts about that because I spared his life, then he couldn't give them my real identity.

"*She's a hitchhiker I found on the side of the road,*" Quern awkwardly stated.

I knew how to lie. I had honed my skill over many years.

Quern had not.

I could tell he was lying from the way he slowly cobbled together each word like he had never formed a proper sentence before. My heart continued to hammer, wondering if these outriders would believe it.

Perhaps they couldn't read human emotions well.

"*Our orders were clear,*" the main outrider stated. "*We weren't to bring others to this location.*"

"*I wasn't given those orders. I was taken hostage by the enemy, and only just barely escaped.*"

"*This female is useless to us—and since she's seen the edge of our domain, we need to silence her, as per Architect Riven's orders.*"

I stepped backward until my back hit the jeep. They were going to kill me just because I knew the Iron-Blooded were here? Goddammit. I turned to Quern again, hoping he would do something to get me out of this situation.

Quern shook his head. "*You can't kill her.*"

"*Why?*" the main outrider asked. "*Is it because she's carrying a child? Architect Riven didn't give that as an exception for execution.*"

Carrying . . . a child?

CHAPTER SEVENTEEN

Oh, no.

No, no, no.

Without conscious thought, I ran my hand over my abdomen, wondering why I hadn't noticed it. I knew the answer to my question immediately—I hadn't been pregnant long. Maybe a few days. Maybe a week. That was enough for the human body to produce new hormones. From all my studies, I knew it required about ten days for the hormones to really saturate the body, and those hormones changed a woman's chemical makeup enough that animals could detect a change in her scent.

These Teth probably smelled the difference in me.

They knew—and they probably weren't wrong.

The main outrider grabbed me by the arm and jerked me close. "*We'll dispose of her body,*" it said in Tethlite.

"*You can't,*" I said in Tethlite. That shocked the outriders, who probably all assumed I wouldn't know their language. "*I . . .*" I would fight everyone with just my fingernails and teeth if that was all I had. I'd never let them touch me without it being an ordeal they'd never forget.

"*Don't kill her,*" Quern stated, his tone grasping for some sort of logical reason.

"*We were going to eat her,*" the outrider stated.

"*No. As a member of the warrior caste, I forbid it.*"

The outriders all growled together—a habit the Teth had whenever they wanted to convey a singular position. It was the human equivalent of clapping or booing. It meant this scouting group was rather discontent with the decision, and they wanted Quern to know it.

"*Human fetuses are filled with nutrition,*" the outrider said. "*And female humans carrying children are quite tasty.*"

"*No,*" Quern growled.

"*At least let us consume some of her blood and insides.*"

They wanted my insides? Some sort of disgusting organ removal? Sometimes the Teth bothered me. I made a mental note to myself to teach my Teth not to view humans as things they could consume.

That was assuming I made it out of this situation alive.

"*You can't kill the child,*" Quern stated. "*Because it's mine.*"

That statement gave all the outriders pause.

Hell, it gave *me* pause. I turned to him, my expression twisted in shock. But I quickly got control of myself and held back a laugh. That was a good lie—because the Teth wouldn't kill kin of different blood, so if this child was Quern's, it was technically a member of the Iron-Blooded.

"*I see,*" the outrider stated. "*Forgive me.*" The Teth bowed its head until it touched the cracked cement. When it lifted its eyeless gaze, it said, "*We will escort you to the heart of our operations, to ensure the safety of your legacy.*"

Quern hesitated. He clearly didn't want to take me, but it was obvious he was running out of excuses to send the Teth away so I could escape. I had to admit—I didn't know what I would say in this moment, either. What kind of lie would result in me separating from the group?

In the tense silence that followed, I could almost hear the gears turning in Quern's head. He was trapped in his own web of deception. I opened my mouth, but he shot me a glare, his eyes filled with cold confidence. Without uttering any words, he had said—*this is my lie; let me spin it.*

Finally, Quern nodded to the outrider. "*Very well. Lead the way, and make sure no harm comes to the woman or her child.*"

In Teth culture, higher-ranking castes could give orders to the members of lower-ranking castes. Since Quern was considered a warrior, the outriders would have to follow his instructions.

The outrider seemed to accept this. "*We will ensure safe passage. The child of an Iron-Blooded is a valuable asset.*"

I got back into the jeep, my backpack slung on my shoulders, just in case I needed to run. Quern slowly accelerated, and the five outriders ran alongside the vehicle. At first, I thought we would outspeed them, but as we continued, it became clear they were much faster than I had previously imagined. They ran with their arms, like dogs, but they used their smaller arms to help cushion their movements.

They ran remarkably quietly. Their claws barely clacked against the cement and asphalt, and they moved with the grace of rabbits—despite the fact they all had to weigh over four hundred pounds.

I scooted over in my chair, staying closer to Quern, my mind racing. His quick thinking had saved us for the moment, but it was only temporary. If the Iron-Blooded discovered my identity, they wouldn't care if I was carrying Quern's child or not.

When I glanced over, he didn't meet my gaze. I wondered what kind of man he really was. His act of claiming the child as his own was either a stroke of genius or pure madness. Maybe both. But it had given us an advantage, a small window to plan our next move.

It was risky on his part—if they found out he was lying, he would also be killed.

We continued forward at a fast clip, the car shaking from the potholes. Asphalt was a terrible material to make roads out of. It was cheap and cracked easily, and before the Forever Winter it had needed to be replaced on a regular basis. But there were no repair crews anymore.

Now the road was practically a hazardous obstacle course.

I held my stomach, suddenly fearful of every tiny bump and movement. Which was silly, I knew, but I couldn't help but feel panic.

"You'll be fine," Quern muttered in English.

The outriders probably didn't know that language.

"Hopefully," I replied in a low tone.

The ruined city loomed around us like a mausoleum. The Iron-Blooded operations center had to be somewhere close, because with each passing second, I felt the weight of their presence, their alienness, closing in around us.

There were more drones. More shadowy areas. Windows boarded up. Suspicious towers on the tops of buildings that I suspected were the homes of snipers.

I shivered.

We drove across a cracked parking lot, weaving between ruined cars, before heading straight to an abandoned department store. It was some sort of buy-everything-in-one-place mega-building, complete with an orchard section, a grocery store, and a hardware department.

Across the parking lot in the other direction, and over a road, was a large concrete wall. The sign on the wall read: *Davis Space Force Base.*

The Iron-Blooded had taken over both buildings and built a makeshift bridge between them. It was made of bricks and wood, and a stairway had even been constructed over the wall of the space force base—probably because the main gates were rubble or ruined.

The department store was clearly more fortified, though.

And everything was covered in a fine layer of plant life, and every exposed piece of metal was red with rust. A barricade had been built around the store, but that wall was shorter than around the base itself.

My time was running out. Whatever move we were going to make, it had to be soon.

My hand instinctively touched my abdomen again, a silent vow that I would do whatever it took to protect the life growing inside me, even if it meant trusting Quern for a short while.

Quern parked the jeep near the front entrance and got out. I joined him, and together, the outriders surrounded us. The lead Teth motioned with his snout. "*This way, kin of different blood. To the barracks.*"

Quern nodded.

Before anything else happened, Quern covertly passed me the 9mm. I held my breath as I quickly shoved it into my pack.

One of the outriders grabbed me. I tensed, but remained calm when Quern subtly shook his head. Then, as a group, we walked toward the warehouse portion of the base. I kept my pace quick and my eyes open. There wasn't much to look at, and the Teth wasn't talkative.

Once we reached the hardware entrance, the outrider dragged me to some poorly constructed barracks, Quern between two of them, as though they were making sure we couldn't go in any unexpected directions. Or perhaps this was just common for the Teth, who were blind, and probably kept in groups by sticking extremely close to one another.

Several Iron-Blooded humans were gathered around cots and using water from gigantic canisters stacked in the corners of the massive room. There were no women here—the Teth never assigned females into the warrior caste. It wasn't because they were sexist, just that they didn't understand dimorphic species.

The hermaphroditic Teth classified themselves based on their physical appearance and differences at birth. They did the same with humans, thinking we worked the same way.

The Iron-Blooded uniform was mostly black. Pants, shirt, belt—even a bulletproof vest. It also had the Iron-Blooded insignia, which was an alien skull with a human skull inside its teeth.

The human men all turned to face Quern and me as the outriders led us to the very back. There were a few rooms there—probably once storage facilities or offices for the store—and the outrider shoved me toward the nearest one.

It opened the door.

The tiny "room" was cramped. It had probably once been a closet.

"You will remain here until you are given further instructions," it said.

I didn't reply.

Quern nodded for me. *"She will."*

There was a cot, and a box, and a couple of magazines with women prominently on the cover.

That was it.

When the door shut behind me, I flinched. It was dark now—too dark to see. But I could hear the others beyond the door. They yelled a few things in Tethlite, clearly speaking to the outrider.

"Why is there a woman here?"

"Quern has returned to us?"

"We need that room for one of the new warriors. You can't just take it."

Quern and the outrider were bombarded with a million questions and statements. All this told me was that I wouldn't be able to leave without walking past dozens of Iron-Blooded lunatics. If I exited the closet, there were only two directions—the way I came, or deeper into the department store. If I went deeper, I'd likely run into the important players in the Iron-Blooded, such as Theon Sellers or Architect Riven.

Just to make sure I wasn't locked in the closet, I tried the handle. The door creaked open a tiny bit without much force.

I peered outside.

"Quern is one of the few warriors who has the ability to pilot the power armor," someone in the crowd of Iron-Blooded said.

"Still. Wasn't he reported dead? How is he here?"

I couldn't see who was talking, and their voices mixed together since so many people were talking over one another.

The outrider was probably just as frustrated. It growled, and the others quieted down. *"The architects will decide what to do. Until then, Quern's offspring—and its carrier—will remain here. Do not harm them. I will return with further instructions."*

I waited for a moment, watching as Quern and the outrider walked out into the hardware department. The other Iron-Blooded humans stayed in a group, whispering about this turn of events. They all carried rifles and handguns. More of a reason not to jump the gun and recklessly escape.

I had Quern's 9mm, though. If it came to a fight, I would have something to defend myself with. Still, I didn't like my odds.

After a long sigh, I shut the door. In the darkness of the closet, I mulled over my situation. My best bet would be to wait until the evening, or whenever most of the Iron-Blooded were away, and sneak out.

CHAPTER EIGHTEEN

I peered out of the closet several times.

While my presence had been baffling and mysterious when I first arrived, it was largely forgotten now. I didn't make any noise, or bother them in any way, after all. Out of sight—out of mind.

It was odd that Quern never showed up to get me.

He was probably speaking with Theon Sellers right now.

It didn't take long until something happened in the hardware department. I wasn't sure what, but after a couple hours of lingering in the darkness like an owl in a trunk hole, an alarm sounded over a couple radios scattered around the store. The alarm was a shriek that echoed throughout the cement building.

"*We got to move,*" one of the Iron-Blooded shouted. "*Ex Cathedra soldiers to the east! Junk hunters to the south!*"

Ex Cathedra?

"*Target the Ex Cathedra soldiers. Leave the judges for the people in power armor. Clean up the junk hunters before they reach the base.*"

Oh, damn. A judge was here?

They grabbed weapons and made plenty of noise as they headed out the door. The alarm sounded a second time on the radios, and I snuck a glance out of my closet another time. Most of the Iron-Blooded had left, but four of them remained to guard the door to their makeshift barracks.

I cursed under my breath.

It would've been *too easy* for them all to leave so I could escape, apparently.

"I'm probably the unluckiest individual in the wasteland," I whispered to myself.

Then I chuckled.

No, the unluckiest individuals were dead. I was just the lunatic that got into every bad situation I could think of.

Instead of exiting out the door, I could head deeper into the department store. There were no guards near the door that led to the interior . . . probably because there were more soldiers within. But I needed to risk it.

So, when the four guarding the door out were busy speaking amongst themselves, and also turning down the volume on the radio, I quietly slipped out of the closet-turned-room and headed for the opposite door.

With my breath held, I opened it, and then went inside.

I kept my backpack on my shoulders and the 9mm in my hands. After an exhale and a deep breath, I moved forward.

This was obviously once a discount department store—with rows and rows and rows of cheap goods on display down dozens of aisles. The plastics and metals lasted throughout most of the Forever Winter, but the papers, fabrics, and cardboard were decaying, mostly from insects that had crawled in through the cracks.

The lights overhead were A-tech, and had obviously been hung recently. The wires on the ceiling were draped like half circles, and I imagined someone with a tall ladder had to put them up there for everyone else to see.

"You'll do fine, Kit-Kat," I said to myself, trying to mimic Bishop's voice.

Why his?

My mind had been on him ever since I learned of the pregnancy. He didn't know. He should know. I wanted to see him more than anything.

Why did I always find myself separated from him? I made a vow to myself to handcuff our wrists together.

I carefully made my way forward, ducking between the shelves that were still standing. Many had toppled over, like dominoes, their merchandise scattered across the tile floor. Lines of ants and groups of cockroaches were everywhere.

The front door to the department store was blocked off by what appeared to be a patchwork of metal sheets, bike racks, and a couple of *Welcome to Wally World* signs riddled with bullet holes. The white smiley face logo had a giant hole through its left eye.

More sirens.

I froze and leapt behind a group of cash registers.

Iron-Blooded soldiers rushed past me and headed to the barracks in the hardware section. Once they were gone, I stood and continued.

The Iron-Blooded had truly outdone themselves with this place, though. I got several laughs out of their redecorating.

Aisle three, previously home to canned goods and nonperishables, was now an armory, stocked with an impressive array of handguns and rifles. The ammo boxes were stacked next to each, and I hurried over.

Nine millimeter bullets were some of the easiest to come by, so I grabbed some and then reached for a rifle and some of its ammo.

Aisle seven, once the go-to spot for camping supplies, was now barren. No cots. No tents. They had all been moved to the barracks, so I kept going.

Aisle ten . . . was mostly for babies. I thought, for a split second, I should grab things, but that was absurd. I didn't have enough room in the backpack.

Instead, I grabbed a book on child nutrition, another book on child rearing, and another on common illnesses. Knowledge always comforted me, and I would need every advantage I could get on every subject.

The electronics section had been transformed into a command center, complete with a wall of TVs that seemed to display footage of the outside. The surveillance cameras, which had previously been used to catch shoplifters, now served as an early warning system.

Clever.

One man stood before the TVs, his attention on a screen that displayed the Iron-Blooded soldiers rushing into the parking lot. I recognized the man.

He wore an old-world business suit and a combat vest that had been painted black. He also wore a pair of skintight black gloves that made it look as though his hand had been dipped in oil. That was Theon Sellers— the man who had the ability to command Teth drones. As far as I knew, he was the only human with that capability.

Sure enough, two drones were sitting in the electronics area, calmly waiting like gigantic Dobermans.

"How are the judges here already?" Theon asked.

I froze in the aisle just outside the electronics area. At first, I thought he was speaking to me, but then I calmed down and realized he had spoken to himself. I glanced between the rusted shelves and rotted merchandise to stare at him and the TVs.

The man kept both his hands behind his back as he glared ahead.

"Dammit," he whispered. "This will complicate things. I must tell the architect at once."

He was rather handsome now that I had time to just stare. With hair so blond it was like the sun decided to take a day job on his head, he was the kind of guy who didn't just enter a room, he illuminated it. Since I had black hair—and had mostly known people with brown hair—Theon's hue was intriguing to me.

Then he turned on his heel and my heart leapt into my throat.

His dark eyes scanned over the department store before he walked out of the electronics section. With a jut of his head, the two Teth drones followed.

I had a rifle and a handgun. Could I shoot him? Even if I did, even if I blew his brains all over the discount canned foods, the drones would immediately attack me afterward, and I wouldn't be able to kill them in time before they shredded me.

No, I had to let him go.

I slumped down and knelt on the tile floor, listening to the click of his shoes as he headed farther down the aisles and away from my direction. He was likely heading to the connector hallway they had made to link the store to the space base . . .

As soon as I couldn't hear Theon anymore, I stood.

Then someone grabbed me from behind.

Ice shot through my veins as sudden panic set in. I ducked my chin, so my attacker couldn't wrap their arm around my neck and choke me. Then I slammed my elbow backward into the man's gut. In the half second I had—where I probably surprised the man—I ducked out of his grasp and rolled away.

When I leapt to my feet, my 9mm was in my hands, ready to go.

Bishop stood before me.

I caught my breath, my heart fluttering.

He straightened his posture, rubbing his stomach and giving me the same grin he always had. "Nice to see you, too, Kit-Kat," he said, a laziness to his tone. "I see you've been using those moves I taught you."

I practically dropped my gun and ran to him. I didn't—I had too much presence of mind to ever abandon a weapon—but I did quickly tuck it away before throwing my arms around his neck and pulling him into the tightest hug I could muster.

"How?" was all I managed to choke out.

How had he gotten here?

Was I dreaming?

He wore a black shirt, dark cargo pants, and a vest similar to the Iron-Blooded, but it wasn't their uniform exactly. The tally marks on his skin—on his arms and neck, poking out from under the fabric—were a welcome sight. I didn't like scarring, they were just uniquely Bishop's, and now my favorite thing in the world.

I dug my fingers into the fabric of his clothes and twisted.

A rifle was slung over his shoulder, and I suspected he had stolen it from the same weapon aisle I had found in the warehouse.

"How *what*, Kit-Kat?" Bishop chuckled as he returned my embrace. "How am I this handsome? How am I so talented? You have to be more specific."

His jokes . . .

God, how I had missed his jokes.

"How did you get here?"

"Drove," he quipped. "I'm good at that." But he could probably tell I was annoyed with his vague answers, so he snorted back a laugh and continued, "As soon as we heard Quern was missin', we knew you had to have gone to the nearest Iron-Blooded stronghold. We talked to some local junk hunters, and came straight here. We've been here a day and a half, but until we saw the jeep driving in, I don't think you were here."

He had been here that long? I supposed it had taken a while for Quern and me to make it this far. We were constantly bogged down by things like gangs and mutant bears.

I stepped away from him and smiled. "I'm so glad you're here."

"Gascoigne is in the Mark VI, and Brecht is holding down our lookout spot with the car." Bishop held his hand out. "Let's get the fuck out of here."

"We need to be careful," I said. "Ex Cathedra is attacking."

Again, he smiled. "You worry too much. Ex Cathedra? They're here because we told them all about the Iron-Blooded's operations. Gascoigne apparently knows the radio frequencies they use—since she's an ex-judge and all—and we got them info enough to cause some major damage. We should be able to get out of here just fine."

I was . . . surprised.

Normally, I was the one coming up with all the plans. It impressed me to know that Bishop and the others would do whatever it took to help me when I was in danger.

"*Huh. What's that?*" someone asked in Tethlite.

Bishop and I turned to glance down the aisle. An Iron-Blooded soldier stood there, his eyes wide, a rifle held in his hands, though it was casually pointed at the floor.

"*What's going on?*" he asked.

CHAPTER NINETEEN

The Iron-Blooded man wore the same black uniform they all did. He was likely a warrior from the barracks section who came to either check on the surveillance TVs or speak with Theon. He seemed baffled by our presence, and thankfully, Bishop *kind of* resembled an Iron-Blooded just standing around in an outfit of mostly black.

"We're discussing the attack going on outside," I said in Tethlite.

The man nodded in response, but then the gears in his mind clearly turned. *"Wait, aren't you Quern's woman? The one pregnant with his child? Why would you be discussing tactics?"*

My heart leapt into my throat.

I whirled on my heel to face Bishop, my eyes wide. I was hit with so much panic it was hard to speak. Would Bishop be angry? I wasn't actually pregnant with Quern's child! What would he think? Would he allow me to explain? I didn't want to have this discussion right now—and under these circumstances.

But Bishop just stared down at me.

He lifted an eyebrow.

"What's wrong?" he whispered.

In English.

Because he didn't understand Tethlite.

I almost giggled like a madman. Obviously, Bishop didn't know what the Iron-Blooded had said—because Bishop didn't speak that language. I had panicked for no good reason. Bishop still didn't know about the child, or Quern.

"*Wait a minute,*" the Iron-Blooded said, his eyes narrowing at Bishop.

But before the man could do anything, Bishop slung his rifle up and fired. The *bang* reverberated off the walls and bounced around the steel and concrete building as if it were trying to escape, ensuring everyone would here.

Bishop had shot the man straight between the eyes, and the Iron-Blooded flew back and hit the ground with a thud. Bishop's aim always impressed me. He had spent years out in the wasteland, obviously, and only people comfortable with violence lasted longer than a few months.

"Did that guy say something that upset you?" Bishop asked.

I shook my head. "N-No. Well, that's not true. Yes. But I was being silly. We, uh, need to focus on getting out of here. But first . . ."

I hugged him again, and kissed him as passionately as I could given the circumstances. Bishop melted into me, always willing to drop whatever we were doing for intimacy.

I broke the embrace and then whispered, "I love you."

He chuckled. "Don't say that, Kit-Kat. Don't you know the rules of the universe? If you say overly emotional things in the middle of enemy territory, one of us is gonna end up a tally mark. Irony will see to that."

"I just . . . had to. For my own mental health."

"Well, since you've already jinxed us—I love you, too."

The barracks door slammed open. Bishop and I ducked behind one of the metal shelves, and then carefully crept to the back. Three more Iron-Blooded soldiers rushed in, but they held their rifles up as they went, and kept their backs to each other as they searched. I kept watch on them through the tiny holes in the shelves.

As the three soldiers neared us, I nudged Bishop. He smiled and motioned to the end of the aisle. We crouched and headed there together, but when we made it to the end, he gestured for me to follow him in the opposite direction. I pointed to the barracks—we could exit that way now that there were no more soldiers.

He shook his head.

With my teeth gritted, I decided to follow him.

Bishop had come out of nowhere to save me—perhaps he knew a few things I didn't in this situation. He led me straight to the back of the department store, and opened up a door labeled *Employees Only*.

It creaked when it opened, and I heard the hurried footsteps of the Iron-Blooded as they quickly searched for the source of the noise. Bishop yanked me into the back, and then closed the door. There were no lights in this back area, just a wall of blackness. He slowly led me down a long hallway that stank of urine and rust.

"Keep kneeling," Bishop whispered. "The ceiling over here gave it its best shot, but after fifty years of holding its shit together, it finally gave up the ghost and collapsed a bit."

"What's the plan?" I asked, also keeping my voice low.

"Insert lead into the face of anyone in our way," Bishop quipped.

I softly chuckled and then shook my head. "I meant more specifically. Where are we going? I didn't know this place existed."

"There's a door that leads to a trash pile out back. The trash had been so solidified and disgusting, it practically fused to the side of the store and was blocking a view of the door. Thankfully, Vega found it and led us inside."

"So we have to crawl over some trash to get outside?" I asked.

Bishop patted me on the shoulder, "Oh, Kit-Kat. I wish I was as optimistic as you. We're going to have to crawl *through* a *lot* of trash to get outside."

Bishop . . .

He always made me laugh. No matter what. No matter the circumstances.

We made it to the end of the dilapidated hallway, and then Bishop shoved open another door. Sure enough, a wave of noxious stench rolled over me. Here it was: our escape route.

Of course no one would follow us out this way. I was surprised Vega had found it in the first place.

The sight that greeted us was . . . unique.

It was a mountain of garbage, decades old, like a grotesque monument to old-world food, returned products, and toiletries. It was a jumbled mess of rusted metal, broken electronics, and unidentifiable refuse that had melded together.

A tunnel had been dug through the pile, and light shone at the other end, illuminating the disgusting path forward.

Bishop kicked the edge of the "trunnel"—the trash tunnel, as I had named it in my head—testing the stability of the trash heap with a cautious foot. A whole hive of insects scurried out, like a living blob of inky blackness. Now I understood why there were so many inside the department store.

"Ladies first?" Bishop offered.

I nervously chuckled. "Chivalry isn't dead, I see."

"Nope. It just smells like it is."

I moved forward, to crawl out to safety, but then my attention snapped to the glint of thin metal. Needles were in the trash, and I shuddered.

Everyone knew there were drug addicts out in the wasteland. They were addicted to all sorts of chems—and some of them required needles to inject the substances straight into the veins. Most of them were homebrew narcotics, but some were actually chemicals from before the Forever Winter. They aged like wine, apparently.

Were these needles from before the winter? Or after?

The fear of getting a bloodborne illness—or worse—from the needles caused me to hesitate. I didn't want to get sick. I was pregnant. I had to be more cautious. Recklessness would get me, and my child, killed.

"What's wrong, Kit-Kat?"

I shook my head. "I'm scared," I whispered. "I . . . I don't want to get cut up on the trash."

Bishop half laughed and half coughed. After he ran his hand down his face, and calmed himself, he looked me dead in the eyes. "Remember that one time you went deep into a building filled with radioactive material? Remember that? You *knew* it was dangerous, and you still went. I couldn't fuckin' talk you out of it."

"I remember," I said.

"And *the trash* scares you now? I just want to hear you say it aloud so I know I'm not going crazy."

"Please, Bishop. I just . . . I don't want to."

I could've explained, but I didn't feel like we had to the time to do so. The Iron-Blooded would surely find this back area, and if we were talking, we'd be in trouble. I just wanted out of here—but over the trash.

Bishop inhaled and then exhaled—which was impressive, due to the smell. But instead of arguing or telling me to buck up, Bishop turned around and grabbed at the collapsing ceiling in the hallway. Long, flat metal panels had once been secured together, but now they were separated and crumbling at the edges.

Bishop sucked in air through his teeth as he cut himself on the debris, but that didn't stop him. He struggled with the metal, making a racket in the hallway and raising the tension of the situation even higher. Finally, he yanked one off and then placed it on the trash, right in the trunnel, like it was a sled.

"Get on," he said.

I heard the door at the far end of the hallway open. Clearly, the Iron-Blooded had discovered our location. Thankfully, the dark hallway, and collapsed ceiling, made it so they didn't have a line of sight on us.

I slid onto the ceiling panel, and Bishop got behind me. He pushed the panel forward, and I slid through the garbage tunnel, sliding over the needles and twisted metal, but unable to escape the stench. So I held my breath and closed my eyes.

Thankfully, Bishop was a strong man. He was able to push me through everything *and* hauled himself through the tunnel. He never even broke a sweat—he just did what needed to be done.

Each inch was a careful negotiation with the unstable terrain. The trash shifted and crunched under our weight. My backpack scraped across the top of the tunnel, and I worried it would collapse. Thankfully, my fears were unfounded.

Thankfully, it wasn't actually very long of a trek—perhaps five feet—and the metal ceiling panel slid out of the trash and hit the cracked asphalt of the parking lot. I pulled myself out the rest of the way and stood. Bishop leapt out after me.

Two individuals were waiting for us.

Brecht and Vega.

As a massive warrior caste, Vega was giant. He stood tall, and his bulky larger arms were exposed enough to see muscle. He was tense and flexing, obviously prepared for combat. Hopefully he wouldn't smell the change in my body's physiology and report on the pregnancy.

Brecht, on the other hand, wore a long trench coat that went to his ankles, and a thick vest underneath. He also wore a scarf—he loved that damn scarf—and tall leather boots. He looked ready to trudge through anything, including a mire.

Brecht held a rifle at the ready, his gaze on the parking lot. He and Vega had been standing guard, obviously.

After sweeping back his black hair with a quick motion of his hand, Brecht glanced over. "Kita? Wow, that was fast. I thought it would take Bishop longer to find you. If, uh, he found you at all."

"You thought I wouldn't find her?" Bishop brushed off dirt and grime from his black clothing. "What's wrong with you? I told you that I'd be right back."

I glanced around, hoping to see Gascoigne, but she wasn't here. As a matter of fact, we didn't have anything here. No vehicle. No stockpile of weapons. No safe location.

I didn't want to just stand around.

"What's the plan?" I asked.

It was the middle of the day, but the overcast skies kept it gloomy. Now that we were outside, I heard the *boom* and *rattle* of an actual fight. The sound of mortars filled the air, and the unmistakable rumble of power armor running across an open terrain caused the ground to tremble. We were behind the department store, and the building blocked my view of the action.

I assumed it was the Iron-Blooded versus Ex Cathedra, but I couldn't confirm for sure.

Brecht motioned away from the parking lot. "Our plan was to extract you and then leave." He glared at the city in the distance. "We have a small base of operations in an old bank building. Gascoigne wanted to be part of the fighting, however. She's out there now . . ."

"As in, she just has a rifle and is fighting against the Iron-Blooded?" I asked.

When Brecht turned to face me, it was with a sardonic look of annoyance. "No. Gascoigne brought our only suit of power armor—and she refuses to get out of it."

CHAPTER TWENTY

That sounded like Gascoigne, all right. When I had first met her—and she was attempting to kill me—she had lived in her judge armor like it was her favorite outfit.

Vega snorted and then motioned with two of his four hands. "*Come,*" he said in Tethlite. "*I smell more of my kind on the wind. They're nearby.*" He turned and headed away from the department store.

"What'd he say?" Bishop asked. "He can speak English, right? Is there a reason he's not?"

Brecht headed after his alien brother and just pointed to the ruined city away from the department store. "Vega said—we need to get the hell out of here." And then he jogged alongside the Teth as they hurried toward an office building.

With my breathing shallow, I glanced over my shoulder. The Davis Space Force Base wasn't far from us. The Iron-Blooded were busy fighting the enemy. Perhaps I shouldn't waste this opportunity . . .

On the other hand, I was hungry, and tired, and I was *just* reunited with Bishop. Perhaps now was the time to recuperate. A good tactician understood the need for rest just as much as the need to seize opportunities. And since they were fighting, it was likely the Iron-Blooded were high-strung and trigger-happy.

I didn't . . .

Want to get hurt too badly.

"We need to go," I whispered to Bishop. "We need to get to someplace safe."

He placed a hand on my back and then urged me to move. Together, we jogged after Brecht and Vega. He gave me frequent side glances until we reached the ruined bank building. The front door was jammed shut, due to the fact the building had half collapsed, the weight of the upper floors smushing the doorframe and preventing it from allowing the door to swing open.

Vega leapt in through a broken window. His Teth skin, black and matte in texture, was too thick to be cut by random shards of glass. The beast effortlessly made it inside.

Brecht had to be more careful. He used the butt of his rifle to smash away jagged teeth-like shards of glass that poked up from around the sill.

The fighting still raged on in the distance. The sounds were like a warzone, and I feared for Gascoigne's safety. Although, if she really was in the Mark VI, she was probably the more protected—and most dangerous—individual on the battlefield.

I glanced up. If I could get to the roof of this bank, which was only five stories, I'd probably be able to get a clear view of the fighting. That was my first goal after I managed to catch my breath.

However, when Bishop and I reached the window, I caught sight of the rusted sill, and the harsh edges of the glass sprinkled all around. My skin crawled.

"Get in," Bishop said. He turned around, his weapon at the ready. He stood lookout while I hemmed and hawed in front of the building. Finally, he glanced over his shoulder. "What's wrong?"

I hesitated, my breath caught in my throat. "I . . . I need a minute." After a brief moment, I formatted a plan.

I unslung my backpack off my shoulder, placed it on the sill to protect my body, and then carefully stepped over it in order to get inside. Bishop watched me with perplexed fascination.

"Is everything okay?" he asked as he effortlessly leapt inside. He took my shoulder, pulled me to the side, and hid by the broken, half-squished door. "You're not actin' like yourself."

"What do you mean?" I asked.

"I mean, you were worried about the trash. And then, once we got outside, I half expected you to ask me to help you steal from the Iron-Blooded. Instead, we follow Brecht into safety. Now you can't risk getting a little cut on the glass? This isn't like you. What's wrong? Are you sick?"

I shook my head.

"Let me guess—Quern didn't feed you? You're feeling weak? What is it—you're obviously being cautious. Way out of character cautious."

It amused me that Bishop knew something was off about me within *minutes* of us being reunited. Out of everyone in the world, he knew me the most. I supposed that was appropriate, given our relationship.

But I still hesitated to tell him about the child. He was right about jinxing things. I knew it was just superstition, but I still felt a great and terrible dread about speaking it aloud, because what if something happened? What if I were shot? The nanites in my blood would likely keep me healthy—I no longer had any bear claw wounds—but would the nanites save a barely formed fetus?

And I couldn't imagine the weight of losing it.

When a wife loses a husband, everyone calls her a widow.

When a husband loses a wife, everyone calls him a widower.

When a child loses a parent, everyone calls them an orphan.

But there was no word for when a parent loses a child—because that was how awful that was.

And it was silly—the child wasn't born, why was I already thinking up haunting scenarios?—but my mind was overactive, and loved to play tricks on me, apparently.

Bishop grabbed both my shoulders. "Kita."

He rarely used my real name. I turned to stare him straight in the eyes. "Yes?"

"What's wrong? Did one of the Iron-Blooded hurt you?" He leaned in close to me. "Because I'll kill every fucker here if that's the case."

"No," I whispered. "I . . . Uh, *we're* going to have a child."

What an awkward way to say that, but I was trying to make it sound romantic. I probably failed, because my voice was shaky, and my whole body cold, but it was the thought that counted. Or so everyone said.

"Seriously?" he asked.

I nodded once.

"Well, not right here, you're not," Bishop said with a confident smile. Then, without warning, he scooped me up into his arms. With a laugh, he held me close. "We need to get you home. That way we can feed you good food. If my grandma were alive, she'd insist on feeding you twenty-four seven, so in loving memory of her, that's what we've got to do."

I wanted to joke and play around as well, but that was when the whole city shook.

The ground, the bank, the roads outside—they trembled as though someone had thrown the whole world a sucker punch. Bishop stumbled a bit, but he held me tight and never actually fell over.

Brecht and Vega, standing in the lobby of this bank building, both whirled around to face us. Well, Vega didn't really have eyes to face us—he just turned his head and sniffed the air deeply.

A powerful rush of hot air *whooshed* in through the window. My hair fluttered around, and I kept my eyes closed.

With gritted teeth, Bishop cursed under his breath. "Motherfuckers . . ."

"What's going on?" I asked.

"Ex Cathedra . . ." He stared down at me, his expression both amused and darkly serious. "They brought bombs to a fistfight."

"What does that even mean?" I whispered.

Brecht and Vega ran over to us, coughing as they went. Dust and debris were flowing into the building now, and without proper ventilation, this place would become dangerous to dwell in.

"The Ex Cathedra lunatics brought plastic explosives and A-tech mini nukes," Brecht said through a wheeze. "That's probably what they're using. *We need to get out of here!*"

"All right," I said.

But Bishop didn't let me down. He leapt out of the building and straight into the billowing clouds of dust. With his eyes squinted, he rushed around the side of the bank and then passed an empty office building. A side on the wall read: *Wi-Fi faster than your home's, coffee better than your ex's! We're your new office away from the office!*

Then spray-painted over that was a poorly drawn bobcat with an arrow pointing out of the city.

I remembered the radio broadcast, and kept the image fresh in my mind as Bishop took me through a back alleyway and then out on another street. He kept going, with Brecht and Vega ahead of us, until he came to a ruined coffee shop. The inside was a complete mess, and the ceiling had partially collapsed, but the brick walls stood firm.

Vega ran to the outside, sniffed it deeply, and then pressed his two larger hands on the bricks. "Up here," he said in English.

Brecht pointed to the fire escape on the side of the building. The ladders and platforms weren't rusted, and it made me wonder what material they were made out of.

Bishop took me to the first ladder, and in an impressive show of athleticism, managed to climb up with me held in one arm. He grunted the whole time, and was obviously pretending not to struggle, but he did it.

"My hero," I whispered to him.

"Easy," he managed to grunt between strangled breaths.

We got to the top of the coffee shop, and I was surprised by how flat and whole the roof was. Vega lowered most of his body, but kept his head slightly perked, as if he wanted to keep his nose in the wind.

Brecht ran over to the side of the roof and set up his rifle. "We need to look out. After bombs comes the suppressive fire—then the cleanup."

Bishop walked over to him and took a seat. While this was only a one-story building, and there were several others in the way, I could see a sliver of the combat down the long roads of this forgotten town.

Ex Cathedra had judges. Judges in Ex Cathedra held a rank equivalent to captain in most other surrounding countries, and they typically were in charge of squads or entire facilities. The JUDGE-X0 exoskeletons were big and impressive, and it was easy to spot them stomping their way through the wreckage the bombs left in their wake. Most were painted black and red, with the word "JUDGE" clearly on their leg, chest, or arm.

The Iron-Blooded didn't bother shooting at them. Bullets wouldn't pierce the thick armor of the exoskeletons.

Instead, the Iron-Blooded released two "judges" of their own—two Teth warriors in Teth exoskeletons took the battlefield. They were built solid and gigantic, even a bit bigger than the human power-armor suits because Teth were just all-around larger.

These suits of armor clashed, but my attention didn't stay on them long.

If Gascoigne was here, she would be easy to spot. The Mark VI of the JUDGE-X0 suit came equipped with a plasma blade—a weapon capable of rending through enemy suits. Unfortunately, it drained the battery faster than a child sucking down juice. If Gascoigne used it for a few minutes, she might run the risk of having her batteries deplete.

I didn't see her, though. No plasma blade, no Mark VI.

"Where is Gascoigne?" I asked.

Brecht kept his rifle pointed out to where our enemies were. "I don't know. She said that if she got into trouble at the bank, she would meet us at the rendezvous."

"Where is that?"

"Out in the woods."

I exhaled. "Then we should go there."

CHAPTER TWENTY-ONE

We were just outside the city, where nature butted up against the waning roads and encroached on the buildings in the form of vines. Although we were probably a mile or two from the conflict, the sounds of the battle still echoed through the streets.

Brecht and the others had clearly planned for this to be a safety location to retreat toward. There was a tent hidden by shrubs, a shallow, dried-up riverbed with a place to make a fire, and a few packs of supplies secured to the higher branches above us.

It was slowing, though. No battle lasted forever—especially not one in close quarters, and with an abundance of explosives.

Brecht, Vega, Bishop, and I waited by a grouping of thin pine trees that were so resilient they had sprouted up through concrete. I placed my hand on one of the trunks and instantly regretted it. The sap caused my palm to become sticky.

Bishop saw what happened, and how I tried to rub my hand against the side of my pants. He grabbed a bottle of water from the side of one of the packs, and then took my wrist. Without a word, he poured water over my palm and then cleaned it off with his shirt.

When I glanced up at him through my eyelashes, he smiled.

"Better?" he asked.

My face heated. "You don't have to do that for me."

"Pfft, it wasn't for you," he playfully said. "It was for the baby."

"The *baby*?" Brecht stepped closer, his eyes narrowed.

Vega loomed over all of us, at least two feet taller than any one of us in the group. With a powerful snort and inhale, the Teth shook his head.

"She's carrying a child," Vega stated. "I wondered why she smelled off . . . I thought it was because of the trash."

I frowned at him—and I was glad he couldn't see.

"This is a good day," Vega said with a hint of finality.

"Why is that?"

"When we were growing up, we were told the CCP would have an army of billions," Brecht stated. "We were told that birth rates would play a huge rule in who would lead Earth after the Forever Winter."

Bishop squinted and frowned at the same time. "What the fuck is the CCP again? You keep saying that, but it just goes . . ." He *whooshed* his hand over his head.

"The Chinese Communist Party."

"Who are they again?"

Brecht sighed. "I, uh, was told they would be a big deal by the many recordings left to us in the bunker. And as you can see, the people who made the bunker weren't as informed as they thought they were." He shrugged. "But they were probably right about one thing—humanity needs to repopulate."

Clearly, Brecht and Gascoigne had been talking extensively. No one was *this* excited for kids if they weren't part of the military. Most people out on the wasteland didn't want the burden of looking after small children, especially when there were so many dangers—and so little food.

That was why Chelsy's father had such a rough time, and why protecting her took so much of my dedication. Children were frail, and the world was rough.

But Sanctuary was different.

We just had to get back.

The rumble of the ground underfoot drew me out of my musings. I glanced over my shoulder and saw a plume of smoke rising in the city. It was difficult to see any details from our location, but Brecht quickly rummaged through his pack and withdrew two rifle scopes. He handed one to me, and then used one himself so he could keep track of the fighting.

I glanced through the scope, but it took me a moment to locate a clear view of the warzone.

The Iron-Blooded moved with a chilling precision. They kept in groups of three, which allowed them to watch each other's back, even as they advanced through the rubble. They were clad in black, their presence ominous and foreboding against the backdrop of destruction. The white skulls emblazoned on their bulletproof vests seemed to mock death itself— or perhaps invite it. As I watched, another explosion went off, and the shrapnel tore through a man's throat so thoroughly I thought he had been decapitated.

I lowered the scope.

"Who's winning?" Bishop asked.

"The crows," I quipped. "There's gonna be a lot of meat on these streets."

He elbowed me. "Do you see Gascoigne at all?"

I hadn't even looked. After a deep inhale, I lifted the scope back up and attempted to get eyes on any exoskeletons. Instead, I found the soldiers of Ex Cathedra, overworked and underequipped, slogging their way down the road. They fought with a raw, unyielding ferocity, even though their weaponry seemed crude when compared to the Iron-Blooded.

Ex Cathedra had access to factories . . .

Unlike a lot of other places in the world, they could still construct things thanks to the A-tech machinery—some machines as large as the five-story bank.

I took a deep breath, and even though we were far from the battlefield, the air was thick with the acrid stench of smoke and the metallic tang of blood.

"Spot her yet?" Bishop asked.

"No," I whispered.

It seemed Ex Cathedra had more soldiers. They practically threw wave after wave of their own men at the problem. I spotted a couple judges who were part of the vanguard—they were breaking the Iron-Blooded's ranks, and separating teams of three.

Another explosion rocked the decaying urban landscape, sending showers of concrete and steel raining down onto the streets. The echo of gunfire was a relentless drumbeat, punctuated only by shouts and screams.

I lowered the scope. With a shaky hand, I gave it to Bishop. He immediately brought it to his eye and scanned the situation.

The Iron-Blooded and Ex Cathedra were my enemies, but it was clear they vastly outmanned and outpowered Sanctuary. And if they were this close already, I might not even have time enough to raise Teth.

But then . . .

What was I going to do to protect my infant civilization?

"It's impossible to see much." Bishop lowered the scope. "Too many damn buildings. Too much smoke."

But then the rumble of firepower slowed. I glanced over, and both sides were retreating.

Yet we still didn't see Gascoigne.

"I'm sure she's fine," Bishop muttered as he tossed the scope to Brecht. "Our *Robot Mommy* isn't going anywhere." He patted my shoulder, and while his words were soaked in levity, his tone betrayed his worry. Just as he had an easy time reading me—I knew Bishop pretty well.

"We'll wait here until nightfall," I muttered. "She might not want to come here, because it'll guide the enemy to our location. If we give her enough time, perhaps she'll make it to us."

We didn't start a fire. There were too many enemies nearby for us to risk that.

Brecht smeared ceanothus flowers all over us while we waited. Most people didn't know, but ceanothus was extremely odiferous. The flowers often attracted a wide variety of insects, and the scent was so potent it hid most others.

It also stank.

But I understood why he did it. Brecht was just trying to make sure none of the Iron-Blooded Teth discovered our location. Most castes within the Teth had a keen sense of smell, but none as keen as the drones who roamed the cityscape.

Our tent was hidden under shrubs, so even if a scout was on the nearby buildings, we'd remain hidden.

Because the weather was slowly clearing up, the evening didn't seem so dark. For some reason, that lifted my spirits.

However, I wasn't feeling entirely comfortable. Vega insisted on sitting next to me, and then curling up halfway around me like a dog snuggling close to their owner. He was large, muscular, and his skin rough in a lot of areas. Despite that, he was pressed up against me like half an inner tube.

Bishop sat shoulder to shoulder with me on the other side, constantly eyeing the Teth.

"Well, aren't we all chums," he quipped.

The only person *not* cuddling in a gigantic pile was Brecht. He sat across from us, with a small flashlight between us for some dim illumination. Because the light was on the ground, all shadows were cast upward, giving everything a spooky vibe, even if it was otherwise mundane and normal.

Like Brecht.

When he glanced over, he looked like a serial killer, mostly due to the fact that he kept his scarf up over his chin and his eyes narrowed.

"Why are we cuddled like this?" Bishop asked.

"In Teth society, the warrior caste is always assigned to protect the vulnerable—such as those carrying fertilized eggs." I glanced over to him. "However, that period doesn't last long with Teth. Once their eggs are fertilized, they carry them for about four months, and then they expel them from their body a few days before they are supposed to hatch."

"*Expelled from the body*?" Bishop snorted back a laugh. "You make it sound like they have explosive diarrhea." He snapped his fingers. "Actually, that reminds me. I found a chicken farm while we were making our way here. We should stop there on the way back. Can you imagine raising chickens in Sanctuary? Great, right?" He nudged me with an elbow. "Genius, even."

"Chickens are good," I muttered. "For outdoors. But there's a reason most underground bunkers didn't utilize them. Most birds have a bad habit of fouling up their environment, and unless our ventilation system is fixed, I don't think we want that *inside* of Sanctuary."

"Outside, then."

I didn't reply to that.

The benefit of Sanctuary was living away from others—hidden in the group, safe from bombs, or the weather, or even outside forces that would do us harm. If we expanded to the outside too quickly, we'd be putting ourselves at risk.

"How close was Ex Cathedra to this location when you radioed them?" I whispered.

Vega stirred. His massive muscles rippled as he lifted his head to answer my question. "*Within just a few miles of this location*," he replied in Tethlite.

"*Gascoigne was surprised by how close they were*," Brecht stated, also in Tethlite.

Bishop glanced around at everyone, his eyes narrowing in sardonic irritation. But he didn't say anything. Instead, he reached into a pack, pulled out a knife and small mirror, and started shaving the stubble on the side of his cheek, completely checked out of the entire conversation he clearly couldn't understand.

"Do we know why they're this far north?" I asked.

Brecht slowly nodded. *"They're capturing entire towns full of people."*

Vega offered a guttural growl. *"There are militia camps around here, all clearly marked."*

"He means with flags and signed," Brecht interjected.

I knew what they were talking about. I'd heard about it on the radio and seen the signs on the side of a building we passed to get here. The weird radio host, Weatherbean, had been insistent that anyone who needed help should go toward the yellow flags marked with bobcats.

"The soldiers of Ex Cathedra have been intentionally targeting these outposts. They kill the soldiers and then secretly take their place. Anyone who comes by is captured and sent back to Ex Cathedra territory to work in their factories and fields."

"How do you know that?" I asked in English, so shocked they would do that I forgot to speak in Tethlite altogether.

Bishop stopped shaving to pay attention.

"The locals," Brecht replied. *"We spoke to a few who saw it happen, but apparently the word hasn't gotten around yet. All we know is that Ex Cathedra has been gobbling up any and all small towns or settlements, all so they can feed the production for their war efforts."*

They were in a long war with U-Cali . . .

Still—that meant they were coming for us. Another reason we couldn't have an aboveground farm filled with dozens of adorable chickens. If Ex Cathedra found us while we were still small—before we had a decent population of Teth—we'd all be captured and forced to work for them.

Well, Gascoigne would be killed for treason, probably. But the rest of us would be made to work.

And thinking of Gascoigne got me worried. We had been in this tent for hours. All sounds of conflict had long since died. Where was Gascoigne? Had she died? Was she captured? I hoped to the good stars she wasn't a prisoner—because then the Iron-Blooded or Ex Cathedra would have the Mark VI, and I desperately didn't want that.

"Maybe we should go look for Gascoigne," I whispered.

Bishop slowly ran his blade along the edge of his chin. "Probably," he whispered as he carefully cut his beard. "She's not usually gone this long."

"How are we going to help her?" Brecht frowned as he picked up his flashlight. "We don't have any more exoskeleton power suits. If we had a spare, I would understand diving back into enemy territory, but right now . . ."

"First off, I've fought both the Iron-Blooded and Ex Cathedra without power armor in the past." I jutted my thumb over my shoulder as I added, "Secondly, there's a space base over there, and according to Quern, they're using it to communicate with all the Iron-Blooded in the area."

Bishop tucked his knife and mirror back into the pack. He hadn't fully finished shaving, and now he looked like he had a stylized goatee rather than a clean face. "Wait, where is that bastard, Quern? I need to make sure he's a tally mark once and for all."

"Uh . . ."

I wasn't entirely sure where he was. He'd left me in the Iron-Blooded barracks and then just . . . vanished.

"It doesn't matter," I finally whispered. "As long as we never run into him again, I'll be happy." I tapped Bishop and then I patted Vega on the top of the head. "I say we break into the space base and interrogate a few Iron-Blooded to see if they know where Gascoigne is. Maybe we can also find some useful information—such as how strong Ex Cathedra is, or the location of more power armor."

Or maybe even parts and supplies for Sanctuary.

CHAPTER TWENTY-TWO

We snuck across the quiet battlefield under the cover of darkness.

The roads were basically just craters, with abandoned vehicles piled in the center, as though they'd rolled in afterward.

The weather really was getting better—sections of the clouds allowed the night sky to poke through. The stars twinkled through the open slivers, but eventually the clouds swarmed back together, closing off the wonder of the night from us once again.

And I preferred staring at the sky because the road was littered with bodies. The tell-tale signs of explosives were everywhere, and it was apparent the most when I examined the corpses. Many of them were missing limbs, especially legs and arms, and several individuals had shrapnel embedded throughout most of their torso.

It was clear both sides had sent people to collect equipment. The Iron-Blooded bodies were mostly naked, and any functioning handguns or rifles were nowhere to be found.

The Ex Cathedra soldiers were a slightly different story. All of them wore a uniform—a brown shirt, brown pants, gold chain on one shoulder, and a black patch on the other shoulder that resembled a throne. They had leather belts and shoes, and they all looked relatively new—because Ex Cathedra raised livestock by the hundreds.

Why didn't they take them? It seemed most were soaked in blood, and most individuals knew the leather would warp and shrink because of it.

I had to keep tearing my attention away from the bodies. They were lined up on the side of the shattered roads, but not buried or treated in any way. It was obvious they were picked clean of goods and then forgotten.

Brecht didn't seem to see them. He hurried forward, using the craters as cover, ducking when needed and then moving through the darkness with a surprising amount of stealth. Same with Vega, who was large and hulking, but somehow graceful. His matte black skin made him perfect for sneaking at night. I sometimes lost sight of him.

Bishop stuck close to me. Like Brecht, he didn't seem to care about the bodies. He had seen hundreds of them, as evidenced by the many tally mark scars across his body. Still, I was little disturbed no one seemed to care about the massive amount of death all around us.

By my count, there were over two hundred bodies here. The only upside was that most of them belonged to the Iron-Blooded.

Once we reached the wall around the Davis Space Force Base, Brecht stopped and waited for us. He moved with a wave of his arm and pointed to the tall barrier that prevented us from just entering the building.

It was mostly brick, and at the top, there was enough barbed wire to create a human-sized blender. I knew of the tunnel that was connected to the department store, but I didn't want to reenter through the barracks— and going in through the front door was insanity.

I hurried over to Brecht's location and glanced around. Perhaps we could construct a ladder? Or use something to help us scale the wall?

Vega sniffed the air. "*Why have we stopped?*" he asked in Tethlite.

Brecht placed a hand on his shoulder. "They have a wall. It looks to be twelve feet high? Maybe more. And there's barbed wire on top. Do you remember our training exercises? I think you might be able to scale it without a problem."

"*I can handle this.*"

Bishop and I knelt next to Brecht, ducking down on the curved incline of a crater, as Vega stood and then lumbered over to the base of the wall. Using his two larger arms, the Teth pulled himself to the top of the wall in one motion. His two smaller arms reached out and grabbed the wire.

If a human had done this, their skin would've been shredded, but the Teth were more resilient. Vega managed to twist the metal in his grasp, and even rip it from its posts on the wall, effectively removing it as an obstacle. He wasn't cut at all—the barbed wire barely did a thing.

Clearly, the Iron-Blooded never thought *the Teth* would try to sneak over this barrier. The Iron-Blooded worshipped the Teth—this was an obstacle meant to keep humans out.

With one of his large, muscular arms, Vega motioned to us.

Brecht went first. He ran over to the wall, leapt up, and Vega grabbed him. With one huff, the Teth hoisted Brecht all the way over the wall. Then Vega helped Brecht slide down the other side.

I was impressed. Vega couldn't even see yet he handled this perfectly.

Then he motioned again.

I stood. Bishop gave me a smile.

"Don't hurt yourself," he said.

After a quick nod, I said, "I can do this."

I shook out my hands and then ran for the wall. I still had my 9mm, but my pack was empty. I had left all my valuable objects at our campsite, so that I would have more options for grabbing things while we were inside. Having an empty pack meant I could maneuver a little better as well.

When I jumped, I managed to get up the wall a few feet. But that was it. I thought I was going to slip back down to the ground and crash right on my butt, but Vega snatched me at the peak of the leap and effortlessly yanked me up to the top.

I caught my breath as he set me down on the bricks. The barbed wire hung limply off to the side, away from my person.

Vega nuzzled his head against my shoulder. My face grew hot as I patted his shoulder. He felt like rock wrapped in flesh.

"*I'm okay,*" I said in Tethlite.

"*You must be careful, kin of different blood.*"

The Teth were clearly programmed to care for pregnant individuals. Since all Teth were hermaphrodites, they probably all went through this stage in their life at some point or another. Even Vega would eventually carry eggs and lay them, so long as an architect instructed him to reproduce.

Still . . .

As a human, this was awkward.

Well, that wasn't true. My grandfather once told me that all humans are kind to children, because all humans remember the struggles of being a child themselves. I supposed, if *all* humans experienced *all the same things*, we would be a stronger species because of it.

"*Thank you,*" I whispered.

Then Vega grabbed my backpack and helped me off the edge into the military base. He released me a few feet from the ground, and I hit with a hard *thud* before tumbling forward. Brecht was there to brush me off.

Harsh spotlights shone over certain areas of the base. There were three spotlights in total, and each was as bright as the sun. One pointed to the tunnel, another toward the main building, and one over the airplane hangar.

Brecht pointed to a metal tower located directly adjunct to the main building. It had several arrays and dishes, and red light blinked near the top.

"Do you see that?" he whispered.

I nodded. "What is it? A communications tower?"

"Exactly."

I recognized the A-tech design. Teth had helped in its creation, which meant it was probably an *Ultra High-Gain Communications System*. The tower utilized directional antenna arrays that could focus their transmissions in targeted directions, increasing the effective range and reducing the power requirements for long-distance communications.

No wonder Quern wanted to get here—and no wonder Theon was stationed here to protect this place. He could speak to the others, probably all the way in Boulder, with this kind of technology.

"Whoa, big guy," Bishop said. "*Whoa.*"

I glanced up and saw Vega effortlessly grabbing Bishop as well. Bishop, practically lifted like a ragdoll, clearly wasn't as keen on this. He struggled a bit as Vega placed him on the top of the wall. Bishop brushed himself off.

"Just keep your claws away from my skin." Bishop traced some of his tally marks, but his fingers eventually settled on actual scars that ran the length of his forearm. "I've tangled with Teth before, and I remember how much your claws hurt."

Vega flexed and unflexed his large hands. Three-inch claws slid from his fingers, the needle points at the tip of each capable of goring a human with ease.

"I will be careful," Vega said in English. "You have my word, squishy one."

Bishop just frowned.

Then Vega grabbed his arm and helped him down the other side of the wall, never even seeing Bishop's annoyance. It almost made me laugh the way they interacted.

Vega was the last to join us. He just leapt off the wall and hit the ground without any fear. His large arms cushioned his landing, as he landed on his hands first. It was an awkward way to go, but perhaps the best way for someone who couldn't see the ground rushing up to greet them.

Once grouped up, I held up a hand to stop people from advancing. Brecht eyed me, but he didn't question my authority—he was just baffled. But I needed to take a lay of the land. I hadn't been in this military base before, even if I had been in many others in the past.

This place was massive, with at least three main buildings, and several tinier warehouses around. The hangar still had aircraft waiting outside of it, and from the tarnish across most of their exteriors, I would say they had waited here through the Forever Winter.

However, as I stared, I took note of their exteriors. They had clear hexagonal honeycomb latticing on the outside—which was highly unusual for human designs, but one of the key indicators that the Teth were involved in the construction process. The Teth always used super-reinforced engineering techniques to make objects hyperdurable.

And most of the planes here were smaller and sleeker, perfectly capable of taking a few hits. The thought of their A-tech thrusters, silently propelling them through the skies with incredible efficiency, sent a shiver down my spine. These weren't just planes—they were silent predators of the sky.

I pointed to the main building closest to the aircraft hangar. "Let's check there first," I whispered.

"Why there?" Brecht asked.

"Because if there's any power armor anywhere on this base, it'll be in the hangar next to the aircraft. Additionally, their computers and communication system are likely all on the same network no matter which of the main buildings we enter, and I'm hoping Theon isn't hanging out next to the planes."

I figured he would be in the administrative building.

"Who is Theon?" Brecht asked.

Vega snorted. "*Is he a human architect?*"

I nodded once. "He is."

"That's impossible," Brecht said with a laugh. "There's no such thing."

Vega sniffed the air and shuddered. "*Something here smells odd. A mix of Teth and human. Disgusting—engineered and unnatural—but stinking of Teth pheromones. I can only describe it as the presence of an architect wrapped in the flesh of a human.*"

Bishop opened and closed a hand, like it was a talking puppet. "*Slurp, slurp, slurp,*" he said, faux mimicking the Tethlite language. "I can speak alien, too, you guys."

I nervously laughed. "I'm sorry, Bishop. We're heading to the building over there, and we need to avoid Theon at all costs."

"Roger," he said with a smile. "But if we *do* run into him, we can shoot to kill, right?" Bishop hoisted his rifle up. It was black, and I just now realized it had a little V spray-painted onto the side.

"Sure," I whispered. "But remember how the Teth claws felt? Keep that in mind—Theon has Teth drones with him at all points, and he'll use them if it comes to a fight."

CHAPTER TWENTY-THREE

As a group, we moved cautiously toward the aviation building. The spotlight's harsh glare sliced through the darkness intermittently, forcing us to pause and blend into the shadows whenever its beam swept close. The spotlight towers were manned by three Iron-Blooded—two at the base, one up operating the light.

We stopped on the side of a smaller building, one that had likely been used as a guard station when the base was still in normal operation. Now it was a ramshackle thing, all the windows broken, and all the radios and computers inside dead.

We waited as the headlights swept by.

I glanced around. The silhouette of the aircraft hangar loomed, large and imposing, not far from us. The planes outside, with their distinctive hexagonal honeycomb latticing, were intriguing, but I didn't spend time dwelling on them.

If I wanted information on how they were built, I could likely get it from the databases inside.

"People used to fly all over the place before the Forever Winter," Bishop muttered as he eyed the planes. "I've seen it in old vids."

"That sounds awful," Brecht whispered.

Vega nodded in agreeance.

"What? It sounds like a fuckin' tactical advantage, if you ask me." Bishop elbowed me. "Tell them, Kita. You're smart."

I snorted out a laugh. With my voice low, I said, "Yes. Flight was a huge advantage in the wars of our ancestors. Also, since the weather is clearing, whoever manages to reconstruct planes first will likely be set to become the next major power."

In the past, flying required vast amounts of fuel. However, since the Teth arrived, with all their A-tech, we could now use things like fission batteries to power a large airplane.

"Still sounds awful," Brecht said matter-of-factly.

Bishop glared at him like he was an annoying ten-year-old. "Why?"

"I just hate . . . the sky." Brecht shook his head, never glancing upward. "Ever since I left the bunker, I just . . . hate it."

He didn't look up, or if he did, it wasn't for long.

Brecht had casadastraphobia—a fear of falling into the sky, basically. It obviously stemmed from the fact he lived underground for so long. He hadn't seen the sky until he was well into adulthood.

But we didn't have time to deal with that.

Once the spotlight swept by, I motioned for them to follow. "Now."

Together, we hurried forward through the darkness. Reaching the side of the aviation building, I paused, scanning the area for any signs of movement or surveillance. It seemed quiet, almost eerily so. Brecht edged along the wall, heading for a side entrance, Vega close to him at all moments.

The side door had no guards.

I wondered why, but then I remembered the many deaths in the streets. The Iron-Blooded were probably low on soldiers—and morale.

I hurried to Brecht's side. He motioned to the door. I carefully tried the handle—it was unlocked. With a silent nod to the others, I pushed it open, wincing at the soft creak of its hinges.

Bishop and Brecht both lifted their rifles.

With a shake of my head, I slid into the building, my heart pounding.

Inside, the air was stale, the musty smell of disuse mingling with the faint odor of machine oil and metal. There was a small desk, and a couple of crumbling chairs, and I wondered if this was an old entrance for personnel who worked at the base—before the Forever Winter, obviously.

With a few quick steps, I crossed the room and tried the door there. When I opened it, I found a dimly lit hallway.

The base still had power.

Did they have a fission battery? Probably. Or perhaps the Iron-Blooded had brought one with them. Either way, if there was power, this would be easier to navigate.

"C'mon," I whispered.

The others nodded and followed me into the hall.

I motioned for Bishop and Brecht to take point, their experience in such situations invaluable. Vega and I followed closely behind. I constantly scanned for any sign of Theon or his Teth drones.

"Tell me if you detect anything," I said as I touched Vega's shoulder to let him know I was speaking directly to him.

"*Indeed,*" he said in Tethlite.

The corridor led us to a larger, open area, probably a common room for the base personnel. Computers and communication equipment lined the walls. Only a few of them still worked, and I figured they were the most advanced of the equipment left behind. I approached one of the consoles, my fingers hovering over the keyboard.

"We're looking for Gascoigne," Brecht harshly whispered.

"I need a moment," I muttered.

Bishop chuckled. Then he glanced over at Brecht. "Listen—you're never going to talk her out of this. She *religiously* checks every computer that's still in operation we stumble across."

"Maybe you and I should continue to search?" Brecht pointed to some doors around the edge of the common room. "This place is gigantic. It would be prudent to secure our nearby vicinity."

Bishop turned to me, worry in his eyes. Then he glanced back to Brecht. "You and Vega search. But don't go too far. One or two doors away—that's it. If you find anything, immediately report back. I'll stay here with Kita. As a guard."

That was all it took. Brecht smiled and happily went for the nearest door, Vega close behind.

I understood why he wanted to go. He and Gascoigne were a couple, after all. And while Gascoigne was a grown-ass woman with plenty of combat training, there was still a real possibility she was being held captive by the Iron-Blooded here.

As Brecht and Vega disappeared through the far door, the hinges groaning, I returned my attention to the console. I tapped the keyboard, and the keys felt as though they were coated in syrup. But it still worked.

The screen flickered to life, illuminating the dim room with a pale, artificial glow. My fingers danced over the keys, accessing the base's internal network. Despite the decay and neglect, the system was surprisingly responsive. Thankfully, this computer ran using the same BIOS and operating system as *all* the pre-Forever Winter computers, and I had spent years and years of life learning how to break into these systems as quickly and as efficiently as possible.

Bishop stood close to me, his rifle at the ready, his gaze scanning the room with practiced vigilance. "So, what are you lookin' for, Kit-Kat?"

"Just give me a minute," I whispered, my focus unwavering.

Data scrolled across the screen, revealing maps, logs, and communication records. My eyes scanned for any mention of Gascoigne or Theon—but also I wanted to know why the Iron-Blooded were here to begin with.

Everywhere I went, there was one constant . . .

The Iron-Blooded only took locations with great uses. They gathered up power armor, raw materials, and even people or wayward Teth. If they were here, it was for a good reason.

And I had a suspicion it had to do with the airplanes.

This was a space force base, not an air force base—which meant these little planes could probably hit higher altitudes than normal.

Sure enough, as I scrolled through the specs of the aircrafts, I realized most of them were designed to intercept bombs that were in orbit. Interesting, but not as useful as I would've hoped. Most of the planes were prototypes, and they were outside because they were meant to have a show for a United States general—right before the Forever Winter took place.

The sound of footsteps echoed faintly from the far corridor.

Bishop tensed, raising his rifle. I paused, listening intently, but the footsteps faded, leaving only the soft hum of the computer in the silence.

"You think that was Brecht?" Bishop whispered.

"No," I replied. "Vega would've been with him. That was someone else."

"Yeah, that's what I thought, too." Bishop smiled, almost sadistically. "I'm gonna wait by the far door to get the drop on the next tally mark who enters here. You're safe at the computer, right?"

I gave him a sideways glance. "No, the keyboard will strike at any second."

He chortled as he walked off, clearly not insulted by my sardonic response. I liked that about Bishop. He never took anything too seriously.

Resuming my search, I stumbled upon a series of encrypted files. They were heavily guarded, suggesting something valuable hidden within. My fingers flew over the keyboard, cracking the encryption layer by layer. Finally, the files opened, revealing detailed schematics of an exoskeleton with the same features as the aircraft . . .

It could fly. And to incredible heights.

My heart pounded—not because this was scary, but because of the possibilities. First off, the planes weren't of use to me because piloting them was a major problem. I wasn't trained to fly—and neither was anyone else I knew. I'd have to teach myself, from old-world books, or I'd need to find a Winter Survivor who still remembered their aviation schooling, which was a long shot.

However, the judge power armor was operated through a connection point on the spine.

I ran my hand over the back of my neck, my fingers grazing the access port built straight into my flesh. I *could* pilot a suit of power armor that could fly . . .

However, a single suit wasn't as useful as a whole plane. It couldn't move many people—or much in the way of supplies—and it was obvious from the schematics it was built to be an anti-missile defense measure.

How could I use this to my advantage?

"Kit-Kat?" Bishop whispered from over near the door. "Are you okay?"

"There's something here about the planes," I murmured, "something about some judge armor . . . I just need some more time . . ."

"Remember to look for Gascoigne."

I gritted my teeth. I'd get to that, I'd get to that . . .

We were interrupted by the return of Brecht and Vega. They slipped in through a different door, entering with an impressive amount of stealth. "Clear," Brecht reported, a hint of frustration in his voice. "No sign of Gascoigne or any Iron-Blooded."

I backed out of the files on the flying Mark VI and instead searched through the recently altered files and communications. The Iron-Blooded *had* sent messages, and it seemed there were several that were sent recently.

One of them was labeled, "Quern."

I opened up the transcript. It read: *Quern has returned to us. As expected, it was the granddaughter of Benjamin Yamasaki who held him captive for so long. Unfortunately, Quern wasn't able to gather any information about her future plans. He was kept underground and restrained until he managed to escape.*

No information? He saw *plenty* of information. Why didn't he report any of it?

I poked at the keyboard.

Another communication, this one received, said: *Quern could be compromised. Act accordingly.*

That was it.

"Well?" Brecht asked as he stood near the computer. "You've been at this for some time. Hopefully you found something?"

There was no mention of Gascoigne. Anywhere.

I logged off the console. "We should look around a bit more, but I'm starting to get the feeling Gascoigne is nowhere here."

"Do you think she was captured by Ex Cathedra?"

I hoped not.

"Let's just keep moving," I whispered.

CHAPTER TWENTY-FOUR

The four of us moved toward the door Brecht and Vega had scouted from. I opened it, and the air that wafted in was filled with musk.

I placed a hand on Vega, and his muscles twitched in response, acknowledging my touch.

"What is this smell?" I asked.

"Teth drones," Vega replied with a growl. "*They were ordered to kill recently, and this smell is from their ferocity,*" he added in Tethlite.

"I'm right here," Bishop muttered. "Don't use your slurp language to talk about me like I'm not."

Brecht slowly turned to face him. "What? No one was talking about you."

With a chuckle, Bishop smirked. "Really? I just assumed Vega said, *Teth drones,* in English, but then followed it up in Tethlite with, *but they're nothing compared to Bishop's rich, and thick, musk.*"

Brecht pinched the bridge of his nose. "Sometimes I wish I were a lone agent, hunting down special forces members of the CCP . . ."

Ignoring them, I tapped Vega's shoulder. "Lead the way."

He nodded his head and flashed his fangs. Vega went ahead, his Teth senses attuned to any hint of movement or presence. His large form seemed to melt into the shadows, which was impressive—like the Teth had evolved to take advantage of creatures who relied on sight.

Brecht followed, his rifle at the ready, eyes darting back and forth. Now that we were indoors, he didn't mind glancing up—and he did frequently, which was probably a good thing. We didn't know what was here, after all.

Bishop stayed close to me, his rifle held in a relaxed but ready grip. The corners of his mouth twitched in a faint, wry smile as he glanced at me. "You know, if you really are carrying our kid, you're gonna have to stay home for a little bit—and leave all this sneakin' around to me."

I replied with a smile of my own, but that was it.

A piece of me knew I needed to do more.

Vega led us to a door and sniffed deep. He gestured to it, and I trusted his judgment. This was where we needed to go. I walked over and grabbed the handle.

Then I stepped through the door, entering another corridor that branched off into multiple rooms. The corridor was lined with closed doors, each one a potential hiding place for danger. The faint hum of the base's power resonated through the walls.

"We split up and check these rooms," I whispered. "But be quick and quiet about it. I'm certain Theon is here."

Then again, perhaps Ex Cathedra had killed way more of the Iron-Blooded than I originally thought.

Brecht and Vega nodded, splitting off to the right, while Bishop and I took the left. Each room I checked was empty, either abandoned offices or storage spaces painted with a thick layer of dust. This place clearly wasn't of interest to the Iron-Blooded, so once Bishop and Brecht had opened a few doors, I motioned them back.

Vega sniffed. "No. It's down that way. The drones . . . they're near the machinery. Metal hangs in the air."

I readied my 9mm, checking to make sure I had it prepped to fire at a moment's notice.

We proceeded down the corridor, our steps echoing softly. Then a large metal double door opened at the very far end of the hall—the type large enough to drive a truck through. Two Teth drones sauntered out, their massive claws clicking on the tile.

Vega flashed his fangs, and his skin rippled, not unlike when the breeze rushes over a grassy field.

Then Theon Sellers walked into the hallway, his blond hair practically glowing under the fluorescent lighting. He didn't have a firearm, but his two drones were the size of horses. His attention immediately snapped to me, and we stared at each other for a fraction of a second—but that was all it required.

He knew who I was.

"*Kill them*," Theon shouted.

Bishop and Brecht opened fire. I took a moment to aim. I wanted to kill Theon. The drones would take ten to twenty shots each if the bullets hit their chest, but Theon could die in a single well-aimed shot to the head. I lifted my 9mm . . .

The corridor erupted into chaos.

The deafening sound of gunfire ricocheted off the walls, the muzzle flashes lighting up the space like a strobe. Theon ducked behind one of his Teth drones, using the beast as a shield. I couldn't get a good shot, so I backed away behind the others.

Brecht and Bishop's bullets hammered into the drones.

Vega . . .

Once Brecht and Bishop slowed their shots, he lunged forward, his claws extended. He slammed one of the drones and sank his large worker claws into its chest. The two Teth screeched, but the drone was clearly smaller and weaker.

The other drone started heading our way, its mouth open, its fangs exposed.

The real secret of the Teth drones were their claws—one slash and it would cause numbness and paralysis both. We couldn't allow the monster to touch it.

The Teth drones were formidable, their thick, chitinous exoskeletons absorbing the impact with frightening resilience. And while Brecht and Bishop fired on the one nearing us, I slammed my back against the wall and searched for Theon. He had fled back into the room with the double metal doors. They swung shut, and I gritted my teeth in irritation.

The hall was wide enough—I could attempt to run past and chase him . . .

But the drones were massive, easily dwarfing a human. One wrong move and I could be fatally injured.

Brecht reloaded swiftly, and Bishop continued the fire. The drone approaching hit the floor riddled in lead. It twitched and didn't move, but then everyone turned their gaze on Vega.

Vega's drone reeled from his assault, staggering back. Vega seized the opportunity, leaping onto the creature's back, his claws sinking deep into its flesh. The drone shrieked, a sound that was both alien and eerily human, thrashing violently in an attempt to dislodge Vega.

Then our Teth warrior ripped out the drone's throat, blood gushing across the tile like someone had shaken a soda and then ripped off the lid.

The monster hit the floor twitching, and Vega quickly dismounted, his fangs crimson.

"We need to catch Theon," I shouted.

Vega, Brecht, and Bishop nodded in agreement. We all ran forward and then slammed our way past the metal double doors, chasing after the human "architect."

But this room . . .

It was some sort of command center. It was a high-tech nerve center of the base with screens and consoles flickering with a myriad of data. Despite all that, the room resembled more of an overused office workspace. There were cracked pillars holding up the ceiling, and every computer was partitioned off with cubical walls that were so old they were now crumbling. The yellowed papers, and the flashing red on some of the screens, painted the whole room in a hue of *urgency.*

Theon, one Iron-Blooded soldier, and two outrider Teth were at the other side of the room, near a cluster of large servers trapped behind rusted cages. The servers hummed with power, clearly designed to last hundreds of years, even without human intervention. The A-tech used in this room was impressive, and extensive.

I almost wanted to take it all.

However, before I could really soak everything in, Theon pointed. "*I said kill them, goddammit! What part of that command was unclear!*"

"*Yes, Architect,*" the outriders and lone soldier all said in choppy unison.

The two outrider Teth, their forms sleeker and more agile than the previous drones, sprang over the cubicles. When they hit the floor, they leapt again, like freakish deer with fangs and claws.

Brecht lifted his weapon, and Vega stepped forward, as if to greet them—but it was only Bishop who smiled.

"*Kill them,*" Bishop shouted, mocking Theon's voice and laughing at the same time.

But the lone Iron-Blooded soldier threw out an object and I panicked. At first, I thought it was a grenade, and I lunged forward, trying to warn Bishop. Vega, who could sense movements, even through the ripples in the air, whipped around and stopped me. He not only shielded me, but he also prevented me from reaching Bishop.

"No!" I shouted.

Thankfully, it wasn't a grenade.

Unfortunately, it was a *flash-bang.*

The non-lethal grenade hit the floor and burst into a blinding dazzle of light. Anyone staring directly at it would be blinded for a minute or so—maybe more. That was the *flash* part. The next thing that happened was a pulse of noise that fucked with a person's inner ear. It was a powerful pulse that left most people stunned or disoriented. That was the *bang* part.

Flash-bangs were fantastic against humans with no protection. Two of the five senses completely taken out of commission? Yeah, it was awful.

Which meant Bishop and Brecht were left blind and shaken, unable to hear the outriders as they leapt over the final stretch of cubicles.

However, flash-bangs did little against the Teth. They had no eyes, and their hearing was far more advanced than humans. Most people thought that it meant the Teth would be *more* affected by the *bang*, but it was the opposite. The Teth's ear canals constricted whenever too much force or sound was nearby, shielding the sensitive parts of their hearing until the sound was reduced.

Vega had shielded me from the worst of it, and while my ears rang, I could still see and tell what was going on.

Thankfully, Vega roared as he whirled around. He charged for the outriders and slammed into one, preventing it from reaching us. But the other slipped by.

Outriders were speedy and precise—and Bishop and Brecht were blind. So I lifted my 9mm and fired, striking the beast in the head. It pivoted on its feet and lunged. I tried to dodge, but two of its claws slashed through my bicep, the hot sting of the injury causing me to catch my breath.

Thankfully, outriders didn't have the paralyzing poison coating their claws.

I hit the floor and then fired up at the outrider, pulling the trigger until no more bullets remained. I struck the beast a couple times, but it leapt backward, hit the wall, and then side-jumped away, fast and impressive, its claws leaving furrows in the building.

The lone soldier, clad in the black gear of the Iron-Blooded, raised his rifle and began firing. His bullets zipped by me overhead, plinking into the wall. Bishop shook his head, his eyes focusing, and then opened fire.

He had nanites in his blood, just like the Iron-Blooded, and those little machines helped the human body recover from everything faster than normal, even the concussion blast of a flash-bang.

Bishop aimed for the soldier, forcing the bastard to take cover behind one of the rusted server cages. Sparks flew from the damaged servers, adding to the frenzied atmosphere.

With brutal efficiency, Vega snapped the neck of the outrider he had been fighting. Then he turned his attention to the other. The Teth enemy leapt over a cubicle, and Vega lunged for it.

I stood and turned my attention to Theon. He was trying to slip away amidst the chaos. I couldn't let him escape—he was too valuable. I sprinted towards him, weaving between cubicles, my heart pounding as Bishop and the soldier kept each other's attention.

Vega caught his Teth opponent and slammed the outrider to the floor. Vega's strength was formidable, but the outrider was nimble, and the thin little Teth slipped from his grasp and attempted to run a second time.

I made it to Theon right before he exited. Instead of allowing him to run, I shot his ankle.

Well, I *would've* shot his ankle, if I had any bullets. I pulled the trigger and it *click-click-clicked* with an empty sound, and I cursed my bad luck. Instead, when I rushed over to Theon, I struck him in the temple right as he was turning to face me.

Blood exploded from his head and coated the wall. He stumbled, and I hit him a second time, this time square on the nose. I heard a crack and he yelled, but the sound was strangled. He fell to the floor, his eyes unfocused, crimson streams of blood gushing from his nostrils and coating his clothing.

I grabbed his vest. "You're not going anywhere."

When I glanced over my shoulder, I realized Bishop was still standing—and the Iron-Blooded soldier wasn't. Vega had pinned the outrider to the floor, and was currently on top of the beast. The two of them were whispering in Tethlite, but I couldn't hear what they were saying.

Brecht . . .

Poor Brecht.

He staggered around, rubbing his eyes and tapping at his ears. The flash-bang had done a doozy on him. It could take two to ten minutes for a normal person to recover from the concussion and flash of those grenades, and some people even experienced permanent damage.

Hopefully he'd be okay.

The room fell silent, the battle over as quickly as it had begun. We were all breathing heavily, and adrenaline was still coursing through my veins. Vega, bloodied but unbroken, stood tall, a true Teth warrior. "This one wants to join us," he said in English.

CHAPTER TWENTY-FIVE

The outrider wants to join *us*?" I asked, keeping my grip tight on Theon's vest.

Vega nodded. "This outrider is unsatisfied with Theon as an architect, and believes Riven destroyed its eggs."

"I thought Teth couldn't betray their architects?"

"The architect's scent controls Teth in the nearby area, but if the architect is too far away, or the Teth has been separated from it for too long, the effects are gone, much like an odor that clings to a cloth."

Ah. I understood.

Architect Riven was *far* from this place. His mind-controlling pheromones couldn't reach here. The outrider was free to run away, so long as he wasn't near Riven. Of course, that meant Riven could retake control if they ever met—but only if the outrider hadn't bonded to another architect. And since we had one, this was a boon.

The outrider got to its feet and then bowed its head until it touched the floor with its snout. All four arms unfolded and then all four hands turned upward, the palms facing the ceiling. It was a sign of submission in the Teth. Normally, they would do this to be accepted into a new hierarchy. Did it really want to join us?

"What's its name?" I asked.

"Leevus," Vega replied. "A young outrider."

I glanced down to Theon. He was still dizzy, and when he stared up at me it was with eyes unseeing. I wasn't that strong—which was why he wasn't fully knocked out—but anyone taking a gun stroke to the side of the head probably wouldn't be feeling well for days.

"Here's the plan," I said. "We're going to find something in this room to tie up Theon, and then we're going to get the hell out of here."

"Why take him?" Bishop eyed Theon with a sneer. "Just shoot that guy. Remember what happened with Quern? Do we really need another kidnapping? I'm getting tired of seeing the Iron-Blooded *again and again*. Let's just . . . burn this place to the ground."

Burning it to the ground . . .

That made me think of the firestorm bombs we had in our possession. I made a mental note of that and pinned it to my thoughts, trying to grapple with the situation while making long-term plans.

"No, I want him." I stared down at Theon. "But maybe burning the place isn't a bad idea . . ."

Theon's eyes finally focused on me. "You won't get anything from Architect Riven," he whispered.

"That's not why I want you."

I motioned for Bishop to take him. Then another thought struck me. "This place has airplanes . . ."

Once Bishop was by my side, he grabbed Theon by the vest. "What about the planes?"

"It's not the planes, per se, that interest me . . . But first we need to find Gascoigne. If she's still wearing the Mark VI armor, we're going to need it."

"For what, Kit-Kat?"

I offered him half a smile. "All my plans." But I kept them to myself for now. If Theon *did* manage to escape, I didn't want him to know a thing.

Bishop dragged the man to his feet. Then he rummaged through his pack and withdrew a nylon rope. He secured Theon so that his arms were behind him, and his feet were bound, but enough to walk. Theon didn't resist much. He was weaker than Bishop, and clearly knew we were at the advantage. But his eyes did flick over to the traitorous outrider more than once, and I wondered if Theon had the power to control it.

Teth architects enforced their will on lower castes through a pheromone system. Supposedly, Theon had that, too. I didn't know how—but I would find out. Sanctuary had a series of labs, after all—labs meant to deal with small components.

My plan was to bring him back and dissect him.

It was . . . a little dark . . .

But if *I* could make myself a human architect, things would be much easier.

Brecht rubbed his face and staggered over. "I think I heard half of that?" He held back vomit. "I apologize—that grenade got me."

"It's okay. Let's just . . . go out the way we came, and hope we don't run into any more Iron-Blooded soldiers."

Bishop motioned with a shrug of his shoulders to the computers, and then to the sparking servers. "You want any of this? Because I was serious about burning it all down."

I held my breath. Then I hurried over to the nearest computer and poked around the keyboard. There were, in fact, piles of information here I would like, we just didn't have time to sort through it all.

In a desperate attempt to save some of it, I quickly searched through the nearby desks. I rifled through drawers and cabinets, my fingers brushing against stacks of papers, discarded tools, and various gadgets.

Then, tucked away in the back of a dusty drawer, I found something worthwhile—a portable hard drive. It was a bit older, a bulky model that looked like it could withstand a small explosion. A military relic from a time when the United States government was likely afraid of nonstop EMP attacks. This kind of hard drive would resist the pulse of electromatic weaponry.

I liked it.

With it in hand, I turned back to the computer, connecting the hard drive with a sense of urgency. The device whirred to life, its small light blinking in the dimly lit room. I navigated through the computer's files, quickly identifying the most crucial data—mission logs, communication records, technical schematics, and important locations and unit numbers.

With a few swift keystrokes, I began the transfer process.

The progress bar on the screen filled at a snail's pace.

Bishop kept watch at the door, his rifle ready, while Vega and Leevus stood guard, their senses alert for any sign of danger. Brecht, still recovering from the flash-bang's effects, sat against a wall, his eyes closed, trying to steady his breathing.

I assumed enemy Iron-Blooded would burst into the room at any minute, but nothing came.

"Anyone else feel like this place is actually a ghost town?" Bishop asked.

Theon, tied up and sitting on the floor at Bishop's feet, glanced up at the man. "The others will know something is wrong shortly."

"They're probably in one of the other buildings," Brecht said, his face pale. He really did look like he was about to vomit.

"Outrider," I said. Then I turned to face Leevus. "The computer records say there's a human judge suit here with the capability to fly. Is that true?"

"Don't answer her," Theon hissed.

Leevus crept around the nearest cubicle, its movements awkward. When it got closer to me, it pointed its long snout in my direction. "*There are several human exoskeletons here,*" it said in Tethlite. "*But we are unsure if they can fly. The battery cells were ruined. We can't power them up.*"

Damn.

I shook my head. "Can you speak English?"

"*I can understand English, but I cannot twist my tongue to make your noises.*" Leevus tilted its head to the side. "*You're carrying a child.*"

"Thank you," I sarcastically replied. "I'm so glad you noticed."

"*You shouldn't be here. You should be in the heart of your domain, safe and protected.*"

"I'll take a break once I finally get there," I quipped.

The outrider nodded, as though this were a satisfactory answer.

"Did you capture a woman in a suit of power amor?" I asked. "In the Mark VI armor Quern used to pilot?"

The outrider shook its head. "*No. Our battle with Ex Cathedra was costly. We lost all our exoskeletons, and we captured no one.*"

"Not even randomly? Outside of the battle?"

Leevus snorted. "*No.*"

That meant Gascoigne really wasn't here.

Theon turned to me, his blond hair stained with his own blood. He glared, but said nothing.

I ignored him. Instead, I returned my attention to the computer. The data transfer seemed to take an eternity, each second stretching out as we waited in tense silence. Finally, the screen flashed a message with *Transfer Complete* and I sighed in relief. I disconnected the hard drive, tucking it securely into my pack.

"I have everything I need," I said. "Let's go."

But Bishop only offered me a smile. He walked around the room, clumping up the yellowed paper and then taking a knife to some of the computers and their wires. Then he threw rotting chairs and bits of the broken desks over, like he was a building a campfire.

A small fire started.

Then Bishop did the same thing over by the servers behind their cages.

Sparks continued to shoot out of the bullet holes on the side, and another fire started easily.

"There," he whispered. "Fuck this place. It'll go up in smoke in no time." Then he chuckled, his smile wide. "Do you think I should put several tally marks on my skin for this one? Or just make a little fire symbol? Or maybe just one *large* tally mark . . . That would be funny."

I never thought any of that was funny, but Bishop had a "delightful" way of thinking about the world.

Setting a fire seemed dangerous, though, considering the forest nearby . . .

But then I remembered the wall the Iron-Blooded had constructed around this base, and the many gigantic parking lots that would act as a stop gate to any major fires.

Although, I still thought it was dangerous if we got unlucky.

"We should go," Brecht said, a slight warble to his voice that betrayed his fear.

"Right." I pointed to the door.

Vega and Leevus went into the hallway first. Brecht and I went second, and Bishop dragged Theon along behind us. As we navigated through the base's corridors, the sound of distant alarms began to echo through the halls. It seemed someone knew we were here and was trying to tell the others.

We slammed through the doors, went straight through the common rooms, and then exited the building the exact way we entered. The spotlights were harsh reminders we weren't safe, and the alarms blared louder out here than inside.

There were Teth and human soldiers already out here—at least nine Teth warriors, but only three human soldiers. They were scouring the area, heading for the other buildings. Normally, I would've ignored them, and hoped to continue past.

But I recognized one of the humans.

Quern.

We all stood in the darkness as a spotlight slid over the ground just thirty feet from our location. Once it went by, I pointed to the portion of the wall we had scaled previously, beyond the high-tech airplanes. We rushed through in the shadows, and while I heard Iron-Blooded soldiers in the distance, they never ran in our direction.

However, I knew the buildings would catch fire.

This place would be engulfed.

And my guilt increased.

I stopped at the base of the wall. Vega leapt up, his claws digging into the stone. He effortlessly helped Brecht, and then Leevus, and even yanked Theon up by his restraints.

It was just me and Bishop, and when Vega went to help me, I shook my head.

"I have to do something first," I whispered.

Vega grunted—it sounded irritated.

Bishop waved a hand through the air. "Don't you hear the sirens? We gotta get out of here, Kit-Kat. C'mon. We got everything we need, right? And Gascoigne isn't here? Let's ditch this hellhole."

"I have to tell Quern," I whispered.

Bishop lifted both his eyebrows until they practically disappeared into his hairline. "The tally mark who *kidnapped you*? That's the man you have to tell? And tell what? You're leaving? *Oh, goodbye, boo—hope I see you next weekend!*" He hardened his expression after the sarcastic tirade. "We should leave."

"He let me escape," I said.

Bishop didn't reply. He obviously mulled over the new information, though it didn't seem to change his opinion much. "You shouldn't risk yourself."

He had a point.

I glanced up at the wall, the sirens still going, the spotlights still flashing. No one knew Leevus had sided with us. "Outrider," I said in a harsh whisper. "I need your help."

Leevus leapt to the top of the wall from the other side and then gracefully landed next to me. Its sleek body, and nimble movements, ensured it made no noise.

"*Yes?*" Leevus asked in Tethlite.

I pointed to the group of warriors. "Go there. Tell Quern about the fire—but no one else. And then return to us on the other side of the wall, all right? Make sure no one knows where you're going."

"*You want me to simply carry a message?*"

"Yes. That's all. Don't fight them. Just say what you have to and pretend you're searching for us. As soon as you can, leave."

The outrider nodded, my instructions absorbed.

I hoped Leevus would understand, because I didn't want Quern to die here. That was stupid though—I knew it was stupid—but he had helped me, and now I wanted to help him.

Then Vega pulled me and Bishop over the wall like he had before. I gulped down breath, my heart racing.

"We should get back to the coffee shop," Brecht muttered.

I nodded. "Lead the way."

On the top of the coffee shop, with the aid of Brecht's scopes, we were able to watch the Davis Space Force Base go up in flames.

The inferno that engulfed the buildings was nothing short of breathtaking. From our vantage point, the fire seemed to dance, painting the clouds above in shades of orange, red, and gold.

It was a sight that was both terrifying and mesmerizing.

"You should definitely get just one giant tally mark for this," Brecht said as he passed his scope over to Bishop. "It's amazing."

After snatching up the scope and gazing through it himself, Bishop chuckled. "I agree. It'll be amazing. I just need to think up where I'm going to put it."

Through Brecht's scope, I saw individual structures collapsing, one by one, into the fiery maw. The heat was so intense that it created a shimmer in the air, distorting the view, making it seem as if we were watching through a dream or a vision.

Vega and Leevus, standing a little apart from us, couldn't watch anything. And they didn't seem interested. Instead, Vega kept hold of Theon, flashing his fangs whenever the man moved. Again, I worried. What if Theon really could force the Teth to listen to him?

They hadn't turned on us yet.

Probably because Theon wouldn't risk it. We could easily put a bullet through his head, even if Vega and Leevus were under his control.

I was happy Leevus had made it back without complication, though it didn't have much to say about the encounter with Quern. Leevus delivered the message and left—that was all it had to say about that. Perhaps Quern didn't believe the outrider, and was caught in the inferno. I suspected I would never know.

As the flames continued to rage, I couldn't help but feel a sense of awe. This fire was a cleansing force, purging the landscape of the Iron-Blooded's influence.

And some of the old world, too.

Purifying flames . . .

Perhaps they really were the only option for me.

CHAPTER TWENTY-SIX

The dawn of a new day.

I woke up stiff, and my stomach churning. We were in our campsite, just outside of town. We had only slept a couple of hours, but that was better than nothing. When I opened my eyes, and rubbed away the grogginess, I realized Vega was snuggled up on one side of me, and Bishop was on the other.

There wasn't any room for the others in the tent. It was just us three, as though we were a bizarre interspecies throuple.

I rolled over so I could face Bishop. He got close and nuzzled my neck, inhaling deep as he half groaned, "Good morning."

"Morning," I whispered.

Bishop gently extricated himself from the tangle of thin blankets and then slipped out of the tent. I watched him through half-closed eyes, admiring his considerate movements designed not to wake Vega. Outside, it was cold, and when Bishop slid open the tent flap, I shivered. But as soon as the flap was closed, Vega scooted closer to me, his warmth a boon.

I lay there for a few moments, listening to the sounds of Bishop rummaging through things. The distant rustling of leaves in the gentle morning breeze could've easily lulled me back to sleep. It was a rare moment of tranquility in our hectic lives, but I knew I couldn't enjoy it too long.

We were still in enemy territory.

I couldn't wait to make it back to Sanctuary.

After a few minutes, the unmistakable aroma of cooking food wafted into the tent. My stomach growled in response, reminding me that I hadn't eaten properly in what felt like ages. Curiosity piqued, I quietly got up, careful not to disturb Vega, and peeked outside.

Bishop had set up a small, makeshift kitchen area. He was skillfully flipping what looked to be fried eggs on a small, flat piece of metal. Next to him, a pot of boiling water was perched over a small fire. It was risky to have any light or smoke, but given the huge bonfire of last night, and the fact it was now day, the risk was considerably lessened.

He noticed me watching and flashed a quick smile. "Thought I'd whip up something special for us. Remember when I told you about those chickens I found?" He winked and then motioned to some supplies he had left here prior to finding me.

I smiled back, thankful for anything other than hardtack. It was these small acts of kindness, these moments of normalcy, that kept me grounded amidst the chaos of my life.

As I sat down at the makeshift breakfast table—which was just a small blanket spread out like a picnic with two logs as seats—Bishop served up four fried eggs for each of us. He presented the dish on a small tin plate with no utensils. I supposed that was why he chose fried eggs—they would be easy to eat with my hands.

The first bite was heavenly, a perfect blend of savory and comfort. I gobbled up the rest of my breakfast like a ravenous animal, practically licking my fingers clean.

I probably looked insane.

Bishop chuckled and nodded in approval. "I know what you're thinking," he said with a smirk. "*Oh, Bishop, you're so funny and charming and attractive and extremely humble. Surely, you can't also cook. That's too much for one person!*"

I couldn't help but smile at him.

Then Bishop leaned forward, no more mirth in his expression. "Okay. Let's get down to business."

"Business?" I asked as I placed the tin plate on the ground. It was a little traveling plate. I recognized it from some of our short treks.

"Yeah. We have serious things to discuss."

I lifted an eyebrow, genuinely curious. Did Bishop want to discuss the information on the hard drive? The potential of flying power armor? What we were going to do about the Iron-Blooded, Vay, or the soldiers of Ex Cathedra?

Or—more likely—he wanted to discuss Gascoigne's whereabouts. She still hadn't returned to us, and the longer it went, the more concerning her absence was.

"We need to discuss *names*," Bishop said. He used his empty plate to point at me. "You hate all my nicknames. You only begrudgingly allowed me to call you something cute when I started calling you Kit-Kat. So, if we're going to have a kid, we need to get this topic out of the way immediately."

Names?

I laughed and shook my head. "Wow. That is a very serious topic. I'm glad you brought it up."

Bishop rotated his shoulders as he leaned back. "You know me. No parties—all business."

"It's funny you mention this, because I had three names in mind that I was going to give the newborn Teth at Sanctuary. Benjamin, Tamura, and Joel."

"*Joel?*" Bishop spoke the name as though he were vomiting at the same time. "What's wrong with you, woman? Who names their child *Joel*?"

"I like it." Then I shrugged. "It was the man who built the bunker I lived in. I thought it was appropriate."

Bishop rolled his hand. "Okay, well, I'm glad you gave it to an alien then. Let's hear what your *fourth* preferred name is."

My chuckling filled the crisp morning air, and I playfully nudged Bishop with my foot. "You're impossible. All right, for our kid . . . How about 'Remi'? It's simple, strong, and it doesn't sound like it belongs to someone who's about to retire."

"Remi," Bishop repeated, rolling the name around in his mouth as if tasting it. A smile slowly spread across his face. "So you're thinking we'll have a girl? Hmm? Little baby girl named Remi?"

"W-Well, I thought it could work either way. Male or female—Remi is a neutral name, isn't it?"

Bishop shook his head. "No. But that's fine. I can make this work. I'll call our kid *Bean Bag* or *Billy* or maybe just *Lump*."

The last one had me stifle back a louder laugh. "Lump? That's the nickname you're going to give our child?"

"Yeah." Bishop playfully nudged my foot with his own. "Little thing is just going to be a lump for the first nine months I know them. Seems appropriate, really. And it's catchy—and a little cute, if you ask me."

I didn't want to admit it, but *Lump* was a cute name. For, maybe, a dog. Not a person. But still.

"But I like Remi. Has a certain ring to it." Bishop stared thoughtfully at the ground for a prolonged moment. "Remi . . ."

I couldn't help but feel warm as I listened to him speak the name. Remi was perfect. I touched my stomach as I thought about the name more.

Bishop leaned in closer, his eyes softening. "I promise, I'll teach Lump to be as stubborn and fearless as her mother."

For some illogical reason, I felt like crying. I took a deep breath and pushed all those happy tears down into my gut. "And hopefully Lump will inherit his father's aim and sense of humor."

"Sounds like we're cookin' up the perfect human being." Bishop smiled as he stood from his log. "Now, why don't you let me clean up a bit, and you can rest some more."

"You want me to rest? Shouldn't we be moving?"

"Seems like Vega and Levi are still sleeping."

"Leevus," I corrected.

Bishop scoffed. "No. That's a terrible name. I hate it—it sounds like *leave us*, which is bizarrely ominous, especially for a traitor. *Levi* sounds like a proper name. I already told the alien he has to change it."

I ran my hand down my face. "And what did Leevus say?"

"*Levi* said that was totally fine, because he hated it, too." Bishop patted me on the shoulder. "Now just get a little more rest. I'll clean this up, chat with Brecht whenever he gets back from scouting, and we'll form a real plan once you're awake."

When I woke up, I was alone in my tent. Vega was awake, and so were the others. I exited the tent, stretching and yawning as I shook away the last of my fatigue. How long had I been asleep? Outside, the campsite was abuzz with activity. Vega was conversing with Leevus, who now seemed to have adopted the name Levi, thanks to Bishop's insistence.

Bishop was busy packing up the last of our gear, his movements efficient and focused.

Just as I was about to ask about Brecht, he slid down the dry riverbank and entered the campsite. He hurried over with a sense of urgency, his boots muddy, and his rifle held tightly in his hands. "I've found it," he said. "I found the Ex Cathedra soldiers and where they set up camp."

"Are they close?" I asked, my heart already pounding, even though I had just woken.

Brecht turned to me, seemingly surprised I was awake. "It's a little ways from here. Outside of town. There's a place that used to be a park, I think, with a chain-link fence that's still standing. The soldiers are in there, along with their judges."

"You're a brave man," Bishop muttered. "Those judges love killing."

"I figured Gascoigne had to be there." Brecht returned his attention to me. "But I didn't see her Mark VI armor . . ."

"Still, it's a good idea to check," I said. "Although, I'm surprised they're sticking around. We watched the Davis Space Force Base go up in smoke. They must've seen that, too. Why stay here?"

"They're picking off Iron-Blooded soldiers who escaped the inferno," Brecht replied matter-of-factly. "I watched them do it all morning."

Ah.

That made sense. Ex Cathedra didn't want any competition in the area.

Bishop looked at me, his gaze hard. "We should check it out. It's our best chance to find Gascoigne."

Vega and Levi, who stood off to the side, nodded once he said that. They didn't have eyes, but their posture and stance told me they were both alert and serious. And while Levi had never met Gascoigne, it was clear to me our new Teth loved Vega.

Which also made sense. Outriders typically served under a warrior.

"We need to move fast and stay under the radar," Brecht said. He hurried back up the dry riverbank. "The terrain around the park will give us some cover, but we can't afford to be spotted, as Bishop so helpfully pointed out."

I turned to the group, feeling the weight of leadership on my shoulders. "Let's get ready then. We'll approach cautiously and assess the situation before making any moves. Our priority is to find Gascoigne and get out without drawing too much attention."

But then I remembered something.

I glanced toward our only vehicle—the car Bishop and the others had taken from Sanctuary in order to find me. Theon was tied down inside. Should we leave him here?

Would anyone find him?

I doubted it.

"We're going to leave our prisoner," I muttered.

"*Are you sure?*" Levi asked in Tethlite. "*Perhaps we should slay the architect before leaving.*"

Levi clearly didn't like Theon. Bishop had been right about that.

"*No,*" I replied in Tethlite. "*We leave him, and we search around. He can't drive the vehicle without our keys, and he was already weak before we brought him here. Without food and water, he's likely exhausted.*"

Levi nodded once.

Bishop grabbed his pack, and then both Vega and Levi moved to flank me. I flinched when they got close, but then I gradually relaxed as I realized what they were doing.

They were moving to keep me protected, no matter what.

Bishop motioned with a tilt of his head. "C'mon, Kit-Kat. The sooner we find Gascoigne, the sooner you and Lump can take a long rest at home."

CHAPTER TWENTY-SEVEN

Before we went to the Ex Cathedra encampment, I decided we should at least have eyes on the Davis Space Force Base first.

We didn't actually go to the Iron-Blooded-constructed wall; instead, we returned to the five-story bank and ascended to the roof. It was awkward, considering the crumbling nature of the building, but once we started up the fire escape, I realized we weren't in any danger. A lot of old-world banks were reinforced and built to last even through fires and earthquakes. While some of the façade was crumbling, the building itself was still sturdy.

Brecht handed me a scope, and I gazed out over the ashes and embers that used to be the military base.

Surprisingly, of the three main buildings, one was still partially intact. It had been burned on the western side, but the inside of the building was mostly made of concrete, and wasn't affected much by the flames.

The other two buildings were mere shells of their former selves, charred beyond recognition. The hangar was gone, but the airplanes remained, blackened from the heat but still standing.

Bishop joined me at the edge of the roof. Without a scope, he couldn't see all the details I could, but it was still easy to see the devastation from our vantage point. "Looks like the fire did its job." He smiled wide. "I'm ready to receive my *thank you* at any moment."

"One building is still partially intact," I muttered. Then I handed him the scope. "It was more fortified than the others. It's probably where all the equipment is—like the faulty power armors."

He took the scope and peered through it, his brow furrowing as he studied the remains. "Okay. Probably. But that makes searching this place way easier. I still think I deserve a thank-you."

"You are very humble and amazing," I quipped. "Thank you for all your kind efforts as our team's arsonist."

With a little twirl, he handed me back the scope. "No problem."

Brecht, who had been scanning the portion of the city between us and the park, openly sighed. "Our main focus should be the Ex Cathedra encampment. We can't lose sight of that goal."

Vega and Levi, who had been circling us like protective sharks, both nodded at that statement. Most Teth wanted to be unified in their goals—and in their location. The importance of finding Gascoigne and understanding the situation with Ex Cathedra was paramount.

We climbed back down the fire escape and then traveled down the twisted sidewalks. Smoke from a smaller, distant fire caught my attention, and I wondered where it was, exactly.

As we made our way through the desolate streets, I saw a few more graffiti signs, but these were more ominous than the ones previous.

They read: *From Sea to Shining Sea*.

Brecht saw me staring, and he nodded once. "We've seen a few of those already. Do you know what they mean?"

"It's Ex Cathedra's motto," I muttered.

"What? Why?"

"They've formed a nation under the belief they're the ones to reunite everyone. *From sea to shining sea.* It's part of a bunch of old-world songs and slogans, and they've adapted the parts of those songs that best fit their desires. Everyone in Ex Cathedra knows them and sings them on occasion—especially since the radio is state-controlled and only allowed to play songs that bolster morale."

I spoke the last few words sarcastically, but Brecht nodded along with them. He touched his scarf, and pulled it tight around his neck, his long coat flowing in the morning winds.

Vega and Levi stayed close to me, their claws clicking on the cracked cement.

"Gascoigne is from Ex Cathedra," Brecht whispered as he stopped at a large intersection and crossed the street, weaving between abandoned vehicles. "Can you tell me more about the nation?"

"I'm technically from Ex Cathedra," I muttered.

"Oh." Brecht eyed me more thoroughly. "I didn't know that."

"Well, I didn't serve the nation, but still . . ." I coughed back a laugh. "Look, there isn't much to tell. They're powerful because of the A-tech factories that survived the firestorm bombs and Forever Winter."

Brecht went ahead, taking point, but never quitting the conversation. "Gascoigne made it sound like Ex Cathedra was quite formidable and advanced."

"I wouldn't use the word *advanced* . . ." I was about to squeeze my way between two vehicles, but Vega, with his absurd strength, actually moved one to the side a few inches so I could easily walk between them. The *screech* of the rusty car being moved was probably more noise than we should've made, but I appreciated his help.

"What's it like, then?" Brecht asked, always returning to the topic, like a dog who faithfully brought a bone back and wanted it thrown for the eight hundredth time.

"One of the earliest memories I have is in an Ex Cathedra hospital. It was so busy with patients—people who were dying from cancer, radiation, injuries, or genetic defects—that they never had enough medicine to go around. There was security everywhere, to stop people from stealing, and the military officers and their families were prioritized. Then the craftsmen, then teachers. Everything was based on rank and authority; everything was to help the nation and not an individual."

As I spoke, I thought about Sanctuary.

I was in charge now.

How would I make *my* nation different from Ex Cathedra? How could I do that? What policies and practices did I need to start *now*—in our infancy—to make sure I didn't end up like a place I hated?

Bishop nudged me. "Don't forget to mention their *fabulous justice system*." He said the last few words with a shake of his hands and the most sardonic tone one could muster.

Brecht shot him a glare. "Gascoigne said that was actually competent."

"Of course she would say that," Bishop replied with a chuckle. "That place is as harsh as Gascoigne is gruff. *You overcook dinner? Congrats, you've just won an all-expenses-paid trip to indentured servitude.* Every crime, no matter how minor, always had you doing forced labor for Ex Cathedra, because they never have enough people to do everything they want."

Brecht stopped at another intersection, this one far more deserted than the last. He glanced over to Bishop with a frown. "And did you live there, too?"

"No. Hell no. I lived in the wasteland—the place between Ex Cathedra and U-Cali." He shrugged. "But I've seen tons of runaways who tell me the exact same stories over and over again. They broke some law, were forced to serve, and instead of working the field for seven years, they ran off. When your options are *run* or *slowly die a painful death in the middle of a corn field*, you'd be surprised to see how many people just pick the *run* option."

Silence settled between us as we crossed the street.

I hadn't seen any Iron-Blooded or Ex Cathedra soldiers. Were we lucky? Or had that many of them died over the past few days?

I glanced toward the sky. It seemed lighter than ever, which really helped my spirits.

"What about U-Cali?" Brecht asked. He turned his attention more to Bishop, but he was still frowning. "Are they the same? Gascoigne seems to think they're awful."

"Oh, she just thinks they're going to lose their war." Bishop shrugged. "She might be right, but don't tell her I said that. She's already got a fat head."

Brecht gritted his teeth together, his grip on his rifle tightening. Then he glanced over to me. "Can you tell me about U-Cali?"

"Well, you might be happy to hear that they speak Mandarin in most of U-Cali."

Brecht stopped walking, whirled on his heel, and faced me. "Are they the remnants of the CCP?"

"Oh, no." I laughed and waved my hand, and then pointed to the road that led out of the ruined city. "U-Cali is a bunch of communities—a few cities—that have all made agreements to help each other, either through trade and goods, or through outside attack, like with Ex Cathedra. And some of those communities mostly just speak Mandarin. Apparently, people fled the CCP right before the firestorm bombs dropped, and that's why there's such a high population of Mandarin speakers there."

"One of the cities has land cannons," Bishop chimed in. "They don't allow anyone to get near U-Cali if it seems they're part of Ex Cathedra. They've been killing *judges* for decades."

I had another bizarre thought then, when I imagined the people of U-Cali. The problem with them—and why Ex Cathedra figured they would eventually win the war—was that only one city was actively fighting. The other cities in U-Cali sent supplies to the front line, but never people. If the cannons ever fell, or too many soldiers from that small city of U-Cali died, Ex Cathedra would finally break in and continue their onslaught until they reached the Pacific Ocean.

Again, I tried to imagine how *my* nation could be different.

What did I need to do to make sure Sanctuary survived?

The problem was all the enemies nearby, and a severe lack of options for dealing with them. I glanced down at my 9mm. We had exactly ten bullets left for my handgun. Once we were out, we'd need to find more, or else this would be useless, just like when I had charged Theon in the command center.

Should I focus all my efforts on getting guns?

Should I focus more on building something beautiful?

Should I force my citizens to help, even if they'd rather not?

Ex Cathedra forced everyone to be unified, even if they didn't want that—which led to people hating their own nation. U-Cali allowed each city to do its own thing—which led to a weaker nation that was struggling to hold its own against another, even though they had superior tech.

Thinking over all these options made me realize something important. I couldn't allow the threat of violence to come to my people. War changed everything. If U-Cali didn't have to fight, maybe they would grow powerful, and if Ex Cathedra focused on using their factories to produce medicine and crafting materials, maybe they wouldn't be so reviled.

I didn't know . . .

"What's wrong, Kit-Kat?" Bishop asked.

"I'm just thinking."

"We can all see that."

When I glanced up, I realized Brecht, Vega, and Levi were all paying attention to me. The Teth didn't have eyes to stare, but that was basically what they were doing the whole time.

"It's fine, I was just thinking about Sanctuary," I muttered. "How close are we to this park?"

"We're not far now." Brecht pointed to a cluster of pine trees not far from us. "There's a road through there, and once we spot all the signs, you'll know we're close." He lifted his gaze—slightly—and then pointed to a couple pillars of smoke before he quickly turned his gaze back to the ground. "You can tell they're in the middle of cooking food."

He was right.

Those were cooking fires.

"All right," I said. "Let's stick to the shadows."

CHAPTER TWENTY-EIGHT

We slunk through the shadowy nooks and crannies of the city's outskirts, ducking behind old farmhouses and even a toppled-over water tower. The closer we got to the city's park, the more the scent of smoke filled the air.

As we stopped behind a rusty tractor the size of a small house, Bishop whispered, "Ex Cathedra doesn't have any Teth as allies, right?"

"They kill any they find," I whispered back.

Brecht practically choked on his air. He whirled on me, crestfallen. "What did you just say?"

"They kill the Teth. En masse." I shook my head. "Ex Cathedra is all about reunited humanity—not the Teth. They see the aliens as the reason humanity fell from grace. They have an entire sermon and religious order about the parallels of *taking the information of the aliens* as *taking the apple of wisdom from the Garden of Eden.* That's why they picked the name they did."

"Ex Cathedra?" Brecht asked. "What does it mean?"

"It means *with ultimate authority*—like, they're infallible and follow God's will. Like the Pope from ancient times would be *ex cathedra.*"

It was awkward explaining this to someone who hadn't grown up in the wasteland. It was obvious to me because I had listened to the many sermons about how A-tech was the undoing of all humanity—but it was said by the same people who used the judge power armor to enforce their will on others. They clearly didn't mind using the A-tech, even if they proclaimed it evil.

"Let's just focus on the task at hand," I whispered.

We moved around the tractor, with Vega and Levi moving with an eerie silent grace, blending into the darkness as though they were born from it. In my mind, it made sense they came from space—they were like a little slice of the void. They led the way into the tree line. Unfortunately, the undergrowth in the forest was so overgrown, it practically came to my waist. The Teth used their claws to clean us a path, though they had to take their time with each swipe of their claws, careful not to make too much noise.

It didn't take long before we came to a chain-link fence that had been so overgrown, it looked like a wall of shrubs. I climbed up the side, wedging my boots into the vines and hoisting myself up to get a better view of the Ex Cathedra encampment.

The park was a beautiful oasis amidst the ruins. Well, it would've been, had the soldiers not been here. There were makeshift tents, small cooking fires, and at least a hundred brown-uniformed soldiers milling about the large, rectangular park. The place had a rustic, almost charming feel to it, like a camping trip organized as a team-building exercise.

I climbed back down the green wall and landed in the shrubs with a *thump*. As I brushed myself off, I sighed.

"I didn't see Gascoigne," I muttered. "But I didn't see any of the judges, to be honest."

"Their power armor is being kept at the other end of the park," Brecht stated.

"Okay. Maybe we should just follow this fence along the outside, then." I pointed through the trees. It would be easy to walk around the park—it would just take a while.

We followed it around. I kept a hand on the fence as we went, just to make sure it actually was still the fence and not random growths of vines that were trying to trick us. Our movements were deliberate and silent, which I thought was a struggle for Bishop. The overgrown foliage provided excellent cover, but it also made progress painfully slow. Every rustle of a leaf or snap of a twig seemed amplified in the quiet morning air.

As we made our way around, I heard the shouts and laughs of conversation in the park. At one point, there was a yell for order. I stopped to glance over the top of the fence again, only to see soldiers mobilizing. Half the forces were planning on leaving.

Or perhaps they were going to scour the city to rid it of the remaining Iron-Blooded.

I slid back down and continued.

The tension in the air was as thick as the undergrowth we navigated through. At one point, the fence was torn in half by a stubborn pine tree that had sprouted behind it. We walked around the trunk.

"I can't believe they see the Teth as a curse," Brecht whispered. "And to justify it with twisted religious doctrine . . ."

"Focus," I murmured. "We can talk about this once we get back to Sanctuary. Right now, we should get Gascoigne and go."

It bothered me how often we were separated from each other.

I blamed the wasteland—or in this case, the Wastewoods—but I knew on some level it was my fault. I should've created plans for situations like this. If I had a recovery plan in place for whenever someone went missing, we wouldn't have to improvise so much.

My list of improvements was growing longer and longer the more we were outside of Sanctuary . . .

We continued our cautious advance, my head practically on a swivel. As we neared the end of the park where Brecht mentioned the power armor might be kept, my heartbeat quickened.

We paused, crouching low in the bushes. Through the gaps in the foliage, I saw a clearing ahead, with a few tents and what looked like an armory. A group of soldiers was gathered there, their backs to us as they busied themselves with their morning routines.

"If Gascoigne is here, this will be her location," Brecht whispered.

Vega and Levi nodded, their alien forms melting farther into the shadows as they stood perfectly still afterward. Bishop glanced over at them, lifted an eyebrow, and then tried to do the same thing. He held his breath and leaned against a tree, holding as perfectly still as he could. He was still fairly visible, but less noticeable than before.

"Kita, you should wait here," Brecht stated. "For safety reasons."

Vega curtly nodded. "I agree. Levi and I will watch over you."

"I'm not fragile," I muttered.

Bishop waggled his hand back and forth. "Eh."

I narrowed my eyes in a sarcastic glare, but I didn't actually argue. We couldn't take the Teth into the park, but Brecht and Bishop might be able to sneak around without anyone catching them.

"Okay, just be quick," I said. "Look for Gascoigne, or the Mark VI, and then get back here."

* * *

I waited in the pine forest outside of the park, in the shadows next to Vega and Levi. It was cold—a terrible chill clung to the wind—and the Teth kept close.

I glanced over at Levi. "Vega told me your eggs were crushed."

Levi nodded. "*Architect Riven ordered the outrider eggs be smashed during the last birth cycle. They were no longer needed, and the food they would require was too much a cost for their existence, so they were terminated in favor of more innovator eggs.*"

That . . . sounded like something a Teth architect would say. They were so cold, and logical, that death was more a number in an equation than a very real life consequence that held emotion.

"I'm glad you joined us," I whispered. "Your eggs won't be smashed while you're with us in Sanctuary."

"*I won't ever have any eggs,*" Levi stated. "*Since I have no architect, I will become sad and barren.*"

"We have an architect."

Levi tensed, clearly interested in this new development. I probably shouldn't have said anything, because it wasn't like I knew much about Levi, but I figured instilling hope into my new follower wasn't a bad thing.

I was about to explain more, when an explosion of sound rocked the whole park. Then the ground shook, and I almost toppled over. Vega grabbed me and steadied me.

For a moment, I thought I was going to bear witness to yet another battle—perhaps the Iron-Blooded versus Ex Cathedra all over again—but then I realized there wasn't *that* much noise. I ran to the fence and pulled myself to the top in order to get a better view. As I hung there, Vega walked over and offered his shoulders, so I had something to stand on. With my boots firmly on his muscular body, I stared out over the park.

Welp—I found Gascoigne.

There she was, wearing the JUDGE-X0 power armor, Mark VI variant. It was a steel alloy exoskeleton, at least ten feet tall, with metal so scratch-free and beautiful, it practically glittered silver. It was the shape of a human, with arms and legs and a helmet that was large enough to hold a head and also provide a screen visor. There were vents on the neck, and lights to indicate the power cell situation.

Everything was working at full power.

Gascoigne was practically in the middle of the park, standing with such confidence it bordered on audacious. She had busted in through the fence on the side of the park opposite of me, clearly not giving a damn that she had to smash her way through tents and a few sleeping soldiers. The legs of her power armor were splattered in scarlet gore.

A plasma blade flared to life on the right arm, jutting out of the wrist on the power armor, glowing with a hot blue intensity.

Her feminine voice, warped by the armor's mask, echoed a bit. "Guess who's back, fuckers?"

Some of the soldiers—foolishly—opened fire on her.

Gascoigne didn't even flinch.

The bullets pinged harmlessly off the power armor. Then she moved with an agility that belied the suit's size, stomp-running towards her attackers, the soldiers who stood absolutely no chance. Technically, the speed of reactions the exoskeletons were capable of was determined by the mental acuity of the driver . . .

Each step caused the ground to tremble slightly.

The soldiers, realizing too late what they had done, darted in all different directions. Gascoigne trampled them, the steel boots of her exoskeleton merciless. The soldiers were shouting, screaming, and some flung themselves out of the park, trying to flee as fast as possible. Two soldiers even ran over to where I was, but they clearly didn't care that I was here. They hurried over the fence and just kept going, barely looking back.

The soldiers who died instantly in Gascoigne's attacks were the lucky ones. A few soldiers were only half stomped, their legs broken, but most of their bodies intact. They lay screaming on the ground, calling for help—one man calling for his mother—but everyone was in such a panic, no one stopped to help the injured.

A few lunatics flung themselves into tents, as though they could wait this out, hidden from view.

Gascoigne's HUD system that made up her face mask could use thermal imaging to detect nearby people. Hiding wasn't a viable option.

Gascoigne lunged, the plasma blade cutting through the air and cleaving through a tent as if it were made of paper. The terrified screams of soldiers filled the air, but were quickly silenced.

I watched, my heart pounding, as two Ex Cathedra judges emerged from the tents. They wore JUDGE-X0 exoskeletons as well, but unlike Gascoigne's, theirs were painted in bright red and black, with the word "JUDGE" written in handprints down the right leg. Ex Cathedra always painted their power armor to give them a "uniform" look and hide any damage they might have sustained over the years.

Bishop and Brecht had been investigating near the judge tent—but I hadn't seen them during all this carnage. I wondered if they realized Gascoigne was even here.

I wondered if *she* knew they were here.

"Goddammit," I whispered to myself.

One of the things I needed to do in Sanctuary was reestablish the rule that everyone needed to carry personal radios around with them. At all times. We wouldn't lose each other if we could use short-wave radio to speak to one another.

Most people out on the wasteland used that, though it was always risky. Other people could hear the communications as well, and some people took advantage of that—especially rail gangs or raiders.

The two Ex Cathedra judges moved to engage Gascoigne, their own suits bulkier and less refined than the Mark VI. They were wearing Mark III variants—I could tell by the clunkier vents and the larger attachments on the shoulders and the hands.

The Mark III didn't have a plasma blade, but it did have a normal steel blade meant to be used as a tool. The judges curled their left hands into fists, and eighteen-inch blades extended from their suits' gauntlets.

Both the judges moved to flank Gascoigne, and they charged with their blades, probably hoping to cut through Gascoigne's armor and disable her.

One slashed at her shoulder, but the *clang* of reinforced steel hitting reinforced steel told the world that the Mark VI wasn't going to be disabled that easily.

In response, Gascoigne was a whirlwind of destruction. They struck at her, hitting with a *clang* and *clang*, but she didn't care. She swung her plasma blade in a deadly arc, slicing through one suit's arm and rendering its weapon useless. The judge tried to back away, but Gascoigne showed no mercy. With a swift motion, she thrust the blade through the suit's torso, the sparks and sizzles filling the air.

I could practically smell the metal melt, and the flesh within cook.

"*We should run,*" Levi said in Tethlite, drawing me out of my thoughts.

I took a deep breath. "No. That's my ally. We're okay."

Levi didn't respond to that.

The judge, seeing his comrade fall, attempted to retreat.

Which was . . . an interesting choice. I hadn't seen a judge decide to flee before. Perhaps they weren't used to fighting such an advanced suit as Gascoigne's . . .

Gascoigne was relentless.

She leapt, her strength and power enhanced by the power armor, and landed in front of the judge, cutting off their escape. The judge tried to fight, swinging a heavy metal fist, but Gascoigne caught it, her suit's strength overpowering theirs. With a heavy swing of her plasma blade, Gascoigne cut through the arm of the Mark III.

It wasn't a clean, easy swipe. It was the kind where she had to drag it through the metal, melting more steel, and then flesh, as the judge thrashed in an attempt to get away. The *clang* of the power armor rang out over the park. Almost all the other soldiers had fled at this point—they left most of their supplies in their haste to save their own lives.

I couldn't help but feel a mixture of awe and fear. Gascoigne, at least in the Mark VI, was unstoppable. She kicked the judge, knocking it off-balance, the *smash* of her blow so loud it shook the park. Then, with a final, swift motion, Gascoigne thrust down with her blade, also puncturing the other suit straight through the chest, killing the pilot.

When she pulled out her weapon, the exoskeleton collapsed to the ground with a bone-shattering thud. Sparks flew out of the chest, meaning the battery cells hadn't been damaged—but everything else was a mess.

I wished Gascoigne hadn't destroyed the suits in the process of gaining a victory . . .

But I wasn't about to complain. The Ex Cathedra judges were some of the worst around. We really didn't want them as enemies lingering nearby.

CHAPTER TWENTY-NINE

Gascoigne switched off her plasma blade, which was a great idea. That weapon drained the suit's battery cells like nothing else.

I hopped down from Vega's shoulders, my mind racing. Gascoigne had single-handedly decimated the Ex Cathedra presence in the park. While it was a victory for us, the display of raw power was a stark reminder of the capabilities of the JUDGE-X0 Mark VI.

I wished I had been the one piloting it—though jealousy really wasn't the appropriate emotion at this time . . .

"Let's go," I said to Vega and Levi. They both hesitated, and I shook my head. "It really is okay. Gascoigne won't hurt us."

"*The exoskeletons remove emotions,*" Levi whispered in Tethlite.

Levi was correct. The exoskeleton power armor had special helmets that connected to the driver's head. They sent electrical signals to the brain, stimulating certain hormone production in their adrenal glands. That kept the judges focused and angry, so they didn't buckle during combat to fear or cowardice.

But that was why most people feared the judges. They were modern-day berserkers.

That was why it had been so shocking to see the second judge attempt to retreat.

Or perhaps . . .

It wasn't a retreat, but more a regrouping. What if there were other Ex Cathedra judges here? It got me nervous.

I scrabbled over the fence. Levi and Vega joined me. With my heart pounding, I quickly scanned the wreckage to see if Bishop and Brecht were here. To my relief, I saw them leap over the far fence and they joined me in the graveyard of Ex Cathedra bodies.

"Good to see you both safe," I called out as Bishop and Brecht approached, their faces etched with a mix of awe and concern.

Brecht wiped his brow, his eyes scanning the park. "That was . . . intense."

Bishop nodded, a rare seriousness to his expression. "Gascoigne's a force to be reckoned with in that thing. But at least she's on our side, right? I'd hate to be one of her tally marks."

I couldn't help but agree, though a part of me remained wary. The power of the JUDGE-X0 Mark VI, in the hands of someone as capable as Gascoigne, was both an asset and a potential threat. "We need to talk to her."

Gascoigne stood, still clad in the Mark VI, in the middle of the park. As we approached, she turned her attention to a few twitching bodies on the battlefield. With all the reverence someone would give a dying insect, she stepped on the dying Ex Cathedra soldiers, crushing them under her steel foot until they popped like overripe ticks.

"Gascoigne?" I called out, stopping a good twenty feet away.

"There you are, Kita," she said through her helmet, her voice distorted with a robotic sound. "Sorry I didn't find you right away. I got distracted."

"Where have you been?" Brecht shouted. "We were worried."

Vega stood tall—he was the only one of us that even rivaled the height of Gascoigne's suit. He seemed on edge, as though he didn't trust that Gascoigne wouldn't hurt us.

After she finished crushing another helpless soldier, Gascoigne pivoted and gave us her full attention, her glittering power armor now stained with the blood of our enemies.

"I got distracted," Gascoigne said again through her suit's helmet. "I realized I knew a few people here, and I needed to pay them a visit."

She pointed with her gauntlet over to the downed judges. They weren't going anywhere—but perhaps we could pick apart their suits for parts . . .

"These two," Gascoigne stated. "And the commander of the forces here. I needed to settle a few debts, so I waited until they were packing up to leave before I struck." When she chuckled, it sounded overtly sinister. Again, I agreed with Bishop—I was glad she was now on our side.

"Don't you think highly of Ex Cathedra?" Brecht asked, clearly baffled. "You talk about them all the time—like your homeland. Something you hold dear."

Gascoigne stomped over to us. When she was within a few feet, the Mark VI knelt, and the front *hissed* as it opened, like two hands with fingers intertwined slowly coming apart. Once fully opened, Gascoigne was exposed to us, just sitting inside like the exoskeleton was her throne.

She stood, and I spotted the cables connected to the back of her neck. She disconnected them, sighed, and then stepped out to face us.

She wore a pair of skin-tight workout shorts and a white tank top drenched in sweat. Every inch of her looked like she had been rolled around in the water before being dumped out of the power armor.

After a few breaths, Gascoigne wiped away the sweat from her brow and glared at Brecht. "I talk about Ex Cathedra because that's all I know. I don't *enjoy* them—they're my homeland because I wasn't lucky at the genetic lottery—and I'd rather they burn in nuclear fire."

"Oh." Brecht rubbed the side of his neck. "I see. You didn't really express your hatred to me when we spoke."

"You asked about my childhood," Gascoigne intoned. "So I told you about my childhood. I kept from being overly negative because no one seems to enjoy that."

Bishop snorted. "Your pillow talk was about Ex Cathedra? You're a hoot."

"You got a better idea?" Gascoigne snapped.

"Yeah. Ask what you can do better next time." Bishop grabbed at his crotch and smirked. "We only live a short time in this world—might as well get good at the only skill that matters."

My face heated. I dragged my hand down the side, frowning. "R-Right . . . Well, I'm glad you're okay, Gascoigne. I was also worried."

"Yeah, well, unlike you, I don't tend to get kidnapped," she muttered.

"Didn't *I* kidnap you?" I lifted an eyebrow. "In Boulder?"

"That doesn't count, smartass. You have a tendency to drag *everyone* you come across along for the ride."

"We have someone again," Bishop muttered, stifling a laugh. "Literally. We left him in the car."

Gascoigne groaned and rolled her eyes. "No doubt one of our enemies."

"It's one hundred percent one of our enemies." Bishop couldn't stop himself from chuckling.

Brecht stepped closer to Gascoigne, ignoring all other commentary. "Well, I'm happy you're here. For a moment, I thought you were going to go back to Ex Cathedra . . ."

Gascoigne's expression softened. She folded her arms over her chest and leaned her weight back onto one of her feet. "My new opinion is—fuck everyone except our new home in Sanctuary. I don't care for any other nations, any other people, or any other things."

"What about the kids of other nations?" Bishop pointed to her and then clicked his tongue in disapproval. "*Tsk*. Got ya there. You can't be a cruel and heartless bitch who hates kids."

Gascoigne sneered. "I'm not a monster. We can absorb enemy orphaned children into our ranks. They make for good workers, after all."

After stepping close to me, Bishop placed both his hands on the side of my stomach. "Hey," he playfully said, "don't say mean things like that in front of Lump. We're trying to teach him—or her—that we're the light in the darkness of the world, thank you very much."

Gascoigne immediately met my gaze, all of her hardness returning. "You're pregnant?"

"I'm glad this is going to be the first thing we talk about with everyone," I sarcastically stated. Then I knocked Bishop's hands away, my face hot. "Do we have to keep mentioning it? I feel like we're bringing it up too much."

"I'm glad you're finally starting to take my advice." Gascoigne smirked as she swept back her short hair with a free hand. "Once you're done baking that one, you should get on another. We need as many as we can get our hands on."

Brecht held up a finger. "You know, I did suggest *other* women could have children."

"I told you—I don't think all my organs work as intended. The Teth *fixed me*, but that's in big fat quotes. I'm . . . broken."

Architect Riven and the others had fixed Gascoigne so she wasn't dependent on power armor to live. Hadn't they healed her fully? It made me sad to think there were still lingering problems.

But then I glanced around at all the death and carnage, and how we needed to get back to Sanctuary. The smell of scorched metal and burnt earth mingled unpleasantly in the air.

"You did well, Gascoigne," I muttered. "Your actions here . . . they've given us an advantage."

"How so?" she growled. "We've probably made Ex Cathedra a permanent enemy. I mean, they were already our enemy, but now they'll know we're powerful enough to kill a few judges. And they won't like that."

"W-Well, that's true. But we can use all their supplies. Even their broken power armor. All of it. We should take it back to Sanctuary and use it all to help our people." I snapped my fingers. "And we should dig through the wreckage at the Davis Space Force Base. Anything there we can take back as well."

Gascoigne nodded once. "Good. I like this plan. We'll need a shit ton of weapons to fight everyone when the time comes."

She took a few steps back toward the Mark VI. Then she glanced over at me.

"We're the only two who can pilot this," she said.

I nodded once. "You should take it." But then I glanced over at the downed judges. "Wait . . . We should take the pilots."

"The corpses?"

Bishop laughed a little harder. "We've moved on from *kidnapping* to *grave robbing*."

I shook my head. "We need them. We can bring them back to DC at Sanctuary." We had an entire lab, and she was a trained medical doctor. The connectors on the back of the pilot's necks could be removed and reinserted into someone else.

Ex Cathedra did that all the time with their judges.

We could do it, too—and then more people besides Gascoigne and me could pilot the exoskeletons.

"Are you sure you don't want to take the Mark VI for a little spin?" Gascoigne asked. "Just for old times' sake?"

"Uh . . . I don't know if the helmet attachment will affect Lump."

The way the power armor messed with the brain, and alerted chemicals, made me fearful. I doubted the suits were designed with pregnant pilots in mind.

Gascoigne smiled. "Fine by me. I hate my soft, fleshy body—I crave the certainty of steel."

CHAPTER THIRTY

It quickly became apparent that we couldn't carry everything in our arms. Ex Cathedra had quite a bit of supplies here, and two downed JUDGE-X0 Mark III exoskeletons were too valuable to just leave behind. We had to move it all, so we spent a lot of our efforts looking for a way. Thankfully, Gascoigne knew where to look—Ex Cathedra had to transport all of this here in the first place, and in their haste to flee the Mark VI, the soldiers had left two of their troop transport vans behind in the process.

If I drove a van, Bishop drove a van, Brecht took Sanctuary's car, and Gascoigne piloted the Mark VI, we could move a considerable amount of material with just the four of us.

None of our vehicles were the type the Teth could drive, which just meant that Vega and Levi would need to be passengers. They were both strong, and capable of moving the ruined judge armor into one of the vans with just the two of them, but it was a shame their lack of sight prevented them from driving human vehicles.

As we sifted through the Ex Cathedra encampment, I grew nervous. We didn't have all the time in the world. Gascoigne was right—they would be back. And all the soldiers who had escaped, and saw us, would report on what happened here. For all I knew, Ex Cathedra could already be sending more troops to this location.

We had to hurry.

Out of all the things here, the best equipment was the munitions. We wanted the rifles, ammo, body armor, and grenades—and boy, did Ex Cathedra have a lot of them.

They had left behind dozens of high-powered rifles, some sleek and untouched, others rugged and battle worn. Alongside them were crates filled with ammunition, even bullets for the 9mm, for which I was eternally grateful.

When I searched through a smaller box near the command tent—well, the *ruined* tent—I found a box of grenades, both fragmentation and smoke. These were some of my favorite types of weapons, mostly because of how devastating they could be when used in the right circumstances. Also, because aiming was a little less important.

"Look what I found," Bishop said in a cheery voice from across the encampment.

He held up a slashed piece of a tent that had a medical cross stitched across it.

"If there's any medical supplies left, take them all," I said.

We could never have enough medicine. Ever. Human beings would get sick from now until the end of time, and the more ways we had to deal with that, the better.

Once I finished gathering the grenades, I walked over to Bishop and found that he had unearthed a treasure trove of valuable items. Bandages, antiseptics, painkillers, and even some field surgery kits. These were as valuable as any weapon, and I was surprised how many of them weren't completely smashed by Gascoigne's rampage.

Once we gathered all that, and brought it to our ever-growing pile of *things to keep*, I realized that Brecht and Vega had found communication equipment. I rushed over, elated they had managed to gather portable radios. With these, we could intercept enemy communications and coordinate our movements more effectively.

"This is perfect," I said as I examined them. They had no damage.

"I was told communication was key for battle," Brecht stated. "It was my first priority when searching."

Which reminded me of the Davis Space Force Base. There had been a communication tower that was far more advanced than anything we had been using. Sure, the fire had probably damaged it, but perhaps—since we now had two vans—we could sift through the wreckage of that location as well, and bring back even *more* supplies.

I liked this plan.

Gascoigne, using the Mark VI, carried over dozens of boxes of nonperishable food rations. In a world where every meal was uncertain, this was a significant boost to our logistics.

Once she set them down, she pointed to a smaller box. "That is a bunch of bullshit I found in the armory tent."

I opened the lid and found a small number of useful items—ten night-vision goggles, a map of Montana, twenty flares, and even fifteen gas masks. I loved gas masks. They outright prevented a lot of chemical warfare, though not too many people used that in the open air of the wasteland.

I touched each piece of equipment and nodded.

"Thank you, Gascoigne." Then I glanced up at her helmet—the only part of her not covered in dry blood. "Let's load this all up, and then take the transport vans over to the military base. I think we can salvage a lot of supplies from the fire. We should, uh, pack the vans and our car with as many things as we can carry."

She nodded once. "And if the Iron-Blooded intervene?"

"Well, you still have power in your battery cells, right? Your job will be to make sure none of our enemies harass us."

The devastated Davis Space Force Base was a much larger area to investigate than the park encampment Ex Cathedra had used. To make matters worse, the day was already half over by the time we drove our vehicles over, and while the sky was too overcast, and the sun barely illuminating the world, it was still better than the light we'd get at night, which meant we'd have to be quick about this.

The spotlights the Iron-Blooded had used were clearly no longer operational. One of the spotlight towers had completely collapsed, and the other two were so charred they were half leaning over, the light face blackened, and the electronics all exposed and mostly melted.

We started searching around the one building that was mostly made of concrete. It had withstood the destruction of the fire, at least mostly, and we all split up in order to sift through the ashes.

Already, we had a use for the gas masks. Bishop, Brecht, and myself each donned one of the masks to move the ashes aside; that way, it wouldn't clog our lungs.

Unfortunately, there were still some live embers around, which meant we had to be careful with where we dug. We hadn't found any good gloves in the Ex Cathedra encampment, after all.

As I searched, I found a room that was mostly protected from the flames. Inside was a sort of mini library of technical manuals and blueprints. I scooped most of them up and stuffed them into my pack, knowing I'd want them for our own personal library within Sanctuary.

I wanted *all* the knowledge I could get my hands on.

The blueprints were mostly detailing aircraft and weapon systems, but there were other useful schematics, including A-tech breathing apparatuses for space travel. Not that we would go to space anytime soon, but still . . .

I also found a storehouse for old United States military uniforms and gear. It was funny to see the symbol of the old nation past. While most were damaged beyond use, a few pieces were intact enough to be utilized for parts or repairs. They reminded me of my grandfather, so I took a few for my own personal use.

Silly, I knew, but I did miss my grandfather more and more, it seemed.

I wondered if he would be proud of what I had accomplished, or just saddened by what the world had become.

I tried not to think about that too much.

"Kita!" Bishop called out, his voice carrying over the ashy ruins of the base.

I poked my head out of the secured storage room and shouted back, "Yes?" The gas mask made it difficult to see everything clearly, and I had to wipe the ash from the glass over my face just to make out the nearby terrain.

"Just checking on you. I'm sending over Vega."

Before I could protest, the Teth warrior bounded over the wrecked bits of the base, kicking up ash and debris into the air as he moved. Once he was by my side, I realized his matte black skin was almost entirely gray from caked-on ashes now.

"You can breathe through all this?"

Vega lifted his head and nodded. "Unlike humans, the Teth require much less oxygen to function. Our bodies filter much of what we breathe before it reaches our lungs."

I touched his shoulder as I spoke—since I knew the Teth preferred physical contact. "Thank you for watching over me."

"It is my caste—my duty—kin of different blood."

Then Vega touched my shoulder with one of his smaller crafter hands. The spindly little fingers felt like a spider's, but I held back a shudder. This was just the Teth's way of showing trust and affection. It would be insulting to be disgusted.

Together, we moved over to the next portion of the base that was surprisingly intact. It was practically a whole shed that was untouched by the flames—it had a standing roof, and walls, and even a door made of thick steel.

As soon as I drew close, I understood why it had survived.

The door had a trefoil mark—the symbol that meant *radioactive materials*. Whatever was in this room was dangerous, and the military forces had clearly been afraid of it catching fire, so they placed it in a room that would never allow the blaze to touch whatever was within.

When I tried the handle, I realized I couldn't open it.

Did I want the materials within? It was probably fuel or chemicals, or maybe even byproduct waste from their high-tech airplanes.

I left the door and shook my head. I didn't need any of that. I needed things to build my civilization, and since we had such limited space to bring things back, I needed to focus on objects that were extremely useful, not moderately so.

"There," Vega said, pointing to a pile of ashes. "There is something underneath."

"You can tell that?" I asked.

The Teth warrior nodded. "I sense it every time we step over this area. The vibrations are off. There's a hollow space there. Something within."

We walked over together, and then Vega did most of the digging with his larger claws. The ash flew through the air, spiraling around like a disgusting puff of snow. I was so happy I had the gas mask, I almost laughed. Imagining all this ash in my lungs almost had me empathetically coughing.

Vega dug with the intensity of a dog searching out a bone.

It didn't take him long to reach a room that was part of a basement section for the base. There was a hatch, and he lifted it up once he had enough ash and debris pushed to the side. It *creaked* open loud enough that my ears hurt.

"Here," he said again.

I carefully walked over, sliding down the little crater of ashes, and then slipped into the basement. There were no lights. The base had clearly suffered too much damage for that.

But the dim lighting coming in through the hatch allowed me to see that the walls of this area were covered in racks that held power tools. There were large tools for soldering big pieces of metal, but also smaller tools for nails, computers, and welding.

These were great finds.

Another useful tool was hanging on the wall—a scouting drone. It was the small kind, about the size of a person's head, and came with a remote control and screen. From what I understood, people used them all the time before the Forever Winter, even for recreation, but since they were so small and delicate, they were mostly gone from the world now.

Here was one, so intact.

"Thank you, Vega," I called up to him. "These tools are perfect."

He snorted—in a happy way.

I took as many as I could and then located a ladder up to the hatch. It was difficult carrying so many things in my pack, but I forced myself up regardless. Vega must've heard me straining, because he took the pack from me afterward.

"*I'll carry it,*" he said in Tethlite. "*Don't strain yourself while you're carrying a child.*"

He seemed upset now.

I didn't argue with him.

"Kita! *Kita,* come quick! You're gonna want to see this."

After clearing the ashes from my gas mask again, I trudged through the ashes and made my way toward Bishop's shouting. He was standing near the half-charred warehouse with Gascoigne in her Mark VI armor. They were by one of the opened doors—the kind meant to allow trucks inside—and they both motioned me over.

It took a while, because the ash gave out under my feet more than once, but I managed to get to them before the sun fully set.

Once I was there, I glanced inside the warehouse. The roof had collapsed, meaning everything was covered in a thick layer of dust, ash, aluminum slabs, and debris.

Fortunately, that wasn't enough to damage the equipment held in the warehouse.

Much like the hyper-advanced airplanes that were here at the base, this warehouse had two advanced exoskeletons. Both were silver—and one shiny—with design elements that clearly resembled a jet plane. They had wing-like attachments and thrusters, and were much sleeker than any power armor I had seen before—almost feminine in design.

And on the side of both exoskeletons were the letters and numbers: JUDGE-Y47 Mark VI.

CHAPTER THIRTY-ONE

I hurried over to examine them, my hands trembling. Levi had told me these were here, so I wasn't *shocked*, I was just in awe at how beautiful they were. Even dirty, they were the most advanced pieces of military equipment I had ever seen. These could *fly*? That seemed insane to me.

I carefully hopped over a piece of debris and touched the side of the armor.

It was cold.

It was hard to believe that these machines, with their aerodynamic forms and thrusters reminiscent of aircraft, were capable of flight. I had a difficult time imagining how I would even pilot that. Flying seemed . . .

Like a thing of the past.

Gascoigne, still within her own exoskeleton, watched me with what I imagined was curiosity. "Never seen anything like these, have you?" she asked. Then she snorted. "They must be special if they have *you* shaking like a leaf."

I shook my head, still trying to process everything. "They're incredible. We just need to, uh, fix the battery portion of the armor. Apparently, they can't take normal cells. The Iron-Blooded would've used them against us if they could've."

"What's with the wings?" Bishop asked through his gas mask. "They can't fly, right? I mean"—he laughed, more to himself than anyone else— "that's silly, right?"

"According to the base's records, these can fly," I stated. "But flying one of these isn't like driving a car. It'll take skill and practice."

"Pfft." Gascoigne stomped over to one. "I can fly this bitch. Just give me a day to adjust to the controls."

Bishop dusted ashes off the second exoskeleton. "Can you imagine the advantage we'd have with these in the air? Just . . . damn."

I nodded, already envisioning the possibilities. These exoskeletons could change everything for us—in combat, in exploration, in asserting our presence in this fractured world. But they also represented a significant responsibility. The power they offered was immense, and it needed to be wielded wisely.

What would my grandfather do?

Brecht slid into the warehouse from one of the side entrances, the ashes kicking up all around him as he moved. He waved his hand through the air, clearing it away until he had a better look at the exoskeletons.

"Are we taking these back to Sanctuary?" he asked, a hint of excitement in his voice that could be heard even through his gas mask.

"Yes," I replied. "We'll transport them along with the other equipment we've gathered. These suits could be the key to our future."

"What if they can't fit? We only have so much room."

"We'll *make* them fit," Gascoigne growled.

I nodded along with her words. We needed these more than anything else we had found so far.

Levi and Vega carefully navigated their way into the warehouse, examining the exoskeletons with a mixture of curiosity and caution. They had to touch them to fully appreciate was going on, and after the two of them had "investigated" the suits, they were practically clean.

As the sun set, leaving us with just the dark, overcast sky, I felt a surge of hope. With the JUDGE-Y47s and the other resources we had salvaged, we had the tools to forge a new path . . .

We just had to get them back to Sanctuary in one piece.

We had a lot of supplies.

Two damaged JUDGE-X0 exoskeletons. Two faulty JUDGE-Y47 exoskeletons. Ammo. Rifles. Medical supplies. Blueprints. A hard drive with Iron-Blooded information. Theon Sellers, a human architect. Body armor. Food rations. Atomic batteries. Two new troop transports. Power tools.

Hell, we even had a new Teth—the outrider, Levi.

In the half a week I had been kidnapped from Sanctuary, I had somehow amassed a metric fuck ton of supplies for my burgeoning civilization.

I wasn't about to get a pat on the back or an award for turning a bad situation into a good one, but I felt like it was becoming my specialty.

It took us several days to make it back to Sanctuary, but along the way, I rested as much as possible. My dreams, restless, were of when my sister was alive—when I was afraid of the Teth. It made it hard to sleep, at first, but then Bishop kept his arm around me whenever I started to nod off, and the nightmares left.

When we made it back to Sanctuary, people came out to greet us.

Grizzled Garret stood in the middle of the group like a bear man, his hands on his hips, his mouth turned down in a slight frown. He did smile once he saw me, though, which was a surprise. I got out of the vehicle and headed over the cracked parking lot. Everyone from Sanctuary hurried toward the vans to start with the unloading process. Many of them stopped to thank me and a few even shook my hand.

"Kita," he called out as he strode over. "Thank God you're okay. We were worried."

"It was nothing. I was just—"

He wrapped me in a bear hug, and my face heated up.

"That crane is workin' overtime," he said as he ended the embrace. "We can't have you gallivantin' off. We need you here."

"I thought . . . I shouldn't be the only one handling everything?" I asked him, repeating his own words with a hint of sarcasm. Didn't he want me to stay away?

Garret shook his head. Then he pointed at me. "Listen here—you should train some people, but that doesn't mean you should disappear. Having a foreman on the job is a good thing."

"Right." I motioned to the vans filled with supplies. "I brought things back with me. For Sanctuary. Once these vans are unpacked, we're going to make massive improvements. I, uh, think we'll need them. For the future."

When our enemies came to attack.

But I didn't say that part aloud. I wanted to keep an optimistic tone and demeanor. This was a good day. We were going to improve. We were going to be a brand-new city with all our demands met.

"We'll get on that." Garret patted me on the shoulder. "You just get some rest. You've got bags the size of the moon under your eyes."

I chuckled and nodded.

Yes. Sleep was priority number one. And then . . . rebuilding.

That was my top priority until all of Sanctuary was in tip-top shape.

* * *

Hunger woke me early.

I turned over in the bed and glanced at Bishop. For some reason, he was sleeping half on the blankets, his broad, muscular, and tally-mark-covered back displayed for the world to see.

I was half tempted to resume my sleeping, but I had a lot to do. Last night, seeing everyone again, had been fun. But given that Ex Cathedra would probably be coming to look for us soon, I didn't have time to waste—I need to start checking items off on my list as soon as possible.

And I *was* hungry.

I threw on some heavier clothing, and headed to the front of our little living space. I wanted to get some of the good food, the fresh—well, fresher—stuff, but my mind was already awhirl with plans. I decided to wait till Bishop was awake for a real meal. Instead, I grabbed a hardtack biscuit, treating my hunger like any other problem to be solved.

It tasted like how the wasteland looked.

That was fine.

I walked from our personal space in Section Three and made the relatively long trek into the main part of Section One as I chewed on the tough and tasteless biscuit.

The lights had been dimmed, since it was still early, but there were enough of them for me to make my way to my first, and possibly most important, stop—Dr. Claire's clinic.

I knocked on the door once I got there. DC answered, surprising me. I had assumed one of her assistants would answer.

"Who's there?" she asked.

"It's me, uh, Kita."

The door opened, and DC stared out at me. I was always surprised by her appearance—she had eyes filled with wisdom, set in the face of a twenty-five-year-old model. I'd managed to find a lot of things, and steal them, on my brief involuntary trip, but I had never found one of the implants that would make me immortal, like her.

Again, that was fine. It was a problem I could solve at another time.

"What can I do for you, Kita?" she asked. She lifted a perfect eyebrow. "You're staring an awful lot."

"I have a quick question. And then a favor to ask."

DC regarded me with a curious look. She didn't normally seem so intrigued. "What question?"

"If I'm pregnant, would piloting a suit of power armor harm the child?"

That was probably too many bombshells to unload on someone, but DC didn't blink an eye. "As long as it's not uncomfortable due to your increased size, the exoskeletons won't harm the development of a child in the womb."

"Oh. Good."

"And what's the favor?"

"Well, I, um, had an idea. It's a bit weird, and it involves . . . bodies. But I was hoping you could help me with it."

Why was I so awkward?

DC smiled. "Well, with an intro like that, I'm intrigued. What's the situation?"

"Well, Gascoigne defeated two judges from Ex Cathedra. And by *defeated*, I mean, *stabbed through the chest with a plasma sword*. The, um, drivers are very dead. But the method by which they expired left their uplinks undamaged—the little implants on the back of their neck required for piloting the power armor. So I was wondering if you could . . ."

"Remove them?" DC asked. "And then, presumably, reinstall them in someone else? Like Brecht or Bishop, I assume?"

I nodded.

DC shook her head. "I don't think so. I can remove them fine, and while it's not my favorite activity, I've worked with more than enough cadavers that it won't be a problem. But I can't reinstall them without advanced medical equipment, supplies, and a fairly advanced facility. I know we have surgical tools here, but this is a *spinal implant*, essentially, hooked to the base of the brain, Kita. I need more. I'm sorry. I wish I could help."

"Well, I don't know if you had a chance to look through the supplies, but we . . . recovered—"

"Looted?" DC asked with a gentle smile.

"—looted a huge number of medical supplies. None of it was A-tech stuff, but we have blood, plasma, antiseptics—"

DC interrupted again. "But no facility?"

I held my breath for a long time. I hadn't shown the facilities to anyone, really. Except Quern, ironically. "Well . . . it'll need some cleaning, but we actually have advanced facilities below, in Section Four."

DC furrowed her brow. "We have advanced facilities and you didn't tell me? People could have *died*, Kita. I should've been informed about this immediately."

She had a point, but the labs weren't currently in working condition. "They're not, strictly speaking, medical facilities. More like . . . genetics labs for people and animals and plants. And a pathology lab, areas to test the experiments as they grew, even xenoscience facilities to work on aliens. They were researching a lot of things here."

I paused. I didn't really want to admit that there were prototype diseases for wiping out the Teth down below.

"Things?" Dr. Claire asked, as if reading my mind. "What does *things* mean?"

If I couldn't trust Dr. Claire, we were all in trouble anyway. "They were researching animal alterations, plant alterations, and . . . well . . . Teth-specific pathogens."

DC raised her eyebrow again at that.

I hurriedly continued. "The facilities they have are *very* advanced. It was all cutting-edge research being done days before the firestorm bombs dropped and the Forever Winter hit. But it has everything we could want. Far more than we need, really, to install the implants."

DC's face had smoothed back to its usual calm bedside demeanor. "Show me the facilities, please."

CHAPTER THIRTY-TWO

"You want me to do *what?*" Westley asked.

He was tinkering with some tools, trying to fix one that had obviously been damaged while repairing Section One. He stood near the wall of the massive "housing development" we had started, and was half paying attention to me, and half paying attention to his work.

I stood close, hoping to just speak with him, and not so loud that *everyone* heard what I was doing.

"I want you to help me repair the Mark III exoskeletons," I said. "I've seen you work with computers before—you've got a good mind, one suited for this stuff."

Truthfully, I could probably have fixed the suit of armor myself, but I wanted to get other competent people comfortable with A-tech, computers, and engineering work, just like Garret had said. If I trained others, they wouldn't need me to do everything per se.

Plus, Westley seemed to have an aptitude for it.

"I . . . I can try," he said. He placed his broken tool back on his equipment box and then stood. He wore a pair of ratty overalls and a clean white shirt. He had the appearance of someone who liked to work on machines—the hardware more than the software.

"Follow me."

I led the way into the back of Section One, where we had taken over some of the stored machines—and I had added some of the computers from Section Three as well as the tools we had taken from the space base and Ex Cathedra's encampment. The result was an impromptu-appearing metal frame in which one of the damaged Mark III was strapped, with a series of computers and cables on cheap tables, all strung together by coaxial cables and power lines. I had loaded all the schematics into the computers we had brought up—including the schematics for the Mark III suit currently clamped in.

It was now hooked to the HUD display of the less damaged suit by a series of cables, and another series of cables ran from one of our atomic batteries to the machine's HUD. The result was to give the computer access to the power suit's internal diagnostics.

Another cable ran to the nano-welder.

I took the nano-welder in my hand. One advantage of the nano-welder was that it didn't generate nearly as much heat as a normal welder, and you didn't need goggles. It could also do rather fundamental repairs if it had information.

"Wow," Westley said, glancing down at it. "Is that what I think it is?"

I nodded. "I'm glad you're excited. That'll make this a lot easier."

The disadvantage of a nano-welder was that you needed special gel, of which we had very little. But I planned to make up the difference by cannibalizing parts from the other Mark III.

I smiled up at Westley. "Okay, tell me what's missing from the suit, and what we can use to repair it with the minimum possible gel cost."

"H-How?" he asked nervously, not looking at me, reminding me of a crane more than anything as he hovered, slightly hunched over, his thick, post-war glasses nearly goggles.

"Just sit at the computer, figure out what's missing, and what components from the suit we could use to repair it—we have a spare."

Westley sat down at the computer. I tried to wait patiently, not focusing on everything else we needed to do, as he looked at the schematics. After a moment, Westley spoke again without looking up from the console. "Actually, the damage was catastrophic to the pilot, but only moderately bad for the suit."

His voice was entirely different when he was talking machines—confident and not at all embarrassed, a change from his usual mild stutter.

"Very catastrophic to the pilot," I quipped.

Westley poked the screen. "The blade went in through a cluster of power lines and a regulator right over the center of the chest. But there is a matching one on the *back* of the armor. You could take the matching cluster from the back of the other armor and simply plug it in—or very nearly plug it back in. The plasma blade vaporized—quite literally vaporized; it turned the metal into particulate matter and dispersed it—the connections to the other power lines."

"Interesting."

I had already known that, but I wanted Westley to feel confident. I waited for him to explain everything.

"But if you take the matching part and place it inside, you'll only need maybe an inch of wire at two of the points, two inches at the third, and the tiniest bit of gel. Most of the other suit will remain intact, although I'm not sure what purpose it would have."

I was impressed with how quickly Westley got it as well.

With some spring in my step, I walked over and pried the back of the spare suit up, carefully unhooking the power regulator and taking it over to the one I intended to repair. I placed it inside the suit, clamped it in place, and then went and got some of the wiring from the spare suit. After a bit, I had put everything where I needed it.

"Now what?" Westley asked, still not glancing up from the screen.

"You'll need to tell the nano-welder what to do. It's going to need to make six repairs to the standard A-tech power cable, so it should have a menu option. I'll hold the device in place, and you can control when it's on and off, getting the read-out from the computer."

"Will do," Westley said.

"You think you can handle this?"

He slouched, and then bit at his lip. "Well . . . I mean, I can try."

"Good. That's the spirit." I patted his arm, hoping it came off as *leader-y* and not *creepy.*

We had a little bit of spare gel, so if he messed up, I could fix everything.

But so far, he was turning out to be everything I had hoped.

The laboratory section was a mess of wires, computers, and extraneous machines, and enmeshed in the center of the mess, like the world's most incompetent spider, was Westley. I had given him a few hours alone, but now I wanted to check up on him.

I wasn't micromanaging, per se—but I was fearful he would damage the exoskeletons beyond repair.

"How goes the project?" I asked.

Westley popped his head up, his hand inside a glove. Another machine, an arm, moved with the glove as he turned to face me, knocking over a bench and sending tools and parts clattering across the floor.

A masculine guffaw came from the back, behind me. My heart briefly leaped to my throat—I'd been ambushed quite a few times in my short life—and I whirled around. Scrapyard Pete stood in the back corner, next to a pile of metal and machinery with far less computer parts.

He was a forty-something-year-old man, but he had retained his youthful vigor. When he glanced over, he seemed done with today, though. He half waved and then returned his attention to the scrap.

"Hello," I awkwardly muttered.

Westley ripped the glove off and dropped it. "Sorry, Kita, you surprised me."

He rushed over to grab some of the tools off the ground but tripped over the bench and went sprawling himself. He picked himself back up, rubbed his glowing red face, and put the tools back.

I felt oddly comfortable with Westley—he was one of the few human beings worse at social interactions than me.

It took the pressure off of dealing with him.

He finally stood again, facing me, his face glowing. "It's all working . . . I think. But without someone to plug in, I can't really test it—not the main part of it, at least."

"But the feedback works over long distances?" I asked.

Westley nodded. "Yeah. And for smaller things, I can make it work fine—like aiming as if something was in a person's hand, sure."

He held up the glove portion of the disassembled Mark III.

I walked over, gave everything a thorough look, and then smiled. I was hoping I was coming across as *approving*, to help encourage him to move faster. Gascoigne warned me relentlessly that we needed these machines. Ex Cathedra had hundreds of exoskeleton suits. We had . . . one and a half?

"But that's the easy part. The hard part will be getting control of an entire facility that's not compatible with human visualization, which is what this suit is set up to do. I'm sorry, Kita, but I have far too little knowledge of these systems to program that."

I sighed, but wasn't too surprised. A few days extra work with A-tech, and a history of poking around scavenged human computers, didn't make him a cyber-systems specialist.

"I guess for the first part, then, I need you," I said, turning to face Scrapyard Pete.

"Well, I've pretty much already put the design for what you want together. We've enough random parts and spare metal that I can easily make it, although it'll take a few weeks of work. Considerably less, if you can lend me the help of one of your boys and their power suit to move all the big parts and hold them in place. This is a hand assembly job, not factory work."

I nodded. "You'll get it done, then?"

"Yup. Won't even be hard, mentally. It's pretty basic, except for running the guts of the judge suit."

"I'll ask Bishop to help you out, once he has finished helping Grizzled Garret with the farms."

Scrapyard Pete looked at me. "You could almost certainly help quite a bit—you've a fine hand for any kind of systems, I've noticed."

I was briefly tempted, but shook my head. "I'm trying to learn to delegate. And I'm not really in a state to be climbing all over huge chunks of jagged metal in the sun regardless."

"It's weird to think we're occasionally getting sun. Downright strange, but I like it."

"You want me to do . . . *what?*" Brecht asked.

We stood in the middle of the gore-fest that was the Section Three labs. Bishop and Brecht were collecting the dead animals and shoving them into garbage bags. Others from Sanctuary—mostly teen boys—were scrubbing down the entire facility.

I should've had them clean this place a while ago. It was my fault the situation got out of hand—I had just been fearful to speak about it.

I needed to get rid of that fear.

"Kita?" Brecht asked, jarring me out of my musings. "What do you want us to do?"

I snorted back a laugh. Then my face went red and I wasn't sure what to say.

Why was I never normal? Who snorted at a perfectly innocent question?

I pulled out the implant from my pocket. It had once been in a judge's body, but now it was in the palm of my hand. DC had practically mutilated the body in order to remove it. I showed the device to Brecht.

Bishop, who was shoving a dead cat into a bag, noticed. He tied the bag shut and then sauntered over, his mouth turned down in a frown. "What's this?"

"It's a piloting implant for the exoskeletons." I turned it over in my fingers. It resembled steel teeth—more like fangs—with little wire hanging from the tips of a few.

Bishop eyed the device with a healthy amount of skepticism. "You want to carve me up and put a machine in my head? A machine from a dead guy's brain, I might add?"

I turned, pulling my hair up and showing him the socket at the base of my skull. "You've seen mine plenty of times, Bishop. It's perfectly normal."

Brecht scoffed. "It doesn't *look* normal, trust me."

I dropped my hair down and glared at him. "I've seen it in the mirror several times—and I've seen it on Gascoigne. It's not *bad*, either. The implant is perfectly safe. Tons of people have them—people get them inserted in Ex Cathedra all the time. And it's normal to pass these on to the next person, I'll have you know."

They couldn't make them anymore. Ex Cathedra had factories but they no longer had the facilities for anything this complex. So, they had a couple hundred and passed them from one judge to the next—whenever they died.

"Oh, so this implant has been in *several* people?" Bishop actually laughed. "Way to sell this, Kit-Kat."

I coughed.

Bishop got back to the subject at hand. "Wasn't yours installed by a Teth innovator in one of the most advanced facilities in the world?"

I motioned to the facility all around us. "Yours will be installed at one of the *other* most advanced facilities in the world, by a human doctor and winter survivor—DC."

"Wow—you're a horrible salesman." Bishop glanced over at the dead animals around the lab. And then to the bag. "You want me to get surgery, here?"

I placed my hand over my still-flat belly. "I wouldn't ask you to do this if I thought there was any significant chance of danger. I don't want little Lump growing up alone in this world. Don't worry—DC looked over the facilities and thinks they'll be very adequate. I mean, Ex Cathedra does it regularly, it can't be too hard."

"And then I'll be able to pilot the judge suits?" Brecht asked. "Like Gascoigne?"

I nodded. "Yes. That's the point. And I can trust you two, which is why I want you both to get the implants. You could even drive them *with* Gascoigne, since the repairs to one of the Mark III suits went well."

Brecht's eyes lit up. "I'm in. Give me a few minutes to let Vega know, just in case, and I'll be back." He quickly left the half-cleaned facility with bounce in his step. Apparently, he had always wanted to pilot one of these.

Bishop held up his hand. "Wait. Wait, wait, wait. Don't these things make you think differently while you're piloting them? Will that happen to me?"

"Only when you're in the suit," I said. "You'll still be the same loveable scamp the rest of the time."

"That's a new one. Loveable scamp, huh?" He rubbed his stubble-covered chin. Then he glanced down at his arms, where some of his numerous tally marks were visible. "I wouldn't have ever believed I would get that reputation, but sure, whatever you say."

"I think I would know most of all," I muttered.

Bishop paused for a moment, but then his mouth firmed. "All right, I won't deny, it'll be awesome to pilot one of those things. What tally marks are you planning on having me hunt? I bet I could get nearly any tally with one of these."

I laughed again, but at least stopped myself from snorting. "Well, it's funny you should mention that. The first tally I'll be sending you after is a beast you yourself found—the fabled chicken."

Bishop blinked. "What?"

"I've decided that we're going to expand the upper portion of the valley. I think I have some good ideas on that, and we can't just hide if we're going to rebuild the world. Your plan was a good one, Bishop."

He raised his eyebrows. "I can't believe you're taking one of my plans."

"I use your plans all the time," I said, frowning at him.

"One of my plans that doesn't involve turning people into tally marks, I mean."

I chuckled. He had a point.

Bishop sighed and stripped his T-shirt off over his head, displaying his broad and muscular—but massively scarred—torso. Then he went and lay face down on the medical table. "All right, let's get this over with."

I held up both hands. "Whoa! Not right now. Only once this place is clean, okay? After that, DC will perform the surgery. She said it would be short—but she would only do it after we sterilized everything."

Bishop exhaled as he grabbed his shirt. "You're always such a tease, Kit-Kat."

I shook my hand back and forth. "You always jump to conclusions."

Once fully dressed, Bishop grabbed the bag with the dead animals. "I'll get on this then, O fearless leader." Then he gave me a faux salute and headed out of the lab.

CHAPTER THIRTY-THREE

Fatigued from all the work in Sanctuary, I wanted nothing more than to rest. But I knew I couldn't do that. I needed to see Chelsy.

While people were still setting up homes in Section One, there was a long hallway of barracks that people used as individual homes. Anyone who was single—or older children who had lost their parents—were given their own room. Chelsy had a room her own, even if she opted to spend all her time with me when I was here.

I went straight there, between all my work, so I could speak with her. The others in Sanctuary nodded and waved as I passed, and I always smiled back.

Hope was like fire—if fed, it would blaze brightly.

I had to keep that in mind. Unfortunately, it was difficult once I reached the barracks.

It was a sad section of Sanctuary, to be frank. Gray walls and gray floors meant it was uniform, but it was also so drab as to be lifeless. I didn't like walking the long hall to Chelsy's room, and I made a mental note to liven up the place once I had any free time or spare people to assign the job.

Chelsy's room was clearly labeled with her name on the door. I stopped in front of it and knocked. The door creaked open afterward, and Chelsy peered through the little sliver of space between the door and the door-frame. When she saw it was me, she threw open the door, smiling wide.

"Hey, Crouton," I said, trying to be lively and playful.

Chelsy threw her arms around me in an emotion-filled, but ultimately silent, hug. Then she let go and ushered me into her space.

It was a small room, but the moment I stepped into it, I was hit with an explosion of color.

Cheerful scenes of green meadows, blue skies, and a sun that seemed perpetually on the brink of dawn, had been lovingly painted onto the walls. Most of it looked like Chelsy herself had been the artist, but a few of the trees, and the little animals in the fields, were too detailed—and of a different style—to be Chelsy's doing.

The blue sky was even painted onto the ceiling . . .

Earth hadn't seen blue skies in years.

I pointed to the ceiling. "Did you do that?"

Chelsy smiled wide. She pointed to the sun, and then to the grass, and even some houses. Then she tapped her chest. Those were hers. When she gestured to the ceiling, and then the trees and animals, she shook her head.

"Let me guess—that was Dr. Claire's doing?"

Chelsy nodded vigorously.

Since DC was a Winter Survivor, she probably remembered when the skies were always blue.

"It's beautiful," I said.

Chelsy stood a little straighter.

Today she wore a pink dress with a pair of ballerina leggings. She also had three necklaces—all of which were shiny and made of a faux gold— hanging low around her neck. Chelsy loved the loud colors, perhaps since she couldn't be loud herself.

In the corner of the room stood a small, sturdy bed, covered in a quilt that was a patchwork of bright fabrics and featured hand-stitched animals, flowers, and even a unicorn. I loved unicorns, if only because they were creatures in old legends that were said to purify away poisons.

"Very pretty," I said as I glanced over her bed.

Chelsy smoothed the blanket, showing me how neatly made it was. I nodded once, impressed with her diligence.

Then she waved her arm to the other tiny corner of her room. It was filled with a small wooden table—something likely picked up off the side of the road and cleaned before being brought here. It was banged up pretty bad. I almost felt sorry for it.

There was a lamp perched on top of the pathetic table, plugged into the power and shining bright for the whole small room. Around the lamp were all Chelsy's treasures: figurines I had crafted for her from wires, smooth stones from the nearby river, and a stack of well-thumbed picture books, though most of them were weathered and on the verge of falling apart.

On the other side of the wooden table, barely able to fit, was Chelsy's notebook. Crayons, pencils, and markers lay neatly organized on top of the notebook, as though she wanted to have every possible color and texture with which to work.

"I really like your room," I said.

The last time I had been here, it had been as gray and as sad as the hallway. I loved that she made it her own.

I took a seat on her colorful bed. Chelsy grabbed her notebook before rushing over and sitting directly next to me.

I placed a hand on her head, my fingers gently stroking her black hair. "I know I said I would take you exploring, but do you mind waiting a little bit longer? Until everything is finished? I . . . I've been tired lately."

Chelsy nodded once. Then she pointed to my stomach, opened her notebook, and hastily wrote something before showing me.

She showed me the words: *You have a baby?*

"That's right," I said.

Chelsy's smile was infectious. Then she closed her notebook, leapt off the bed, and stood directly in front of me. She motioned with her hands.

Sign language.

I didn't know it, so I shook my head in response. Chelsy didn't seem to care. She grabbed my hands and held them in front of me, poised with the confidence of a seasoned teacher.

"You want to teach me?" I asked.

She nodded.

She waved her hand in a gentle arc. I did the same. Chelsy clapped, then grabbed her notebook, and wrote: *Hello.*

That was the sign for *hello*, I supposed.

Then Chelsy crossed her arms, with her hands facing up, one arm resting on the other while touching one elbow with the fingers from the opposite hand. It was like . . . she was cradling an imaginary baby in her arms. Then Chelsy rocked her arms from side to side.

When she grabbed her notebook, I already knew what she was going to write.

She showed me the word: *Baby.*

I mimicked her gesture, and Chelsy hugged me tight. Then she pointed to my stomach, and signed the words, *Hello, baby!*

I understood now. And while I had never been keen on learning a language that involved my hands, I didn't mind learning for her. It had been infinitely more difficult to learn Tethlite—if Chelsy preferred sign language, I would do that for her.

"Do you have more words to teach me?" I asked.

I wanted to spend time with her, and if this involved also sitting down, I counted it as a win.

Chelsy became so happy, she clapped a second time. She grabbed her notebook, and pointed to a series of words, from *friend* to *bird*, and then started frantically signing them all.

I watched and listened, still exhausted.

But I'd sleep when I was dead.

"I have a new project for you, Westley," I said, my voice cutting through the early morning stillness of the workshop.

Westley, absorbed in his task, was bent over his workstation like a scholar poring over ancient texts. The glow from his computer screen illuminated his concentrated expression, casting a soft light in the dimly lit room. Beside him lay the remains of a Mark III suit, its components spread out in a meticulous array. It was as if he were conducting an autopsy of the machine, and needed every bit of it exposed.

It was still early, the hour when night hesitantly hands over to day.

Bishop had just been escorted to surgery with DC to undergo his implant procedure, leaving me in a state of restless concern. I needed a distraction, a project to immerse myself in, to quiet the worry gnawing at my mind.

Despite the fact I was standing right next to him, Westley remained utterly engrossed in his work, his fingers moving deftly over the keyboard as he analyzed the schematics we had retrieved.

"What can I do for you?" Westley finally responded, his voice steady and focused, without even a glance in my direction.

"We retrieved a drone from the Davis Space Force Base."

That got Westley's attention. He stopped reading the schematics and turned to face me. "Really?"

"It's a reconnaissance drone that uses an atomic battery to stay aloft for very nearly ever. I wanted you to take it up and do a survey of our surrounding area—programmed such that I can have a map of the area, tens of miles in every direction, as soon as possible—and at least the basic pictures downloaded for me to look at in the next couple hours."

This took Westley a few seconds to absorb. "Do we have something like that? A program to make survey maps, I mean?"

"If we do, it'll be in the computer. If not, just take the pictures and work something up—but get them to me either way."

His excitement got *me* excited. Westley returned his attention to the workstation and started hammering at the keyboard. "*All right!* Just give me a few more moments and I'll get on that right away."

"Good," I said, feeling proud of myself.

I did know how to delegate, it seemed.

If I could use this drone for scouting, we'd have yet another major advantage.

I knocked on the infirmary, and waited till an exhausted-looking DC opened it, staring at me with wide eyes. She was so much taller, and I always felt better in her presence. I leaned on the doorframe as I spoke to her.

"Hello," I awkwardly said.

"Kita, you look like you haven't slept in hours."

I shrugged—I could sleep when we were safe and prosperous. "Is Bishop still okay?" I asked.

"Bishop and Brecht are both okay, and Bishop will likely be able to walk. Brecht will need about two weeks since he isn't blessed with nanites."

I nodded, briefly ashamed I'd forgotten to ask about Brecht.

"Did you want to see him?" DC asked.

I shook my head. "Let him sleep. I actually came to ask you something else—another favor of your expertise."

She smiled encouragingly. "Go on." She even leaned against the other side of the doorframe, as if putting me at ease with our mutual postures.

I took a deep breath. "I . . . want to be like Theon. Theon Sellers, our prisoner. I want to be a human architect. He has something in his body that allows him to produce the pheromones that can control the Teth . . . and let them breed."

DC blinked. "I'm a doctor, not a xenobiologist."

"But you could at least remove the parts from him?" I asked. "And either put them in me or perhaps study them, with Jack's help, in order to be able to reproduce them?"

DC pushed away from the doorframe and then shuddered. "Probably, Kita. But . . . will Theon survive the process?"

"I don't know. But it's not my first priority. He has opposed me, and humanity, at every turn for his own benefit. Now he can at least do some good."

I mean, I remembered when he tried to kill me multiple times. And then, in the Davis Space Force Base, he was ready to do it again. We were enemies on opposite sides of the war, and unlike Quern, Theon was a danger to Sanctuary.

Dr. Claire's expression was aggressively neutral, but she nodded. "I'll . . . handle it. Please assign me guards for when we try and put him under. But tomorrow, please."

"I'll send you Gascoigne."

But not all of rebuilding of Sanctuary was just adding new toys and supplies to the preexisting structure. And I wanted to get as much as possible done before I had DC operate on me. What if I needed lots of time to rest?

A part of rebuilding would be using the toys we already had—like the farms and plants.

Descending the damp, concrete stairs into the subterranean depths of Section Three's prison, I felt an involuntary shiver ripple through me, not solely from the clammy air that clung to the walls like an unwelcome specter. Gascoigne walked behind me, her footfalls heavy. She didn't seem to notice my discomfort—or if she did, she didn't say anything about it.

This was where Quern had escaped from, and it reminded me that I either needed to improve the prison, or do away with it.

"Try to steer clear of kidnappings and near-death experiences this time," I mused to myself.

"Who's there?" Jack's voice echoed up the stairs from the shadows. "Kita, is that you? *Are my plants okay? Are they still alive?*"

Gascoigne, following closely, almost collided with me as I halted at the foot of the stairs. "Keep moving," she growled. "We've got bigger issues than this crackpot. Ex Cathedra won't be sitting on their hands for long."

That was all she ever talked about—Ex Cathedra's inevitable attack against us. Sometimes I wondered if she had attacked those judges just to get us entangled in a conflict, but the fear in her voice whenever she mentioned them told me I was probably wrong.

I thought Gascoigne was just inherently more restless than I was.

It was difficult to understand her sometimes.

But I had picked her to accompany me into the prison because of her reckless, and somewhat menacing, demeanor. Bishop and Brecht were still recovering from their surgery, and Jack was an unpredictable lunatic, or else I would've done this myself.

As we approached his cell, Jack sat disheveled on a makeshift bench, his wild, graying beard and untamed ponytail giving him the air of a deranged prophet. His cell, reinforced with sturdy bars and robust padlocks—likely Pete's handiwork post-Quern escape—was rather barren.

"You attract a lot of crackpots," Gascoigne quipped.

I cleared my throat, ignoring her. "Jack, your plants are doing fine. We're even considering introducing some to the surface. You'd like that, right?"

I hoped this partial truth might coax him into cooperation.

His reaction was both immediate and intense. "Outside?" Jack flung himself toward the bars, his eyes wild. "My *legacy* will finally spread its roots in the new world?"

I forced myself to chuckle. "That's right. But just a few. Little baby steps."

"Why not all of them?" Jack asked, pressing his face against the bars.

Gascoigne watched this whole exchange with a sneer. She didn't want to be here. Every cell in her body was screaming it.

"We need your expertise, Jack," I said. "To ensure your plants survive in their new environment."

Jack's expression flickered between suspicion and hope. "You haven't harmed them, have you? *Have you?*"

Gascoigne slammed a fist on the bars, rattling them loud enough to hurt my ears. Jack leapt back, shivering. She glared at him, warning the man to keep his composure.

I stepped closer to the bars. "We need to discuss *fertilizers*, Jack. You know . . . soil enrichment. I've read some of your research. I know you know what I'm talking about."

He hesitated, but then moved closer to me. "Fine. But I need to see them. Verify their well-being."

With a deep breath, I unlocked his cell. Jack slowly wandered out, glancing around as he did so.

Gascoigne, wrinkling her nose at the pungent odor wafting from the man, said, "A bath and new attire are in order. Even his plants have standards."

"Lead me to my plants," Jack said.

Gascoigne grabbed his upper arm like she wanted to tear it off. I motioned to her to ease her grip. "He's had a rough time," I whispered. "His instability comes from mental degradation, not a desire to irritate you."

She exhaled, rolled her eyes, and loosened her grip. "All right. I'll take him there—and I'll *baby him*."

Jack didn't seem to mind.

"Okay, take him to the Section Three labs. DC said she would help him. And the *D* stands for doctor, so please just do whatever she says if Jack acts up."

"I already said I would." Gascoigne huffed as she stopped past me. "Are you going to join us?"

"I will . . . once I inspect the prison. I'll be there soon, I promise."

I waited for a bit, while Gascoigne took Jack up the stairs. Again, I was delegating, and I was proud of myself for it, but I definitely needed to do more.

More.

Constantly . . . more.

I didn't want anything to happen to this community.

I watched from a distance, standing mostly in shadows at the corner of the lab, as Jack delved into his work with an almost frenetic energy. He was at the computer, typing wildly as he searched through his research data.

DC and Gascoigne flanked him, with Gascoigne tense and ready for any sort of violent outburst. Yet, as Jack immersed himself in his plants, his erratic behavior seemed momentarily forgotten.

Jack stopped on one file. "These specimens," he whispered, "aren't my most potent creations. They're efficient, yes, but they lack the vigorous growth of my true masterpieces."

"Don't ever say the word *vigor* again," Gascoigne growled.

DC gave her a sidelong glance that conveyed only confusion.

But then Jack was at it again. He opened a blank document and started outlining plans not just for plants, but an entire ecosystem in Section Two—from bacteria to small animals and birds.

"It's an oasis," he muttered.

DC watched with a lifted eyebrow. "It all seems coherent so far."

"Based on our current resources," I said, "we have around twenty-five hundred acres of arable land nestled within a valley-like area. If we need to do some farming aboveground, we can do it nearby, and probably protect it."

DC watched the screen while she spoke. "In a world filled with enemies, every peaceful acre counts."

"Under optimal conditions, historical data suggests four million calories per acre. Our land, however, would yield half that. There's a lot of trees . . . But with Jack's help, we could potentially reach three million calories per acre."

Gascoigne eyed me like I was speaking a third language. She clearly didn't like that I was discussing farmland in terms of calories—I just couldn't help it. That was the easiest way to understand our growth potential.

"That's enough to sustain a population of ten thousand," I said—for her, so she could understand.

DC furrowed her brow. "That's ambitious. We barely have two hundred people here."

"The Teth need more food. We should be thinking about them, too."

"Still . . . You should be careful. The more supplies we have, the bigger the target we become."

"Ex Cathedra *will* attack us," Gascoigne muttered.

She hadn't dropped that, even if she said it less lately.

"Even at twenty percent efficiency, we could comfortably support two thousand people. That's more than enough for the foreseeable future." We could grow with that amount of food.

Jack's sudden interjection snapped us back to reality. "Forget your population! This land belongs to my plants!"

I ignored his outburst, focusing instead on our agricultural strategy. "Our goal is to allocate about three percent of our population to farming. It's slightly higher than the pre-winter world, but our plants and A-tech should balance the scales."

"I thought you weren't going to want to expand at first?" DC asked. "Isn't it risky?"

"I've come to the conclusion it's riskier to hide and not grow. Someday, someone will come for us—and as Gascoigne keeps reminding me, it's probably Ex Cathedra. Besides, we've got new babies to feed, human and Teth."

Jack kept typing away on his machine, barely paying attention to what we were talking about beyond his one outburst. I preferred him this way.

Gascoigne, on the other hand, laughed.

"Yeah, Ex Cathedra knows that truth. You punch above your weight, Kita, I'll not deny—but we're still in a tiny, tiny weight class compared to them. I still have no idea how you plan to stop them for coming for you— and all this"—she swept her arm at the computer—"is just going to make them hurry here faster."

I shrugged. "Let's just focus on this for now. I want to use the chickens that Bishop found, and Jack's plants, to make some test farms."

I had some ideas on how to stop invaders, but I wasn't ready to share just yet. But I also needed some lower-threat means of stopping the basic bandits and such until we were too strong to mess with.

I needed to make sure the JUDGE-Y47s were up and operational. They were huge boons we needed to have online just in case we were attacked.

Or at least . . . one of them.

With Westley's help, I stayed up late.

Always staying up late . . .

It was really taking its toll on me—but I needed this. We used the cranes to put the two JUDGE-Y47 armors side by side in Section One, and then we had Gascoigne move the Mark VI down with it. They took up the whole back end of the massive warehouse, but we were far enough away from the homes that we weren't bothering anyone.

The fish farms were almost done being set up, and I feared if we didn't do this now, we could risk shattering the glass enclosures . . .

Westley walked around the three exoskeletons, drinking them all in with his wide eyes. All three were silver, which I was now coming to associate with the Mark VI model. They seemed to want it to be sleeker, more streamlined, and even more feminine in curvature.

I motioned to the Mark VI. "This is the only one that works."

"So what do you want to do with these other ones?" Westley asked.

"I think . . . I want to remove the part that holds the battery cells from the Mark VI and place it into one of the JUDGE-Y47s."

"That's a mouthful," Westley muttered. He glanced at the ones with jet wings and even grazed his oil-stained fingers along the length of one. "Why not give these ones a different name? We could paint it on. Maybe call them a *cardinal*? Instead of a judge suit?"

"Why cardinal?" I asked.

"They fly?"

I waited for more of an explanation. When none came, I shrugged. "Sure. They can be the cardinal suits. We can paint it on. But . . . I need to get one up and running, first. We need to take it apart, get the battery cells from the Mark VI into one, and then start it up. Can you help me with that?"

"Yeah. We might need Garret's help, too. He's a lot stronger than me. And these parts are going to be heavy—*way* heavier than the Mark III."

I kept my mouth shut as I examined the cardinals. I doubted they'd be heavier—they were meant to fly—but the Mark VI was probably heavier, yeah.

Westley turned his attention to the gauntlets. "Do these . . . have some sort of energy blade? Or tool? Look at this . . . They have the means to heat up *something*."

"Yeah. The Mark VI has a plasma blade."

"The cardinals have it, too. On *both* their gauntlets. That's insane. Why would you ever do that?"

"I imagine they wanted these to kill a lot of people." I laughed at my own dark joke.

Westley glanced over the arm of the cardinal and stared at me like *I* had killed someone. I stopped my chuckling and walked around the side of the Mark VI to hide my embarrassment.

"Okay, well, since these exoskeletons are completely intact, I think it'll be an easy operation." Westley rubbed his hands on the pants of his overalls. "Let's get to work."

CHAPTER THIRTY-FOUR

I sat around in the industrial-sized kitchen in Section One, waiting for all my plans to come together.

The entire room was almost entirely made of stainless steel. The appliances, the counters, even the hoods that caught the heat were all the gray, shiny material for clean cooking. Only the walls and floor were made of white tile.

Brecht, Vega, and Gascoigne were all by one of the stoves, attempting to make food for a few hundred people. Usually, the people of Sanctuary were responsible for their own meals, with some people assigned to restock the pantry whenever it was getting low. However, while we continued with construction, it came to our attention that tomorrow was the *Springtide Jubilee.*

I had never heard of this holiday until I started living in Richfield. The people there said it was a tradition started after the Forever Winter—a holiday meant to celebrate the end of the snow and cold.

That made sense, I had just never celebrated before them, so it was rarely on my mind. Every year, people would make huge meals and feast together as a community, typically outside. Sanctuary was underground, so we'd stay indoors for this year's celebration, though we were going to go to Section Two and sit around the greenhouse roses to simulate a wonderful spring.

"I think you're stirring it too much," Gascoigne snapped, dragging me out of my thoughts.

The three of them were prepping a slow-cooked stew. In theory, they were placing all the meat and vegetables into several pots and allowing them to cook over a whole day so that the ingredients were tender when we all ate them for the *Springtide Jubilee*. Unfortunately, nothing ever seemed to work as planned.

Brecht glanced over with a frown. "Stirring *too* much? Isn't that better than not enough?"

Vega, who towered over both Brecht and Gascoigne, emitted a low, rumbling sound that might have been a chuckle in Tethlite. "Human cooking is peculiar."

"You're doing it wrong," Gascoigne said, practically growling. "You're making it flavorless. I know what I'm talking about—I've made food for hundreds of soldiers before."

"What should I do then?" Brecht asked.

Gascoigne moved on him like she was going to take over, but Brecht narrowed his eyes in a glare.

They had at least fifteen industrial pots filled with gravy, chunks of freshly cut up chicken, and fresh vegetables. They could both cook at the same time, but Brecht seemed insistent on doing it all.

"Use more spices," Gascoigne commanded. "Spices will hide all of your terrible cooking skills."

Vega sniffed one of the pots and then turned his head to smell another. "Aren't humans picky eaters? Who enjoy simpler foods they spice themselves to their preferences? That was what I was taught."

Gascoigne huffed. "Trust me, no human wants half-cooked stew that tastes like paper. Not even the Teth like that bullshit."

The stainless-steel surfaces gleamed under the fluorescent lights. I felt awkward even being here. Should I say something to them? Offer my own advice? I shook my head. I had no advice. All I cared about was that we weren't eating hardtack.

"Do you want to cook the food?" Brecht asked, indignant.

"Yes," Gascoigne snapped.

As if she were playing into his hand, Brecht glanced over with a smirk. "I'll let you. If you're nice to me and apologize for being so rude."

Wow.

Now I felt *extra* awkward. Were they flirting? These two—they had the weirdest relationship dynamic I had ever personally witnessed.

"Oh, is that what you *really* wanted?" Gascoigne stepped close to Brecht. She grabbed him by the waistband of his jeans and pulled him over until their hips touched. "You didn't have to play 4D chess with me in order to get it. All this bickering—for what? Foreplay?"

Brecht's face was as red as the sliced tomatoes on the counter. He glanced over at me, only briefly, and I wished he hadn't. Clearly, he was bothered to have company—just as much as I was bothered to *be the company.*

Gascoigne pressed her mouth to his, her tongue in his mouth long before he could voice anything.

"Vega," I said as I turned on my heel and went for the door. "I think we're needed. Somewhere else. To gather more supplies for the *Springtide Jubilee.*"

The Teth snorted and then lumbered after me. He said nothing on the matter happening behind us, which escalated at a disturbing rate.

Not even Bishop was that audacious.

But it made me laugh, at least—and the fatigue of all these repairs and improvements had been momentarily forgotten.

Even Gascoigne hadn't mentioned Ex Cathedra's inevitable revenge.

Maybe it wouldn't happen.

I prayed it wouldn't happen.

I sat in my office, spinning in my chair, watching the three Teth eggs. I had removed them from their glass canisters and set them on a plush blanket on the middle of my desk.

The eggs had absorbed all the orange gel that had been in their canisters. Absorbing the gel had "brought them back to life" after they had been in cryostasis for so long.

They were due to hatch at any time. It was the middle of night, while most of Sanctuary was sleeping, and while I was also tired, I couldn't stop watching the little leathery eggs. I just couldn't.

The *Springtide Jubilee* had gone off without a hitch. Several people had brewed some moonshine to pass around, and I thought that was probably a bad idea, but everyone had loved it, so we didn't stop it from happening.

Bishop . . .

Had way too much moonshine.

He was in the office with me, sitting on a chair, asleep on my desk, his face in a pool of his own drool. It was adorable, really. I reached over and brushed his dark hair with my fingers. He snorted something, too asleep to wake.

Bishop had stuck by me this entire time, and insisted on being here for the birth of the Teth babies. I appreciated that about him. He had a *care about nothing* attitude at times, but he never faulted when it came to me. He cared. Deeply. And I loved him so much for it.

As I continued to stroke Bishop's hair, the eggs began to jiggle. My heart skipped a beat. This was it. The moment I had anxiously waited for.

I leaned closer, my eyes fixated on the tiny fractures spreading across the egg's surface as they were torn open from the inside. The room was silent except for Bishop's even breathing.

Slowly, painstakingly, the first egg tore open, revealing a tiny, wet creature inside. It was a Teth architect, no bigger than my hand, with delicate translucent skin that revealed dark organs within, and tiny, fluttering limbs. It had no eyes, but it moved, alive and sensing its new world with its four little arms and two chubby legs.

"Hello, Benjamin," I whispered.

I held my breath as the other two eggs started to hatch. One by one, they opened up, each revealing a fragile new life. Next was the Teth innovator—Tamura—and last was the Teth warrior—Joel. The little babies were mesmerizing, their small bodies so strange in the dim light of my office.

The Teth didn't like light . . .

Their flailing made me think they were in pain.

So I shut off all the lights in the room as fast as I could. The office was thrown into a pitch-black state, and I had to feel my way back to the desk.

The little Teth made squeaking noises. Happier noises. I chuckled to myself as I gently patted their heads and then used the blanket to clean all the egg fluid from their bodies.

Bishop stirred beside me, lifting his head groggily. "Huh?" He was clearly baffled by the lack of lights. "What's going on?"

"*Shh*!" I hissed. "The babies hatched and the light was bothering them."

Bishop groaned. "The lack of light is bothering me."

I gently picked up one of the Teth, cradling it in my palm. It was warm and vibrated slightly. Then I grabbed Bishop's hand and carefully handed him the Teth. The little baby squirmed, but Bishop was careful. I felt him use his other hand to make sure the baby was secure.

"It's so . . . gross," he said with a playful *aww* at the end of his words. "I bet it looks like bologna, just like human newborns."

"Human babies don't look like that."

"They do for the first few days after they're born. Just gross little piles of meat." Bishop spoke like he was talking to his favorite pet, his tone high-pitched, his words insulting, though he said them in a loving way. "Are you my precious little disgusting alien? Huh? Huh? Who's a gross little nugget? *You are!* Yes you are!" Bishop made little kissy noises at the Teth.

The noises the baby made in response seemed happy. It squeaked and cooed and I wondered if the Teth just appreciated the sounds Bishop was making.

Then Bishop handed me the baby back and I tucked it into the blanket.

"I'll make sure Vega and Levi help with raising them," I muttered. "And hopefully we can find some more Teth around, so they can breed."

"Yeah, I love talking about breeding to a bunch of aliens who were just born," Bishop quipped.

I smacked him on my shoulder. "You know what I mean. I . . . just want to keep my focus on the future."

"Well, it'll be an interesting future, Kit-Kat. You've already seen to that."

The next morning, I stood outside Sanctuary, a couple thousand feet from the entrance. The pine trees smelled sweet, and the weather was better than usual. The sun peeked through some cracks in the clouds. It was wonderful.

And somehow, we had advanced A-tech computers powered by atomic batteries, but no way to make *paper*. Which was just unfortunate.

I would have to rectify that. There were pine trees all around, so I was sure we'd get there soon, but for the moment I was just showing my companion, Grizzled Garret, my plans on the portable computer.

Behind me, Bishop was learning to drive the Mark III. He stomped the boots on some plants, and even walked across the parking lot as though he were in an old-world fashion show. It was amusing—in a bizarre way.

Brecht was still convalescing, but it was a miracle how much the nanites in his blood could repair, and how quickly. The machine itself was so advanced that "learning to drive" was more like "taking out for a test drive," but he was happy, at least. And whole.

"I want you to clear half a mile by half a mile," I said, "a hundred and sixty acres. Then we need to build a huge chicken coop and a massive area for farming various kinds of food—I have the list here, in this file—" I tapped the screen, moving it to a different list, one with food types, space allocated to each one, and appropriate methods of planting.

"How am I supposed to do that?" Garret asked.

I stared at him, trying to muster every bit of "commanding" I could. "I'll authorize you to take six guys from inside, to use Bishop or Brecht as movers and workers, and also to take the cranes out of the machine storage area in Section One—as well as one van. That should be enough, especially with the power armor."

Bishop's voice came blasting from his machine. "Wait, I'm not a farmer!"

I turned to Bishop, smiling up at him. "Well, when he's better, I can have Brecht do it—but until then, it has to be you."

"The things I do for your visions, Kita," he said. "Besides, can't Gascoigne handle this?"

"She is still driving the Mark VI, and might be needed for combat. I can't have everyone doing this."

Garret looked out over the space. "So how do you want me to do it?"

I braced myself. "I gave you a plan, tools, and a labor force, Garret. You said you wanted me to not have to personally handle everything. So I need you to put your big boy pants on and make this happen. Without any more oversight from me."

Garret snorted but didn't say anything.

I continued, hoping the tactic would work. "I gave you the *what*. Bishop will be back tomorrow, along with the vans, and you guys can start working then. So you have twenty-four hours to figure out *how*."

Garret turned to me, and I was relieved to see he was smiling—but I tried not to show it to him. *You've got to be a leader, Kita*, I told myself.

"Well, I'm glad you've figured that out. Yeah, I'll make sure it gets done. I do have a question though—you brought us here from Richfield to keep us safe. How do you plan to do that if we're just farming in the open, without even walls to protect us?"

"I have plans for that, too—and my first stop is to talk to Scrapyard Pete and Westley about it."

Garret nodded. "Well, I guess I'll trust you. You came through in spades on your promise to take care of the atomic batteries, for sure." He motioned to the farm. "In fact, you're coming through in spades on all of the promises you made when we left Richfield. I'll get this done for you; you handle whatever you need to handle."

I felt my cheeks heating. I couldn't even take a compliment like a normal person. "Thank you, I'll, um, make sure I don't let down your trust."

I was *so* awkward.

But I did seem to have done the trick of making my people like me, at least to some degree.

CHAPTER THIRTY-FIVE

As part of my work on Sanctuary, I moved around the security cameras. It wasn't as difficult as I thought it would be. The cameras were designed to be modular, which I hadn't known until I inspected them personally.

Instead of keeping the cameras inside, I opted to move them outside. That caused problems—so many problems—but I found workarounds so long as the cameras were within a certain range of Sanctuary. Admittedly, that wasn't very far, but the ability to see *outside* of our facility was 100 percent required.

Unfortunately, I only had five cameras for the outside.

I sat in my office, in Section Three, away from most of the others, while I observed their feed. Over the last few days, there had been signs of movement outside. Tree branches that were snapped, tracks in the mud, and even pathways that were clear. The patrols I had set up reported them, but it wasn't until I set up the cameras that I discovered the source.

Vay drones.

Much like Teth drones, they operated on limited intelligence. The Vay drones, a little larger than the Teth, were about the size of a cow, and did things in a peculiar way. They sniffed around the area, always coming back in the same pattern, walking the same trails, before veering off for a short distance and then leaving.

After observing their behaviors through the camera, I came to the conclusion the Vay drones were mapping the area. They couldn't speak, but I assumed they were leaving trace amounts of pheromones on the ground where they walked—similar to how ants left trails—so that other Vay could follow the pathways they laid.

When ants found a food source, they would lay down heavy amounts of pheromones as a message to all other ants. It would work as a "call" and the ants of the colony would amass on the trail and start ferrying the find back to the nest.

These Vay drones were clearly looking for something. I feared it was a way into Sanctuary that wasn't the front door.

The door to my office opened, and I tensed.

"It's just me, Kit-Kat."

I relaxed again and returned my attention to the monitors. There was a Vay drone sniffing down a trail currently, and I watched it intently, wondering when it would turn around and leave. Much like the Teth, it was black, and difficult to spot in the darkness between the trees, but it was much too large to go by unnoticed, even if it had natural camouflage.

Bishop walked up behind me and placed his hands on my shoulders. He massaged me, but it didn't help.

"We need to deal with the Vay," I whispered.

"What do you want to do about it?" Bishop stopped rubbing and then leaned against my desk next to me. He crossed his arms and tilted his head to the side. "We've got some power armor now—we can go clear these pests if you want."

I wasn't entirely sure if that would work. I didn't know what the Vay used for their own defenses.

"Why don't you talk to them?" Bishop asked. "You speak *alien*. Maybe we can strike a deal."

"They don't speak Tethlite." I glanced over at him. "They speak *Vayuu*. And I don't know that language. I mean, I know a few words, because my grandfather taught me them, but that was a long time ago."

"The aliens speak different languages?"

I narrowed my eyes into a sarcastic glare. "Humans speak different languages, too."

Bishop snorted back a laugh and shrugged. "I never said we were smarter. It's all dumb." He clicked his tongue. "*Tsk*. You know what language everyone understands? Violence. If you set up enough defenses, they'll leave us alone. Porcupines had been doing it for generations."

I mulled over his statements, thinking about what I needed to do. Information was paramount.

"I'm going to have Levi and Vega follow these trails back to their home location," I whispered.

"They won't get eaten, or something?" Bishop sounded both nervous and baffled.

"Their heightened sense of smell will allow them to follow the pheromone trails left by the Vay. Additionally, drones don't take complex commands. If they've been ordered to find places of interest, they'll likely not engage in combat. They're more programmable machines. They *can* fight, but I doubt it'll come to that if Levi and Vega keep their distance."

"Pheromone trails?"

I stood from my chair, patted him on the shoulder, and nodded. "Yes. Don't worry, I think I understand what's going on now. You just stay here, continue your training with the exoskeletons, and leave this to me."

Bishop chuckled. "I like it when you get things done. Crazy shit usually results."

It was night, and I'd decided to take some of the lab equipment outside to collect samples.

The Vay left trails on the ground, marking everything with their pheromones, and I wanted to do some testing with that. So, while Levi and Vega were out tracking them, I went outside with Brecht and Bishop as my guards.

I figured, if I gathered enough of the pheromones, I might be able to make something that confused the Vay—a grenade or spray or gas that overwhelmed their senses—but I would need to know what the pheromones were made of first, and then either re-create it, or perhaps have the Teth help me "make more" with their own brand of pheromones . . .

I crouched along the ground, gathering up the freshest samples. My cameras were a definite boon, since I could catch the Vay coming in and leaving. I rushed straight outside once they were gone.

The pheromones they left behind had the slight scent of a skunk. As a human, I could only really detect it when it was fresh, and only when I leaned down with my nose close to the soil. The smell was faint to my much smaller nose, but I didn't care. I just needed to get some of this.

"Are you sniffing the ground?" Bishop asked as he walked by. He shone a flashlight over the area I was carefully investigating.

"I-I just need time," I said, strangling my embarrassment. "Stand watch over there, please. I think light might damage the samples."

That was probably why the Vay did this all at night. The clouds overhead were growing thinner every day, which meant the sun was able to shine more and more. The Vay probably needed their pheromones to soak into the ground before the sunrise for this trail to be effective.

"All right," Bishop said with a groan. He walked over to a far cluster of trees and leaned against one of the larger trunks. Brecht was there too, cleaning his rifle in between glancing around.

I felt safer with them nearby, but also hated being interrupted in the middle of my musings.

Sometimes I just wanted to be alone to dwell on my problems.

I carefully scooped up the soil and placed it into vials that I sealed. Vial by vial, I collected as much of the fresh pheromones as I could, carefully creeping along the trail, practically crawling around trees and searching out the best sources.

And while I probably looked like an animal rooting out truffles, I didn't care. I'd do anything to solve the problems plaguing Sanctuary. That was my job—my privilege.

I had a satchel I'd taken from the lab that was designed to hold several glass vials without allowing them to knock around. Each little vial had its own protective pouch, and I went to great lengths to make sure I had everything I needed.

A stick snapped.

I glanced up, confused by the noise. I hadn't realized how far I had gotten from the others. I was out in the pine woods, my senses on high alert, my nose filled with a noxious odor I couldn't seem to shake.

"Bishop?" I whispered. Then I cleared my throat. "Bish—"

Someone grabbed me. They slammed a hand over my mouth and dragged me to my feet in one clean motion. I grabbed my attacker's arms, and kicked backward, but I didn't struggle long. The person holding me had just a nub of a thumb . . .

Quern.

I stopped resisting, wondering why he'd come back. Why would he ever come back? There was no reason to do this.

Once I was calm, Quern released me. I stepped forward, and then turned around to face him, confused by his presence.

"What're you doing here?" I asked in a whisper.

He stood before me in his Iron-Blooded uniform, the alien skull and human skull prominent on his body armor. He glared down at me with his light-colored eyes that practically glowed in the darkness of the forest. He was also so intense—never relaxed, like Bishop.

He had a rifle slung on his back.

"Kita," he said.

And nothing else. Which was the epitome of Quern.

"Why did you come here?" I asked.

We had left things between us tense, but not hostile. I'd figured I'd never see him again, frankly.

"Commander Dannik and Herin'Kay have been assigned to bring back the Mark VI," he muttered. "And so have I."

"Well . . ."

This was more than awkward, considering I had used the battery cell component from the Mark VI to power the JUDGE-Y47. The Mark VI was still mostly intact, but it wasn't functional at the moment. We could repair it, eventually, but it would take time.

Additionally, it wasn't like I was going to let the Iron-Blooded have it back.

"Wait," I whispered. "You came here to warn me about this?"

Quern nodded. "I was told that if I didn't retrieve the armor I had lost, the Iron-Blooded would consider me a failure. I was assigned to work with Commander Dannik, since I had the implants needed to pilot the power armor. Herin'Kay was assigned to the commander for the same reason."

Ah.

"Herin'Kay" was no human name, which meant they were bringing a Teth warrior suit. They really wanted their Mark VI armor back. I couldn't blame them.

"Are you *just* warning me?" I whispered. "Or are you wanting to help me?"

Quern didn't answer.

He probably didn't think I was going to make this offer. Hell, I wouldn't have thought of this offer three months ago, but here we were. I had too many problems—and not enough allies—to make sure Sanctuary would thrive. If I could somehow get Quern's help, I'd take it.

"You can join us," I said. "You—and any Teth who want to leave the Iron-Blooded. I know Levi wasn't satisfied there."

"Levi?" Quern asked. "Who the fuck is *Levi*?"

"Oh, uh, sorry, *Leevus*. He wasn't satisfied with Architect Riven's performance. Now he's with us. If you, or any of the other Teth, want to join us, we'll take you."

"I came here just to warn you of what was happening."

That was . . . unfortunate. We *needed* more Teth so that when Architect Benjamin was mature, we could produce more on our own. Without more Teth, they ran the risk of dying out—becoming extinct—and I didn't want that. I wanted us all to thrive together.

"*Kita?*" Bishop shouted from a couple of tree clusters over. "Where are you?"

I hesitated, feeling torn between insisting Quern join, and just leaving the option open. However, I didn't want to get into an argument. "When are the Iron-Blooded planning to take back the Mark VI?" I asked.

Bishop shouted again. "*Kita?*"

"I'm coming," I shouted back. "Just give me a moment."

That seemed to placate him.

Quern sneered. "You're still with that buffoon?" He asked the question like he was holding back vomit.

"Jealous?" I meant it sarcastically, but when Quern glanced down at me, I realized I had hit a nerve.

"Commander Dannik is investigating this area as we speak," Quern said, curt. "He knows about Sanctuary, but he doesn't know your full capabilities. His current plan is to round up some people, force them to seek refuge in Sanctuary, and then have them open the gates, so to speak, when they attack."

"I see," I muttered.

"He thinks that if he attacks while you're off guard, with a Teth in power armor, he can gain the advantage. He doesn't want to actually fight you on the field, because he doesn't want to damage the Mark VI too much."

"I understand."

A chill ran down my spine. I didn't like this. How could I turn it around?

"Where is Commander Dannik staying? The Iron-Blooded don't have any bases nearby. You've been decimated, from the bomb at the Hoover Dam, to the mining operations that were busted, to the Davis Space Force Base . . . How much longer can you all go? I'm still surprised you're operating at all, to be frank."

"It's a lot worse than you think," Quern whispered. "That's why they want the Mark VI back."

Hesitantly, I placed a hand on his shoulder. Quern glanced down at my touch, as though debating what to do about this. I was *trying* to be charismatic, but sometimes it didn't work like it did in my head.

Why couldn't I just lie my way through everything?

I gently squeezed Quern's thick bicep. "You should join us. You know you should. Tell me where Commander Dannik is. We can sneak up on him when he isn't prepared—when his Teth warrior isn't even in his suit. Once they're out of the picture, I know—*you know*—the Iron-Blooded will have to leave us alone. They'll *have* to regroup. Or fall apart. Either way is fine by me."

Quern shifted uncomfortably, avoiding my gaze but never pulling away. He was quiet for a prolonged moment. When Quern finally glanced over, I held my ground, hoping he would see reason.

"How's your child?"

That . . . wasn't what I had thought he would ask.

I placed a hand on my stomach. "Everything is fine. We have a doctor—a Winter Survivor—who has been making sure there are no complications."

"And the buffoon is the father?"

Another question I hadn't thought he would ask.

"That's right," I replied.

Quern pulled his arm from my grasp. Then he glared at me. "When Leevus told me about the fire, he said he was leaving with the humans who claimed to have an architect. Is that true? Do you have one? Or did you lie to Leevus to get him to cooperate?"

"We have one," I said. "Architect Benjamin."

I could tell, by the look on Quern's face, that was the worst name *ever* for a Teth architect. But I didn't care. It was my grandfather's name, and it was appropriate for the situation. It was probably the best name we could give an architect that would live side by side with humanity.

Quern exhaled, his shoulders relaxing. "I'll speak to the Teth. If they want to join you, I'll leave instructions for how to find Dannik right here, in the woods. If the Teth *don't* want to join you, then just know you've been warned on their plans. I've done everything I can to help before the attack."

"I'll wait for your note," I said.

"Kita?" Bishop's voice was closer now, laced with concern.

Quern scoffed before backing away into the pine forest. He fled between a couple trunks, leaving me in the small clearing, standing over dirt that had been soaked in Vay pheromones.

"Over here," I finally called.

Bishop slammed his way past a few branches, the pine needles falling to the forest floor. He was half-covered in sap and his eyebrows were furrowed.

"What're you doing?" he asked. "You're just . . . standing here?"

I nodded, trying to appear calm despite the adrenaline still coursing through my veins. "Quern came to visit me . . . and we need to prepare. There's a slight chance the Iron-Blooded are planning to attack us."

CHAPTER THIRTY-SIX

While I waited for a message from Quern, I decided to keep myself occupied with work.

We'd be fully prepared.

So, now that one of the cardinals was up and running, we needed to test out its flight ability.

Gascoigne walked the suit outside, beyond the parking lot for the entrance of Sanctuary, and beyond the trees to the road that was just beyond the valley.

Our chicken farm was finally up and running. Bishop and Brecht had removed enough trees to create an opening, and Garret—plus Scrapyard Pete and other denizens—had come together to make enclosures that could be hidden by the remaining trees. They *also* set up a gun stand, and someone to sit and guard the little birds. Well, they took turns, so that there was a guard at all times, but still.

We drove by the chickens, and I wondered how many we would get. The goal was to have a huge farm for eggs and meat, but I did still worry about the Vay. It would be so easy to destroy since it was outside of our underground lair.

Bishop, Brecht, and I rode in the car alongside Gascoigne, her stomps shaking the nearby trees and disturbing the birds. They flew off in groups, hurrying away from us.

The shine of Gascoigne's armor was mesmerizing. The jet-like appendages on the suit were a little awkward, but I assumed they would help control her movement once in the sky. The type of thrusters for the suit meant it was slow to rise, but fast to propel forward. In theory, the suit was probably meant to be carried on an airplane into the sky, and then leap out the back end like paratrooper.

Taking off from the ground would be a little more difficult, require more energy from the power cells.

Fortunately, we could recharge them in Sanctuary. Unfortunately, that wouldn't do anything for Gascoigne while she was up in the air. If she ran out of juice mid-flight, it was all over. There would be no recovery from that.

We reached a long road that was free of ruined cars. It was cracked, and wasn't the safest place to stand, but it would work for a takeoff pad. Gascoigne stomped over until she was directly in the middle of the road.

Bishop pulled the car over into the dirt and killed the engine. The Sanctuary car was just a little electric thing with four seats and a spacious trunk. The fabric on the seats was crusted a bit, but otherwise it was a smooth and mostly quiet ride.

I slid out of the passenger's seat, and Brecht followed suit. We all walked over to the side of the road.

It was overcast, but the clouds were a little whiter today.

"You ready?" I called out.

Gascoigne turned the whole exoskeleton to face us. She nodded, her helmet moving with her interior action.

"I've got this."

"Do you think they sent people into training to pilot something like this?" Bishop asked, half sarcastically.

"The onboard computer has been telling me what to do, jackass," Gascoigne snapped. "Just stand back and watch me make history."

We waited. Brecht wrung his hands the whole time, and I wondered if he thought this was a foolish idea. Since Gascoigne had the most experience with power armor, this was probably the best choice for a test pilot, but I could understand his nervousness. There really wasn't a scenario where something went wrong, and Gascoigne survived.

Gascoigne activated the thrusters. A bright white and blue light burst to life. Things in the wing appendages opened up, giving the suit a wider silhouette, but also tilting the thrusters downward. I shielded my eyes as I stared at the bright intensity in the engines. JUDGE-Y47 slowly lifted off the ground, hovering.

The sound of the thrusters was a deep, resonating hum, powerful yet controlled. The suit ascended in an awkward way, as though Gascoigne were trying to maintain her balance, hovering a few feet above the earth before going even higher, accelerating into the sky.

She was going . . . just straight up.

The force of her thrusters disturbed the whole area. The branches on the nearby trees rustled, the dirt on the ground kicked up, and it was difficult to keep my black hair out of my eyes.

"It's working," Bishop said, half in disbelief. "I can't fucking believe that."

"You thought this would fail?" Brecht turned to him with a frown. He held a hand over his eyes, trying to stop the wind from bothering him.

"I didn't think she would get off the ground."

I had to admit, my whole body felt icy with exhilaration. I almost couldn't believe my eyes. Gascoigne kept going higher. She was at least thirty feet from the ground, just hovering around in the sky. This was incredible.

I wanted to ask her if it was difficult, but then she went even *higher*.

When she was about two hundred feet, the wing-like section of the exoskeleton shifted again to allow the thrusters to tilt, so she would move forward. Sure enough, Gascoigne took off, moving through the sky at a decent clip.

Brecht half ran down the road, following her for a distance before her suit started to wobble.

"Something is wrong," he immediately shouted.

"She's probably just getting her balance," I said.

Bishop ran to the car and turned on the engine. He drove it onto the road, and then stopped in front of me. I climbed in. Once we had Brecht, too, we drove after Gascoigne, watching her in the sky as her wobbling worsened. The whole suit flailed for a bit, and the thrusters powered down, allowing the suit to come back to the ground.

She came faster than expected, though.

Bishop slammed on the brakes, and we almost flew straight into the windshield.

Gascoigne struck the road in front of us with a *slam*, her legs first, her steel alloy boots cracking the asphalt even further and digging two deep holes into the road. The thrusters *whirred* with a soft sigh as though they were dying and finally shut off.

The cardinal just stood there for a moment before it went to one knee and then opened up, revealing a shaken Gascoigne.

This was one of the rare moments I had ever seen Gascoigne so unsteady. She trembled as she pulled herself out of the interior and then stumbled onto the road.

Brecht flew out of the vehicle and rushed to her side, offering his shoulder. Gascoigne took it and leaned on him while she gulped down air and regained her balance.

I also got out of the vehicle and hurried over. "What happened?"

"My head . . . and stomach," Gascoigne muttered. "I felt like I was going to vomit constantly."

Bishop exited the vehicle and sauntered over with a smile. "Did you get motion sick?"

"I doubt it," she hissed. "I've ridden in exoskeletons for years. I've never gotten *motion sick* because of it."

"It was the height, wasn't it?" I whispered. "It was too high."

Gascoigne didn't answer me, but I knew my guess was correct. The sky had disoriented her, the vast openness and height unsettling her seasoned nerves.

Brecht kept a firm hold on her. "Do you think you can work through it?"

"How the hell should I know?" Gascoigne asked.

I pointed to the opened suit. "I'll try."

Bishop practically leapt in front of me. "No. No, I think we should just let Gascoigne pilot it back to Sanctuary, and then we should focus on the repairs and upgrades. You don't need to do anything with *flight* just yet."

His tone was the most fearful I had ever heard—and I had heard the man talk like he was about to die. Was he just worried about me? I supposed he was right. While DC had said the suit wouldn't harm the baby, *falling out of the sky* sure would.

I glanced up.

The overcast sky seemed to press down upon us, its weight almost tangible. The air, tinged with the scent of burnt electronics and hot metal, felt heavier, though.

I glanced over at the cardinal, its once-gleaming surface now marred by scuffs and dirt from its harsh landing. The cockpit was open and ready for a pilot. Eventually, Gascoigne leaned away from Brecht and walked back over. She slapped her cheek a few times before sitting inside the exoskeleton.

"I got this," she said. "I'll walk it back to Sanctury. And we can practice again in a few days."

"Sounds good." Bishop stared down at me. "Right? Sounds good? This is good?"

"Yeah," I whispered. "Let's go."

Now that I had the Vay pheromone samples, I sat in the lab.

Without all the dead animals making this a horror show, it was much easier to concentrate. Sanctuary had a lab assistant system in all its computers that greatly sped up the time for chemical analysis and breakdown. The lab also had several centrifuges, which were perfect for separating fluids—gases or liquids—based on density. I used the machines to get the pheromones from the dirt, and then used the lab asset to help me with the chemical makeup.

Once I had all the information I needed, I sat in front of the computer, contemplating how I would get more chemicals.

The door to the lab opened with a *hiss*, and I glanced over to find Brecht had entered.

I sat up. "Is everything okay?"

He nodded as he neared me. Even while inside of Sanctuary, the man chose to wear his long coat. Brecht even wore his odd scarf, like he hated being parted with it, even though Sanctuary was temperature controlled and definitely not the type of place that needed additional layers.

"I came to check on your efforts. And also to make sure you ate enough."

I hadn't noticed until that moment, but Brecht held up a small hand-sized container from the kitchen. There were cooked eggs within.

My eyes widened as he set the container down on the desk next to me.

"Thank you," I whispered.

"I knew a lot of people who worked in labs like you do," he muttered. "When I . . . well, when Vega and I lived in our underground bunker. All the people there were focused on making things. Preparing for war. Making sure *I* was prepared for war."

I listened, wondering where this was going.

"They worked themselves to death a lot of the time," Brecht finally said with a dark chuckle. "So, I was worried when I heard you were in the lab so long."

"I think I found a solution to our Vay problem." I motioned to the liquid I had extracted from the dirt. "I'm making pheromone bombs so we can disorientate them. And also liquid pheromones to lead them into traps or other places away from Sanctuary. I think, if I can get research from this lab all sorted, I can even make pheromone bombs that make the Vay sick. If we can just—"

Brecht held up a hand. I stopped talking.

"Maybe just eat a little bit first," he said, scooting the container closer to me. "Everyone wants that. Everyone would like that."

I softly chuckled and then nodded. "All right . . ." I pulled the container close. "I'll do that. Thank you so much, Brecht."

Then Brecht awkwardly nodded to me. After a few moments of prolonged silence, he tapped the desk and then started shuffling toward the door.

"Nice speaking with you. Good luck on the bombs." He left after that.

And while I probably could've been more charismatic, I appreciated that Brecht took the time to look out for me. I had come a long way since I lived in that homebrew bunker out in the wasteland of Ex Cathedra.

I needed to run a test to make sure the Vay wouldn't harm us. I had made a promise to Vega, after all. Not only that, but if we were going to have Teth everywhere in Sanctuary, I needed to make sure the Vay—who already had proven themselves capable of genocide—wouldn't come for our citizens.

"So, what's *supposed* to happen?" Bishop asked.

We sat together in my office, watching the camera screens. My five cameras outside were all ready and transmitting their recordings. Gascoigne was outside in one of the Mark III suits with over a dozen of the pheromone bombs strung along the gauntlet of her armor's left hand. She waited, in perfect stillness, on a trail I knew the Vay drones would take.

I pointed to that screen. "So, once the Vay drones get close, Gascoigne is going to throw a bomb. Depending on how the drone reacts, she might have to throw another."

"What do you mean *depending*?" Bishop sat in a chair directly next to mine. He had a bowl of peanuts, grown from Section Two, that had been shucked and roasted. He grabbed a handful and then proceeded to plop one at a time in his mouth as he stared at the screen.

"I think one bomb might not be enough." I sighed as I stared at the screen. "I haven't tested these at all, and while I tried to make them as potent as possible, I think I might've fucked up."

"You? Never."

I laughed once. "Well, I think they might be too weak to affect the drone. I'm hoping when she throws the bomb, it'll upset the Vay drone and it'll leave."

"And you think Gascoigne will have to throw multiple before that'll happen?" He threw a couple more peanuts into his mouth and chewed.

I nodded once. "Yes. But let's watch."

The screen barely flickered as the time crept forward. The drones always came at about the same rough time, so surely it would be arriving shortly.

Some of the trees swayed, and I scooted to the edge of my seat. "Okay. Here it comes."

Bishop leaned in closer, his casual demeanor giving way to focused attention. The occasional crackle of a peanut between his fingers was the only sound in the otherwise silent room.

A Vay drone emerged from the darkness, and it moved with eerie grace, its muscular form slipping through the underbrush with a predatory fluidity. Its skin was shinier than the Teth's and it reflected the dim light of evening, casting fleeting glimmers as they neared Gascoigne's position.

My heart picked up pace. Would the pheromone bombs work as intended, or had my calculations missed the mark?

Gascoigne's arm moved with mechanical precision, lifting one of the bombs. With a flick of her wrist, she launched it towards the advancing drone. The bomb arced through the air and then hit the dirt in front of the alien.

The explosion of scent was almost visible, but not really. It was probably just my imagination. The pheromone bombs had liquid and gas inside, but it would all be invisible to the naked eye. Only creatures with highly developed olfactory sense would be able to detect the change in the air.

The drone halted, its alien form recoiling as if struck by an invisible force.

"Think she'll need another one?" Bishop asked as he ate another peanut.

And then the drone started thrashing about.

Just . . . thrashing.

As though it was being electrified.

It slammed into nearby trees, knocking down pine needles, and then into the ground, as though it were trying to destroy the bomb with its face. My camera feeds didn't offer any noise, but I could practically hear the *wham* and *slam* of the drone's body as it shattered a pine tree's trunk in a single blow.

I didn't have a way to communicate with Gascoigne, but she clearly wanted to say something to me. She turned the Mark III to face the camera and then visibly shrugged with the exoskeleton, obviously baffled.

Bishop let out a low whistle. "This looks like a *super* success to me."

The Vay drone turned and fled into the darkness.

Which was really the point. The bomb had also contained trace amounts of the disease that Sanctuary had been working on—that Jack had been working on ever since they let him out.. It was a sickness meant to kill Teth, but I thought I had altered it with the Vay pheromones to affect their cells more than the Teth's. Would this sick drone run back to their nest and infect the rest?

I hoped so.

But even if it didn't do that, I could always produce more of the bombs.

I swiveled my chair to face Bishop. "Okay. New plan. We explode a bunch of these bombs around to deter the Vay from coming in this direction."

Bishop ate another peanut. "Right now?"

"In the morning. When we have time—between improving everything."

He nodded once. "Sounds good to me. Although, when are we going to hear from Quern? Or do you think he's sticking with the Iron-Blooded?"

"I think we'll hear from him tomorrow," I whispered. "I have a feeling . . . that's what he'll do."

Bishop rolled his eyes. "I don't know. He seems pretty uptight. I've got money against it."

CHAPTER THIRTY-SEVEN

The next morning, a message was left on the same pheromone trail where I had seen Quern. It was a piece of paper with poorly written English that I suspected was from Quern himself. It gave us the rough location of Commander Dannik's operation, which was the basement of a larger ranch home half a dozen miles from the entrance to Sanctuary.

The ranch house had once been the estate of a wealthy family. According to Quern's note, there was a ditch that was once a pool, a basement as large as the floor level, a barn for holding over twenty horses, and an underground shooting range.

Commander Dannik had picked the location to house himself, a few soldiers, and a dozen Teth so they could carry out their operation. Quern warned that Dannik intended to move on his plan within the next day, and that speed would be the key to catching him off guard.

I sat in my office, with Brecht, Vega, Gascoigne, and Bishop around me. I sat in my chair, Gascoigne leaned on one side of my desk, while Bishop sat on the other end. Brecht paced around Vega's large size, while the Teth warrior just stood in the middle of the room.

The Teth babies—Benjamin, Joel, and Tamura—were with Levi in the infirmary. Once my meeting was over, I'd visit them to make sure everything was okay before heading out to confront Dannik.

That was—if the others would stop fighting me on this.

"You should just stay here," Bishop stated. "C'mon, Kit-Kat. You're needed here. Let the rest of us deal with this. Gascoigne will run in like a lunatic—as usual—and Brecht and I will clean up afterward. It'll be easy. You don't need to be there."

"What if Quern is double-crossing us?"

"Triple-crossing?" Brecht held up a hand and slowly counted his fingers, as if trying to understand how many times Quern hadn't been loyal. Then he shrugged. "I thought you said you trusted Quern's word?"

"I d-do," I said. "I just . . . What if I'm wrong? What if you all go there, and never come back, because Quern quadruple-crossed us?"

"I don't think he's betrayed that many people," Bishop muttered. "Unless you count *disappointing your own mother* as a betrayal."

Gascoigne snorted out a laugh, smiled, and then nodded.

"Didn't you say he would bring Teth with him?" Vega asked.

I nodded. "That was the plan. He wanted to bring Teth over from the Iron-Blooded."

Architect Riven was too far from here to control them all. If they all defected, and allowed Architect Benjamin's pheromones to permeate them, they would join with us permanently. It was a good plan on paper, but I worried. If I was there, at the ranch house, perhaps I could help if anything went wrong. Perhaps I could convince Quern *not* to betray us again, if he was currently considering doing so.

"Perhaps we can bring Levi with us," Vega stated. "The outrider will likely have sway with the others of his blood."

"I also want to go," I said.

Bishop slid off my desk and stood in front of me. "C'mon, Kita. Listen to yourself. You know this is insane. You should stay here. Sanctuary needs you. Lump needs you—to be whole. We can handle this."

"To be fair, we don't have the best track record," Gascoigne muttered. But then she shrugged. "But you've given us a huge advantage. Two suits of power armor, one of which can *fly*? A surprise attack? You know we can do this. You don't have to be at the ranch house, watching everything with your own damn eyes."

I clenched my fists, feeling torn between the need to be present at the ranch house and the responsibility to stay safe for Sanctuary and my unborn child. "I know you're all capable, but this is a critical moment."

I had always lived alone, making every decision, deciding my fate. It felt odd to leave it to others. But wasn't that the plan? I had been improving everyone around me, so that I wasn't the *sole individual* doing everything.

Brecht stopped pacing and faced me squarely. "Kita, you've prepared us well. We know the stakes, and we know what needs to be done. Trust us to carry out your plan." He had a lot of military precision in his voice.

I glanced between everyone in the room, weighing their words. "I suppose you're all right . . . I can't be reckless anymore. Not with Remi."

"Who's Remi?" Brecht asked.

I exhaled and glanced over at him. "Our baby."

"Oh. Right. Of course. *Lump* isn't really the baby's name. That's absurd. I knew that." He spoke the last few sentences with a nervous laugh, though no one joined in.

Bishop's expression softened, and he took a step closer. "We'll bring the Teth back, and we'll deal with Dannik. We won't let you down."

I held my breath, the weight of their trust and confidence in me settling in my heart. "Okay. Go, and be careful. I'll be here, coordinating with Levi and keeping Sanctuary secure."

While the others raided Commander Dannik's hideout, I waited in the infirmary with the Teth infants.

DC had turned her own personal office into a safe space for the Teth children, and several little cribs and play areas had been set up for them. She kept the lights off in the office for long periods of time, since that was more comfortable for the babies.

It had only been a few months since their birth, but when I entered the office, I found that all three of the Teth were the size of large house cats, their once-translucent skin now shiny black and practically glittering.

The warrior, Joel, was the largest, and sat in its playpen, ripping the stuffing out of a doll that DC had given it.

The innovator, Tamura, was the smallest. It was on the floor, next to Chelsy, carefully stacking blocks using its smaller crafter arms. Chelsy watched and clapped each time the Teth innovator managed to get another block to balance.

The last one, the Teth architect, Benjamin, was asleep in its crib. Unlike the other two Teth, the architect had a mane and crest made of bone-like spines. The spines started at its head and ran down between its shoulder blades, reminding me of hair.

The mane wasn't just for show. Architects could create a gas that wafted from their mane, deadly to anything but the architect itself. It was also where the architect had its pheromone glands, potent enough to control virtually any other caste and crucial to the Teth's society.

I didn't know if the architect could create deadly gas as a baby—nor did anyone else—but so far that hadn't happened.

From what my grandfather had told me, architects controlled which of the castes could breed through the pheromones in their manes. Back in Teth history, before they were space travelers, before they came to Earth, they lived in tribes, the architect their leader. If the architect wanted more warriors, it stimulated the warriors to procreate. If the architect wanted more innovators, it would do the same with them. Each architect built a society based around their perceived needs, building complex social structures exactly as they deemed necessary.

That was how they got the title of "architect," because they were engineers of towns and culture, not of buildings.

As I stepped deeper into the office, I realized the baby Teth weren't the only ones in here.

Himiko Akia and her two children, Alex and Hiro, along with Chelsy and Levi, were all crowded in the corner, sitting on the floor near the little innovator.

Himiko was in her thirties, and had lived a rough life, but she retained much of her beauty. She had long black hair, and dark eyes that were softened with kindness. When she glanced up, she had a look of concern that quickly melted away.

"Kita," Himiko whispered. "Welcome. Come join us."

The moment Chelsy spotted me, she lit up and motioned me over.

I walked to them, a little hesitantly, since there were so many people here.

Himiko was our resident teacher. She knew how to play musical instruments, and had quite a bit of knowledge on plants. It made sense she was here—the Teth babies would learn alongside the human ones.

Alex and Hiro both resembled their mother. They had black hair, dark eyes, and smiled a lot. They both sat close to Chelsy, and she tapped Hiro on the shoulder once to sign something to him.

To my surprise—because I thought *no one* knew sign language—Hiro, who was only nine years old, signed something back.

"We've been teaching all the kids," Himiko said as she followed my gaze.

"Right," I muttered.

Levi sat on the floor, near Chelsy, his size considerable when compared to her. He looked *awkward*, with his large legs folded, and his two bulky arms half behind his back. With his thinner arms, he handed the innovator little blocks.

Whenever the Teth touched, they lingered for a moment, feeling each other's skin.

When Himiko handed Tamura a block, the little innovator would spend *longer* touching her palms, as though confused about why it was all different.

"*How are the babies?*" I asked Levi in Tethlite. Then I took a seat on the floor next to everyone.

Levi replied in soft Tethlite, "*They thrive. They explore their surroundings with curiosity and adapt quickly. It is fascinating.*"

Tamura carefully placed a block atop her tiny tower, using her little hands to feel the structure. A human baby at this age would not have this level of fine motor control. It was impressive Tamura could do so much. The other two Teth didn't develop as quickly as she had, though . . .

Although, calling her a "she" was incorrect, considering they were hermaphrodites, but it sounded better to me. Tamura had been my sister, so . . . Tamura felt closer when I imagined a part of my sister as one with this Teth.

Chelsy beamed at the Teth infant, encouraging it with gentle pats on the shoulder. Joel, in his playpen, had abandoned the doll and was now amusing himself by biting down on a squeaky toy.

"They seem happy," I said, wondering if it was natural for the Teth warrior to seem doglike.

Levi snorted. "*They are learning quickly, and their interaction with the human children is beneficial for their understanding of our new kin of different blood.*"

Alex, a mere eight years old, turned to me and nodded. "All the little aliens are happy. Mom says we have to socialize them, so that they're comfortable around humans." Alex placed a hand on his chest. "I talk to them all the time. I'm teaching them English. And also a secret code!"

"That's . . . good," I said.

Chelsy tugged at my sleeve, pointing to Tamura and then to her own small pile of blocks. Then she made the sign for *friend* and smiled.

I nodded. "Yes, you need to be friends with all of them."

Chelsy nodded and resumed helping the little Teth.

I wanted to keep myself distracted, so I didn't think of the others and their assault against the Iron-Blooded. We had radios now, but it was impossible to use the small short-wave devices while I was in an underground bunker and they were several miles away.

I had heard there were A-tech devices that functioned similarly to radios, except their broadcasts could go through most solid objects, but we didn't have them here. I wished we did. I wanted to speak with Bishop the entire time through this dangerous mission. It was *his* life I worried about the most. I had almost asked him to stay beside me and allow the others to handle this, but he was one of the few that could pilot the power armor, so of course this mission would fall to him and the others.

And he had been a junk hunter for several years before I knew him.

He was capable.

I didn't have to worry.

Yet my hands shook nonetheless.

What was wrong with me?

"*You should calm yourself,*" Levi said. "*Teth can sense your anxiety.*"

When I glanced over, I realized all three of the Teth babies were still, even the architect in its crib. Joel was no longer chewing on the toy, and Tamura no longer stacked blocks. They were all "facing" me with their eyeless faces, as though my worrying had caused them a small shock and they all needed to investigate what that was.

Once all the Teth were still, Alex, Hiro, Chelsy, and Himiko all faced me as well.

It made the room feel even smaller than it was.

I stood and brushed myself off. "Ah, well, I just wanted to make sure they were okay, so I'm going to head back to my office. Thank you, everyone. Especially you, Himiko—for taking the time to socialize the babies. Take good care of the little ones until I get back."

The others nodded in acknowledgement, and as soon as I headed to the door, the children resumed their activities. Everyone had told me I didn't need to do everything personally, and perhaps they were right. I had thought *I* would need to teach the Teth babies all the ins and outs of human society, but I had forgotten that was why we had a teacher. That was why we had doctors.

Everyone had a role to play.

Now I had to play mine.

CHAPTER THIRTY-EIGHT

I couldn't sleep.

I watched the outside cameras the entire time in my office, my eyes hurting since I refused to blink. Why was I so emotional about this? I couldn't explain it. I just . . . wanted to know when they came home. I wanted to know what they were doing. I couldn't rest until the worry over their safety was gone from my mind.

The *instant* I saw signs of exoskeletons approaching the front of Sanctuary, I pushed away from the desk and ran out of the office. I hurried my way through Section Three, through the gardens of Section Two, and all the enhanced growth of the plants and the creation of fertilizer, and then I dashed through the newly made homes and fish tanks in Section One.

People waved and spoke to me.

I smiled, waved back, made statements about being late, and then continued. I hoped the citizens of our new little home would understand and not think me rude, but that was far in the back of my mind.

I ran up the stairs and then out the front door into the parking lot outside of Sanctuary, the rusted sign greeting me as I gulped down the cold evening air. I was winded from all that running, but I wasn't able to stop until I made it outside.

The ground trembled as three exoskeletons walked their way over to me. Behind them was an Iron-Blooded transport van, and in the driver's seat was Quern.

I held my breath until I could see the shine of the cardinal, and the paint of the Mark III. These were my people.

Gascoigne and Brecht stopped their power armor in the parking lot. There were two *hisses* as the exoskeletons cracked open to allow their pilots an escape. I watched as they crawled out of the inside, both of them a little sweaty, but looking confident.

Quern parked his van at the beginning of the parking lot. As soon as he did, he hopped out, went to the back, and opened it up. Eleven Teth leapt from the back, each carrying a pack or a box. There were six warriors, three outriders, and two innovators. All the castes were just *shaped* differently, with the innovators being the shortest, the outriders being the thinnest, and the warriors the most muscled.

Bishop also hopped out of the van, though his expression was a little more grim than the others.

"It worked?" I asked. "Everyone is okay?"

Brecht unplugged the exoskeleton from his neck and then walked over to me. "Everything is fine. We handled it."

Bishop sauntered over like he owned the place, a smile chasing away the gloom he'd once had in his expression. "I told you we'd make it back, Kit-Kat."

He pulled up his shirt and showed me a new scar on his ribcage—he had clearly burned it into his flesh less than ten hours ago. It was an X on his lowest rib, different than the other tally marks around it.

"I'm gonna need new symbols for all the bullshit I've been killing lately," he said with a chuckle. "This is for the Iron-Blooded and Teth commanders." He patted his chest. "I got the killing blows on them, by the way."

Gascoigne rolled her eyes so hard she looked like she strained something. "Only after I smashed my way in first. This *ham* wants all the glory."

"I just like *kill stealing*," Bishop said, obviously to irritate her.

Brecht coughed. We all turned in his direction. With a frown, he pointed back to the van. "We should tell Kita about the problem we ran into on the way back."

Problem?

My heart sank into my gut. What problem? Everything was going so well so far. We didn't need any more complications.

Quern leapt into the back of the van and then stepped out with a shaken teenage boy dressed in the brown uniform of the Ex Cathedra army. The teen was roughed up—one eye so swollen he couldn't open it—and most of his brown uniform was stained dark with blood. He walked with a limp as Quern dragged him over.

Once they were close, Quern shoved him. The teen fell and hit the cracked asphalt of the parking lot on one knee. He was so shaky that it took him two attempts to stand back up.

"You found an Ex Cathedra soldier?" I asked.

"*His* squad found *us*," Gascoigne said matter-of-factly. "We chewed through half of them before they surrendered. Then this one stepped forward and said they were just messengers. *General Melvin of the Western Border* has declared Sanctuary an enemy of Ex Cathedra."

I glanced over to the teen. He gulped down some breath and stared at me with his one eye. "I'm here to deliver a message to the leader of Sanctuary."

"I'm the leader," I said. "Architect Kita Yamasaki."

I hadn't yet learned how Theon was a human architect, but I figured it was only a matter of time . . . Taking the title of "architect" was just the next step in establishing myself as the true leader of Sanctuary.

The teen boy seemed confused for half a moment, but when no one said, *just kidding*, he moved on. "General Melvin is demanding your unconditional surrender," he said, his voice unsteady. "You killed several of our judges, took our equipment, and actively impeded our advancement toward the coast. If you surrender, General Melvin will allow all civilians citizenship into Ex Cathedra, whereas your soldiers will be required to serve for seven years before they're freed."

"And if we don't surrender?" I asked.

"I-If you don't surrender, then we'll decimate your army, and wipe out all men in your civilian ranks."

"He means *decimate* in the archaic sense of the word," Gascoigne intoned. "Where they'll kill ten percent of our armies *and then* force the rest into hard labor."

Ah. Ex Cathedra really loved their history books. Back in ancient Rome, the term "decimate" meant to "kill one in every ten of a group of soldiers as a punishment for the whole group." Since then, the word had morphed to just mean *mostly destroyed*, but Ex Cathedra wanted to go old school with their threats, it seemed.

"Is there any chance we could negotiate?" I asked.

Gascoigne ground her teeth. "Don't. Fucking. *Negotiate.*" She stomped over to me, like she was ready to punch me in the face. Bishop leapt between us, his body tense.

Gascoigne looked him up and down. While she was muscled, and tough looking, Bishop still had her beat. She sneered up at him.

"We should never have any dealings with Ex Cathedra," Gascoigne barked. "I was a judge with them for years. Their tactics are underhanded, and they don't want a long-term relationship with us. They want us to bend the knee."

Brecht frowned. "Does this General Melvin have many judges under his command?"

The evening winds howled around us, as though the world was darkly chuckling. I shivered, rubbed my arms, and then turned my full attention to the teen messenger.

He shuddered before saying, "He has a platoon of them under his command."

The size of a *platoon* varied from one nation to another. In most countries, a platoon was four squads of soldiers, which in turn could be made up of six to twelve individuals, depending on the organizational patterns. Instead of guessing the strength of Ex Cathedra's platoon, I just faced Gascoigne, hoping she'd fill me in.

"That means he has eighty judges," Gascoigne stated. "Which is probably *all* the judges assigned to the western border." She glared at me. "I seriously doubt he would order the whole platoon to attack Sanctuary."

"General Melvin knows about your advanced judge suit," the teen weakly said. "As part of your surrender, you need to hand it over immediately."

"What if I wanted to speak with General Melvin?" I asked. "Is there any way to get in contact with him?"

Gascoigne folded her arms over her chest, her glare intensifying. "You want to speak with him? After what they've done? After what they're threatening? Fuck. Them. If you give them *anything* they're going to take until there's nothing left."

Brecht held up a hand. "I think Kita's idea has merit. We should talk to them. At least buy some time. We're still growing—still building. We can't fight *eighty judges*."

"We can't fight *eight* judges," Bishop quietly quipped.

Gascoigne spat on the asphalt. "We could take *eight*. Fuck it—*I* can take eight. The more we rip them apart, the stronger we'll get. Kita has already proven that by scavenging the remains of our enemies. We should never surrender to Ex Cathedra. *Ever*."

Bishop, still standing protectively close, added, "Well, I don't want to fight eighty judges, but I think Brecht has a point. We should probably talk to the general just to get more time. Or maybe just see how quickly they want to mobilize against us."

The teen soldier, still trembling, nodded. "We were keeping in touch with General Melvin through a radio at our forward base. It's, uh, an A-tech radio we use. You have to use it outside." He pointed to the sky, as though both understanding how to use the equipment, but not understanding at all how it worked.

Bishop glanced over at me. "I'll go get it." He poked me in the shoulder with his pointer finger. "You stay here. All right? Once I get back, you can speak with the general, and then we'll formulate a plan. Together."

He didn't want to put me in danger. After a long sigh, I nodded once. While Bishop was away getting this A-tech radio, I would think up a few bargains for Ex Cathedra. We couldn't fight that whole nation . . .

Well, that wasn't true.

Gascoigne was right. We *could*. I just didn't want to. I wanted to grow—I wanted to build. But if Ex Cathedra forced my hand, I'd make them regret they ever spoke to me.

CHAPTER THIRTY-NINE

They brought the radio back a few hours later.

It was a large box-like stand with the radio on top. It must've weighed fifty pounds, but it reminded me of the communication tower I'd seen at Davis Space Force Base. I almost wanted to take it apart to see how it worked—and reverse engineer it—but I pushed that thought from my head.

Gascoigne carried it over using her cardinal armor. Those exoskeletons made everything look lightweight. She probably could've thrown the radio over the nearest mountain, if she really wanted to.

She set it down in the parking lot just outside Sanctuary's front door. I stared at the device, wondering if I just *used* it or if there was a certain procedure.

Fortunately, I didn't have to wonder too much. Quern dragged the teen messenger over so *he* could use the radio.

Brecht stayed in his Mark III suit, standing watch over the group, and Bishop stayed close to me, even as I approached the Ex Cathedra soldier. The teen was looking worse than ever, though. I suspected no one had fed him or given him any water, because his complexion was wan and his stance weak.

I glanced up.

Night.

"Will General Melvin even answer at this hour?" I asked.

The teenager nodded. "He's waiting for our r-report. We were supposed to give you the message and see what you had to say. Our instructions were to radio in the moment we had your answer."

I walked over to the box. It had several buttons, but each was conveniently labeled as though someone suspected a child might need to use it. One knob had the words *FRONTLINE BASE* under it, while another knob had *DON'T TOUCH THIS FREQENCY*. Someone had also taken a pen and written *DO NOT USE FORCE* on the side.

I switched on the radio and then picked up the receiver. After clicking it on, I said, "Hello?"

I clicked off, and waited for a response.

Static on the other end, and then a man replied, "This is the Frontline Base. Identify yourself."

"I'm Kita Yamasaki, the leader of Sanctuary."

The man took a moment to respond. "One moment."

The night was cold, and I didn't want to have to sit around forever for some general, but I also knew this couldn't be avoided. The occasional *bwak* of chickens could be heard in the distance, over by our hidden chicken range. I wondered who was on guard duty, but I shook it from my thoughts. Now wasn't the time for that. I had to be ready for the general.

I had to—

"Good evening," a voice said over the receiver.

It was probably the iciest voice I had ever heard in my life. It was the kind of voice you only needed to hear once and you'd be able to identify it in a crowded room. It was like the man hated speaking—hated conversation on a deep level—and his tone was laced with that contempt. His words were perfectly articulated, though, and he spoke with such an even cadence it would be impossible to misunderstand him.

"Good evening," I said in response. "To whom am I speaking?"

"General Melvin of the Western Border and military advisor to the justicar. I assume I'm speaking to the leader of the town Sanctuary?"

The "justicar" was the name most military people used for the president of Ex Cathedra. It was a weird title, given all the injustice going on in the nation, but I wasn't about to argue the fact.

"I'm Kita, yes." Then I took a deep breath. "Your messengers ran into my soldiers. We thought you were attacking, so some of them unfortunately didn't make it. I apologize, but—"

"Never mind that," General Melvin stated, cutting me off.

The teen boy shuddered.

Everyone else around me exchanged cold glances. Except for Gascoigne—she just stared at the radio like it had killed her father and she was mentally preparing revenge.

"I sent messengers to offer you a chance to surrender," General Melvin said. "I assume they conveyed the conditions?"

"I heard them," I said. "You'll decimate our forces if we resist, and you'll kindly integrate my citizens if I don't."

"That's the gist, yes."

There was a short moment of silence between us. I had read once that silence was a form of dominance—and that making the other person speak first was a way to assert authority over another. If that were the case, it seemed as though we were playing the same game, and Melvin grew tired of it faster than I did.

"I assume you'll be surrendering?"

"How about we negotiate?" I asked.

Gascoigne turned her knife-glare on me. I shook my head and motioned to the radio. I just wanted to see what he had to say.

"Do you think you have something that would interest me?" General Melvin asked.

"Yes."

"Then why would I negotiate? Why wouldn't I just take it from you when I come to take everything else?"

Ah, the classic *threaten their lives* tactic.

"I don't want to fight you," I finally said, though I regretted wording it that way. It made me sound weak, like I was *afraid* to fight, even though that wasn't what I meant.

"Then surrender," Melvin said with a hint of faux sweetness to his words. "We're already the largest nation on the continent. We're growing more powerful by the minute, and your tiny sad sack town doesn't stand a chance."

"We killed two of your judges recently," I whispered into the radio receiver.

Everyone around me stiffened. Except for Bishop, who actively started chuckling, like this was all one big game that he was happy to take part in.

General Melvin also chuckled. "I heard you had some sort of rare and advanced judge armor. We'll be taking that as well, trust me."

"You think you can handle it?" I asked.

"What makes you think we don't have a couple ourselves?"

I caught my breath and then glanced over at Gascoigne. Her expression was unreadable, and I wondered if she knew that. *Did* they have their own version of the Mark VI? It was plausible. Surely the United States military didn't make just *one*. But did they have their own *cardinal*? I doubted it. And that was the most important thing.

Flying was our biggest advantage.

"I don't care if you have a million exoskeletons," I said into the receiver. "I'm not going to surrender, and if you knew what was good for you, all of Ex Cathedra would leave our area on the map alone."

I spoke each word with a calm and casual tone, as though I were speaking to a friend or making an order for food. But deep in my gut, there was a fire—a rage—that anyone would dare to threaten the safety of Sanctuary. I had worked tirelessly to make this place bigger and better, and I was going to make sure it was the beacon of hope in all the wasteland.

Ex Cathedra thought they could fuck with us? They had another thing coming.

But General Melvin just laughed. It was a deep and guttural *not giving a damn* kind of laugh, the one that an evil villain would've done at the end of a children's vid. I didn't care. I allowed him to get it out of his system, listening to the full chuckle until he wound himself down.

"You've got balls," he eventually said. "So I'll just make a note in my records that you said *no* when I offered you a peaceful surrender. How does that sound?"

Gascoigne ripped the receiver from my hand and clicked on. "*You can go fuck yourself, Melvin,*" she growled. "We'll fight you to the very last man, destroying as many judges as we can get our hands on. You understand me?"

Once she was done, Melvin switched back onto the radio. "You sound familiar . . . Gascoigne? Cherry Gascoigne? Is that really you?"

Bishop couldn't stop himself. He laughed—it was so loud—and nearly folded over with chuckles. "*Cherry?*" he half shouted. "Your first name is *Cherry?*" He hit Brecht with an elbow. "Did you know this?"

Brecht shrugged. "Yes."

"You did? *And you never told me?*" Bishop laughed through each word, as though it were uncontrollable. I was happy he was having a wonderful time, but it was clear that Gascoigne was not.

She stared at the radio, no emotions on her face, her cold demeanor intensifying worse than the Forever Winter.

"We'll never surrender," Gascoigne said. "Because if I ever see you in person again, I'm gonna castrate you in front of all your men."

That sentence calmed Bishop down in a hurry.

Even Quern seemed unsettled by her dark proclamation, and nothing seemed to faze the man.

"I'll be sending a welcome wagon your way," General Melvin said with a chortle. "And you better hope you die before we see each other face-to-face again, Gascoigne. I won't be so nice next time."

CHAPTER FORTY

General Melvin switched off his end of the radio, leaving it dead. I poked at the radio and gave serious consideration to switching the frequency, just to see if I could pick up anything else.

Gascoigne threw the receiver down and stormed away from the radio.

I turned around to face her. "Are you okay?" I asked. "What the hell was that? We should've at least *tried* to make them go away."

She sucked in some air through her teeth. "I can't. I can't go back."

No one else said anything.

When I waited for her to continue, Gascoigne finally said, "You heard him. Anything you have that he wants, he's just going to take. There is no negotiating. They think they have the upper hand."

"They do have the upper hand," Quern drawled.

We all turned to the face the Iron-Blooded defector.

He sneered and then motioned to the area around us. "You made a big show of being *protected*. That's how I convinced the Teth to join you—by telling them of your architect, and your safety. Now what? Huh? We can't fight Ex Cathedra."

"I can," I stated.

Quern looked me up and down. "How?"

"Kidnap them and develop a close-knit bond, obviously," Bishop quipped.

"Shut up," Quern hissed at the other man. "This is serious. We don't need your *buffoonery*."

Bishop snorted back a laugh. "That's a new word for me. I like it, though. I might have to burn some tally marks into that word right over my ass. It'll make for a good story."

The more Bishop joked around, the more Quern seethed.

I didn't care, though.

"Listen, I need to go inside," I whispered. "I'm going to prepare for what needs to be done. And then . . . we'll discuss how we want to do it."

"What do you want to do about the radio?" Brecht asked.

"We need it," I stated. "I'll have to speak to the general again. Keep it close."

"What do you want to do with the messenger?"

I glanced over at the teen, almost sad he was involved in all of this. "Put him in the jail. The opposite of Theon. We'll . . . do something with him later."

The prison was going to become crowded at this rate. I really should've looked into improving it.

I sat in my office, staring at the camera screen. Lately, I had been watching the outdoors, looking for the Vay or trying to spot the chickens. Fortunately, the Vay hadn't returned, and the chickens were more hidden than ever.

Now, I was watching the feed of the inside. I had a camera specifically in Section Five, to watch the firestorm bombs.

I had lowkey thought about them since I found them. They were the most devastating weapons ever created, and the reason the world had fallen apart. Even one of the bombs could level a whole city—maybe even a megacity—and the fires would specifically burn through organic matter much more than normal.

They were the peak of A-tech weaponry.

And I had some.

Before, I hadn't known what I was going to do with one, since driving it around in a van seemed like a suicide mission. They weren't remote detonated—they were the type of missiles that detonated upon impact. That meant they were normally loaded onto planes, and then dropped over a location.

Technically, before the Forever Winter, some of the firestorm bombs had been launched from the space station that orbited around the Earth.

The missiles launched from there could hit anywhere in the world, whereas the planes needed to be capable of flying over their desired location. Any place with antiaircraft defenses was mostly safe.

Mostly.

The fast fighter jets—the ones with the A-tech stealth—had delivered most of the devastating payloads during the war.

I figured I'd never be able to use a firestorm bomb, even though I had them, because I had no way to deliver them.

But now . . .

Now I did.

The cardinal could fly.

However, it was just a single power-armor suit, not really meant for carrying a missile in its arms. Would I really send someone to fly over Ex Cathedra carrying a deadly nuclear missile? And who would do it? Gascoigne wasn't capable. She barely made the suit fly a few hundred feet before vomiting.

And I hadn't ridden in a suit since I learned of the baby.

Would I have to suck it up and do this myself?

Another one of the screens flashed with light. I glanced over. It was a camera pointed to the outside. The clouds over the nearby forest . . . They parted and allowed the morning sun to trickle down onto the pine trees. It was beautiful, if only for a moment.

It reminded me of how far we had come.

Humanity was recovering. Sanctuary was a beautiful place. If I wasn't willing to fight for these things, who was?

I needed to make sure no one would come to bother us.

Then I saw something troubling appear on the screen. More exoskeletons. Four this time. They walked toward Sanctuary as though on the warpath, and each of them was painted black and red with the word JUDGE prominently splattered on the legs of their power armor.

Three of them had large vents near the helmet, which betrayed the fact they were Mark III suits of armor. The last one—the one suit in the lead—was definitely a Mark V, and was holding a large railgun. The type meant to be wielded by power armor. The devastating railgun was a weapon that used electromagnetic force to launch high-velocity projectiles, sometimes with enough force to blow through multiple buildings at once.

This was an anti-power-armor weapon.

"Oh, fuck me," I whispered.

Ex Cathedra wanted to start a war. And they were already here.

I poked at my computer and immediately hit the alarm function. All of Sanctuary blared with a warning noise and small red lights started flashing from the corners of all rooms. I leapt from my office chair and ran for Section One.

Bursting into Section One, my heart pounded against my ribs like a frantic drum. The warehouse was alive with activity—residents of Sanctuary scurried in every direction, all of them trying to secure their new homes. Overhead, the red lights pulsed in time with the wailing alarm, casting an ominous glow across the stark gray walls.

As I sprinted for the front stairwell, the metallic clang of my boots echoed sharply. My breath came in quick and shallow gasps. Adrenaline surged through my veins, sharpening my senses to a razor's edge. I felt every vibration of the alarm.

"*Kita!*"

I stopped just before I reached the front door. Bishop was running after me. He stopped once he reached my side and then grabbed my shoulders so he could examine me. "What's wrong?"

"Ex Cathedra is here," I breathed.

The air was thick with the smell of oil and metal, and I turned to see Brecht suiting up into the Mark III. Once the power armor had closed around him, he stomped his way over. The warehouse was so tall, he didn't have to duck. People pointed and shouted.

"I'm ready," he said, the helmet mildly distorting his voice.

Gascoigne was already halfway into her suit, the cardinal armor encasing her like a second skin. The sleek, metallic surfaces reflected the red emergency lights, giving her an almost demonic appearance.

"They're here," I shouted to Gascoigne. "That welcoming committee. It's four judges. They have a weapon to take down other exoskeletons. You have to be careful."

I was vomiting up the words because I just couldn't speak fast enough. Panic flooded me. I didn't want to lose them—or anyone—and I certainly couldn't afford to lose the cardinal suit.

"We'll handle this," Gascoigne said, her voice equally distorted by her helmet. "Let's give them a welcome they won't forget."

Both Brecht and Gascoigne stomped past me, shaking all of Section One as they strode out the door and then up the massive stairs that led out of Sanctuary.

"Where are you going?" Bishop asked. "I'll stay with you."

"I . . ."

I wanted to go outside, but what was I going to do? Only the exoskeletons could fight them. I wouldn't stand a chance with just a gun.

"I'm . . . going to head back to my office." With spare energy swimming in my panic-filled veins, I *ran* back to my office. Bishop stayed close, clearly panicked as well.

Once I'd burst into my personal office in Section Three, I threw myself back into my chair and turned to the monitor that had caught sight of the four judges to begin with.

"Are they already fighting?" Bishop asked as he grabbed a chair and dragged it over to me. The alarm continued, the red light even flashing in my office.

That was fine.

We would be fine.

Gascoigne, clad in her gleaming cardinal armor, raced into the view of my camera. Beside her, Brecht, donning his less advanced but still formidable Mark III, rushed in to fight the four judges.

This was a smart tactic. The judges hadn't been prepared to see them, and Gascoigne knew they couldn't stand at a distance, lest they be taken down by the railgun. They had to stay close.

The lead judge, wielding the anti-armor railgun, pivoted to target Gascoigne, the railgun flaring to life as it charged. My cameras didn't pick up any noise, but I could imagine it humming with power. Those damn guns were always so loud.

Gascoigne's armor was wider than most, but lightweight. She moved to the side faster than the enemy could swivel and pivot, and she managed to close the distance between them.

Brecht, in his Mark III, moved with less finesse but with no less determination. He bulldozed towards the nearest judge, his armored fist raised in a telegraphed punch.

Gascoigne reached the lead judge just as the railgun fired. The projectile, a streak of light and force, grazed her armor, sending sparks flying and leaving a seared mark on its surface. Gascoigne ignited her plasma blade. Unlike the Mark VI, which had a blade of hot blue, the cardinal lived up to its name with a blazing red blade that extended a good twenty inches.

She stabbed at her opponent, but didn't quite hit his torso. Gascoigne slashed the arm of the machine, devastating it.

Brecht engaged his target with brute force, his armored fists pounding against the enemy suit in what I assumed was a symphony of metal on metal. Bishop grabbed the edge of my desk and pulled himself forward. He never blinked as he watched the fight.

I didn't blink either. Hell, I didn't even breathe.

I just watched.

The enemy judge, taken aback by Brecht's sheer power, staggered but quickly regained composure, responding with a series of well-placed strikes that tested the limits of Brecht's armor. The enemy unleashed a steel alloy blade, and it made me wonder why Brecht didn't use his own.

Probably because . . .

He wasn't used to piloting the power armor. He wasn't *Gascoigne*, who had lived in an exoskeleton for years. He barely knew how to drive the thing—he was punching because that was amateurish.

Damn.

I should've been the one out there.

While I hadn't been paying attention, the other two Mark III judges had maneuvered to flank Gascoigne, their steel blades already extended. Gascoigne, obviously aware of the encroaching threat, twisted and turned, her movements a whirlwind of tactical evasion and offensive prowess.

In my office, I watched the scene unfold with bated breath, my fingers gripping the edges of my desk.

CHAPTER FORTY-ONE

The two flanking Mark IIIs lunged at Gascoigne. She dodged one, but the other struck her with the steel blade. That was fine—her armor was strong enough that it left just a scratch—but if she sustained enough of those, she could be in trouble.

However, the enemies hadn't been prepared for her *second* plasma blade. The red-hot weapon shot out of her other arm, and Gascoigne stabbed it through the chest of one of her attackers, killing the pilot instantly.

These plasma blades . . . seemed more devastating than the one on the Mark VI.

Brecht grappled with his opponent, trying to wrestle the other to the ground. The trees around them shook. The enemy judge escaped the grapple and then swung his alloy blade through the air, aiming for a weak point in Brecht's armor, but Brecht deftly maneuvered to avoid the strike.

The other Mark III judge lunged, aiming a swift jab at Gascoigne's side, while the railgun judge circled around, attempting to trap her. Gascoigne countered with a spin, her plasma blade cutting through the air, narrowly missing the first judge's armor.

Brecht, meanwhile, found an opening. He delivered a powerful punch that sent his opponent reeling backward.

Back in my office, the alarm continued its relentless blare, but I barely heard it.

The Mark III judge managed to land a solid hit on Gascoigne, knocking her off-balance. However, Gascoigne quickly recovered, her suit's thrusters firing to stabilize her. I hadn't known they could do that.

She swung her plasma blade around, a line of red illuminating the area as she decapitated the enemy judge. The helmet was cut clean from the rest of the body, taking the pilot's head with it.

The railgun judge opened fire on Brecht, the bullets ripping through more of his suit as though he wasn't even there. Brecht hit the ground.

"Oh, fuck," Bishop whispered.

Gascoigne threw herself on the railgun judge. She slashed down on his head, and then his chest, and then his railgun, using both the plasma blades like they were sticks for a drum set, gouging and ripping apart the enemy in a matter of seconds.

Sparks went everywhere. The armor holding the railgun was practically melting from the plasma heat.

Then Gascoigne leapt off the Mark V railgunner. The thrusters on her suit allowed her to really *jump*, and when she came back down, it was practically on top of the last judge. The resulting *crash* of steel on steel shook the whole damn forest. I swore I felt it, even inside Sanctuary.

Again, like a berserker unleashed, Gascoigne pounded the hell out of the other judge, tearing through his armor as though it were wax and she were a flame.

Only once she tired herself out did Gascoigne stop attacking.

All four of the judges were dead. Some of them *very* dead and melted.

Brecht's suit *attempted* to open, but the damage from the railgun had left one side unable to move. The machine struggled, but only the right side slid open to reveal a bloodied Brecht. He wasn't moving.

Gascoigne used the plasma blade on her power armor to cut away the other half. Then she deactivated the blades, knelt, and scooped up Brecht from within. The exoskeletons weren't designed to be gentle, but it was probably the fastest way to get him out.

She ran from the battlefield toward the entrance of Sanctuary.

I stopped the alarms.

"We have to go get DC," I said to Bishop.

He was already to the door of my office. "Yeah, c'mon. Let's do it."

Bishop and I stood in the infirmary waiting area.

Not only had we lost our only Mark III suit, we couldn't even use the suits that Ex Cathedra had sent because Gascoigne had mutilated them all. I didn't blame her—I would've done the same—but it was unfortunate.

Brecht wasn't dead, but he wasn't awake, either. DC had operated on him, and stitched him up, but Brecht had lost a lot of blood. He also didn't have the nanites, like the rest of us, and I should've taken that into consideration when Ex Cathedra attacked.

I should've . . .

Sent Bishop.

But then I remembered the railgun firing through the steel plating of the power armor and I shuddered. Should I have sent Bishop to deal with that? Would that have happened if *he* were fighting? I didn't know—all I knew was that I couldn't deal with it.

Not when I had Remi to think about.

"I need to speak with General Melvin," I whispered.

Bishop, who had been pacing around the waiting room, glanced up at me. "Why? You're going to make a deal now?"

"No. I'm . . . going to give him one last chance to leave us alone."

"And then what?" Bishop asked.

I met his eyes.

I loved him more than anything in the world, and the thought of him dying made me want to ensure his safety. Really, I wanted to ensure *all* our safety. Chelsy, the Teth, Quern, Gascoigne—I couldn't imagine any of them dying. It shook me too much.

"I'm going to hit them with a firestorm bomb," I whispered.

Bishop chuckled. Then he got serious again. "Really?"

"I can deliver it using the cardinal."

Apparently, Bishop hadn't thought of any of this. Probably because I hadn't spoken about the firestorm bombs much in the way of a tactic. Regardless, it was our final option.

If General Melvin sent four more judges—*forty more judges*—we would all die.

I couldn't allow that.

"I think you should let Gascoigne do it," Bishop said. He placed a hand on my shoulder. "I think it's insane for you to go alone."

"Gascoigne isn't good at flying the suit," I murmured. "But I know I'll be able to handle it."

Heights had never bothered me. This was my plan—and I'd be the one with all the blood and nuclear fire on my hands.

Bishop took in a deep breath. "Why give them a warning? Why not just take a bomb now? Go to their capital or something?"

"I don't want . . . their civilians to suffer." I shook my head. "If I warn them—if I give them a chance to surrender—I know I'll have at least *tried* to deescalate this. If I don't warn them, I'll feel like a murderer. Even if we are at war."

"These lunatics brought guns to our doorstep and threatened to kill everyone. I don't think you need to use kid gloves with them."

"They didn't know who they were messing with," I whispered. Then I glanced up and met his gaze. "If a child slapped an adult, would you think it okay for the adult to shoot the kid with a gun?"

Bishop darkly chuckled. "Man, I hope we're the adult in that metaphor."

"We are. Which is why I have to go warn the general." I turned and faced the infirmary door. "Stay here, Bishop. Let me know if Brecht recovers, okay? I won't deliver the bomb until everyone knows what I'm doing— and I have a chance to discuss it."

"Okay. I'll hold down the fort. Good luck with the general."

I waited a few hours before I attempted to contact General Melvin.

Quern joined me outside to use the radio, and Bishop brought the teen messenger as per my request. When he was hauled out into the parking lot, I glanced him up and down. He was looking better, if only because people were feeding him now.

"What's your name?" I asked.

"Rory," he muttered.

"Sorry about this, Rory. But you're on the wrong side of this conflict."

He had sandy blond hair and sad green eyes that looked like they had been drained of all their vibrancy. His brown uniform was only dirtier than the last time I saw it because it was clear no one had given him any new clothing to use.

"You can't beat Ex Cathedra," Rory whispered.

"They said I couldn't beat the Iron-Blooded either, but look what happened."

Rory stared at me, confused, and then glanced around. There were Teth in the forest, some of them tending to the surroundings, one of them even guarding the chickens.

It seemed to occur to him then that we were a different kind of city.

"I'm going to contact the general," I said.

Rory nodded.

"You think he'll talk to me? Will he negotiate?"

"No."

Even though everyone said he wouldn't, I still needed to try. I switched the radio on, and then I made sure the frequency was set before I clicked the receiver.

"Hello?" I asked.

And then I waited.

Static. Then a male voice responded. "Please identify yourself."

"I'm Kita Yamasaki. Leader of Sanctuary."

The radio went to static again before it flared to life. The general's unmissable voice rang out from the speaker.

"Good afternoon, Kita. I assume, since you're speaking to me, that my judges have left?"

"If by *left* you mean *left this world and moved on to a nicer place*, then yes. They've left."

The radio was silent for a lone moment.

"I see," the general finally stated. "Then you'll be happy to hear your little hovel is now my top priority."

"Here's the thing," I said, not wanting to go back and forth with this. "I didn't want to hurt you, but you've left me no choice. I'm going to bomb the nearest Ex Cathedra city. And not with a pipe bomb, or little fission bomb—I'm going to hit it with a firestorm bomb."

No answer.

I assumed he was laughing on the other end, but I would never know. I gave him a chance to respond, and he didn't take it, so I continued.

"You have a day to surrender, but if you don't, that's what's going to happen. If you don't surrender after *that*, I'm just going to bomb another city. And then another. Until Ex Cathedra is blown back into the Forever Winter."

I hadn't realized it until then, but my voice was louder than normal, and more pointed. The others were staring at me as if I were a mass murderer, but I didn't care. This was the price of threatening everything I cared about.

I was warning them. I was giving them a chance.

Would they take it?

"You expect us to believe that?" General Melvin asked. "I hate to break this to you, but bluffs only work if they're plausible."

I didn't reply.

"We're never going to leave you alone. We're going to burn down that mud hole you call a home, and then we're going to take all your citizens and put them to work in our mines. If you want to salvage something of your life, you'll rethink all your choices that brought you to this moment."

"Is that your answer, then?" I asked.

But the radio cut out.

The general never replied.

That was fine. I gave them the warning, and now I was going to follow through.

CHAPTER FORTY-TWO

Garret and Westley used the cranes to drag out two of the firestorm bombs. Bishop and Quern were there in Section One, ready to help with the whole process.

Everyone had to be careful, because if one of these bombs went off, we were all dead. All of us. No one would survive that. Fortunately, it required a massive impact to break the shell of the warhead. Only then would it explode.

However, to ensure an exoskeleton would carry one of these warheads, everyone gathered up as much rope and bungie cord as they could find. I was going to strap it to the cardinal, fly it over, and then cut the cords with a plasma blade in order to drop it.

We didn't need to be too accurate. The blast radius on a firestorm bomb was extreme. If I hit in just the near area of an Ex Cathedra city, we would level it and everything around it with ease.

Before the warhead was secured to the suit, I had to get in it.

Taking a deep breath, I ascended into the heart of the JUDGE-Y47 exoskeleton. The suit was kneeling, its cockpit like a regal throne that was just waiting for me. Settling into the seat, I reclined my head slightly, feeling the connectors align seamlessly with my neck. With a sharp and decisive *click*, the suit bonded to my spine, resonating with a mechanical precision that echoed in my ears.

A sudden, electrifying pulse surged through my body, a jarring wave of energy that coursed from the tip of my nose down to my toes. It was like a ripple of static electricity, both startling and invigorating.

The suit then came alive, its limbs pulsing with newfound energy. I slid my arms into the sleek "sleeves" and guided my feet into the armored legs.

This suit was very much like the Mark VI, and the powerful feeling it gave me was a delight.

The suit's interior hugged my body with a gentle firmness, its soft padding securing me in place. With a hiss of finality, the armor encased me completely, a cocoon of advanced warfare technology.

As the helmet secured over my head, the world momentarily faded to black. An anticipatory void.

But then the helmet's visor activated, and a new world opened before my eyes. My surroundings were transformed into a high-definition display of tactical data and environmental awareness.

The JUDGE-Y47's system intricately mapped the terrain around me, alerting me to the fact I was in an underground facility. Red light flashed on the nearby warhead, indicating it was a potential threat that could easily eradicate the power armor.

I appreciated the suit's attention to details.

Its thermal scan painted a vivid picture of the ambient temperature, highlighting warmer areas in a spectrum of colors.

The exoskeleton's user interface was a marvel of design—intuitive and unobtrusive. As my gaze settled on the surrounding people, they were crisply defined against the backdrop, with essential data like distance and status subtly appearing at the periphery of my vision upon focus. This suit was not just a shell of metal . . . it was an extension of my senses, a fusion of human and machine that opened up a realm of unprecedented capabilities.

It was better than the Mark VI.

I thought it was because this suit was meant to fly. It needed *more* information and a *better* connection with its pilot.

Inhaling deeply, I initiated my first movement. The power armor responded instantly to the mere intention of walking, its advanced systems translating thought into action with seamless precision.

As I advanced, the helmet's display affirmed that all systems were operating at optimal efficiency, hovering near the 100 percent mark.

Garret and Westley waved their hands around. They motioned me toward the warhead.

With each subsequent step, I became increasingly aware of the intricate neural connectors at the nape of my neck. These connectors interfaced directly with the suit's computational matrix, interpreting my intentions and preempting my physical movements. The suit's artificial intelligence, which had startlingly acknowledged me by name, seemed to be synthesizing an array of data about me, creating a symbiotic relationship between man and machine.

"Welcome, Kita Yamasaki," a soft, feminine voice spoke into my ear.

"Hello," I replied, already familiar with the exoskeleton's little AI helper.

As I continued, a subtle yet noticeable change began to cloud my consciousness. The JUDGE-Y47 exoskeletons were equipped with a neural feedback loop designed to suppress fear and anxiety—as were all the judge suits, really. This system ensured that the pilots remained undaunted, even in the most harrowing of combat scenarios.

I felt its effects taking hold . . . My heartbeat decelerated, a calming rhythm in contrast to the adrenaline of the situation. A sense of exhilaration began to replace the initial trepidation, a manufactured courage flowing through me . . .

Which was great, because now I had a warhead to deliver.

"Please be advised, Kita Yamasaki," the onboard AI said. "A deadly warhead is in the nearby area and has the capability to destroy the JUDGE-Y47. You should avoid it at all costs."

"Thanks," I said again. "Please keep suggestions to a minimum."

"Reducing warnings."

Garret, Bishop, Quern, and Westley used a combination of the crane and sheer brute force to get the warhead onto the front of the cardinal. It took them a short while to painstakingly attach it, but once I had the suit's arms around it, the work was easier.

They said encouraging things to me, but my heart pounded so loud, I couldn't hear them. Instead, I focused on the task at hand.

We had used our little drone to fly over the nearby area. With the distance scope, I had seen the nearest Ex Cathedra encampment. Our plan was for me to ride in a van all the way to the Ex Cathedra border, and then fly over their territory and drop the warhead.

Once the firestorm bomb was in place, I carefully walked it out of Section One. It was probably ungraceful, and more like a waddle, but no one was around to see it. Everyone had locked themselves away in their new homes, leaving us to this task.

No one wanted to get involved with a firestorm bomb, after all.

With shallow breaths, I went up the long stairway to the surface, and waited for the others to bring the van around to our parking lot. I loaded myself into the back, lying down next to my deadly payload, and then I closed my eyes.

Destroying an entire city was a terrible thing.

I wished it hadn't come to this.

I also wished I hadn't stuck myself in the exoskeleton before we reached the border. It took longer to get there than I wanted. Fortunately, the power armor could do things like filter blood and take human waste, but it wasn't the easiest to eat while inside.

Bishop spoke to me the whole way, but again, I barely heard him. I just thought about what I had to do, and how I was going to do it, all the way until we reached the border. When the van stopped, I had hardened my heart to the reality of the situation, and I was ready to do what was needed.

I stepped out the back, and watched as both Bishop and Quern pointed me in the right direction. My helmet's HUD system displayed everything in the nearby region, and when I asked it to select a location, and then guide me there, it did so.

After several gulps of air, I waved to the others and activated the thrusters.

The initial lift-off was a challenge, the suit's balance and weight distribution altered by the deadly payload I carried. The thrusters roared to life, a cacophony of power that resonated through my entire being. The whole suit shook, and I glanced at the battery cell indicator on the HUD.

I still had over 80 percent power.

The sensation of ascending was surreal. The ground receded rapidly as I climbed higher into the sky, the landscape sprawling beneath me. The HUD flashed intermittent warnings, reminders of the precariousness of my flight. Yet, despite the complexity of the task, the exoskeleton responded intuitively to my commands. A slight lean forward, and the thrusters adjusted, propelling me onward.

It took me a moment as I wobbled, and my HUD said both Quern and Bishop remained below me, no doubt watching.

But I had to do this, so I leaned forward and embraced the awkward feeling of shooting straight over the terrain.

It worked. Even with the warhead . . . it worked.

I soared through the air, the cardinal armor moving and adjusting to keep me in the air, even though I didn't know what to do myself. The world below transformed into a patchwork of colors and shapes, distant and detached. My heart raced with a mixture of fear and exhilaration.

"This is amazing," I whispered.

"It is," the computer replied.

Which was awkward, and it caused me to nervous laugh, but I didn't mind.

It was . . .

Longer than I thought it would be . . .

Too much time to reflect, really, which was why I chose not to do it . . .

As I navigated through the air, the landscape below shifted, revealing the sprawling expanse of the Ex Cathedra territory. My HUD gave me all the information I needed, which was fantastic because all the dots down below me were too tiny to distinguish from one another. If I didn't have the HUD, I never would've found the appropriate location, or even known what it was.

The city . . .

I didn't know its name.

Well, that wasn't true. The messenger, Rory, had said its name, but I hadn't heard properly. Once my mind had been set, it had filled with white noise.

At 60 percent battery cell power, I activated one of the plasma blades and cut the firestorm bomb from my exoskeleton. The deadly bomb flew off me and plummeted to the ground. My visor highlighted it the whole way down, pointing at it like I hadn't seen it on my body this whole trek, trying to warn me how catastrophic it would be if I were caught in the blast.

Without the bomb on my person, I tilted the thrusters up and continued to climb.

The cardinal suit was designed to handle the changing of pressure. The interior of the suit held me snug, altering the pressures to keep me from experiencing the worst of the ascent. It also filtered and stored air, so as I went higher, there was no danger of losing oxygen and then passing out. The exoskeleton had thought of it all.

It wouldn't last forever, obviously, and my HUD kept track of all my resources, including the air I could breathe.

It also kept track of the bomb as it reached terminal velocity and just kept falling.

I closed my eyes.

The whole exoskeleton *screeched* and buzzed with warnings. The moment the firestorm detonated, everything in my power armor wanted me to get out of this place. It urged me to go, whispering more warning than ever before. But I waited a long moment, letting this all sink in.

Then I tilted the thrusters forward and started the bizarre spiral descent toward the border. I didn't look at the devastation, even though it kept flashing across my screen.

Not only was it a bomb, but the "firestorm" aspect remained long after the detonation. It would burn up organic material, leaving nothing but charred earth behind. Then there was the dangerous sand-like radioactive particles known as *fallout* that would linger long after all the fire had been blown away.

The land the city had been on wouldn't be used again for generations.

It was dead, just like the citizens who had once dwelled there.

I flew back to the others, hoping that General Melvin would finally capitulate.

CHAPTER FORTY-THREE

Back in Sanctuary, I sat on my bed, trying not to think about what had happened. We still had multiple firestorm bombs. Nine more, to be exact. Which was too many—and perhaps not enough. When the door to my room creaked open, and Bishop slipped inside, I barely gave him a second glance.

"Kita?" he asked, using my real name. "Are you okay? You've been resting for over twenty-four hours now."

"Do we still have Rory? The messenger?"

He crossed our small room and took a seat on the tiny bed next to me. He was so large, and I wished I could just disappear into him until my mind felt well again. Bishop wrapped an arm around me, and I appreciated every second of his presence.

"We still have the messenger," he said, mulling over my question. "I think. Yeah. In the prison."

"We should release him—but only after we tell him everything that happened."

"So he can tell the world?"

I nodded.

We needed the word to get out that Sanctuary wasn't a place to mess with. We were a civilization that would destroy anyone and everything that dared to threaten us.

"Have you heard from General Melvin?" I asked.

Bishop shook his head. "Quern has been using the radio every couple hours, but they don't respond." He chuckled as he said, "Do you think that maybe you got him with the bomb? Huh?"

"No," I whispered. "I doubt it. I wouldn't be that lucky. I'm *never* that lucky."

"So, you want your own tally mark now? A little mushroom cloud?"

I glanced up at him, not in the mood to joke about this. He must've sensed my dour attitude, because he forced another laugh and then shrugged. "Sorry, I thought you would appreciate that. You've had a dark sense of humor in the past."

"It's not a laughing matter . . . I just don't want us to be harmed."

"I'm pretty sure you prevented that."

I hoped so.

Bishop grabbed me and rested me back on our bed. He curled up next to me and held me tight.

The only solace I took for all of this was that no one had this responsibility but me. I had protected them—from our enemy, and the consequences of dealing with the enemy. I would be the one who was known for this attack, not Bishop or Gascoigne or any of the others. Just me.

So when I closed my eyes, I tried to come to terms with it all.

I would do whatever it took to save my people.

When people finally answered the radio again, it had been three days since our attack.

I stood next to the radio, as did Bishop, Gascoigne, Quern, and now even DC.

Brecht was alive, and would probably recover, but he'd be half paralyzed. The railgun had chewed up some of his spine, and he couldn't handle it. Gascoigne, more wrecked over this development than I was over attacking Ex Cathedra, paced around the radio as though she were losing her mind.

When the static flared to life, everyone went totally silent.

"This is Kita Yamasaki," I whispered into the receiver.

But no one answered.

They were there, we all knew, but no one had said a thing.

"Do you surrender?" I asked. "If you do, know that we don't want anything from you. All we ask is that you leave us alone. There's a mountain range to the east of us, a small collection of hills that are covered in pine forests. To the south, there's a salt desert. Those are our borders in relation to you. Ex Cathedra cannot cross those boundaries."

That would give us a huge chunk of territory, larger than the old-world state of Idaho. But it was also out of the way for Ex Cathedra. They could still cross to the west, and fight U-Cali if they wanted, but they couldn't touch *us*.

But no one answered.

"Do you surrender?" I repeated. "I need to hear you say it. I need to know you're going to leave us alone. If you don't . . . I'll have to destroy another city."

No answer.

"Please," I whispered into the receiver. "Don't make me destroy another city."

Would they believe me? Would they realize they were outclassed and outmatched? I hoped they would. I wanted this to be over. I wanted to go back to worrying about the chickens and the babies and Remi . . .

The cost of war was high.

Sometimes much too high.

"They're not going to surrender," Gascoigne said. She resumed her pacing. "They're not. They never do. They're relentless. That's their fucking motto. We're never going to be free of *any* of our enemies—because they all remember and hate us for it."

"The Iron-Blooded aren't going to pursue you anymore," Quern interjected. "I know. I heard them speak about you, and your efforts. You're too costly. And I think, by using that bomb, you've made yourself too costly for even Ex Cathedra."

DC shook her head, her blonde hair catching in the wind. "Funny, how some things repeat themselves . . ." But she had whispered it more to herself than anyone else.

When the radio finally flared back to life, someone was on the other end.

"This is the justicar," a woman on the other end of the radio said. "And Ex Cathedra agrees to your terms of surrender."

EPILOGUE

*"History repeats itself, but in such cunning disguise that we never
detect the resemblance until the damage is done."*
—Sydney J. Harris

Over the span of a decade, Sanctuary transformed from a cold and quiet
hermit bunker to a bustling city, both over the ground and underground. Everyone knew of Sanctuary, because I paid junk hunters and
travelers alike to spread the good word.

Theon Sellers was a human architect because of a device in his pituitary
gland. The A-tech device was a complex onboard computer that added
instructions to bloodborne nanites, and allowed for the body to create and
excrete concentrated pheromones.

It wasn't a difficult surgery to remove it from Theon, and it wasn't a
painful surgery to have it inserted into me. And once I had it, the Teth of
Sanctuary felt more at ease with my presence as their leader.

So, when I walked through Sanctuary, the Teth all greeted me as one
of them.

"Hello, Architect Kita," one of the innovators in the labs said. The
innovators, as with everyone else here, spoke near-perfect English. She
worked alongside the new nurses that DC was training, and they were
actively cultivating more antibiotics, which we always needed.

I waved back and smiled, strolling through just to make everything was
okay.

"Should we inspect everything further?"

I turned to face the Teth following me. Architect Benjamin. His mane
had fully come in, and the spines were nearly three feet in length. He was

prominent and distinct in such a way that *everyone* turned to face him whenever he walked by.

"You want to look at the medicine?" I asked.

Benjamin shook his head. "I want them to know we're paying attention and happy with their progress."

"When people are busy, it's best to let them just do their work." I motioned to all the lab attendants at their stations, and how focused they were. "We can look at everything when they're done."

The Teth architect touched me with one of his smaller hands. "Yes. Let's continue our walk."

Every week, I walked through most of Sanctuary, hoping to greet everyone. Benjamin joined me each time, familiarizing himself with every human and every Teth. He was smart enough to remember them all, even though most faces were a blur in my mind at this point.

We walked into the greenhouse portion of Section Two to find it was mostly a jungle of fruits and vegetables. They were larger this yield than they were the previous one. As I walked through, more people waved, including a couple from Eagle Nest.

That whole city had been absorbed by Sanctuary, and I smiled as I walked by.

"Good afternoon, architects," one of them said.

Benjamin bowed slightly in their direction. "Good day, Mary. Good day, Drew."

I had forgotten their names—but not Benjamin.

There were more than just people from Eagle Nest. I noticed individuals from Boulder, like the pawn shop man—Pawn, people called him— and the lady who once ran Dodge City. They were here because Sanctuary was larger and safer. Even now, people were in the greenhouse to pick food just so they could eat it, because it was so ripe.

We utilized advanced agricultural techniques, integrating Jack's genetically modified plants with traditional farming, resulting in bountiful harvests every time.

I stopped and plucked a handful of raspberries from a bunch that was growing near the door. "You want some?" I asked Benjamin.

He shook his head. "No. I don't want the *scent* on me."

The use of A-tech, salvaged and repurposed from other bunkers, had allowed us to fix the damage done to Sanctuary, including the air filters, without having to develop or make our own. For some reason, it made the

Teth more fastidious. If the air was clean, *they* wanted to be clean, so they avoided foods and activities that would cause them to have lasting scents.

We had plenty of Teth here. As we strolled through Section One, I noticed there was a whole section for outriders here. They were the fastest breeders, and loved to do things in groups. They took turns caring for the chickens, and had become so good at it that we now had a holiday to eat chickens just to keep the population from exploding.

"Hello, architects," Levi called out from the group—his English perfect. "We were just on our way to Himiko's classes."

I touched each and every outrider that walked over to us, letting them know that I appreciated their presence. Benjamin did the same thing. The touch helped reinforce the bond, and once the outriders were happy, they continued to the expanded classrooms we had built.

Cultural integration became a cornerstone of Sanctuary's identity. Humans and Teth shared knowledge, leading to a fusion of ideas and customs. Schools and research facilities were established, where human and Teth scholars worked side by side, unraveling the mysteries of A-tech and developing new technologies.

Scrapyard Pete taught them about building, DC taught biology, I taught history, and even Quern had an entire course on guns and shooting. We had everything the kids could want, and more.

"Do you think they'll finish building the play area?" Benjamin asked as we headed for the long steps to the surface.

I patted his shoulder. "I think it'll be finished before spring, when the new Teth are born."

"Excellent."

Remi, my son, and Alain, my daughter, both came running down the long steps. Remi laughed as he went, not even looking forward. He was about to crash right into me when his sister pointed.

"Remi, look out!"

I grabbed my nine-year-old son and stopped him from tumbling down the steps. He was a large kid, though. Like his father, he was just too much meat and bone for one person. And when he smiled up at me, it reminded me of Bishop all over again.

"Hey, Mom," he said he brushed himself off. He'd inherited all my looks, though. Black hair. Dark eyes. But the smile . . . that definitely belonged to his father. "Are you okay? Just working?"

I nodded. "That's right. Are you helping out?"

He saluted me. "Yes. I'm currently bringing word back that we've successfully replaced the battery in the jeep."

"Good." I ruffled his hair and turned my attention to my daughter. "Are you helping?"

Alain reminded me of my sister. Long inky hair like black waterfalls, and larger eyes than I had ever seen on a child. She was cute. Always so adorable.

"I was helping," she whispered. "But I was about to go see Chelsy. I help her with the newborn Teth today."

As I watched Alain and Remi bound off, their youthful exuberance a bright spark in the growing city of Sanctuary, I couldn't help but marvel at how much they had grown. It felt like just yesterday I was worried about whether they'd make it, and now I couldn't wait to see how they'd change the world in their time.

Architect Benjamin walked beside me as we continued up the steps. We made our way up and out of Sanctuary, exiting onto the new entrance platform that had been built to better accommodate trucks. The air was crisp now that we were outside, and the sky was a vibrant blue.

It was so amazing to see beyond the overcast clouds—so amazing to see a world not covered in gloom.

Off in the distance, we had borders that were well guarded, to make sure no enemy nations marched against us. I made sure Sanctuary's military and defense capabilities grew as well. The city harbored a formidable force, a combination of human strategy and Teth prowess.

It was almost a moot issue, though. Ex Cathedra didn't move on us again, at least not in the ten years since I started expansion. They left us alone, as did the remnants of the Iron-Blooded. And with my new anti-Vay technology, there was no one left to bother us outside of simple raiders or thieves, and *they* were no match for our power armor.

"You're worried," Benjamin stated.

I exhaled. "Yeah, I make myself anxious sometimes."

"You're among friends."

The Teth said that to me a lot. Whenever I would get worried, or doubt the future, they would remind me of their presence. *You're among friends.* It was my new personal motto—and it was way better than what I had before, let me tell you.

Socially, Sanctuary had evolved into a melting pot of ideas and beliefs, just as my grandfather had always wanted. While there were challenges and conflicts, the shared goal of creating a better future forged a strong communal bond. Festivals, markets, and public forums became common, places where humans and Teth could interact and celebrate their joint achievements.

As Benjamin and I continued our walk, the sounds of laughter and conversation from the BBQ area filled the air, along with the smell of grilling meat. I noticed Gascoigne and Brecht by the outdoor BBQ. Their little girl, Momo, was also with them.

Brecht leaned heavily on a cane, his right leg unable to support his weight, but that didn't matter. Gascoigne kept close, and helped him whenever he needed it. Momo watched the food cook, her six-year-old gaze sharp, even if she didn't speak much.

Gascoigne had thought she'd never have children, but she had been wrong. DC found a way to make sure she was fertile.

I waved to them.

Gascoigne jutted her chin up at me. "Don't overwork yourself."

Always aggressive.

"Don't burn the meat."

"I *never* burn anything."

"We'll make something for you too," Brecht called out.

And I appreciated that about him. No matter what happened, he cared for everyone.

Vega eventually came over and joined them for the meal. While he was a warrior Teth, and stayed with the other warriors the majority of the time, old habits died hard. Vega was next to Brecht most of the time, and played with his daughter whenever he could—even giving her piggyback rides.

Quern was nearby, watching from one of the other BBQs over. For whatever reason, he always remained close, but never close enough to engage in much conversation. He was like a shadow—there, but easy to forget. He seemed to like it that way.

Then a familiar figure caught my eye, approaching from the direction of the main gates beyond the road. It was Bishop, his stride confident and his smile unmistakable even from a distance. He was making the rounds, walking with everyone, and sometimes delivering mail from the cities over.

He was a junk hunter at heart, and loved to do trades.

My heart leapt in my chest, a mix of surprise and overwhelming joy. It had been a while since I last saw him—his wheeling and dealing often took him far from Sanctuary.

"Bishop!" I called out, unable to contain my excitement.

Benjamin sniffed the air in the direction of the approaching figure and gave a respectful nod before excusing himself to attend to other duties.

As Bishop neared, his signature grin widened. "Hey, if it isn't my lovely and super beautiful wife." He brushed back his dark hair as he sauntered over. "Kit-Kat, did you miss me or did you *super* miss me?"

He seemed the same yet different. His hair was slightly longer, and there was a new scar on his cheek—or maybe it was a new tally mark. I didn't know. But his eyes still sparkled with the same mischievous light, and his presence exuded the same reassuring strength.

Despite all that, I ran for him.

He laughed as I rushed over and threw my arms around his torso. Once upon a time, I had always been alone, and now it felt like I would never be alone again.

"Where's our kids?" He glanced down at me. "I mean, I love you so much, but like, I want a big group hug from my little nuggets, ya know?"

I nuzzled his chest and laughed. "They're down below."

He clicked his tongue in disappointment. But then he embraced me a second time. I felt the rough fabric of his travel-worn jacket and the solid strength of his arms around me.

"Missed you," he murmured, his voice muffled against my shoulder.

"You don't have to go, ya know," I whispered into his chest. Then I pulled back to look him in the eye. "But we don't have to talk about that. You're here now. You're among friends. Let's just celebrate that."

Another lesson I learned about the wasteland—celebrate everything. Why not? You never know when you might lose it.

Bishop chuckled, his eyes scanning the bustling life around us. "It looks like everyone is already celebrating something. What is it? Chicken Slaughter Day? I hope I didn't miss Chicken Slaughter Day."

I smacked him on the shoulder. "That's not what it's called."

He snorted back a laugh. "That's what I call it in my head." Then he elbowed me. "C'mon, Kit-Kat. Let's get something to eat."

I couldn't help but smile in his presence. "All right."

He nodded, his gaze lingering on the BBQ where Gascoigne, Brecht, and Momo were. "Seems all my friends are here."

Momo beamed up at him. All kids liked Bishop—he just had kid-like energy to spare. He hoisted her up, placed her on his shoulders, and then licked his lips at the BBQ.

"You want your meat properly cooked?" Gascoigne asked.

"Just make it as black as you make yours," Bishop muttered. He spun in circles, delighting Momo as he made his way to a table.

As I walked by his side, I couldn't help but feel complete. Bishop was my soulmate, even if it didn't seem like that to outsiders. If it hadn't been for him, I would've given up on life in the wasteland. I would've . . .

I would've thrown it all away.

So in part, Sanctuary's success was *his* success.

Bishop eyed me. "Stop thinking weird things," he said in a singsong tone. Because he knew me too well.

At the BBQ, warm greetings and laughter awaited us. Vega playfully ruffled Momo's hair as she giggled, and Gascoigne raised an eyebrow at Bishop, her usual tough demeanor softened by a small smile.

We all sat down to eat at the table.

While we had only been here a decade, Sanctuary was unrecognizable from its humble beginnings. The city was a marvel of A-tech, a center of trade and learning, and quickly growing into something beyond what I had hoped for.

My grandfather would be proud.

AUTHOR'S NOTE

My name is Shami (yup, just those five letters) and I was born in Utah, but grew up in California with my mother and little brother. Now I live in Kansas, and I couldn't be happier! After graduating high school, I went on to earn my BA in History from Stanislaus State, and then my Juris Doctorate from the Laurence Drivon School of Law.

My favorite novel as a child was *Island of the Blue Dolphins* by Scott O'Dell. It opened my imagination to possibilities I had never considered, and to this day I can still remember the impact it had on me. My second-favorite novel was probably *Say Cheese and Die* (the Goosebumps tale) and my third was *Where the Red Fern Grows*. However, the moment I read science fiction, that was all I read for years. At least until I graduated high school—then I moved on to all the most epic fantasy you can imagine.

As an adult (albeit still a kid at heart), my favorite novel is *Stranger in a Strange Land* by Robert A. Heinlein. His take on a perfect world again opened my mind to possibilities I had never considered, and Jubal Harshaw is the fictional character I most aspire to be.

I love telling stories, playing video games, reading, and writing about myself in the third person. My top three favorite video games are *Super Mario RPG*, *Mass Effect* (the first one), and *The Legend of Zelda* (the whole franchise). They really captured my imagination when I played them, and they still have a special place in my heart to this day. Special shout-outs to *Fallout*, *Elder Scrolls*, *Pokémon*, and *Fire Emblem*. Those games all really helped me out of dark places, and are among my favorites. Also, in case it wasn't obvious, *Fallout* and *Dies the Fire* were huge inspirations for this series.

As an author, nothing gives me more pleasure than hearing others enjoyed my work, so here's hoping you find something you enjoy!

Lastly, if you wish to support me, and help build my burgeoning career as an author, please consider supporting me on Patreon! I provide early access to chapters, and short stories set in the universes of my stories. Thank you!

Patreon: patreon.com/shamistovall
Twitter: @GameOverStation
Facebook: facebook.com/SAStovall
Email: s.adelle.s@gmail.com

ACKNOWLEDGMENTS

First and foremost, to my remarkable husband, John.

Without his unwavering support and belief in me, the title of author would have remained an elusive dream. In moments of doubt, when shadows of despair seek to engulf my creative spirit, John is always there to remind me I'm just being dumb, because *of course I was born to do this.* He is the warmth that combats the cold, the hand I hold when my dark thoughts threaten to steal all my happiness, and the man I will always love.

John embodies a rare combination of gentle kindness and tenacious advocacy, making him truly unparalleled. Our shared past as attorneys is a testament to our deep connection; we are soulmates, mirror images of each other, even when our similarities present challenges. Yet, there is no one else with whom I'd rather share my life—except for maybe the many cavapoos he so lovingly adopts.

Second, to Drew, my agent, a kindred spirit in every sense. Had fate made us neighbors, I have no doubt we would have become fast friends. Another fellow attorney, his passion for literature and his love for Final Fantasy have resulted in several three-hour phone conversations. It was *The Half-Life Empire* that first captured his attention and for that, this grand finale is in part due to him.

Last but by no means least, this dedication extends to Podium. They have not only published this series, making it accessible to a world of readers, but have also brought the epic tale of Kita to its glorious conclusion.

They probably also have attorneys on retainer, so everyone here is somehow related to law. That's, uh, a theme? Right?

And so, with heartfelt gratitude and anticipation, and a little bit of awkwardness, I hope you enjoyed *The Half-Life Empire 3*!

ABOUT THE AUTHOR

Shami Stovall is an award-winning fantasy and science fiction author. Previously, she taught history and criminal law at the college level and loved every second. When she's not reading fascinating articles and books about ancient China or the Byzantine Empire, Stovall can be found playing way too many video games, especially RPGs and tactics simulators. She loves John, reading, and writing about herself in the third person.